Inherent Nature

Inherent Nature

Steve Baumler

Illustrations by Scott McDaniel.

Library of Congress Control Number: 2008910338
ISBN: Hardcover   978-1-4363-8564-0
                 Softcover   978-1-4363-8563-3

This book was printed in the United States of America.

To order additional copies of this book, contact:
Xlibris Corporation
1-888-795-4274
www.Xlibris.com
Orders@Xlibris.com
52825

To my wife Kristina

Without her support I would not have come so far

PROLOGUE

The reflection of the night sky in the silent water was obscured by the midnight's mist just beginning to rise. Within minutes, a layer of webbish, semitranslucent filaments floated several feet above the surface of the stilled lake. The blackness of the water, coupled with the lack of life therein, created a flawlessly reflective surface that, while seemingly as fathomless as the sky was tall, effectively conveyed a complete lack of depth to the lake itself. No bird flew in the night over or through the mist above the lake. No fish broke the surface in search of insects that were not there. No animal prowled along the perimeter or investigated its image in that reflective surface. This area of the world held no living thing to prove it really existed. Nothing, save the expanse of the lake and its six sisters nestled in the foothills of the Dead Mountains. A single spring sprang "life" to what some called the Seven Seas of Sterility. From this aquifer arose a creek that cascaded down the Dead Mountains, meandering its way through a region known as the Barren. Here, scorched earth from a war waged over a thousand years ago split the stream into seven parts and saw their termination in the seven lakes known more commonly as the Dead Pools. It was said a survivor of that ancient aggression claimed that the seven lakes, at that time only pools, were formed from the depressions left by the devastating power of the seven wizards who religiously eradicated each other from the world. Few things living felt neither the need nor the desire to descend upon this portion of the world. The emptiness alone emanated enough fear to ward off wandering beings and animals, but the reputation of the pools for being overrun with death, disease, and decay made them a landmark largely and purposely avoided.

For this reason alone, many would call Morgan a fool and a dead man. For this reason alone, all would shun him if they knew of his sojourn to the Seas of Sterility. Morgan snorted at this as he silently poled his skiff along the edge of the smallest of the lakes. His boat's passage rippled the surface of the water, but only for a few feet; such was the stillness of the lake. With his gaze outward, he did not notice the disturbance he caused, adding to the lake's apparent deadness and mystery.

Morgan found it intriguing that he was drawn to the lakes. He found it intriguing that he had to pull the veil of mystery away from this place and stare blindly and unprotected into the face of this horror. Days of impatient travel across the land to this place had knotted his stomach and resolve until he reached the edge of the wood that bordered the southernmost lake, some two miles from the actual shoreline. Here he had feverishly constructed a small raft and dragged it and his horse toward the lake. His animal had died of fright by the time he reached the water, and he spent that evening replenishing his dwindling food supply. Water was a different problem.

Water, it rolled slowly down the shaft of a long straight sapling he used to propel himself around the lake. The liquid seemed to stain the wood as it wound its way back to the whole from which it came. Towering nearly seven feet above the bottom of the raft, Morgan looked misplaced, like a twig standing on end atop a pond lily. What he had hoped to find hidden, or even evident, here, he did not know. Disappointed at discovering nothing, no mystery, no horrific abnormalities, he dropped to his knees and wearily lowered his head, lightly hitting the hard wood. The quake of adrenaline and the edge of anticipation gave way to the gnaw of hunger and the bite of cold. He tied a leather thong around a knot on his pole and wrapped the other end around his leg, letting the pole remain in the water. Even after all that he had seen here, or better yet not seen here, his superstitions would not let him dare to touch the tainted liquid.

Slowly, almost hesitantly, he reached for his rucksack and pulled out a tightly wrapped leather bundle and began to unwind the cord that held it together. What was it about these lakes that proclaimed such power over his thoughts? What lay submerged in the black belly of this body of water that refused to reveal itself to him? He lifted a sliver of smoked horse haunch to his lips and passed it through to his mouth. The meat revolted his senses, stimulating a violent upheaval of whatever was standing in his stomach, mostly acid, which he was barely able to keep down. Depleted of all strength and desire to think, he turned over and slept. While he slept, the raft rested as well. It rested in the same spot to which he had last poled it. The reflection of the motionless boat on that motionless body of water would have looked, to anyone who might have gazed upon it, to be part of the whole.

Waking early in the morning, Morgan's lips were taut and dry. He grabbed his bota bag and shook it lightly. He had very little water left, not enough to bother conserving. By day the desolate lake looked less mysterious and more barren. He glanced at his leg and noticed that the leather thong he had placed there the night before was gone. It lay floating on the surface of the lake a few inches from the side of the raft. The water seemed just as black in the light of day as it did during the dead of night. The only notable difference was the fact that the sun's rays successfully penetrated the gloom of the water to a depth of an inch or two, giving the entire surface of the lake a black opaque quality that released no reflections. Morgan stared at the sapling he had used the night before. It floated motionlessly only a few feet from his boat. He looked at the shore of the lake; he was still about twenty feet from dry land. He turned back to the sapling.

Reaching into his rucksack, he removed his wound supply of leather line. His longest piece was a section about seven feet in length. He pulled a coin from a pouch at his waist and examined it. Not satisfied, he returned it to its receptacle and removed another. This copper piece he kept out. He said a silent prayer to Kasparow for all the cheap people in the world who greedily shaved the edges of coins. The irregularly shaped circle provided several sections around which to wind his leather strap. He secured the coin to one end of the leather strap. A few inches up from this point, he tied a loop in the line, leaving the coin dangling from the end of an open circle about three inches in diameter, just enough to fit over the end of the sapling. He gazed at the sapling. Taking hold of the other end of the line, he began to spin the coin in a circle. He had to spin it slowly and make sure he didn't put too much of an arc on it. Too high an arc, and the length of the line would run out before the coin reached its target. One chance was all he had to get the coin over the edge of the pole. After that he would be forced to come in contact with the water.

He let go of the spinning coin and watched as it passed through the air almost too shallowly. The coin came to rest on the farthest side of the pole, resting there, refusing to drop into the water. He grimaced, as if the coin's lack of movement hurt him physically. Lightly shaking the line from side to side, he eventually coaxed the coin into dropping off the wood. With a thick *plop*, the copper coin hit the water and pulled the line taut with its weight.

Morgan pulled the line in slowly, keeping as much tension on the leather as he dared. The pole began to move toward him, its progress slow. He realized that the boat was being pulled toward the pole as much as the pole was moving toward the boat. An eerie feeling came over him, as if the resistance of the water was negligible. It seemed to shun away anything that was not of itself. Slowly he brought the pole to the edge of the boat. Standing erect, he grabbed a portion of the line that had not come in contact with the liquid and held it aloft. The coin sought the surface of the water like it meant to die there. Lowering the coin to the surface of the lake, he brought the circle within reach of the end of the pole. Stooping, he grabbed the pack of meat he had tried to consume the night before. Letting the horseflesh drop to the bottom of the raft, he covered his hand with the leather. Slipping the circle of line over the end of the pole, he worked it down along the sapling's length. When he had gone one-third of the way down the pole, he stopped. Morgan lifted his hand slowly, raising the end of the pole out of the water. He crouched and dropped his covered hand, draping the leather over the wood. Grasping tightly, he pulled the sapling up a few feet and shoved the other end back into the muck that lined the bottom of the lake. In this manner he was able, one handed, to propel the boat toward dry land. Satisfied, he tossed the pole onto the ground and stepped off the raft.

The same eerie nonresistance he had experienced when pulling the pole toward him returned. The boat moved away from him as he went forward, cutting his step short. His boot came down in the water. He hit bottom and immediately reacted, jumping forward onto the soil, sending several droplets of dank liquid in different directions around him. He was prostrate on the ground, breathing heavily, when he realized he had held his breath through the entire episode. He closed his eyes and tried to control his pulse, slowing it down to a normal level. The sweat on his brow rolled into his squinting eyes, seeping through the crack between his eyelids with a strange conviction. The salty secretion scorched his eyes, burning into his brain.

He stood up violently and wiped his eyes clear, his vision blurred. His reasoning raced, his soul screamed. *I'M NOT SWEATING!* He brought his hands to his face and inhaled tentatively. A pungent odor offended his senses. Not *sweat*, he thought as he knelt and began searching for the sapling that had spent the night immersed in the lake. His hand groped along the barren ground, eventually coming in contact with the wet wood. He snatched it off of the ground and stood, slowly moving the sapling toward his face. He inhaled and froze. The odor was the same. Dropping the stick, he knelt. His legs getting wet as water slowly seeped into his boots. He looked back across the lake's landscape.

From the bottom of the lake, a green glow began to cut through the still blackness. An urgency burned its way into his brain, and he found himself wandering into the water. His awareness closed in on itself, swallowed by the bleakness of the lake. His consciousness tunneled down to a bright emerald pinpoint that commanded his movements. In blindness he reached to embrace it. The energy that flowed into him made him gasp and gag on water. His lungs burned, and he felt as though he was injected into the green light. It infused itself into him and became all he knew, all he was.

CHAPTER 1

The burning passed in what seemed like an instant. Time had meaning again. There was pain in his chest and the chill of evaporating water on his skin. His muscles moved, and he marveled at the sensation of having weight. For the first time in how long he did not know, Malchom opened his eyes and gazed upon a world that had thought him vanquished. The light was dazzling but did not hurt him as he sat up, amazed at the diversity of colors and shapes that surrounded him.

His lungs filled, and he screamed, "I'm free!" His hands rose up before his face, almost on their own. "I live, I live!" Malchom stood and looked around him. The dry, cracked earth continued as far as he could see. He caught an odor and smelled his hands. He reeked of death. A wave of ecstasy rolled through him. He turned to find a body of water behind him; there was a small raft nearby. At his feet lay an emerald the size of his fist. He grinned. "You fools have failed! I'm free, do you hear! Free! I told you I would make it out. Do you hear me? I told you, do you hear me!" The sound of his voice was entirely alien, but it was his. "But you can't hear me because I'm out." He leaned over the gem. "You're no longer in control of me. I'm free." Malchom paused, touched his face.

But who am I? he thought. *Am I still myself? ALTAIR! Hear my plea. Grant me the power to return home. Hear my plea. Grant me the power to conjure water.* He kneeled and raised his eyes to the sky. *ALTAIR! Hear my plea. Grant me the power to conjure food. Hear my plea. Grant me the power to call a steed.* He lowered his head and cleared his mind, preparing for the impact that accompanied the rush of arcane knowledge that would soon be entering his thoughts. He cleared his mind and waited. For what seemed like hours, he waited. His resolve began to fade.

"ALTAIR! Why do you not answer me? Do not punish me for this lapse. I beg of you, I was imprisoned," he sobbed imploringly at the heavens.

I must sacrifice, he thought. *I must regain* His *attention.*

Standing weakly, he decided to examine the raft. It was resting near the waterline. A small thing, it looked hastily made and contained a backpack; he opened it and dumped the contents on the ground. He reveled in the feel of a metal cooking knife. Some spare underclothes held his attention entirely too long as he caressed his skin with the thin cotton. A bound leather book was filled with a precise script, unreadable. Inside a cloth sack was a bundled waxed canvas that when unrolled revealed four metal spikes, a block of flint, and a striking stone.

The last item intrigued him most. It was a miniature circular shield, about six inches in diameter and made from a single piece of platinum. Was this an emblem or insignia of some sort? The design on the face of the shield was painted in gold. It depicted an upright sword that acted as the fulcrum of a set of scales; below this was a single dagger. He repackaged the rucksack and stood, noticing for the first time that he wore a long sword at his side. He drew the weapon. It was finely made, the blade etched with an unreadable writing.

I will have to learn this language, Malchom thought. *This blade feels good in my hands. I feel so strong!* He looked at his body the best he could. His torso, arms, and legs were covered with tough, layered leather armor. On his breast was the same sword emblem that emblazoned the platinum talisman. Flexing his arms, he waved the sword about. *I wish I knew how to wield this thing*, he thought as he sheathed the sword.

Some dried meat was littered on the boat's bottom. He sampled the dried meat and found himself eating it all. The food's flavor filled his senses in a way he did not remember his senses had ever been filled before. He returned to the emerald. He had to have the gem; it was going to make a fine weapon. But how to secure it without touching it? For touching it would capture your soul and exchange it with the soul contained within. Who had touched the gem? Whose soul now resided there? He opened the backpack and emptied the cloth sack; its sturdy thickness would be enough protection, he hoped. He fluffed open the sack and scooped the gem up into it. For added protection, he broke apart some of the dried earth with one of the metal spikes and packed the emerald in a thick cushion of dirt.

I will not touch the gem. Never again will I allow myself to be imprisoned so, he thought as he placed the sack at the bottom of the backpack.

The sun had risen higher into the sky. He now examined his new surroundings. The land was dry and desolate. In what he guessed was a western direction was a forest several miles distant. Having no other direction, he headed for the wood. When he reached the edge of the forest, he marveled at how well his body withstood the burden of heat and the lack of water. The forest was very sparse, as if the desolation of the area around the lake permeated even to this point. He found the travel through the wood easy and quite pleasant.

Malchom traveled the rest of the day in what was a westerly direction before he encountered another person. He had found a trail, which led to a road that eventually brought him to a farm. The light was dim, and he had to squint to make out the figure in the field. Malchom hailed a greeting and approached the man. The man was dressed poorly and showed the age of many years.

"You there, might you assist me?" said Malchom.

The man stared at him in confusion, then replied with some sort of gibberish that Malchom could not understand. *Damn! Can't read, can't understand this language at all! Altair, please help me!* Malchom moved his hands to his mouth in an imitation of eating and drinking. His chest emblem reflected the fading sunlight into the old man's eyes. They went wide with excitement.

The old farmer began bowing and babbling at a breakneck speed, motioning for Malchom to follow him. He was led to a farmhouse not too distant. It was a long, single-storied wood building; two barns were built against a wood that backed the house. The old man jabbered the entire time. Malchom could almost pick out some of the words. He seemed to be vaguely familiar with the language, but not enough to grasp any concepts.

As they entered the house, the old man called out; and an elderly woman and a younger woman, whom he assumed were his wife and his daughter, entered from a side room. Luscious smells wafted in after them; dinner was obviously being cooked. They listened to the old man, gazed at Malchom in astonishment, and began bowing when they caught sight of the emblem on his chest. *This body I have leapt into obviously belongs to a person of power, or at least high in standing. Could this emblem be one of rank? Or possibly it represents an organization? The local government or military perhaps?* They ushered him to a table next to an unlit hearth, and the two women began bringing in food of all sorts to lay in front of him. Malchom placed his backpack on the floor and unbuckled the sword belt out of a strange reflex. He sat. He was ravenous and ate accordingly; all the while the old man continued to talk at him.

Eventually Malchom figured out that the man was attempting to introduce himself. It sounded like "Arin." "Malchom," he replied, pointing to himself. The man smiled brightly and repeated Malchom's name while bowing. "Do you understand dwarven?" Malchom spat in the ancient dwarven tongue. The man did not reply. "How about elven?" he asked in the other tongue. This time the man reacted slightly. "Well, that's about the extent of my ability unless you happen to know the Orcish languages," he said to himself. The remainder of Malchom's dinner passed in silence.

After the meal, Arin led him into another room. Arin motioned Malchom to sit and called to his wife and his daughter. When they entered, Arin introduced them as Shell and Shar. The daughter, Shar, held an infant in her arms. She brought the child forward and showed Malchom. The child was very fair skinned and had high cheekbones. *Ah . . . the child has some elven blood in it. This could be most profiting,* he thought. Shell put the child in his arms and spoke the name "Zeddidiah."

"Little Zeddidiah," Malchom said. "You just might be what I have been needing." A plan began forming in his mind. He cooed at the child for a few minutes before handing it back to the daughter. The child had Shar's eyes.

A voice from the doorway caught their attention. Looking up, Malchom saw a short, thin figure enter the room. It was an elf. Zeddidiah's father? Shar rushed to the Elf and squawked at him hurriedly. The elf listened, and when she was finished, approached Malchom.

"Shar says you understand elven," said the elf. "I am Zorin. I and my family welcome you, Sir Knight." Zorin then bowed deeply.

Knight! Ah . . . good, so I am a person of standing. I wonder what this elf will believe. "I am Malchom," he said with as much pompousness as he could. "And I am blessed by your hospitality."

"Well then, Dun Malchom, be at home. I'm afraid Shar's story of your arrival is somewhat confused. She says you do not understand the common tongue?"

"Uh, yes, that is true. My native tongue is not as similar as yours."

"How is it that a Dun Lian knight does not know the common tongue?" Zorin asked uneasily.

"Well"—Malchom's mind raced for an answer—"that is a long story, and I have been traveling long—"

"Yes," interrupted Zorin. "Shar says you came from the east. Were you near the Dead Seas?" Zorin was obviously very suspicious.

"Dead Seas?" *That desolate place I found myself this morning?* "Well, as I said, it is a long and interestingly involved story. Would you mind if I rested first?"

"Of course, Dun Malchom. A Dun Lian knight," he said the words with a somewhat mistrusting tone. "Would bless us in many ways by bedding down in our home." *Was this Elf attempting to imply something?* Malchom decided it would be best to retire into solitude to work a plan through.

"Thank you Zorin. I require a private room so that I may . . . *meditate.*" He hoped this would seem fitting for a *Dun Lian knight.*

"Of course, this way." Zorin led him through the house to a small simply furnished room. "Call if you need anything, Dun Malchom," he said, bowing as he left the room.

Dun Malchom. A Dun Lian knight? Malchom searched his memory for any hint of a knighthood named such. He found that when he concentrated he could remember much that Jux had told him. He stripped himself of his armor, his hands moving reflexively. A knock at the door stopped him short.

"Yes," he said in elven.

"Dun Malchom," came the Elf's voice. "Forgive my intrusion, but you left this in the other room." Malchom moved to the door and opened it to find Zorin standing there with the long sword and backpack in his hands. In the background, Malchom spied Shar peeking around the corner, her eyes wide with amazement.

"Thank you, Zorin. Now please do not disturb me until the morrow."

"Of course." Zorin bowed as Malchom slammed the door.

He does not believe me, thought Malchom. He finished removing his armor and prostrated himself on the bed. Closing his eyes, he relaxed, began breathing deep and slow. The routines of meditation returned to him as he remembered the art he practiced what must be long ago. His thoughts slowed, and pieces of his consciousness fell away. Sounds departed as he declined to hear them. He was aware of an argument taking place outside. Colors faded to black as he declined to see them. Blackness consumed him as he remembered the events of an age long ago.

He stood on a slight rise, grassy rolling plains spread out before him. He recalled the events as clearly as if they were happening anew as the memory of that long-concluded conflict washed over him . . .

Lightning crashed around him as he reviewed his intentions. *I will obliterate them all,* he thought. *I will bring down the power of Altair as none of them dare or have ever seen. There are too many of us, too many parasites plaguing Him. Too many of us drawing His power down. With so much fragmentation, His power is diminished. I shall be the only one to do His bidding. And I shall be ultimate in my domination of those left.*

Malchom looked out across the plains. Six other figures stood in the distance. *Only six, someone has become the coward.* Each occupied a hillock of their own. Although they were far off, he knew all six were preparing for the same battle, and in the same way.

"Altair! Hear me! Grant me far sight that I might see my foes! Grant me lightning that I might raze my foes! Grant me earthquakes that I might bury my foes in a tomb of dirt! Grant me tornadoes that I might blow my foes into oblivion! Altair! Hear me! Grant me invisibility that I might evade my foes! Grant me the sun that I might strike fire down upon my foes!" Malchom continued to chant, praying for powers that would terrify any ordinary man. The wind whipped around him, whirling his cloak about him. A form coalesced from the wind.

"Hello, Malchom," the form said. Its voice reverberated in Malchom's bones.

"Mighty avatar! Grant me all that I have prayed for! I am ready. Infuse me with thy God's power!" Malchom braced himself for the influx of power that was about to be his.

"Actually, Malchom, before that happens, you need to be aware of a few things." The avatar glared at Malchom.

Malchom winced. This was not normal. Was Altair about to abandon him? He gazed at the avatar's face. It was almost featureless; the brilliance of his visage all but washed out his facial features.

"Speak, avatar! For as are you, I am a servant of Altair, and I do his bidding."

"So true, so true. I hope you remember that always." The avatar again glared at Malchom, his voice booming. "Know then that Altair is not pleased with the path your petty arguments with the others has taken. All of you have the desire to be supreme in Altair's eyes and have thus lost sight of your true goals. Altair has decided that only one of you should be the vessel of His power. Eternal torment waits for those who lose. Your requests for power will be granted, but only those requests that are not echoed by any of the others. Altair has given all seven of you five minutes of prayer. Think creatively, Malchom, for any duplicated request will not be answered. You have five minutes!" The apparition faded.

Five minutes? His mind raced. Silently he prayed for every power he had ever used. New torments sprang to mind. Twisted forms of creatures and forces of death sprang from his mind. He would be victorious in this fight. He lifted his head and arms to the heavens and prayed as he had never done before.

Lightning struck him, and he felt himself infused with power. He marveled at the number of his prayers that were answered. *These fools, are their minds so weak that they can't conceive of any varied power?*

His head snapped forward, and he flung an earthquake at his closest foe. *Gorwin. Die! Be swallowed whole by the earth, and be crushed to death. I command it!* He saw Gorwin sink into the ground. A green light flashed above his head. An emerald fell at his feet; he ignored it. He commanded the wind to stiffen around him, to form a barrier against physical attack.

Two of the other wizards were gone. Fiery hail the size of a man's fist rained down upon another. Malchom raised his hands and conjured a nightmare of a dragon in front of the wizard that seemed to be burning alive. *Brolio! Die!* he thought as he sent the dragon rushing forward. Brolio turned, fire cascading all around him. The wizard spread his arms wide, and a ball of fire formed between his hands. As the dragon plummeted to strike, Brolio hurled the fireball at Malchom. Malchom searched his mind for a defense against the fireball but had found none when the ball impacted with his wall of wind. The explosion catapulted him backward as it blew the hillock into dust. The earth shook, and a geyser erupted from a hole that Gorwin had disappeared into. Malchom landed with a thud that forced the air out of his lungs. The fist-sized emerald landed on his chest and rolled toward his face.

Malchom tried to breathe but couldn't. He tried to breathe and found he did not need to. Around him was blackness. He felt as if he was floating. There seemed to be substance to his thoughts, but he could find no solidity to his body. A tingling ran through his mind, as if his brain was being tickled with a feather. The tingling became faster and faster. The sensation became a torment as something sifted through his mind. He screamed without sound.

"You are a most interesting person," a voice said. It seemed to reverberate with the tonal qualities of several individual voices meshed together, as if a crowd was speaking to him at once.

"Who are you?" he replied.

"I am not a who, but you may call me Jux. It is a name that seems to have stuck with me."

"Why can't I move? Where am I?"

"You cannot move because you no longer have a physical body." Jux's voice seemed to move through his mind and pause at specific spots. The tingling sensation followed the voice's movements.

"Are you in my mind?" Malchom asked.

"No. You most likely are inside of my mind."

"I don't understand, what's happened to me?"

"Well, what do you *remember* happening to you?" said Jux.

"We were fighting, the other wizards and I. Altair had decreed that only one of us was to survive. Did I fail? Are you another of Altair's avatars?"

"No. Continue."

"The battle was quick. I assume I only lasted for a minute or two. I remember Brolio hurling a fireball at me. It exploded, and I was thrown backward. Then everything went black, and you spoke to me shortly thereafter. I felt as if you were sifting through my mind."

"That I am. Your mind and I are now one."

"But I still don't understand. What happened to me?"

"Can you remember anything else?" prodded Jux.

"I'd used the wind to create a wall around me, just after an emerald fell at my feet. It just seemed to appear before me. I don't think any of the other wizards threw it at me. It didn't do anything."

"Did you touch it?" asked Jux.

"No, it fell to my feet. I think it was caught in midair while I was casting my wind-wall spell."

"Well, the emerald obviously touched your skin at some point, for it is within that gem that your soul now inhabits. The emerald you encountered is a magical gem that traps the soul of any creature it touches. You are here, so the gem touched your skin at some point."

"I think . . ." Malchom's recollection of the battle seemed to jump to life as Jux's probing found the specific memory.

"Here it is. The explosion blew you back, and the gem landed on your face. At that time, your soul was transferred to the gem." Jux replayed the memory several times before speaking again. "Do you now understand?"

"What's happened to my body?"

"That I do not know. I have no connection to the outside world. All I can tell you is that the soul that was previously filling this gem was transferred into your body, much to my relief."

"You mean somebody else has my body?"

"Not exactly," said Jux. "The previous tenant was not a person. The mind was very crude, not very intelligent, and as far as I can judge, was a rodent of some sort."

"You mean a *rat* lives in my body!" exclaimed Malchom.

"As far as I can tell."

"But if this gem switches souls around, who are you?"

The memories faded. Malchom opened his eyes, the eyes of his new body. *How long ago was it that I was imprisoned in that gem? Long enough that Altair no longer hears me. The child. The child's blood drew his attention, maybe the Elf's as well.* He decided to try just the child, somewhere away from the house, well after the family went to sleep. Malchom closed his eyes and continued to pray to his god.

The moons had begun to set by the time he woke. Standing stiffly, he quietly dressed and belted the sword to his waist. *White. Humph, I should have known this person was a knight.* With his knife, he cut open the crude pillow and emptied the down onto the floor. The pillowcase he shredded into several strips and tucked them in his belt. He stuffed one of the bed's blankets into his backpack and slipped his arms through the straps. He took a deep breath.

The house beyond his bedroom was silent and still. Despite the suspicions that had clearly manifested themselves in Zorin's reactions, the elf evidently did not feel threatened enough to watch over Malchom. He left his room and plodded down the hallway as carefully as he could. *Damn!* he thought. *Where would the child be?* He wished he had paid more attention when Shar had brought the baby out. He reached the common room where he had dined and noticed that the main door was open. A breeze flowed freely through the room. Was someone awake, or was this just to cool the house? He heard a faint banging noise beside him and turned toward the sound. The shutters were open, and one of them softly swung against the moorings that held it against the outside wall. An idea came to his head, and he left the house as quietly as he could.

Outside he cautiously circled the house. Every window he came to had its shutters propped open. One by one he peered into the portals looking for the child. His hopes rose when he came to the window to the child's room. The child was alone in the room. It slept soundly in a wooden crib covered by a thin gauzy insect net. The window was very low to the ground, and Malchom's large frame made it easy for him to step into the room.

The door to this room remained open, presumably to let any sound the child might make filter to its mother, and allowed the breeze to flow through here as well. The room was all but empty of any furniture or other items. A collection of small articles of clothing rested inside an open chest. Malchom picked up one of the baby's shirts and ripped off a section. Moving to the crib, he wadded the fabric into a ball.

"Little Zeddidiah," cooed Malchom. "Come to Malchom, good boy, good little Zed." He wondered if the child was male. Male blood would be much more preferable. He drew aside the bug netting and carefully picked up the child, who stirred and began to make noises as it began to wake. "Ah ah ah . . . none of that now." Malchom stuffed the clump of cloth into the child's mouth and hurried back to the window. A strong gust of wind blew through the house as he awkwardly climbed out the window. Despite the bundle in his hands and the wind outside buffeting him, he successfully made it outside and was rushing toward the woods before he realized that he had gotten away unnoticed.

No alarm was raised from the house. No screams of surprise or anguished cries answered the banging shutters or whistling wind that continued to echo through the night. Only the muffled, spasmodic jerking of the child and his own controlled, heavy breathing could be heard above the rustling of the nearing trees. Reaching the wood, he plunged behind a tree and turned to observe the house. No change, no sign of pursuit.

"We got away," he said, looking down at the child. Zeddidiah's nostrils were covered in snot and flared in and out violently. Malchom realized that the cloth was choking the child. He removed the fabric and again attempted to soothe the child. "There there, little one. Shhh . . ." Out of curiosity, Malchom checked the gender of the child. Male. Good. Altair would be happiest with male blood. "You, see little one, Altair, who is my god, and much more powerful than any other, utterly abhors elves and the other demihuman races. Spilling the blood of an elf in his name is a very powerful thing to do, indeed. He especially likes it when male blood is spilled, for every male elf that is sacrificed reduces the amount of seed that the soiled race has available to it. You will bring His attention back. I want to thank you for your selfless deed. First, we must build a fire." He walked farther into the wood, to a small clearing he felt was well shielded from the house. He placed the child on the ground and began gathering wood for a fire. By breaking dead branches from the surrounding trees, he soon had enough kindling to provide him with adequate flame. A few seconds later, he had sparked life to the fire and was soon waiting for the flames to build. While the flames grew, he returned to the child and used the strips of cloth tucked in his belt to fashion a harness around Zeddidiah. When he thought the fire large enough, he grabbed the knife out of his backpack and held the child as high as he could over the flames.

"Altair! Hear me! With this elven child's blood I call to thee! Hear me! Grant me power!" He brought the knife to the child's throat and silenced its growing screams. Blood poured onto the fire. "Altair! Hear my prayers! Grant me the power to return home. Grant me the power to understand the language of this day. Altair! By the power of this blood spilled, grant me the ability to create food and water, Altair! Hear me!" The child had ceased to move, its blood had quickly drained onto the fire. The fire popped and nearly sputtered out as blood splashed down upon it. Malchom released his grip on the child's harness. The lifeless body fell to the fire, flinging sparks outward and nearly dousing the flames entirely.

"I don't understand, Altair! Why do you not answer me!" Malchom fell to his knees. Why was Altair not answering him? Could his god have forsaken him entirely? Surely Altair knew of his imprisonment inside the gem. How much time had elapsed since then? Was Altair gone entirely from this realm? He staggered to his feet. A physical weight stemming from his plummeting spirits dragged him down. He felt abandoned. Altair was never going to answer him.

"Malchom!" He whirled to find Zorin standing at the fringes of the firelight. In the elf's right hand was a short fat sword, in his left was a long thin dagger. "What manner of evil is this? Who are you talking with? Where is my child?" By the anguish on Zorin's face, Malchom reasoned that the elf already knew what had happened to the infant.

"Can't you tell, elf? Does the smell that hangs in the air not tell you what has befallen the little one? Take a deep breath, elf." He inhaled deeply. "For this is a smell that shall soon be as common as the smell of wildflowers in a country glade."

"What kind of knight are you?"

"KNIGHT! No, not a Dun Lian knight any longer. I worship the god Altair! And your blood shall help me gain his favor once more."

"Altair? You're mad! That religion has been dead for over a thousand years."

"Not dead, elf, just sleeping."

"And it shall continue to sleep!" rasped Zorin as he rushed forward. Malchom sidestepped the elf, the long sword instantly in his hand. A natural fighting instinct seemed to be instilled within his new body. The elf spun and swung the short sword in a shallow arc, which Malchom saw and effortlessly parried. He did not see the dagger as it slipped inside his stomach. The elf was off balance, and the thrust held no power behind it. It penetrated Malchom's leather armor, but not by much. Malchom punched Zorin with his left fist and caught the off-balanced elf squarely in the jaw. Zorin crumpled to the ground with the force of the blow. Malchom placed a booted foot on the back of the fallen elf's neck.

"Thus, it begins," he said casually as he slammed the sword's pommel onto the elf's skull with a sickening crack, rendering the elf unconscious. He dragged the elf's body to the fire. It had almost gone out. He could not understand why Altair had not answered him. More twigs and branches were thrown onto the flames. An elven child should have been enough to bring an avatar to hear his prayer at least. He crouched low and blew hard on the base of the flames. *If one child will not call Him down, then perhaps I need to spill more blood, spill blood until he once again looks in my direction.* He added wood to the fire until he thought it was strong enough to burn the two elven bodies. He then sliced open Zorin's neck and traced a circle of blood around the fire before tossing the lifeless body onto the flames. Zeddidiah's corpse was next. When he was done, he seared his knife in the fire, burning the last of the blood off the blade. Malchom prayed to be heard throughout the entire episode. Gathering his scant belongings, he crept back toward the house.

Lamps had been lit, both inside and outside the dwelling. As he drew nearer to the house, he could see Shar through a window, pacing back and forth. Shell sat at the table, stress showing around her tired eyes. Arin was nowhere to be seen. Malchom stole his way past the window and approached the front door. His hard-soled boots echoed too loudly on the wooden landing of the front steps. He drew the sword and decided to do it quickly. He heard an excited voice at the door and, with a swiftness of action that continued to surprise him, kicked the door open.

Shar was thrown backward with a bang and crumpled against the side wall. At the table, Shell stood and screamed. Across the table knelt Arin. He had been attempting to start a fire but now stared up at the doorway, fear oozing from his face.

Malchom wasted no time. In two strides he was upon Shell. In one stroke, she was down, grasping her stomach as she struggled to keep her intestines within her. A quick leap onto the table, and he was slashing down at Arin, nearly severing the man's head. Blood was rapidly reaching across the floor, sinking through the spaces between the floorboards. Dizzy with excitement, he dropped to the floor and disemboweled Arin as well, allowing as much blood to rush out as possible. Malchom was in a frenzy. He dipped his free hand in blood and wrote prayers to Altair in his now-ancient tongue upon the walls. A warped thought came to him. He drew the Dun Lian symbol on each wall and the outside door with the old couple's blood. He then chopped off their heads and placed them on the stoop.

Shar groaned. Again, instinctively, he cleaned and sheathed his sword and approached Shar. He grabbed her and hauled her into the chair next to the lifeless form of Shell. Shar's eyes fluttered open.

"Good morning, pretty one," Malchom said. "You know you deserve to die. Befouling your body by letting that *elf* beget a son by you. I should torture you just to purge you of sin."

Shar began babbling. Her pleas fell on Malchom's uncomprehending ears. Only the word "Zeddidiah" had meaning for Malchom. Malchom noticed she held the Dun Lian medallion from his backpack in her hands. She must have taken it before Zorin had returned his things.

He wrenched the piece of metal from her hands as she began to mutter "Dun Malchom" over and over.

"You see this!" he raged at her, holding the medallion in her face. "You see this! You think me one of them? Look around you, would one of your knights do something like this? I am Malchom Jamias!" he bellowed. "You cannot see who I truly am." He waved the medallion in front of her. "All you can see is this! Well, if you cannot see the truth, then you truly should not see."

Malchom held her head in his long left arm. With his new body's strength he was well able to keep her head immobile in her weakened condition. He used the medallion to gouge her eyes out. She screamed and struggled through the first one, but had passed out by the time the second eye popped loose and hit the floor with a satisfying squish as he tossed the medallion on top of it. She was still breathing when Malchom finally left the house, having raided it for supplies.

He moved to the barns, found several horses in one and picked what he thought was the best. It was a large beast, young and thick with work-hardened muscles. The sun was just coming up by the time he started down the road. In the light of the new day, he could see that he was very bloody. Dried blood covered his hands and most of his forearms. His leather armor was punctured at the stomach; caked blood was encrusted on the tear. His left arm, from elbow to shoulder, was covered in blood, Shar's, he assumed. The emblem on his chest was red; it glowed eerily in the morning light. Even though he enjoyed his condition, almost craved for more, he thought it unwise to wander into a town decorated as such.

It was midday by the time he came across a small stream in which to bathe. Removing all of his clothing for the first time, he marveled at how honed his muscles were. Despite the fact that he seemed to have retained some amount of this knight's training, he decided he would have to begin learning the ways of the warrior. He would do it for no other reason than to keep his new body in such superb shape. Although, with the possibility of not recovering his former powers, the prospect of earning his keep by the sword held a lusty appeal all its own. He had always had an affinity to death and killing, and as he washed the dried blood from his body and clothing, he decided he really liked being able to physically take the life of another. His former body had been fairly frail and unimposing. The powers granted him by his god had always conveyed his control over others. The possibility of pairing physical prowess with a sword and the magical abilities he hoped to soon have restored rejuvenated his resolve.

He camped that evening by the stream. The sky was clear, and the stars were out. They looked the same. If the spot where he emerged into this new body was the same spot in which he was originally imprisoned, then his castle, if it still stood, would be but another week's travel to the west.

The stars reminded him of Shar. He wondered why he had not ravaged her. She was not a comely creature, but it had been a while since he had been with a woman. Over a thousand years, from what the elf had said. *Altair? You're mad! That religion has been dead for over a thousand years,* the elf had said. A thousand years since Altair's influence had died away. What had happened to the others? Had they killed each other off? What of Altair's proclamation that only one would survive to continue on in His service? He would have to enlist the services of a sage. After all, he had a thousand years of learning to catch up on. Who had thrown the gem at him? Where had the artifact come from?

He fingered the bottom of his backpack. The gem *would* make an excellent weapon, once he discarded the soul within it currently. What would he do with it? He could hold the gem up to a small animal. Would the transference take place if his skin did not touch the gem itself? He felt daunted by the amount of work he had in front of him.

The following afternoon, he came upon another traveler on the road. It was a dwarf mounted on a stocky pony, which Malchom found unusual. The dwarf was stopped on the side of the road, his eyes searching the skies, when Malchom approached him.

"Greetings, dwarf," he said in the dwarven tongue.

The dwarf shielded his eyes with a heavily gloved hand while he watched Malchom approach.

"Greetings, Sir Knight," the squat creature replied.

"I take it you are far from home."

"How so?"

"One does not usually find your kind mounted."

"That is true," admitted the dwarf. "But when I fly my birds, I like to roam far."

"Ah, a falconer. That would explain the gloved hand," Malchom said, looking to the sky, seeking the dwarf's animal. An idea came to his mind.

"I have a question and a favor to ask." Malchom nudged his mount closer to the dwarf.

"Ask away." The dwarf's pony shuffled to one side, agitated by the nearness of Malchom's bulky beast.

"A few days ago, I came across an emerald of exquisite size. I wonder, would you happen to know anything of appraisal?"

"As much as any of *my kind* would know," snorted the dwarf contemptuously. "If that's what you mean."

"Uh, yes, please, excuse my rudeness." He dismounted. "I have it here in my backpack." Malchom unslung his pack and began removing its contents as the dwarf spied his bird and whistled. Malchom placed the sack containing the gem on the ground. The bird alighted on the dwarf's leathered hand. Malchom waited nervously as the dwarf affixed the bird's hood.

"That certainly is a mighty big gem, if that's all that is in that sack," said the dwarf as he dismounted, placing the hooded hawk on his saddle's pommel.

"I packed it in dirt," Malchom explained. "I did not want to damage it." He upended the sack, spilling the clump to the ground.

As if on cue, the dwarf knelt, pushed some dirt aside, and poked the gem with his gloved hand. Nothing happened. The dwarf reached for the gem with his other hand.

"Please don't touch it!" Malchom started forward, stopping the dwarf by placing a hand on his shoulder.

"Well, how do you expect me to examine it and answer your question if I don't touch it?" asked the dwarf grumpily.

"Actually," Malchom said, drawing his sword, "you have told me all I want to know."

Sometime later, someone would find the pony's body, lying on the side of the road, its decapitated head pointing in the direction Malchom had come. Even the bird's skull pointed east.

"Altair!" Malchom screamed silently several hours later. "Altair! Hear me! Hear my cries and witness my sacrifice!" He moved around the clearing he had found just off the road. He held the dwarf aloft so that the body was suspended with its face toward the flames of a small fire. Malchom brought the knife up to the dwarf's skin and slashed open the throat, spilling the too-rapidly-coagulating blood. The fluid poured onto the fire. The flames leapt and danced as the blood fueled the fire into a frenzy of spitting and popping chaos.

"With this dwarven blood I sacrifice in Your name, hear me, Altair! Accept this dwarven male's blood in exchange for the powers I ask! Hear me and grant me the power to understand the common language of this land. Grant me the power to return home. Grant me the power to create food and water.

Grant me the knowledge of the history of the world since I was imprisoned. Grant me these things, and more blood shall be sacrificed in Your name! Altair! Hear me!" The fire had raged higher and higher and now began to consume the flesh of the dwarf. Malchom's own hands began to burn. He let go of the body and it fell into the fire.

The body bounced on the burning wood and created a slight explosion that startled Malchom; he staggered back several feet as sparks speckled the day around him. The tiny pinpoints of fire swirled past him. They circled the clearing several times before forming a fiery figure that floated above the flames.

"Ahhh!" sighed the form with an earthy voice. "Dwarf blood. Young male dwarf blood." The figure's blazing eyes turned toward Malchom. "You have the look of a Dun Lian knight, but your soul is blacker than that of any I have seen in a while. State your name, mortal!" the voice boomed in Malchom's head.

"Great avatar of Altair, I am Malchom Jamias. My mind is open to you. Look upon it with yours, for the telling of my story would take too much time." Malchom cleared his thoughts and began to replay the events that had brought him to this point. He awaited the avatar's touch. A fiery, disembodied hand reached out of the flames and found Malchom's forehead. Fire ripped through his mind as the avatar drew the information out of Malchom's thoughts.

"So, Malchom Jamias, you've been returned to the land of the living. This world is not as it was when you last walked upon it. Altair's worshippers have all died. He has turned His attention elsewhere. I was left here to gaze wearily decade after decade upon these mortals, should any decide to call upon His grace once more. I thank you for having relieved my boredom and regret that I cannot return you to your former glory."

"What do you mean?" Panic began to rise in Malchom's mind.

"Altair is too busy on other worlds to direct any attention or power to this plane of existence. Especially for a single worshipper."

"But you are here," he said desperately. "Surely you can do something. Can you not tell Altair of my return?"

"True, I do have the ability to infuse you with lesser powers, but nothing that would rival the power you once wielded. And I am afraid it would be too little to begin converting the people of this world back to His worship enough to entice Him to pay attention to this world again."

Malchom fell to his knees. His resolve faltered. "No powers," he mumbled. Despair entered his heart, and he began to sob. What would he do without the power of Altair to back him? How would he exert his control over the souls of this world? He sighed, composed himself, and rose to his feet. "Well then, avatar, give me what you can. Fill my soul with your scant power that I might begin my work." *My soul*, he thought. *The gem! I knew it would be a powerful weapon. I will use it to enslave the leaders of this nation. They will help me avert Altair's eyes back upon this world.* "Yes, avatar! Give me your power, for I intend to bring such a slaughter to this realm that Altair will have no choice but to acknowledge me once more! Yes, that will do it. With your help, avatar, with your help and your powers, I will decimate any who oppose me!"

"So be it," boomed the voice of the avatar. Malchom dropped to his knees as the familiar surge of power rushed into his being.

Two days later, awash in cheers and praiseful greetings, he rode into a village. One of the first things he had done after receiving his god's blessings was to peruse the previously unreadable book he was carrying. It turned out to be a journal. He was titled Dun Lain, an adaptation of his secular name "Morgan Mclain." He was a recently commissioned knight of the Dun Lian Brotherhood. From what he could fathom, the Brotherhood was a piously aligned organization dedicated to upholding justice. Morgan's descriptions of his intense desire to join the Brotherhood revealed just how revered the Brotherhood was, as was evident by the reactions of those Malchom had met so far.

It seemed the Dun Lian Brotherhood was "for hire," as Morgan had made several mentions of hopefully attaining duty rotations on other continents. Evidently, against the wishes of a knight by the name of Dun Loren, Morgan was off "in search of adventure" when he encountered the pools and the gem.

So with his newly granted understanding of the common language, renewed powers, and an idea of his standing in this society, he rode confidently into the happy hamlet. Half of the population seemed to have turned out as news of the arrival of a Dun Lian knight was shouted up and down the streets. He smiled, returned as many greetings as he could, and asked for directions to the town's inn or tavern. He found his lack of having any currency unimportant as many a drink and several meals were bought for him by the inn's patrons. Neither was the evening's accommodation a problem. He accepted the proposal of a remarkably attractive woman, and as he followed her upstairs that evening, he thought to himself, *Thus it begins.*

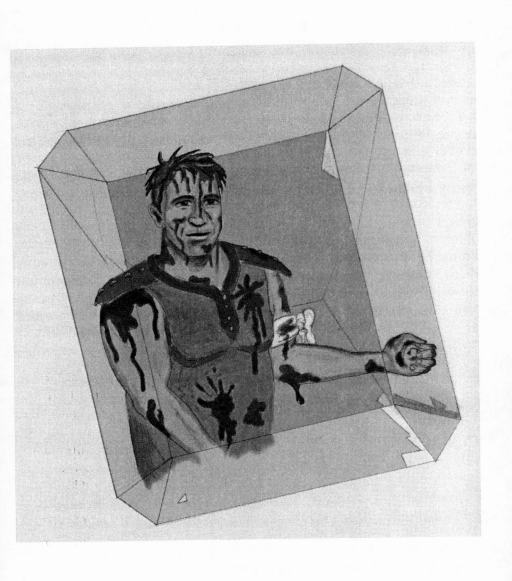

CHAPTER 2

The burning in his lungs ceased and was replaced with a burning within his brain. The sensation of blazing fire ripped through his mind as easily and as quickly as if he was running his fingers through sand. An unseen force sifted his memories, the individual particles of his past. He could see nothing; he felt nothing. Morgan tried to move, attempted to sit up. Nothing. There was no response from his limbs. So complete was the lack of sensory input that Morgan couldn't even be sure he still had a body. He wondered what was happening to him, where he was.

"No, you do not have a body any longer," a voice said. "What has happened to you is easier to explain than where you are," the voice continued after a pause. It seemed as if Morgan's mind was afire. The sensation flared with each sentence the voice uttered.

"What do you mean I don't have a body anymore?" Morgan asked with some difficulty.

"You no longer have a physical body," said the voice, and pain rippled through Morgan's mind.

"Why does it burn when you speak?"

"That will pass as you become accustomed to being without physical substance."

"Explain to me why I don't have a body . . . how am I still alive if I have no body?"

"Well, you are not exactly alive. But the simple truth is this: Your body came in contact with an enchanted gem. This gem has the power to siphon souls into itself. Your soul is no longer contained within your body. It is trapped, within this gem. You, therefore, have no physical body."

"Gem? How did this happen?"

"That I do not know."

"Where was this gem? The last thing I remember I was on the edge of one of the Dead Pools and touched the water by mistake." Morgan searched his memory for what happened next. "And I felt the need to walk into the water. There was this green glow, was that the gem?"

"Most likely."

"Where did it come from?"

"I do not know."

"Are we stuck in here?"

"No, only one soul can inhabit the gem at a given time. At the time of transference, the old soul is forced into the empty body formerly occupied by the new soul."

"But who are you?" Morgan asked.

"I do not know that. But long ago, one of the first souls to be imprisoned within named me Jux."

"Jux?"

"Yes, I remember he named me Juxtaposition," explained Jux. "We speculated that a little bit of every soul imprisoned here is left behind when it leaves. I am what appears to be the combination of those bits and pieces. Not really a who, you see. I seem to retain the memories of all who inhabit the gem, and as each new soul enters, I find myself hungry to explore the memories they bring along with them. I am actually quite pleased to have a new soul. The memories of the last one were getting quite old."

"The last one?"

"Yes, his memories were quite violent, and I found that I did not wish to review many of them. He wasn't much to talk with either."

"How long was he in here?" inquired Morgan.

"I do not know. It is impossible to keep track of time here. After a while, everyone gives up on the notion of time."

"Who was this person?"

"He called himself Malchom Jamias."

"Jamias! He died over a thousand years ago!" exclaimed Morgan. He was not sure he had even raised his voice.

"No, Morgan, you cannot raise your voice as you do not have a voice anymore. You are but thought now."

"You can hear my thoughts?"

"Since thought is all you are, yes. Remember, we are one now. What you think I can hear. What you know, I can know."

"Wait a minute! This means that *he* is in *my* body!"

"Yes," Jux said with dismay.

"In my body! Damn! I've got to get out of here."

"You cannot. Not unless another creature touches the gem."

"But where is the gem now? It was at the bottom of a lake. I don't want to end up in a fish. Can that happen? Does a fish even have a soul?"

"I do not know, though the minds of animals have been trapped in here. They tend to be very boring. I do not know where the gem might be. I have no way of seeing outside the gem."

"In my body." A dark thought passed over him. "Can Jamias perform magic in my body?" he asked.

"I assume so. His power came from his god. Here, see for yourself." A window opened. Morgan was reliving a memory. It wasn't one he had experienced, but it came from within him. He was seeing through Jamias's eyes; he was Jamias at that point.

He stood in front of an altar. A slab of veined and cracked obsidian rested upon grotesquely carved legs of gold. A trough was chiseled down the center of the volcanic glass. The altar was surrounded by a moat of fire. In his arms was a limp body. Even though it was a child in his arms, he had difficulty depositing the body facedown upon the altar. Morgan saw bony arms as he quickly pulled away from the flames. The body on the altar was still breathing.

"Hear me, Altair!" he was saying. "Accept this sacrifice, and grant me the powers I ask!" Again, he moved to the altar and this time pulled on a chain. A golden blade swished out from the back of the altar.

"Hear me, Altair!" he screamed as blood poured down the trough and spilled onto the fire. "Accept this blood and grant me the power to view my enemies!" Morgan wanted to vomit. The window closed.

"He performed sacrifices to gain the powers he desired," said Jux. "At times he did not need to do so, for lesser powers, I assume."

"So if he starts making sacrifices again . . ."

"Then Altair will answer."

"And *he* is in *my* body. I will be making sacrifices. I will be killing people. At least, that's the way it will look to the rest of the world, to my brothers. My god, all hell will break loose."

"Your brothers?" inquired Jux.

"Yes, my brothers. I am a Dun Lian knight. Don't you know this? I though you know what I know?" Morgan asked, perplexed.

"The mind is a vastly complex thing. It will take a while to know all of it. I have but scratched the surface. So you are a knight. Think back, back to how you became a knight, so that I can understand."

How did he become a knight? He had always wanted to be a knight. He remembered when he was a boy. A Dun Lian knight had visited his father's shop. The memory was replayed with a clarity that he had never before experienced.

*   *   *

Ansel was standing at the counter talking with a customer. Father was at the doorway to the back room, watching Ansel with pride. Morgan was unpacking a crate of lanterns and arranging them in a display near the entrance to his father's supply store. This was the newest of four shops owned by his father. His family had moved to Rivingwyre in the late winter, his father wishing to oversee the opening of the new store.

His father had been in business for nearly two decades selling hunting and fishing supplies. Rivingwyre was a young town on the edges of civilization and was an excellent place for a business such as his father's. He watched his older brother with a large amount of envy as he meticulously stacked the hooded lanterns on top of several of the empty crates. The family business was very successful. This new store was expected to do very well, as the demand for camping and hunting supplies was very great here at the edge of the world.

"And it's all going to Ansel," Morgan mumbled under his breath. Being second born had left him with little hope when it came to inheriting the family business. Managing one of the stores was about all that was in line for him. It had been suggested that he become a scholar. Father said he would pay for all of Morgan's learning if he wished it.

"Humph. Let *Ansel* shove his nose in a library full of books while *I* become the rich merchant."

"Talking to yourself is a trait of the old." Morgan jumped, knocking over several lanterns. His father grimaced in his direction and saw the same thing Morgan did.

Looming in the doorway was a massive figure that shed light all around him. A messy mop of blond hair and reddish beard framed a suntanned face. Deep blue eyes stared down at him. Morgan shielded his eyes as his brain slowly registered the words spoken by this vision.

"And clumsy too," said the figure as he knelt and neatly set the fallen lanterns upright. "I'm Grant. And you would be . . . ," he said, taking Morgan's hand and shaking it firmly.

"M-m-morgan," he stuttered.

"Well, Morgan, you must be the proprietor of this wonderful shop. A bit young to be an established merchant, but nonetheless, I require supplies. Can you call one of your assistants to act as my porter?"

"Well, actually, I'm eight," he said, his fear melting under Grant's respectful, confident gaze. "Actually it's my father's store."

"Ah. And where might your father be?" the man said, standing with a clanging of metal armor.

"At your service, Sir Knight," interrupted Morgan's father, who had hurried over. "I am Abram Mclain," he said and bowed nervously. Morgan had never seen his father act in such a way and his awe of this metal-clad behemoth deepened.

The memory blurred.

It was several days later. He was outside the store, busily slaying an invisible dragon of immense size with a wooden slat from one of the packing crates when his father and the knight exited the building. They were shaking hands as if they had known each other for years.

"Morgan, come here," his father called.

He fought his way through multitudes of imagined foes to his father's side.

"Killing monsters, eh?" said Abram, engulfing his son in his arms. "You've become quite handy with that sword in the past few days."

Morgan shook his head vigorously.

"How would you," continued his father, "like to go with Dun Loren and learn to be a real knight?"

Morgan looked up at his father. "Can I?" was all he said.

The two men burst in laughter.

*   *   *

"I was to find out later that it was a deal arranged by my father," Morgan said to Jux, interrupting the memory. "Dun Loren needed a new squire, my father wanted the knight's business. Eventually, Dun Loren began sending other knights to that shop in Rivingwyre. I believe it is still the sole supplier to the garrison stationed there."

"You sound as if you have not been back."

"No. I haven't. I didn't want to return until I had something to show for myself."

"You became a knight."

"So. Well, I guess that was enough. Should have been anyway. I guess I was too anxious to do something once I was accepted." The memory of his knighting ceremony surfaced.

*   *   *

The courtyard was filled with over a hundred knights. It was the morning of the summer solstice, and scores of brothers had arrived to participate in the annual festivities.

As was tradition, Morgan sat with his fellow squires in the center of the grassy courtyard. Large by any standards, the walled courtyard of the Dun Lian Brotherhood's home garrison was crowded with people. The squires had been sitting here for almost a full day. A sword lay unsheathed across each squire's knees.

A day before his knighting, a squire was to begin a vigil, emulating the final day in the life of their Order's founder, Dun Lian. At the conclusion of the ceremony, each newly knighted member of the Order would take a name by which he would be known for the rest of his life. Traditionally, a knight would take some form of his last name and mix it with their founder's first name. Morgan had chosen to be known as Dun Lain.

Above the main entrance to the courtyard, a platform had been erected. It was from here that Dun Lian, the head of the Order, would officially welcome the squires into the Brotherhood. The current leader of the knighthood had been in power for twenty-one years. Being named the head of the Order was a lifelong position and allowed each leader to choose his own successor. Since the beginning of the knighthood, each leader had chosen the title of Dun Lian to honor their founder. The head of the Order was not bound to choose the name *Dun Lian*, but as the centuries passed, it became one of the longest-running traditions in the Brotherhood.

Morgan's arm ached. He was sure every other squire's arm ached as well. The gash on his upper arm would heal slowly. It would also leave a scar. His sponsor, Dun Loren, had cut him and then applied a poultice to aggravate the wound, again to imitate Dun Lian's last day. Every Dun Lian knight had a scar on his upper left arm.

And there he had sat, through the day and into the night. He sat with his fellow squires keeping vigil. As tradition dictated, they were supposed to be attacked sometime before dawn. Dun Lian had sat as they did now, in a grassy glade, his left arm nearly severed, awaiting the mob that would end his life.

The gaining light of the day became bright enough to begin reflecting off of the assembled knight's armor. For hours now, the knights had been gathering. Slowly, one by one, they filled in the ranks that surrounded the squires. At odd intervals, every knight had drawn his sword and held it, ready to strike. Light glinted off of armor and sword alike; the courtyard was ablaze with reflected sunshine.

He knew it was only ceremony, that no harm, other than the cut in his arm, would befall him. But the slow gathering of knights and the sporadic grating of drawn weapons unnerved him. Morgan wanted to know what was going to happen.

As the sun broke the horizon, Dun Lian appeared on the platform. He inspected the gathering. Without a word, he drew his great sword. It was a massive weapon, believed to have belonged to Dun Lian himself and held magical abilities and granted certain protections to the one who held it. Only the Dun Lian was ever allowed to touch the weapon, and only the Dun Lian knew what those abilities might be. The assembled knights crowded in. They slowly and noisily closed the ring that circled the thirty-five squires who had jumped to their feet, swords held ready. Morgan backed up, as did the other squires, until they formed a circle. Dun Loren was standing directly in front of Morgan, his sword in Morgan's face and an exaggerated grin on his own. Each squire faced his sponsor; row upon row of knights encircled them now.

In unison, all thirty-five sponsors roared and dropped to one knee, their swords clattering with the squires' blades. At the same time, the remaining knights dropped their weapons and raised a small round red ball above their heads.

Chaos erupted as the sponsors began jabbing swords at the squires' feet. Distracted in attempting to fend off Dun Loren's advances, Morgan did not see the multitudes of incoming balls.

They broke over his helmet, they broke on his sword, and they broke when they hit his shoulder piece. Dozens of small bladders filled with red poisonberry juice erupted all around him, soaking his armor in the color of blood, seeping through to his skin and staining it. In seconds, every squire and many of the sponsors were covered head to foot in sticky red berry juice.

The roars turned to laughter as the mock fighting died down suddenly. Swords were retrieved and sheathed as the knights gathered in on the stunned squires. Dun Loren stepped up to him. In his hands was a medallion. Made of platinum and covered in berry juice, it reflected the morning's light with a slight reddish hue.

In the memory, he heard Jux chuckling.

CHAPTER 3

The parchment felt heavy in his hands. He looked up at Dun Lian. Amazed, he asked, "When did you get this?"

"It arrived this morning. Now you understand why I summoned you. This is by far the most heinous circumstance that has befallen the Order since its conception nearly a millennium ago. I fear that there can be no relaxation of our traditions in this matter."

"Yes, yes," he replied and read the letter again.

Dun Lian,

It is with regret that I confirm the rumors surrounding the recent killings I informed you of in my last dispatch. As I reported earlier, seventy-one of the Maralat townsfolk were slaughtered before the suspect fled west. It has been confirmed that the death toll now stands at seventy-seven. Six more were added to the list today.

The remains of the first body were found several miles out of the village. A slaughtered horse on the roadside prompted our men to search the surrounding woods. The burnt body of a dwarf was found in a nearby clearing.

Continuing east, our scouts came across a farmhouse about a day's ride from the Dead Pools. In the woods surrounding the farm, a campfire was discovered. The bones of an elf and an infant were littered about the campsite. Inside the house were two decapitated bodies and, surprisingly, a female survivor. Her eyes had been plucked from her head. She did not survive long enough to give us any information.

Painted in blood upon the walls of the common room was a writing, which we have not yet deciphered. In addition, and most disturbingly, the Dun Lian Scales of Justice were also sketched in blood upon the walls and door to the building. All in all, it was a most gruesome scene.

Again, I regret to inform Your Honor that the rumors concerning the identity of the culprit are now confirmed. The young woman, before she expired, relinquished from her grasp a Medallion of Merit. The platinum shield was bloodied, and bits of flesh still clung to it. It appears that the shield, our gift to newly commissioned knights, was the implement of the young woman's torture.

These facts confirm the rumors that it was a Dun Lian knight responsible for the massacre at the village. Surviving villagers have all described the knight with unwavering accuracy. There can be no doubt that Dun Lain is responsible. May Kasparow have mercy on his soul.

I have placed the village of Maralat under quarantine in an attempt to keep knowledge of these events from spreading. I await further instructions.

Your servant,

Dun Dison

He let the letter drop to the table. The majestic council hall of the Dun Lian Brotherhood seemed cold and harsh. The evening sunlight streamed in through the vaulted stained glass windows and refused to warm his skin. A shiver ran through him as Dun Lian, head of the Order spoke, his voice echoing throughout the chamber.

"You were Dun Lain's sponsor, were you not?"

"Yes, Dun Lian," he said heavily.

"You understand your duties, then, Dun Loren."

"Yes, Dun Lian." He bowed his head as Dun Lian spoke to the scribe seated to his left.

"Let it be recorded, then," said Dun Lian formally, looking back to the dejected knight, "that Dun Loren, as Dun Lain's sponsor, has accepted responsibility for Dun Lain's actions. He is hereby charged with the duty of bringing Dun Lain before me to be judged. Failure to do so within three calendar months will result in the forfeiture of Dun Loren's holdings and title. How respond you, Dun Loren?"

"I accept the charge, Your Honor." He kept his head low as Dun Lian continued.

"This came for you as well." Dun Loren looked up. Dun Lian held another letter in his hand. "I suggest you leave as soon as possible."

"Yes, Dun Lian." He left the council chamber and read the letter as he walked. It was short; he finished it before he reached the stables. He found his horse and began to ready it. He was agitated. He was having a hard time buckling the saddle. His horse sensed his restlessness and was jumpy, making his job even harder.

"Why the hell did you have to go to those damned pools?" he said to no one. He finally secured his saddle. He pulled a small apple from a bin hanging on the wall and palmed it in front of his horse's mouth.

"Here you go, boy. We're all finished."

Two young men burst into the stables; both were breathing hard, wild looks on their faces. He turned to them. He was always amazed at how exactly alike they were. Not just twins physically, but even every detail of their mannerisms was mirrored in each other. He was still amazed. The twins had said that their mother could tell them apart. He couldn't. So when they had come to him as his new squires, the first thing he had done was to order one of them to shave, and keep shaved, his head.

"Dun Loren!" said the bald brother. "We were getting your supplies together. We didn't know you wanted your horse readied immediately!"

"Please forgive us!" said the other brother.

"Boys, relax. I *needed* to do this myself. Clerents, check his shoes."

The bald-headed brother moved to the horse and began his task in silence.

"I can imagine," said Justin, the other brother. "Rest assured, Dun Loren, this is something you will never have to do with us."

Dun Loren studied the squire. That was a little brazen, wasn't it? Justin was a bit more brass than his brother was, probably the only difference between the two. That, and now the fact that Justin had long brown hair while Clerents had a brown scalp. Justin's boldness had gotten him into trouble already. On the right side of his head, around the temple area, was a gray discoloration, the only other way to tell the boys apart. Justin had received that mark during his first month as a squire.

One of the trademark weapons of a Dun Lian knight, the Malta, was a small handheld, spring-loaded tube that fired a single poison-coated dart. It was a single-use item that was to be used only as a last resort, to save a knight's life. Once drawn, tradition required that it must be fired. If the weapon was drawn without reason, or rashly, the knight was required to discharge it at his own person. The dart could be removed and the weapon dry fired. Dry firing a Malta against skin left a characteristic mark as the spring slapped against bare flesh and embedded small bits of lead just under the surface of the skin. It was considered somewhat of a dishonor to have a Malta mark. If correct penance was made, a knight with a Malta mark was allowed to cut away the embedded lead, leaving only a normal scar at the temple.

Justin had drawn his Malta in anger at his brother. Both boys had frozen when the incident occurred. They remained completely still, not knowing what to do, for nearly an hour before Dun Loren found them. Administering Justin's punishment had proved very difficult for him to do. To be a knight branded with a Malta mark was one matter; to be just a squire and so marked carried a very heavy stigma.

In the thousand years since the Order's conception, only two members of the knighthood, the McAri brothers, Dun Zona and Dun Ari, had acquired a Malta mark before their knighting. The stories of those two knights were well known, and not just amongst the Dun Lian knights. It was a tale told around many campsites and by many storytellers. Dun Loren had spun the yarn several times himself, including twice to his current squires.

The first time had been during the twin's first night in the wild. The boys had been born and raised in the city of Rendarin, which was one of the five great walled cities of the Kingdom of Aplarlan. For all of their lives, before becoming Dun Loren's squires, the boys had lived entirely inside the city. Trees, small creatures, and the sounds of nature had been unsettling to the twins on that first outing. Dun Loren thought the story of the two knights would calm the boys. Dun Ari and Dun Zona had been brothers as well, adding a bit of affinity to the story.

The second time he told the story to the boys had been at their request, shortly after Justin had received his Malta mark. Chatter and speculation spread rapidly through the knighthood after Justin's marking. Many believed the twins to be doomed to repeat the actions of the McAri brothers.

The horse winced. "Careful, Clerents," he said. He wondered if it was true. Was Clerents doomed to bring dishonor to the knighthood on a scale that the McAri brothers had? "Justin, are your horses readied?"

"Not yet, Dun Loren."

"Well then, get to it. I have a small errand to run, and then I want to leave. Actually, fetch a scribe to my room first." He left the stables and headed for his apartments.

A shadow of clouds drew across the courtyard as he walked, accentuating his mood. Now dark and gloomy, the courtyard had been the sight in which he had participated in, what was it, fifteen knighting ceremonies so far? He wondered if he would see another; would he be able to make it through to the twin's knighting? If he failed to retrieve Morgan, then he would be stripped of his knighthood. Justin and Clerents might not be able to finish their training. His disgrace would extend to them as well, and who would want to take on two squires tarnished as such? Especially one with a Malta mark.

Regardless of the result of *his* charges, what would befall the Order? If Morgan continued this murdering rampage, what ramifications would it have on the order's worldwide standing and reputation? A for-hire force that prided itself in its pious perpetuation of justice and law, the order might never survive such a scandal. He knew of at least two kings and one religiously ruled government that would immediately sever relations with the order. And what of the order's rivals and enemies? How would they abuse this event? He hoped that Dun Dison's quarantine would work, at least until he could locate Morgan.

"This can't be right," he mumbled to himself as he opened the door to his apartments. His living quarters at the Dun Lian Brotherhood's main castle of Lianome was by no means lavish. A modest three-room apartment, it was sparsely furnished. The washroom contained only a shower and privy stall. The bedroom was just as vacant with a single straw-filled futon, its only piece of furniture. He never spent much time at Castle Lianome, and when he did, it was mainly to attend to clerical affairs. Which is why the drawing room was the only chamber of the three that he had spent any effort in furnishing.

In front of a large set of yellow stained glass windows was his desk. Finely crafted of stained polished wood, the desk dated four hundred years old and was one of his favorites. The drawer handles were made of gold. A railing of gold ran along the edge of the tabletop. His Medallion of Merit was displayed on the desk, along with several other mounted commendations he had earned throughout his twenty-one-year tenure as a knight of the Dun Lian Brotherhood. In front of the desk were two purple silk-covered chairs that were studded with generous-sized emeralds. The chairs were almost as old as the desk. Two oil paintings, one of himself and one of his wife, hung on either side of the window. If one peered closely enough at the paintings, the artist's name could be seen in the lower left-hand corner. Pep was a contemporary artist whose recent acclaim was rapidly raising him to the status of Master Painter.

He stepped in front of one painting. Pep had done a wonderful job at capturing his wife's beauty. Her distinctive high cheekbones and angular jaw, the gentle slope of her shoulders, her deeply raven hair, and her slim waist called out to him as they always did when he viewed this painting. The memory of her voice was as crisp as a spring morning. At times he had a hard time believing that she *wasn't* calling out to him. He sighed and turned at a knock on his door.

"Come." A tan-robed, tan-faced scribe entered the room, carrying one of the castle's hallway sconces. The candle within was lit despite the time of day. The golden light streaming in through the yellow glass gave the scribe's skin a putrid-looking orange color.

"You desire my services, Dun Loren?" the scribe said in a well-rehearsed manner as he sat at Dun Loren's desk, placed the sconce on the table, and opened the top drawer, removing several pieces of parchment in the process.

"To Abram Mclain, Proprietor, Wilderness Outfitters, Rivingwyre," he started in a cool, mechanical manner. Rosen Kirkland was a competent scribe, one that he used quite often. Without need of preliminaries, Rosen had snatched a quill off the table, opened the inkwell, and began his transcription before Dun Loren had finished the first sentence. "Heavy is my heart and hand as I write this letter to you." The light in the room dimmed as the clouds continued to gather outside. "The clouds outside my window mock my mood, and even what warm sunlight is left refuses to warm my soul. I fear the darkness may soon gather around your heart as well." He paused to take a deep breath.

"As you can tell from the tone of this letter, the news is not good. There is no easy way to phrase this, so I will come to the point. Your son Morgan has done . . ." He stopped and thought for a moment. He turned toward the scribe. "Strike those last three sentences.

"Your son Morgan has always been one of my favorites. As you know, he was knighted several months ago and set out to make a name for himself. I do not believe you know, however, that he set his sights on the Dead Pools to the east of Aplarlan. What evil lurks in that region is a mystery, which may be what drew Morgan to them. Whatever evil might be there, *evil* has befallen Morgan. Know that he has entered into a situation from which he cannot extract himself without assistance from the Brotherhood. I am, therefore, leaving within the hour to bring him home." He realized he had been pacing and stopped. "When we return, I will see to it that he explains all. Until then, rest assured that I will do all I can to return him home safely. As this is an internal matter, all details are being kept confidential. Please do not heed any rumors that may filter through the realm as their accuracy will no doubt be in question. Respectfully yours, Dun Loren, Castle Lianome."

Dun Loren closed his eyes and breathed deeply again. *And pray as hard as you may, Abram. Pray that Morgan is not responsible for these deaths.*

Rosen was in the process of writing a final copy as Dun Loren walked up behind him and peered over his shoulder. The scribe's script was impeccable; he was truly a master of his trade. Dun Loren had even allowed the scribe to forge his signature at times; such was his trust in the man. When Rosen had finished the letter, he reached over and signed this one himself. The scribe held the paper up and lightly waved it back and forth to dry the ink. He then carefully rolled it and slipped it inside a hollow tube of bone he had removed from the top drawer.

"Do you wish me to wax the ends, Dun Loren?"

Dun Loren nodded. The scribe removed the candle from its holder and slowly dripped the hot wax around the edges of one end of the bone. He continued this slow process until both ends were completely clogged.

"Have that dispatched as soon as possible. And do me a favor, come back in an hour and wake me."

"Yes, Dun Loren."

CHAPTER 4

"First, transport me to my home, the castle I once lived in when I last walked this land."

"Certainly," said the glowing form of the avatar. The incarnation of Malchom's god bowed and waved his hand. Malchom's vision blurred.

"This is not my home!" Malchom cried, dropping his rucksack as his vision refocused. He was in a small clearing. Slightly rolling hills were in the distance.

"Look closer, Malchom. A thousand years have passed." Malchom turned slowly, carefully examining the surroundings. There was a lot of rubble behind him. He recognized the stone. An enormous pile of weathered, cracked, moss-covered bloodstone rocks was all that remained of his once-magnificent castle.

"But . . . but my castle was impregnable, its walls unassailable, its gates unyielding. It can't have been destroyed so completely. It was protected by magic!"

"Protected as long as Altair was present in this world. I told you he has moved on to other dimensions."

"What of the catacombs?"

"They fare better, I believe."

Malchom sighed and sat on a rock. "Then I can work with that."

"Will there be anything else?" inquired the avatar.

"I sacrificed an entire town! You'll grant me more than simply teleporting me here! I now realize the depth of what you have been telling me. I'll need to engage in genocide to bring Altair's attention back. Give me the knowledge of the whereabouts of all the towns within, let's say, a hundred leagues of here. I also want the ability to transport myself and several others at will to any location I choose. And I want that ability to be permanent." He paused for a second. "And I want the ability to create my own food and water. Plus, I want the knowledge of the location of the entrance to the catacombs below me."

"You ask a lot for a mere eighty deaths. Remember that I am Altair's only point of influence on this plane of existence. My powers are limited. I shall grant you the knowledge of the surrounding villages and towns, the ability to sustain yourself, and the ability to transport *yourself* at will. And that will be all."

"I am your only worshipper on this world, avatar!" seethed Malchom. "How many hundreds of years have you been waiting to do something? I now live in the body of a strong, highly trained knight. I can walk into any town and receive the worship I am due. I can make a living well enough on my own. I do not need you. How would you like it if I abandoned you and Altair? What would you do with yourself, then? Give me what I ask for."

"I know you, Malchom Jamias. You could no further pretend to be good, let alone live a life of good. These powers will last for seven days. You must make sacrifice before then if you wish to keep them."

"So be it, I shall do your bidding, *great* avatar."

"May you meet with success." The avatar shimmered slightly for a moment then vanished. Malchom growled and looked around him.

"Avatars used to *prostrate* themselves at my bidding." He sighed. "I can rebuild this. It will just take time. Now where can I go that would openly welcome a *Dun Lian knight*?" He said the name with disgust. He searched his memory. "Ah, the hamlet of Jourlean. Eighty-seven leagues to the west, population three hundred and twenty. Now how to kill them all . . ."

CHAPTER 5

"Show me more of this *Dun Lian*," said Jux. "Malchom had no knowledge of this person, or of his following. He must have come to power after Malchom's time."

"It was Dun Lian who instigated the change. In Malchom's time, the god Altair was widely worshipped in the land. His followers thrived on death and cruelty, but then, I guess you know this."

"Yes."

"So widespread was Altair's power that several of his followers became quite powerful. Eight, to be exact. Eventually, the desire to be supreme in Altair's eyes drove the eight to warring with each other. As their need for power to do battle grew, so did the deaths. Whole cities were eventually sucked empty to the sacrifices the eight wizards made."

"Yes, this I do know through Malchom."

"Dun Lian was a fighter for hire. Just before the time of the massacres, he was in the village of Olmar, along the Ruinwhite River at the base of the Snow Mountains. That year a wave of trolls had flowed out of the Snow Mountains. Dun Lian was being paid by the villagers to keep the town safe. He was quite good at it, and many families from the surrounding countryside had migrated to the village seeking his protection. In months the village grew in size and became a hub of local activity and trade. Its location on the Ruinwhite River provided excellent access to the North Sea.

"The original townsfolk suddenly found themselves in a position of great power. Their council unanimously voted to raise Dun Lian to the status of lord and gave him vast amounts of the surrounding land in return for his continued protection of the village, which now called itself the city of Olmar.

"He became the law in the town. He took in several men as squires and began to train them to be his deputies. Traffic to and from the city grew.

Its reputation grew. Dun Lian's reputation grew as well. After a short while, people began to show up looking to be trained by Dun Lian.

"Realizing that Olmar's continued growth would eventually attract the attention of the warring wizards, Dun Lian began seriously training his followers, eventually knighting them into what he called the Brotherhood. Now numbering in the hundreds, the Brotherhood began the task of fortification. A massive wall was erected around the city.

"Many believe that it was the construction of this defensive wall that caught the attention of the wizard Kharrie. Olmar was within Kharrie's range of influence, so the wizard decided that the city's inhabitants should contribute to his war effort. He sent a detachment of men to secure a certain percentage of the city's population for his sacrifices.

"They were not prepared for what they encountered. They were handily dispatched by the Brotherhood. Too engrossed in the war, Kharrie simply sent a larger force of men. Again, they were no match for Dun Lian and his knights. This time Kharrie paused long enough to send his son, infused with magical abilities, to finish the little annoyance that was quickly becoming a problem, for news of Kharrie's failed attempts was spreading. Increased numbers of recruits surged into the city. I guess Dun Lian became a magnet too strong for the downtrodden to resist."

"And you too felt this pull.'

"I guess. There was something about Dun Loren when I met him. When I first saw him, I could have sworn I saw light radiating from him. Almost as if he were a blessed, holy being. I think now that it was just reflected light from his armor. But I would like to think that there was something else involved, some reason that I felt so drawn to the Brotherhood."

"Why?"

"I don't know . . . I just . . . I would like to believe that there's something bigger at work here than just pure chance. Like my decision to go to the Seas of Sterility. I was *drawn* there for some reason. After a knight enters the Brotherhood, he is expected to journey abroad and find some *just* cause to spend his first year engaged with, again to simulate Dun Lian's life. After that year, he is allowed to return to the Brotherhood and become a full member.

"When I was knighted, Dun Loren handed me a medallion. It's called the Medallion of Merit and is given to all new Knights of the Brotherhood. When I touched this medallion, I felt something weird. It almost tingled and felt heavy in my hands. When I looked up into Dun Loren's eyes, my vision blurred, and all I could see were his eyes. They were like great big blue pools of water."

"So this is what told you to go to the Dead Pools?"

"Not exactly, at least not right away. There were several days of celebration after the knighting ceremony, and it seemed that every time I saw anything that resembled a body of water, my vision would cloud over, and the image of a this pool of water would dominate my sight. For a while, I tried to pass it off as a result of the drink. But when I had a vision several days later, sober and newly refreshed in the morning, I sought Dun Loren out."

"And he was the one that told you these visions were of the Dead Pools."

"No. He could make no sense of it either. It was that evening, when I dreamed, that we were able to make any sense of it at all. In my dream, I saw mountains, and a set of pools below them, both so completely barren that I woke screaming that I had died. Dun Loren was sure that it was the Dead Mountains and the Dead Pools that I dreamed of. So the next day, I set out for them."

"And here we are." There was a pause. Morgan felt a tingling in his mind.

"Jux, what are you doing?"

"I am looking for the memories of what you have just told me, I want to relive it myself—ah, here we go." The tingling intensified.

"What are you doing? I can tell you're doing something, but it's not like before. I'm not remembering anything. Have you found it?" The tingling stopped.

"Yes, I have found it," Jux said. "But I am reliving the *emotions* you were feeling, not simply the memory as you experienced before. When you think of something, you do not usually include the actual emotions behind the actions." The tingling resumed. Morgan tried to connect with what Jux was doing but couldn't. He concentrated on the memory of his dreams. He could sense that Jux was near him, almost next to him, but he couldn't quite reach that spot. He brought up all the memories associated with his knighting ceremonies, the following celebration, and his decision to leave Castle Lianome. Jux's presence always seemed to be just off to the side, just out of his reach, or his comprehension. He thought he caught a glimpse of terror. He almost *felt* afraid.

"I see now what you mean," Jux said.

"What did you do? Why couldn't I do it as well?"

"Like I said, memories do not normally include emotion. The next time, try concentrating on just emotion. Forget what the memory might be and think in terms of feeling. In this case, the memory of the dream was accompanied by a feeling of terror. Forget the actual memory and concentrate on what terror feels like. Once you have set your mind to terror, you can then search through every instance of terror you have felt and relive the emotion, as well as the memory."

"Wouldn't that take a long time, to think through every instance of terror or joy or whatever that I have ever felt?"

"Time? I do not know. I have nothing to base that against. Time is irrelevant, and besides, thought is almost instantaneous. Try it."

Morgan cleared his mind and tried to relax, but found that relaxation was difficult. "Just clear you mind," Jux said. "Your natural means of relaxation, deep breathing, the release of tension—these things do not work. Remember, you have no body. All you have to do is concentrate."

Morgan cleared his thoughts again and concentrated on what terror felt like. Several pinpoints began to appear in his thoughts.

"That's good," said Jux. The pinpoints grew in number and intensity. Some seemed distant; others were closer and in a way brighter. When the number of pinpoints seemed to stabilize, he tried to focus on one. He picked the brightest and closest; it seemed like the logical choice.

He was engulfed in pain, stunned to a point that he could not stop the memory as it played out for him. Cowering on his knees, he sat on a rough rock. Cold wind whirled around him so violently that his eyes blurred and burned. Around him were barren, jagged rocks—some towering above him, some hundreds of feet below him. There were people, with wings, hovering all around him despite the wild winds. He was absolutely afraid of the beings, which he could hardly see through the slits his eyelids had become.

A creature, vaguely human, rose out of the stone in front of him. Its head was massive. Two huge protruding lidless eyes dominated most of the head. A small recessed mouth, filled with blunt teeth, dripped a yellow slimy substance.

"WHY HAVE YOU COME HERE?" its voice boomed, sending pain lancing through his head. Morgan screamed; the shock brought him out of the memory.

"What was that?" he said after a long while.

"That was one of Malchom's memories," Jux replied. "As I said, all he knew, you have access to."

"I felt the pain, the horror. It was, I was—*what* was that memory?"

"I believe it was the first time that Malchom met his god face-to-face. You will learn to distance yourself from distasteful memories like that. I suggest we get back to the story of Dun Lian and give you more time to get used to things."

"Okay, so, where were we?"

"Right here," said Jux. Another window opened in his thoughts. His words were replayed for him. *Increased numbers of recruits surged into the city. I guess Dun Lian became a magnet too strong for the downtrodden to resist.*

"That can come in handy. Yes, so more and more recruits came to the city. Rumors began to surface of a face-to-face confrontation between the wizards. Everyone knew what this would mean: if it were true, there would be an enormous increase in the number of sacrifices as the eight stocked up on spells and magical abilities.

"Kharrie's defeats by the Brotherhood attracted more and more refugees. The city became a packed mass of depressed people. When Kharrie's son, a man named General Zar, approached Olmar, he found a massive tent city surrounding the defensive wall of the city. General Zar was a competent military officer and seemed to be in no rush to get things done. He, along with the seven hundred soldiers he brought with him, camped within several hundred yards of the tent city.

"Dun Lian couldn't extend protection to those who couldn't fit within the city's walls and was surprised when General Zar didn't immediately attempt to capture or slaughter those left outside. Dun Lian waited to see what the general would do.

"They waited for weeks. It was a bizarre siege, if you could call it a siege. Zar's men, by day, seemed to be having a huge celebration. Laughter and music, men drinking and engaging in games of skill—it was as if they were trying to lure the townsfolk out of the city. Many inhabitants of the tent city did wander over during the day. Those that bothered to return came back with reports of a great classic party right down to the proverbial wine, women, and song.

"Those cramped inside the city heard these rumors. Food and water were running out. More and more people were leaving the tent city for Zar's encampment. Tensions were stretched very tight, and the thought of such a release began to eat away at the resolve of a large number of the besieged people. Large groups began to demand that Dun Lian open the gates and begin negotiations with General Zar.

"And here is where things got bizarre. During the day, the revelry continued, but at night, strange things began to appear. It started one night, about three weeks into the siege. A strange sound came from the encampment—a low moaning, not a moan from a person or creature, but what seemed like a moan from *hundreds* of people. The next day, the rumor mill churned out the idea that all of the tent city folk who had ventured over to General Zar's camp were being tortured.

"When the moaning continued, louder, the next night, any thought of joining General Zar was blown out of everyone's mind. In fact, those remaining in the tent city began to howl themselves. They begged and screamed to be let inside the city's walls, claiming that whispered voices on the wind had told of demons that were coming at night to take people away. Despite the lack of room, Dun Lian let them in.

"And the demons did come. They drifted from the camp slowly, shadowy figures of grotesquely deformed people. Floating like wisps of clouds, they began circling the camp, howling continuously. Eventually, they turned toward the city. They screamed toward the walls and raced up and over the stone as effortlessly as the wind. Terror filled the streets as they rampaged through the masses.

"The demon's bodies were not corporeal. They were almost gaseous and would pass right through flesh. Those unfortunate enough to be touched by the demons were found to be missing the next day. At least they were thought to be missing until, when the afternoon came, the party in Zar's camp resumed. This time, all those in attendance at Zar's bizarre party proved to be all of the missing townsfolk.

"They were all disfigured. Limbs were missing, eyes hung out of sockets, flesh had been charred or flayed off of bone. And yet they celebrated. They drank, laughed, and acted as if they were having fun, despite the obvious pain and horror that covered their faces. The noise rising from the camp took on an evil chatter that made the day just as horrific as the night. For a week, the demons came and spirited people away. And for a week, the number of living corpses in the camp of General Zar grew.

"Then one day, the party stopped. That evening, General Zar appeared at the edge of his camp. He stood facing the city for several minutes before drawing his sword. One of the captured and crippled townsfolk stepped forward. General Zar skewered the person, demonstrating that the disfigured hordes could not die. When he withdrew his sword, he barked a command, and several scores of the zombies rushed forward, howling with the despair of the damned.

"Dun Lian's knights had lined the city's walls despite their fear and showered a rainstorm of arrows down upon the corpses as they neared the fortifications. Blood appeared to erupt from every wound on every animated corpse as they were struck, more blood than should have been physically possible. They reached the city walls and began climbing with the slow dexterity of insects, leaving a stain of blood behind them as they rose.

"Seeing this, Dun Lian ordered oil and torches to be brought up and used against their attackers. The walls and crawling creepies were coated and then lit ablaze. Unable to effectively grasp the oiled stone, the zombies fell one by one like crimson leaves dropping on an autumn day. They squirmed and scrambled, attempting to reclimb the wall until the fire consumed them entirely.

"It had become nearly dark by the time the corpses finally expired. General Zar, sadistically satisfied that the small sortie had sufficiently scared the citizens of the city, retired to his tent, smiling. That night, the demons came with a venomous zeal, spiriting away more people than ever before. No one slept that night, and in the morning, Dun Lian, accompanied by his squire, climbed the ramparts of the city and called the people to attention. Without ceremony, he came bluntly to the point.

"'We cannot hold thusly against such a foe,' he projected. 'Therefore, when General Zar appears this evening, *regardless* of whether or not he appears this evening, I shall lead the Knights of the Brotherhood into his camp to end this evil tonight. Our squires will remain behind should we fail.' He turned to his squire and removed a medallion from around his neck. 'I raise you, Alexander Arjet, to the title of Knight of the Brotherhood and charge you, should we fall, to knight the remaining squires and defend this city until the life runs from your body.' 'I accept your charge Dun Lian, and take the name of Dun Jet to show my pride in your brotherhood.' Dun Lian smiled, turned back to the crowd, and continued, 'We shall fight, every last one of us, until only the *just* remain standing. I ask that every single one of you spend the next day in prayer. Perhaps a mass vigil will aid the Brotherhood to victory this day.' With that, he left to prepare his knights, leaving Alexander to watch for signs of Zar's approach.

"You tell this story very well," interrupted Jux.

"I do. It is a well-remembered story, taught to all squires of the Brotherhood for a thousand years."

"Your brotherhood seems to be steeped in traditions."

"It is. Not much has changed since Dun Lian's time. Anyway, that evening, when General Zar emerged from his tent, he found the gates to the city of Olmar open and nearly four hundred armored knights of the Dun

Lian Brotherhood slowly and regally filling in ordered ranks along the field between him and the city.

"Alexander watched from above the gates as General Zar, smiling gleefully, ordered his own men into positions opposite the Brotherhood, confidently leaving the hundred or so zombies in the camp, staring painfully, aimlessly at nothing. Seeing this, Alexander ordered the squires to the ramparts with bows, and as Zar commanded his troops to attack, they were set upon by scores of arrows. Buoyed by the help from behind, the Dun Lian knights charged and engaged the battle that had been brewing for over a month.

"The battle lasted well past midnight. In the end, only Dun Lian remained alive. He had slumped against a tree, his left arm nearly severed, and was hidden by the darkness. Both sides, General Zar's and Alexander's, thought everyone to be dead. General Zar, enraged at losing every last man, sent the demons in with a vengeance. Over a hundred people were taken that night. Alexander and his former squires, now declared knights, attempted to maintain order and urged everyone to pray as hard as they could for he knew the zombies would attack in the morning. Outside, against a battered tree, surrounded by bodies and covered in blood, Dun Lian prayed as well.

"Dun Jet was on the city wall that morning and watched a crimson sun rise over a crimson field. He watched as General Zar lined the zombies up along the edge of his camp and took a position behind the tortured townsfolk. General Zar raised his arms, chanted something, and a bolt of lightning struck the city gate, scattering it to the winds. Alexander was almost blown off of the wall.

"Zar chanted again, and an awning of stone appeared above the gates, presumably to protect his zombies as they marched into the city. That protection was never put to the test for as General Zar urged his animated army forward, Dun Lian rose from his resting place and proclaimed for all to hear, 'General Zar, by all that is good, by the God of Light, Kasparow, I forbid you and your evil minions from entering this city and hereby banish you to the hell from whence you came!'

"This infuriated the general. He ordered all of the zombies to attack Dun Lian. Alexander acted quickly and yelled for his own forces to charge the field, but they never had the chance. General Zar, chanting a spell, brought the awning down, effectively preventing a quick exit from the city. Alexander watched as two hundred zombies descended upon Dun Lian.

"With his good arm, he swung his great sword. It moved with a speed no one could believe and seemed to glow and hum as it sliced through body after body. The zombies, once cut down by the sword, disintegrated into ash. Alexander knew that the prayers had been answered. When all of the attackers were gone, Dun Lian, exhausted, stood in the middle of the field and defiantly challenged General Zar to come forward.

"General Zar snickered, raised his arms again, conjured a fist-sized ball of fire, and flung it at Dun Lian. The flaming sphere sailed toward Dun Lian, reached the tip of his sword and fizzled. Dun Lian smiled, the people watching from the city cheered, the general scowled. Dun Lian began walking toward the aggravated spellcaster.

"This time General Zar chanted for several moments, a black globe growing in front of him as he spoke. Sweat rolled down the general's face as he concentrated, willing the sphere to move slowly toward Dun Lian. Again, the incantation came in contact with Dun Lian's sword and disappeared. Shock covered the general's face as several shafts from a volley of arrows pieced his flesh. The general died.

"Cheers echoed through the city. Dun Jet, seeing Dun Lian collapse to his haunches, ordered the gate to be cleared as quickly as possible. The excavation was slow. He feared that Dun Lian would expire before they could reach him. While they were engaged, clouds began to gather, the wind became cold.

"Dun Jet was watching when a form materialized in front of Dun Lian. It was a tall being, thinly built. He had blond hair and was extremely fair skinned, as if his flesh had never seen the sun. He was clad in very light, brightly colored robes. The person knelt beside the body of General Zar. Dun Jet had no doubt this new arrival was the wizard Kharrie himself. Alexander became worried. He screamed for a coil of rope, and when it arrived, used it to rappel down the city wall. Hitting the ground, he sprinted toward the clearing, yelling for as many knights to follow him as possible.

"'Tell me who you are, so that I might know the murderer of my son when I kill you,' the wizard was saying when Alexander reached Dun Lian's side. Dun Lian waved the knight away and stood. 'I am Dun Lian, leader of the Brotherhood, protectors of the city of Olmar. We have defeated your son and shall defeat you as well.' Despite his waning life, Dun Lian's voice was strong and full of conviction.

"'So be it, Dun Lian. Now you will die.' The wizard raised his right hand; in it was a hollow metal rod. He pointed it at Dun Lian, and a small dart sprang from the tube, striking Dun Lian in the chest. Alexander shrieked and launched himself at the wizard, tackling the frail man to the ground. The wizard flicked his wrist, and another tube emerged from his sleeve. Alexander knocked the weapon from the wizard's grasp and was jolted by a force of energy when the wizard shouted, casting a spell that flung him backward to land on top of the still body of Dun Lian. Alexander reached for the fallen leader's great sword.

"Several knights were arriving as the two combatants regained their feet. As his mentor had done, Alexander held them off with a wave of his hand.

"'And tell me who *you* are that I might know your name before I kill you,' sneered Kharrie.

"Alexander straightened, holding the sword ready. 'I am . . .' He paused, regarding Dun Lian's battered body. A white froth had formed on Dun Lian's lips before he died; he had been poisoned. 'I am Dun Lian, leader of *the Dun Lian Brotherhood*. We have defeated your son and shall defeat you as well.' He moved forward slightly and brandished the sword in Kharrie's face.

"The wizard held his ground, obviously unafraid of the weapon. He laughed for several moments at Alexander's actions. When his overconfident chuckling concluded, the pale, thin elegantly dressed wizard slowly mumbled a few words, confident this knight was no match for him.

"A dark liquid leapt from his outstretched hands, floating on the air like smoke toward Alexander. The knight smiled as he watched the liquid slowly approach. He held the sword out to his right and chuckled himself, mimicking the wizard as the spell was drawn toward the sword and disappeared into it. The smile left Kharrie's face, and he screamed something, bringing a dome of shimmering energy into being around him.

"'Your magic has no place in the world any longer, wizard,' the knight said, striding forward, breaking the barrier of the dome. 'We shall see to that,' he concluded as he brought the sword down upon a stunned Kharrie."

"Ah, so that is why there were only seven wizards at the last battle. Malchom often pondered over the fate of Kharrie," said Jux.

"Unknown at the time to the people of Olmar, it would only be a few short days until the wizards gathered and obliterated each other."

"What happened next?"

"Can't you tell? Don't you know my memories?"

"Well, yes, but this is not exactly a memory of yours. You are retelling a story. I might be able to find the memory of the time that you *heard* the story, but it is much easier to let you tell the story. Besides, you are doing a good job."

"Well, several days later, the remaining seven wizards gathered. They fought, flinging great amounts of power at each other. When it was all over, they were all dead. When the news of this spread, many thought the terror was over. Celebrations sprang up everywhere. Many of them lasted for weeks.

"But the evil hadn't been quenched. Dozens of smaller, lesser wizards sprung up—many of them were direct subordinates of the original eight—all of them attempting to seize as much of the power of their former masters. If Zar had been alive, there was no doubt that he would have become quite powerful. With these power struggles ravaging the land, a more destructive chaos than had been felt under the eight wizards threatened to destroy all semblance of civilization.

"With the death of Kharrie and his son at the hands of the Brotherhood, the influx of worshippers and those wishing to join the Brotherhood again increased. Dun Jet, who had continued his leadership of the Brotherhood, decided that he would retain Dun Lian's name and use the Brotherhood's growing reputation and strength to eliminate the upstart wizards and return the land to sanity. That is the story of the founding of the Dun Lian Brotherhood."

CHAPTER 6

The door closed silently behind him and latched automatically. He had been employed as a scribe by the Dun Lian Brotherhood for over a quarter of a century and had known this particular knight nearly since the start. He had never seen Dun Loren so distressed. Rosen Kirkland hiked up his robe and left the knight's apartments as quietly as possible. *Damn robe is too long,* he thought. *Damn traditions.* The Brotherhood was as good a place as any to hold a job. They paid well, especially for loyal service, but these traditions . . .

He walked through the corridors, oblivious to all, the rolled parchment in his hands. His familiarity with this castle allowed him to study the bone-encased letter even as he negotiated his way from the castle's living quarters to the stables at the front gates. Had he been able to observe himself, strolling through the halls, half his attire in one hand, the wax-covered bone in another, he would have laughed. As it was, he was too lost in thought to consider the humor of his appearance.

What had agitated Dun Loren so much? He hadn't come right out and said it in his letter. Something to do with Morgan. Dun Loren couldn't even tell Morgan's father at this time. Pretty serious stuff if the Brotherhood needs to take care of it internally before any news spreads. As a scribe, he was bound by honor to *forget* everything he put to paper. Usually he was excellent at this, but this situation threatened to linger in his mind for a while. Should he, *could he,* break the sanctity of his profession and ask Dun Loren questions about what was going on?

He emerged into the courtyard, into the waning light of a summer's evening sun. He crossed the grassy enclosure, passing knights and squires involved in all sorts of training. Groups of men swung padded and unpadded weapons at each other. Grunts and clangs echoed in the courtyard. This was the first time he looked up since shutting Dun Loren's door. He quickly counted the men, sixteen pairs. Only a quarter of this class's students. There were typically two graduating classes each year. These days, around 150 knights were admitted into the Brotherhood every year. There were currently just over 100,000 knights in the Brotherhood. A decent number, considering the way the world worked these days.

He remembered a time in the past when he first had come to the Brotherhood. A war was being waged overseas. The Brotherhood was involved as usual. His first task with the Brotherhood had been to transcribe hundreds of flyers that were used during an enrollment push. One of the warring governments, the *just* and *righteous* of the two involved, had hired over half of the Brotherhood's forces during the first year of the war. They had paid handsomely for that many knights on such a short notice. Hundreds of knights had to be pulled from other assignments to fulfill the request. No, there were not many recruits these days, but he had seen graduating classes that numbered in the thousands.

He reached the inner gates and passed through them into the outer courtyard. To each side was a large archway that led into the castle's stables. A squire stood at a podium in front of one of the archways.

"Picking up or dropping off?" the squire said. Rosen stared blankly at the colorfully clothed squire. "Sorry," apologized the squire. "Just attempting to vary the boredom." Rosen handed over the tube of bone.

"This goes out to Abram Mclain, Wilderness Outfitters, Rivingwyre. As soon as possible."

"Hold on, hold on, let me get my paper out." The squire fumbled about for his records and finally found what he was looking for. "Never as prepared as I should be, eh?" Strong smells were coming from the stables. "You think it will hamper my chances at making knight?" Damp hay, urine, and the odor of dung were heavy on the air in the outer courtyard. "Haven't heard of many squires that actually failed to make knight, you? You've been around a long time, haven't you?" The odors reminded Rosen of the first time he had lain with his wife. It had been in these very stables. "Here we go. Okay, you said it was going to Abram Mclain. Any relation to our Mclain? What was the address again?"

"Wilderness Outfitters, Rivingwyre."

"Rivingwyre. All right then, got it." He wrapped the parchment around the tube of bone and tied it off with a strip of leather. Then he tossed the whole thing into a basket beside the podium. "Evening dispatch is going out in an hour or so, any more?" Rosen shook his head and walked away, much to the chagrin of the talkative squire. "Evening, then."

The evening dispatch, one of three daily departures from the castle. The Brotherhood employed a large number of scribes and horsemen to ferry their messages around. Their postal system was even used by others outside the Brotherhood. It was expensive, but fast and dependable. The Brotherhood, between their mail carrier system, educational institutions, and their knights-for-hire, had built quite a profitable enterprising empire. Who said that the good and righteous couldn't also be wealthy?

The walk back to his own residence passed without incident or memory. The meeting with Dun Loren was affecting him very strongly. He hoped that it was a situation that he would be made privy to eventually. He had rather liked Morgan, the few times he met him, at least.

The rooms he and his wife occupied were set apart from the servant quarters. A large number of those that took care of the day-to-day workings of the castle preferred to live outside the stronghold, in Reitner, the village that surrounded the home of the Dun Lian Brotherhood. His vocation required him to be on hand nearly around-the-clock. Several of the knights, including Dun Lian himself, preferred his work to the other scribes employed by the Brotherhood.

He opened the door and was assaulted by the smells of dinner. If nothing else, Zora was a good cook. He was never dissatisfied with what she prepared for him, and his bulging stomach would attest to that fact. He scanned the room looking for her, but of course, she would be in the kitchen.

The front room was not large. His entire five-room apartment was not large, but he had spent a lot of money to furnish it completely. Each room was filled with the finest silk-covered furniture he could find, cleaning of which was a nightmare, and he ended up reupholstering the more used pieces every several years. Magnificent paintings hung in every room. He even had several by Dun Loren's favorite artist, Pep. Gold and silver wall sconces adorned the walls of each room. His study held a first-century writing desk made of pure scentwood, still potent in its aroma even after nearly nine hundred years. Even the lavatory was lavished in luxury. Andonesian red marble lined the floor and walls; gold and platinum fixtures controlled the flow of running water to the bath and toilet. Overall, his apartments outshone many of the more wealthy knights in finery.

His wife outshone most other wives as well. He caught a glimpse of her as he passed by the kitchen on his way to the bedroom. She was tall for a woman, almost as tall as he was. She was a true beauty—very long jet-black hair, golden brown skin that tanned without wrinkling, eyes the color of a cloudless sky. Her face was as distinctive as her bright, light blue eyes. She had high cheekbones, a thin angular jaw, and a modestly sized nose that tapered to what he thought was a cute little point. Her eyebrows were very prominent and peculiar, very dark and thinly defined; they served to draw his attention to her eyes when he gazed at her face.

She was very beautiful. They would have had beautiful children as well, had she been able to produce offspring. An accident two years ago had claimed the life of their unborn child and left her unable to have more. Children were important to him; they had planned to look into adoption, but for some reason, had never gotten around to it.

He entered the bedchamber and removed his robe. He opened his wardrobe and wandered through the garments within. He opted for a light silk shirt and thin cotton breeches, tossing the robe into a small scentwood hamper.

"Hungry?" she said softly from the doorway, her deep voice rolling through the room.

"Yes. But I have to return to Dun Loren in about three-quarters of an hour. When will it be ready?"

"I can drag it out until after then. Will you be long?"

"No. Do me a favor, wake me in forty-five minutes." He collapsed onto the canopied bed and cleared his mind in an attempt to sleep, which, after a few minutes, he decided would not happen. He thought he was tired, or should be tired; he had been up since before dawn. His mind would not stop, would not allow him any rest. He continued thinking about Morgan. He considered Dun Loren a friend, and the knight's apparent agitation with this matter had to be the reason it was affecting him this way, but something kept telling him that it was more serious than that. Zora entered the room and lay down next to him.

"Not gonna fall asleep, are you?" she said.

"No."

"Well, how long will you be with Dun Loren?" she asked, folding up his sleeve and lightly fingering his arm. Her left eyebrow rose.

"I just have to go back and wake him."

"Another tired little boy?" Her fingering turned to a light scratching. "How's he doing?"

"He said to say hello, by the way." He shifted.

"How's the Lady Giarianna?" she said, following his shift in the conversation.

"As busy as ever, I suppose." He looked at her, took a deep breath, exhaling slowly as he closed his eyes. "Didn't talk much about his family." Her light scratching had migrated over to his chest; he breathed deeply again. "He was in a hurry, tired, wanted to sleep before he left." Her fingers reached his face. He tried to clear his mind again. "Be sure to wake me in thirty minutes or so."

"Of course," she said. This time he fell asleep.

CHAPTER 7

Dun Lian sat back in his seat and looked across the table. Painted on it in a very basic but accurate manner was a map of the world. Polished figures about three inches in height were scattered over the map in a representation of different forces. The figures were made of every type of metal that could be molded and crafted with relative ease. There were a few figures, however, that were made of wood. Some were poorly carved, some painted, and a couple rivaled even the metal ones in craftsmanship.

He was studying one that looked as if it had been carved from a piece of tightly compacted cork. It was the sole odd figure in a line of tin skulls. Tin, a thin metal, was usually used for coverings and such. Tin represented hollow things. Had it been lead, Dun Loren might not have been as worried. Lead was poisonous and represented naturally occurring things. As it was, the meaninglessness of the murders warranted tin skulls.

Dun L'lsen regarded the cork figure. "Where is he now? We knew where he was last."

"And he seems to have left a specter of sorts hanging around." Dun Loren looked up at Dun L'lsen. The ceiling behind the knight rose above him nearly twenty feet. A thin balcony encircled the room. Twelve feet from the floor, the only access to it was a spiral staircase behind his chair. He often stood on that balcony, viewing situations on the table from what he called his "detached perspective."

"A specter?"

"Well, it seems he is continuing to be spotted, but those reports have not been confirmed," said the big knight. "Some of the local people say late at night, you can find him wandering around the ruins of an old castle looking for something. Others say you can see his *ghost* lurking around *during* the day. As I said, unconfirmed reports."

Dun Lian looked back to the table. It occupied nearly the entire rectangular room, leaving no space for chairs, except for one at either end. Two large heavily brass-reinforced wood doors were deeply set into the thick long wall to his left. The war room served both as a staging area and an audience hall. When he wanted to meet with those he did not trust, it was easy to line the walls with knights in such a way that someone entering from the double doors had to walk to the opposite chair, unless that person wanted to climb on top of fifteen or so armed knights to proceed in his direction.

When he had negotiated the Rivington peace treaty fifteen years ago, he had used this method. He scratched his beard and remembered those times. War was war; lots of people died for what was basically no reason at all. Two governments were upset with each other, and both began making noise of some old quarrel, thousands of years gone, most likely in an attempt to simply crush the other. Those had been hollow deaths, during that war, but they still did not warrant the use of a tin marker. What Morgan had done—this, this was as hollow as tin.

"What is he doing? If Morgan isn't brought in, how do you suggest we respond?"

"Create a scandal and denounce him?"

"You think *mass murder* in this case isn't a scandal?" he snorted.

"I mean, in his personal life, Dun Lian. Paint him to be insane, off-kilter."

"Again, you don't think mass murder in this case is insane. You think Morgan is *on* kilter?"

"What I mean, is to overemphasize his personal life and background so that the public's view of him becomes detached from the Brotherhood. Or since he is a newly commissioned knight, of what . . . two months?" The knight paused, waiting for a reaction from Dun Lian. "Being a newly commissioned knight," he continued after a while, "no one outside the Brotherhood would know he *was* a knight. Say he's an impostor—he stole the medallion and everything, killing the real Dun Lain. How many people could know what he looks like? Eighty recently knighted brothers, Dun Loren, a few other knights and servants, regulars here at the castle? I don't think many outside the Brotherhood, with the exception of the survivors of Maralat, know of the incident. Even those in the vicinity of Dun Lain's last known whereabouts don't really know what is going on. Keeping a couple hundred mouths shut could be a lot easier than attempting to dodge all the arrows that this scandal will set loose."

"Not to mention what G'Zellan will do. I don't think being on another continent will slow down his learning of, or acting on, this incident. It's him I'm most worried about—he could sway several governments. And I'm sure his first strike would be at Andonesia. A foothold in our front yard would cripple us. We hold power here mostly due to our reputation. I don't want to turn the countryside into another hollow political battle."

"Yes, but if it came to that, local recruits would flood our gates. We could easily boost our numbers for anything the Andonesian military could throw at us."

"*Local recruits* don't shape national policies and laws."

"Laws, council members—these things can be changed."

"Direct insurrection is not the way we go about doing things," he said roughly; he was getting irritated.

"But if it is what the general public wants?" the big knight exploded, gesturing wildly with his hands; he too was getting irritated.

"We support the *good*, not the *majority rule*. What the majority of the public wants is not always right. Don't let the painfulness of this situation start to sharpen that edge on your feelings. *Morgan* has done evil things, not *the Brotherhood*. Keep that in mind, Dun L'lsen."

"Yes, Dun Lian." The knight's voice was tense. "If you will excuse me, I have a few errands to complete." Dun Lian dismissed the knight with a wave of his hand, returning his attention to the table.

"Where are you?" he muttered, his whisper drowned by the slamming of the great double doors as Dun L'lsen exited the room. "And what the hell has gotten into you?"

*   *   *

"Come!" he responded to the jangling chimes outside his chambers. The heavy mohair rug was pushed aside, and T'Lanizen, G'Zellan's *first officer*, stepped into the dimly lit, musty chamber. G'Zellan dismissed the females that were pampering him with soft caresses. As king, the living embodiment of their god, G'Angelepp, he was entitled to any female he wished. Indeed, he was expected to mate with as many as possible to spread his god's seed. The four females left, and he stood, gathering his fur cloak around him as he strode to the dying fire in the center of the room. Despite the continually burning fire, the largest room in the vast complex of caves the G'Angeleppan race called home was never warm. It was a good thing he didn't mind the cold. He tossed a log into the fire, not caring where the embers splashed and fell around him, smoke rising to the multitudes of cracks in the ceiling.

"You summoned me, Sire?" The first's voice echoed in the great chamber as he placed a small container on a large almost-flat stone outcropping near the room's entrance. It was a subterranean, penetrating voice, like that of all G'Angeleppans. Their ancestors had been creatures of the earth, barely intelligent beings that were more suited to burrowing in the dirt than ruling a nation. Then only a handful of generations ago, G'Angelepp was born. The spark of intelligence burned as bright as lava within him. G'Angelepp fell in love with the things of the surface world and, believing, and declaring, himself a god, led his people in a conquering crusade that lasted two decades.

Now the G'Angeleppan Empire ruled nearly a third of the continent. The usurped governments still existed in exile, but G'Angelepp's intelligence and desire to possess the things of the surface world burned within him as it had burned within all of G'Angelepp's successors.

"Have a seat, T'Lanizen. We've had some rather interesting news from the Dun Lian stronghold." He walked to the wall and ran his hand over the rough rock. It was slick with moisture, which leaked in from the same cracks and crevices that the smoke escaped through. He put his racially concave face to the wall and lapped in the water.

"A pox on those damned *Dun Lian knights*," T'Lanizen spat with disgust.

"Yes, well, their continued presence on this continent may soon come to an end." He dried his hand by running it through the thick red hair on the back of his neck. He turned away from the wall and reached for the precariously balanced container of large dead insects that T'Lanizen had brought with him. The two thumbs of his four-fingered left hand missed the container's handle, and the bowl toppled to the damp floor. T'Lanizen leapt to his feet and rushed to pick up the dead bugs.

"Forgive me, G'Zellan, I should have been more careful." G'Zellan, the "Living God," stooped and plucked a large insect out of the muck that was the floor and popped it into his mouth. He hated the way he was treated, but it was necessary to help perpetuate the illusion of his godhood. He knew he was no god, and he knew his people would eventually mature enough as a race to abandon the concept. But for now, for the next several generations, especially while they solidified and secured their hold on their newly formed nation, it was absolutely necessary.

Dun Lian knew this as well; *every* Dun Lian since G'Angelepp's time had known that none of his race's leaders had been gods. Of course, he knew that the Knights of the Brotherhood simply realized that gods usually did not walk the earth in material form, but every knight did seem to have some sort of divination ability. They were able to sense when one of his race was near, even if that G'Angeleppan was using its innate ability to transform into the likeness of another being. The Knights of the Brotherhood could see through this deception, they could see through the G'Angeleppan force of will that made it appear as if one of his race was anything but a normal human being, or a being of any other race, for that matter. This was probably—no, was definitely why his enemies on this continent employed such a large number of Dun Lian knights.

He was working on this, however—working on negating the effectiveness of this power the Dun Lian knights had. The grand experiment was going on now, had been for a while. It had been going on for years. He was in no rush; he wanted absolute proof that the magic he purchased from the wizened old ogre shaman would suit his purposes before he paid the nasty creature's price. Sacrificing regular numbers of G'Angeleppans to satiate the ogre's hunger would not sit well with his followers. If it meant being able to throw off the onus of the Brotherhood, then his status as a god could probably endure the pressure from his people for a while, at least until he conquered the continent.

"What news then, Sire?" said T'Lanizen. The G'Angeleppan ability to polymorph into another being was an illusion, an outward appearance that was accomplished through force of will, but the ogre had promised that his magic would make the transformation real, possibly even permanent, which G'Zellan did not really wish. As a G'Angeleppan, he could see through this psychic blurring that his race was able to project. What would happen if he could no longer block out the illusion? He did not trust the barbaric nature of his followers. What if one of *them* came after *him*?

"Sire, what news, from the Dun Lian stronghold?" repeated T'Lanizen.

"Yes, well, it seems there is an internal turmoil erupting at the castle." He took the bowl of bugs from T'Lanizen, picking through the insects as he walked to the heap of moss that was his bed. "Something has happened that they are attempting to keep an extremely tight mouth about," he said as he plopped onto the mound of moss. "Luckily for us, we have our inside source. The message was brief. He evidently did not have much time to spend in meditation. It seems that the Brotherhood has begun a manhunt for one of their own. We are not sure why, but Dun Lian is very agitated and desperately wants his knights to apprehend a newly commissioned knight known as Dun Lain." The bugs crunched loudly as he chewed. "But we do know that Dun Loren has been dispatched to personally oversee the operation."

"Dispatched to where?"

"Somewhere near the village of Maralat." T'Lanizen stared at him blankly. "Near the Dead Pools." T'Lanizen's ignorant stare continued. "The Dead Pools, at the base of the Purple Mountains."

"Is that near here?" asked T'Lanizen.

"No," he said condescendingly. "It's on *their* continent." *Could* he really be *that* much more intelligent than the rest of his race? Typically, it was the direct descendants of G'Angelepp that held the military positions. They were supposed to be more intelligent than the rest, but he would never have guessed. T'Lanizen himself was one of G'Zellan's many uncles. Even though they were related, T'Lanizen would never be in a position to claim the G'Angeleppan throne. Only the offspring of the king's first mated were eligible for succession. And considering the short gestation and long-lived nature of his people, even a second-born son to a king would have a hard time assuming the throne.

"What can we do about it, then, happening so far away I mean?"

"We may not need to do anything. While an internal scandal would never persuade our enemies from discontinuing their use of the Brotherhood, it could facilitate enough unpopularity on *their* front as to cause a withdrawal of some, if not all, of their forces here."

"And what can we do about it? You don't intend to remove our agent from their castle, do you?"

"No, I intend to send another. This would also be a good opportunity to continue to test the soundness of our shaman's magic."

"He will want a living G'Angeleppan for payment."

"I know, that is why you will go to the nursery and take one of the females to him. Find one that is close to giving birth. That way, we can say she died during childbirth. And do it during the night tonight, before the nursery awakens. Be sure none of the others see you taking her."

"And who do I take with me to be transformed?"

"Well, whoever goes, will not have the benefit of magical communication with me. So I will need to send someone I can trust, and someone that will be able to think for himself." G'Zellan looked up at T'Lanizen meaningfully. *This is the best that I have to work with?* "I mean to send you." He continued when T'Lanizen failed to catch his meaning.

"Me?" T'Lanizen said, shakily. "But I am your *first*. I . . . I'm sure I'll be needed here."

"As my first, you have only two directly under you. I will raise one of them to be my first." T'Lanizen turned his back to G'Zellan and leaned against the stone table. Both of his second officers were idiots as well; maybe he *was* that much more intelligent than the rest of his race. The G'Angeleppan military hierarchy consisted of ten levels of officers. Each level had as many officers as its number indicated—one first officer, two second officers, all the way down to ten tenth officers. These fifty-five officers controlled his entire military. At times it seemed as if he needed fifty-five officers just for one division.

"Will I still retain my status as first officer?" G'Zellan was amazed that T'Lanizen could continue to speak to him with his back turned; he was being very rude to a god.

"No. You will need to give up that position." He waited as T'Lanizen thought, or at least he assumed T'Lanizen was thinking. His first was visibly shaking. All of his hair, from the back of his nearly bald head down his neck, until it disappeared under his clothing, was quivering slightly. He was really afraid.

"I don't wish to leave your service, Sire," T'Lanizen said at last, weakly.

"You will still be in my service. Actually, yours will be more of an honor than shuffling about these dank tunnels day after day as you do now."

"But I command your forces, Sire."

"And now you have the chance to be directly responsible for the downfall of the Dun Lian Brotherhood. And of our ultimate triumph."

"But this will require me to spend *all* of my time outside—in the sun, the wind, the *rain*."

"I might expect such cowardly behavior from one of my backswill concubines, but not from my *first!*" G'Zellan raised his voice in mock anger, which had the desired effect as T'Lanizen spun around to kneel, facing him.

"No, Sire, don't get me wrong. I . . . I'm not afraid. I simply meant that I wouldn't be able enjoy being in your presence while I am gone . . ."—his voice lowered—"while I am . . . wandering . . . on the surface . . . a-away from your brilliance."

"GOOD!" he bellowed. "Then you will get started before the morning comes. Show me what form you will take." He watched as T'Lanizen closed his eyes and attempted to relax. Slowly, and with what G'Zellan was sure was a lot of effort, T'Lanizen's form shifted away from its natural features to mimic those of a human. His nose grew as his head shrank and sprouted hair. The coarse black hair on his neck and back receded into his skin, which lost its dark reddish brown color. His arms shortened half their length, and one of the two thumbs on each of his hands shriveled and disappeared. He grew nearly twelve inches in height, and his clawed feet elongated while becoming half as wide. The dirt-covered brown claws on his feet disappeared and were replaced with clean white toenails.

To G'Zellan, this transformation was a hazy one, almost completely see-through. He could see the changes, but if he concentrated even slightly, really focused on T'Lanizen, he could clearly see his first beneath the disguise. To another creature who was not G'Angeleppan, T'Lanizen was nothing more than an ordinary human.

"Good. Go to the hoard and take a pouch full of Andonesian gold crowns. A hundred or so should finance you quite nicely."

"And what am I to do? What exactly are you looking for?"

"I'm not quite sure. At the very least, you need to go to Maralat and learn all you can. If they want Dun Lain so badly and want to keep it secret, then we will at least benefit from taking him ourselves. I will find a way to contact you. At the very least, if you discover something, use the Brotherhood's own messaging service to notify me."

"But I don't think they would deliver messages here."

"Send them to the Dun Lian castle. We do have a contact there, remember? He will be able to teleport you there the next time he contacts us, which I expect to be in the early morning. Be ready."

"Oh yeah." T'Lanizen lowered his head. "Well then, I had better get started, unless you have any other words for me."

"No, you may go." T'Lanizen left the chamber. His first was obviously ashamed of his ignorance, and this was the best with which he had to work. He thought it was amazing his race had come so far and done so much in the few decades since G'Angelepp had crawled out of the muck and into the sunlight.

T'Lanizen slinked through the very dimly lit passageways. He didn't need the faint light the burning fagots gave off to negotiate the tunnels. No G'Angellepan needed artificial light to see in the dark. When G'Angelepp had brought his people together to attack the surface world, he had insisted on making several changes. Changes that were supposed to make the G'Angeleppan race more *civilized*.

Wearing clothes was the first change he had instituted. Of course, to wear clothes, they had to make clothes, and no G'Angeleppan had ever done either. So G'Angelepp had bought the knowledge of clothes making. G'Angelepp had bought a great many things. Which wasn't a problem. One asset the G'Angeleppan race *did* have was its natural ability to tunnel and burrow underground. Once they had been trained properly and knew what they were looking for, a select group of G'Angeleppans had been given the task of locating and excavating as many gemstones as they could find. Those gems had financed the Great Coming, as it was now called by the worshippers of G'Angelepp. The gems had financed G'Angelepp's rise to power and his subsequent crushing of the nations of the surface world as the hard colored rocks were greatly valued by the races that dwelled solely on the surface.

That thought made T'Lanizen shiver. He couldn't imagine spending his entire life exposed to the chaotically changing weather of the surface world. The perpetual cold and snow of his mountain home was enough for him. Down here in the caves, things remained the same year round—damp but not overly wet, chilly but not too cold, plenty of light without being blinding.

He much preferred his life here. Even as G'Zellan's first officer, with duties that sometimes required him to make forays into the wilderness above, he was still able to spend most of his time underground.

He was G'Zellan's first, at least for a few more hours. Then he would become something else. The ogre shaman would transform him physically into the likeness of a human. He had heard that there was a chance the change was permanent. That thought was terrifying. Humans were horrific in appearance, let alone in the way they lived. That soft skin and tender flesh could serve no purpose except to be hurt.

He rounded a corner and entered the treasury. Gemstones of all sizes were piled in two clusters in a corner. Rubies, sapphires, amethysts, jade, opals, bloodstone, moonstone, jacinth, emeralds, and even diamonds, one pile of cut gems, one pile of raw stones. Every couple of years, G'Zellan would employ a dwarven gem cutter to restock the supply of cut stones. T'Lanizen didn't much care for dwarves, but being tough, somewhat-subterranean creatures themselves, they were certainly better than humans. Against another wall of this cave were piles of coins. There were all sorts of coins—Andonesian gold and silver crowns, Chunyan marks, even a nicely sized pile of Wetookian platinum pennies.

It amazed him how much value humans and the other races put in these metals. Andonesian gold crowns were accepted nearly everywhere, even on this continent. He wondered how the Andonesian government could allow so much of its valued gold to be freely taken out of the country and used elsewhere. He opened a sack the size of his head and filled it with as many gold crowns as he could stuff it with. He examined a coin, holding it up in the faint light. On one side was an octagon surrounded by eight small circles. This was supposed to represent some sort of group. On the other side was the profile of Dun Lian. He shoved the coin into his sack and tied it off at his waist. Why the Andonesians worshipped this man, he had no idea. Dun Lian had to be a god; he had been around for hundreds of years. From what he understood, Dun Lian had founded his brotherhood nearly a thousand years ago. He had to be a god to live so long. Even G'Zellan wouldn't live that long. And he *was* a god.

Leaving the treasury, he made his way to the nursery, pouch jingling all the way. He was in luck; the nursery matron was nowhere to be seen. She was a cranky sort of creature. He could only guess that having to deal with so many pregnancies had taken its toll on the woman. Over three dozen pregnant women were currently present. It was a small number, considering how easily a female G'Angeleppan became pregnant, especially with G'Zellan's wanton appetite. T'Lanizen was sure at least half of the women in this large cave were carrying G'Zellan's seed. He almost envied G'Zellan's right to mate with as many females as he chose.

He walked silently among the sleeping females. It would be easy to pick out the right one. When it was near the time of birth, a female's skin would change color, signaling the time of delivery, as well as the gender of the child. The quick gestation time drained a lot of energy out of the pregnant female, who spent most of her time asleep, reserving what energy she did have. It would be very easy to pick out a suitable female and spirit her away without the knowledge of those present.

He stopped next to a female whose skin was a dark green. By the deepness of the green color, he knew she would give birth within a day, and it would be male. He shook her, roughly. The sleep would be too deep to rouse her easily.

"Uh . . . wha-what is it?" she said groggily when he finally woke her.

"G'Zellan has summoned you." He hoped that would be all that was necessary to get her on her feet and moving. The other females in the room might be just as comatose as she was, but he didn't want to take any chances.

"What!" Her voice echoed and sounded loud enough to wake the dead.

"Shh. The others need their sleep."

"G'Zellan? Wants me? But I'm not even carrying his child. Pethla, Pethla, wake up." She started shaking a neighboring female violently.

"Leave her be," he hissed, grabbing her arms a little too late as the other female began to stir.

"Jella, what's going on?"

"G'Zellan wants me! He's summoned me, Pethla, me!" T'Lanizen yanked Jella to her feet and peered over the still-sleepy female.

"Go back to sleep," he said, taking on the appearance of the nursery matron. "You must preserve your strength. What would G'Zellan say if you miscarried?" He knew Pethla could see through his illusion, but he hoped she was still too groggy to know the difference. He herded Jella out of the room and flung her roughly against the tunnel wall.

"You will keep your mouth shut and follow me, woman. You know who I am?"

"Y-you are G'Zellan's first officer."

"That's right, and as his first officer, anything I tell you to do must be obeyed, as if G'Zellan had said it himself."

"Yes," she stammered. "I understand."

"Good." He seized her arm and dragged her beside him. "Now follow." At this time of night, there was no one wandering about the main passageways. If anything, G'Angeleppans were not nocturnal.

As usual, there were only two guards at the main entrance to the G'Angeleppans' home network of caves, caverns, and tunnels. The surrounding mountains were massive and snow-covered nearly year round. Accessing the main entrance here, so far up, was a task that few of the other races had ever tried, allowing for the almost-total lack of fortifications.

The difficult task now was to sneak out with the female and keep the two guards oblivious to the fact that he had anyone with him. G'Zellan had made it clear that he didn't want anyone knowing one of the females had been taken. He stopped a few hundred feet before the entrance and shoved the terrified female into a recess along one wall. Hopefully she would not be noticed. Emerging into the cold night air, the two guards snapped to attention as soon as they recognized him.

"Greetings, sir," they said, nearly in unison.

"I'm . . ." His thoughts raced, attempting to come up with a reason to dismiss the two. "I'm going to inspect the camps below. I seem to have forgotten it was so cold out here. Would one of you go fetch me a heavy covering?"

"Certainly, sir." One of the men quickly darted into the cave entrance. T'Lanizen waited a few moments, lightly humming to himself.

"Oh, and on second thought, could you go grab me a lantern. There's not much of the moons out tonight."

"Uh, a lantern?" the guard began.

"Yes, a lantern, just in case. I don't want to lose my footing in the snow."

"As the first wishes." The guard bowed slightly and left, not as quickly or confidently as his partner had. T'Lanizen watched as he disappeared down the tunnel. Satisfied, he retrieved the female and started down the trail that led away from the caves.

The female studied him as he dragged her roughly along. He was sure she was full of questions but lacked the courage to speak to him. The females were always docile, as should be, especially when in the presence of anyone of authority. They even shied away from the nursery matron.

G'Zellan had told him several times that most of his people were weak. *They are as sheep*, he had said. *Weak and herdlike, most are incapable of any truly independent or creative thought. If I weren't continually pushing them to change, most would be content with digging in the dirt for bugs until the mountain fell around their ears. This is why we attack the surface races. This is why we adopt their ways. We will change them, T'Lanizen, mark my words. We will become as strong as the other races.*

Slowly they made their way down the mountain, along the side path that led to the ogre shaman's own cave. G'Zellan had suggested to the shaman during their first meeting that a tunnel could be dug to connect the smaller cave to the G'Angeleppan complex. The shaman had declined, stating fearfully that he did not want the additional uninvited and unwanted disturbances that such a connection was bound to create.

Dozens of mountain goats crowded around them as they walked. For some reason, the sturdy, wool-coated animals liked him, or at least it seemed they liked him. Perhaps they simply liked all G'Angeleppans, or maybe they liked all creatures. Just about all of the clothing worn by his people was made of their wool. G'Zellan preferred the feel of silk, a strange material made by worms, or so he had been told. How mere worms could weave fabric, or make patterned clothing of varying colors, he had no idea, but that's what he had been told. G'Zellan himself had told him. Silk was soft, and G'Zellan liked the feel of it next to his skin; he wore a layer of it underneath his thicker mohair clothing all the time. Rumors said he had his females dress in the garment when they mated with him.

By the time they reached the shaman's cave, the female was struggling. Her pregnancy had sapped most of her strength, and the two-mile hike in the cold had taken the rest. T'Lanizen had to pick her up and carry her into the cave entrance.

"Shaman! Wake up! I have something for you." The female's fear shone in her eyes.

"I've heard rumors that G'Zellan sacrifices people to a monster! Where are we? Where is G'Zellan?" she whimpered weakly.

"Silence," he hissed. "Silence, or you'll never see your son born."

"Son? I am with daughter, and it is weeks before the child is due."

"But your dark green color," he began. "Regardless, hold your tongue, woman!" He continued to inch his way inside the cave. "Shaman!" The cavern was not large, barely taller than he was, which was surprising as the ogre was at least twice as tall as any G'Angeleppan. Every time he had seen the monstrous creature, it had been sitting. Sitting in the back of the cave. He wondered how the thing moved around.

"I am back here," came a high-pitched, grating voice. That was another odd thing about the ogre. He was old and weak but still should have had a deeper voice than he did. The cave opened up a little, perhaps twenty feet across, and the ceiling rose to about eight feet in height. It was still too shallow to allow the thing to stand fully erect.

It was sitting on a pile of mohair rugs, between two tapestries. Five tapestries depicting battles between great numbers of creatures of all races hung on the walls. The ogre had expressed an interest in such things. Two of them, bought with a couple of large diamonds from a dwarven gem cutter, had been a gift from G'Zellan several years ago. The ogre was settling himself on the mohair rugs, as if he had just sat down. One of the tapestries behind and slightly to the right of the shaman swung lightly as if moved by a slight breeze. Perhaps there was another chamber beyond that great rug?

There was plenty of light in the cave. A glowing orb suspended by thin chains anchored with iron spikes hung from the ceiling. That light had fascinated T'Lanizen on his first visit here. It was one of the several displays of magic the shaman had performed for him and G'Zellan. This cave had always been empty and unused until one day, almost three years ago. A sentry had returned, reporting that something had taken up residence in the cave. The guard had lost his companion, who had entered the cave but not returned. The sentry reported to G'Zellan that he had heard his companion scream out in terror, which was followed by sounds that the guard could only describe as "something being eaten." Terrified, the sentry had run all the way home.

The female, weak as she was, was becoming just as terrified. In the abundant light, she was able to fully see the ogre. It wasn't a horrible-looking thing. Tall and muscular despite its supposed age, it was far better-looking than any human he had ever seen. A huge curled and yellowed horn protruded from its forehead and bent back along its bare skull, curling around the thing's left ear. The ears themselves were huge, almost wing-shaped flaps of gray skin. The ogre wore no clothing, but thick hair populated its waist, giving the illusion of clothing. Its hands were gnarled, bent in contorted unnatural positions, and ended with extremely thick, stubby yellow nails. A thick gray tongue was currently licking jagged, razor-sharp teeth.

"Have you brought me something to eat, First Officer?" The high-pitched voice was thin and rasping, the words slightly slurred as they passed over the carnivorous teeth. The female struggled uselessly in his grasp.

"I have come at G'Zellan's orders. This female has come at his orders." He dumped Jella on the ground roughly and sat next to her. She tried to scramble away. Terror was oozing from her in the form of a faint squeal. T'Lanizen reached out, cuffed her upside the head, and dragged her back into her place before the ogre.

"Relax, child," the gray creature cooed. "Here, have something warm to drink." The ogre stuck his arm behind the tapestry to the left and pulled out a gourd fashioned into a tall bowl. It was filled with a steaming yellow liquid. "Here, drink, relax," came the somewhat-soothing voice of the ogre. Jella took the bowl with trembling hands and sniffed suspiciously, never taking an eye off the ogre. The tension seemed to melt from Jella's face. She drank the entire thing rather rapidly. "That's better. Would you like some more, child?"

"Yes, I would." Jella spoke with a mellow relaxed tone. The ogre pulled a jug from behind the tapestry and took the bowl from Jella and filled it to the brim. Placing the jug on the ground, he moved the bowl to his lips and blew lightly. When he handed it to Jella, it was steaming. She drank the contents of this bowl just as quickly as the last.

"You need to sleep, little girl," said the ogre. "Sleep." The shaman pulled a small mohair rug out from the pile he was sitting on and unfurled it beside him. "Come here and sleep." Jella rose obediently and settled herself on the rug and was asleep almost instantly.

"Now," slithered the ogre, "what would you have of me? Obviously, you need something, for you wouldn't have brought me such a sweet morsel. And pregnant, I see. She is due in, what, two weeks, with a girl?"

"How do you know that?" Was this ogre *that* smart?

"Why, by her color of course. A green color signals a female child, and the deeper it gets, the closer to giving birth is the mother. Now what is it you seek?"

T'Lanizen steeled his shaken nerves and spoke, "We need another to be transformed and transported to the Dun Lian stronghold. Can you do this? I've brought the girl and her child as payment."

"Of course we can do this!" the ogre shrieked. "I have told G'Zellan time after time that I can transform as many of his people as he wishes. One live G'Angeleppan as payment for each transformation. It is a simple pact. And considering the rate at which you people seem to reproduce, I would think it a small price to pay for the advantage it would give G'Zellan over his enemies. You tell G'Zellan that I am sure *others* would be willing to meet my *needs*." He stroked Jella's dark hairy back. "Plenty of others would be willing to feed me thus for such power. Make no mistake in that, my weak-willed first officer."

He just might be weak willed, and he might be frightened by the thought of what the ogre was going to do with Jella but he had never seen this creature act so forcefully before. The ogre had all but trembled in G'Zellan's presence.

He had conceded to nearly everything G'Zellan had asked for, almost begged for mercy, trembled when G'Zellan spoke. How dare this shriveled, frail old thing treat him like this? "You will have to address G'Zellan with those facts," he said with confidence, sitting up stiffly; after all, he *was* G'Zellan's first officer. "For now, since you've got your payment, you *will* deal with me and do as I say."

The ogre eyed him, still stroking Jella's coarse hair. "So, the little first officer does have some strength in him, after all."

"My title is First Officer T'Lanizen. You will address me as such."

"So be it, *First Officer T'lanizen*," hissed the ogre. "I take it *you* are the one to be transformed."

"Yes, after which you will transport me to the same place within the castle that you transported the other G'Angeleppan."

"Do you wish to have magical communication with G'Zellan as that one has?"

"Can this be accomplished?"

"It can," started the ogre, "but it will mean another payment." He finished by plucking one of Jella's black back hairs and used it to pull debris from between his sharp teeth. The ogre pulled the hair back and forth vigorously, cutting his gums in the process. Blood spilled down over the yellowed teeth, dripped onto the dingy white goat's hair, staining it further.

T'Lanizen swallowed audibly. "I brought only one for payment. But . . . but if you wait two weeks, there'll be two—"

"Yes, I guess there is that. I will consider it. Won't you have something to drink?" The ogre picked up the jug and poured some of the yellow liquid into the bowl. He held it out for T'Lanizen to take.

"No . . . I . . ."—he looked at Jella, breathing deeply—"I'm not thirsty." The ogre chuckled. With his high-pitched voice, it was nearly a squeal.

"Don't trust me, do you? The drink had nothing to do with her going to sleep. Have some, it will make the transformation easier." T'Lanizen remained still, shifting focus from the ogre to the sleeping female.

"Oh," the ogre said in frustration, "the drink is harmless. She's pregnant, and you dragged her all the way out here. Of course, a warm drink in her belly would help her get to sleep. She had no strength to stay awake. Her fear was all that kept her eyes open, and once that subsided, its quite tasty, see." The ogre drank what was in the bowl. "See, I'm still awake." He poured some more. "Here, take it." T'Lanizen refused again. "Very well," he said, putting the bowl down. "If you insist on doing things the hard way." The ogre sat back against the cave wall.

"Now stand up and show me what form you wish to take on physically."
T'Lanizen stood. "You understand, *First Officer T'Lanizen*, that there is a
slight chance that this transformation will become permanent."

"Let's hope not," he said quickly. Concentrating, he formed an image
in his mind of the human he had become for G'Zellan. He saw the ogre
concentrate on him, on the change he knew to be happening. After a few
moments, he looked down at his hands. Superimposed lightly over his own
hands were the single-thumbed hands of a human. He could see through this
illusion, could the ogre?

"Very nice, very nice. That will pass sufficiently for a human. Have you
any thought as to what you will clothe yourself in? Or how you will sustain
yourself?"

"I have coin." He shook the small sack at his side.

"Ah, Andonesian crowns. Beautiful gold, yes, that should be enough for
you to live like a king. For a while, at least."

"How does the transformation work?"

"Relax, it will come. You must learn a little more patience. Well, I guess
it doesn't really matter anymore. Dorvain, have you been paying attention?"
the ogre called over his shoulder, surprising T'Lanizen. There was another in
the cave? "Careful, First Officer T'Lanizen, don't lose the illusion. You must
keep it going for the transformation to work. Keep concentrating. Dorvain."
This time the ogre actually looked over his shoulder at the tapestry to his
right. "Dorvain, are you ready?"

The colorful tapestry moved aside, and a figure stepped into the room.
He was human! T'Lanizen stumbled backward slightly, losing the illusion,
he was sure. He squatted slightly and growled, showing his teeth and claws.
This human was unarmed; its soft flesh would be no match in a hand-to-
hand fight.

"T'Lanizen, stop!" The ogre rose to his feet with a grace and ease that
continued to surprise T'Lanizen. The ogre towered over him, even though
he was crouching in the crowded cave. "Take a closer look at this human,
you simple-minded muckbeetle of a creature!"

Muckbeetle! T'Lanizen's rage began to return, and he nearly attacked the
ogre. A fierce heat seemed to come from the ogre, who was close enough to be
breathing on him; it was a hot breath. He peered past the ogre. The tapestry
had been pulled back; the figure was standing in the entranceway to another
chamber. It was a much larger room than the one he was in. It was decorated
lavishly. A quick glimpse was all he got. The figure stepped forward and let
the tapestry fall when he caught T'Lanizen studying the other room. The

figure was human, and it did appear to look like the image he had formed in his mind for both G'Zellan and the ogre.

"Now concentrate on that image so the transformation can be completed." The ogre crouched, roused the sleeping Jella, and walked with her toward the room behind the tapestry. "You can handle things from here, Dorvain," he said as he dropped the tapestry behind him.

"I am Dorvain. I will help you make the transformation, but you must concentrate. Here, drink this, it will help." Dorvain handed the bowl to T'Lanizen. A little dazed, he took the bowl and drank it without complaint. There was a very sweet, appealing odor to the fluid. The yellow liquid stung as it went down his throat; it seemed to catch everything it touched on fire. This feeling lasted for only a few seconds; the burning was replaced with a warm, comfortable feeling. He began to go numb, starting with his throat and spreading though his entire body. It was a wonderful feeling; he had never felt so good, so peaceful before.

"Okay, drink some more." Dorvain had taken the bowl from him and refilled it. He had no desire to resist. In fact, he was eager to drink more. This time there was no burning sensation, only peaceful numbness. His mind wandered; he found he couldn't focus on a thought, let alone his sight. Dorvain became a blur; T'Lanizen felt as if he might collapse.

"You feel fine," said Dorvain, and he did—he felt fine, but he felt empty. He needed something to fill the emptiness. "You will follow me." Follow Dorvain. That would fill the emptiness. "Follow me this way." Dorvain moved the tapestry aside, and the two entered the other room.

A few minutes later, a form materialized in one of the apartments of the Dun Lian stronghold.

"You must hurry," said the person, who was waiting for the new arrival. "I can't let you linger. I have places to be. Put this on, it should be enough to get you out of the castle unmolested. Is everything okay? Yes? Is your telepathy intact? Good. Is your memory intact? What's your real name?"

"I am Dorvain," responded the figure.

"Good, I think the master will be pleased. Here is the quickest way out." A flash of thought was transmitted between the two, a mental picture of the route the new arrival would take and possible responses to any challenges Dorvain might happen across as he fled from the Dun Lian stronghold. "Now go."

CHAPTER 8

"I see you worship a god as well." Jux's voice sliced through the silence.

"Was I sleeping?"

"Not in a real sense. I was going through your memories . . ."

"You were?" interrupted Morgan. "I didn't feel anything."

"Even though you do not have a physical body, your mind can still become weary. I have noticed that people tend to simply shut down when this happens. As I said, I was going through your memories. I see that you worship a god much in the same way that Malchom did."

"I would hardly call my methods of worshipping Kasparow the same as how Malchom practiced his worshipping. He murdered hundreds of people on a regular basis."

"Did it ever occur to you that to kill in a sacrificial ceremony dedicated to your god might not be considered murder? Perhaps those followers of Altair that Malchom killed volunteered and felt that it would put them closer to their god."

"Closer all right—closer by being dead."

"And if you died while in service to Kasparow?"

"All that we do when we worship Kasparow is *pray*."

"And if part of your prayers required you to spill blood?"

"Then I would choose another god to worship. Speaking of praying, through all of this, I have neglected my own prayers. I wonder how long I have gone now without meditation. Is there any way to tell how many days have passed?"

"Not really, unless you wanted to start counting. And how accurate would that be? As I said before, time has no real meaning here."

"I just realized that I haven't felt Kasparow's presence for some time now. A long time must have passed. He must be displeased with me."

"What makes you say that?" asked Jux.

"Well, as you pointed out, it's much like when Malchom would pray to his god. He would pray, make sacrifices, and Altair would reward him with power. I spend several hours a day in meditation, praying to Kasparow, singing his praises, and professing my love and devotion to him. In return, he comes to hear me pray and fills me with his presence."

"What gifts does he give you for such prayers?"

"Well, the goodness of his presence, for one. All Dun Lian knights pray to Kasparow and are granted this gift."

"But what does his presence do for you? I mean, Malchom would get very specific and *potent* powers. What does your god grant to you?"

"Nothing like that, at least not to me."

"It seems to me then that Malchom's way, although you may find it disgusting, is far better. Perhaps with that kind of power, you would not have become trapped in here."

"But he was murdering thousands of people for that power!"

"Again." Jux paused. "Again, you are assuming they were murders and not self-sacrifices."

"Who in their right mind would want to kill themselves so that a lunatic like Malchom would gain unearthly powers?"

"One who worships Altair? But that would be just a guess. You said that Kasparow did not give you any powers, but it sounded as if he might to others that worship him?"

"Dun Loren explained to me that the greater the worship, the more attention Kasparow would give and the longer he would remain with you. I believed he meant louder and longer prayers. I would spend half my day in meditation, inwardly singing to Kasparow. Not once did I feel any increase in *His* presence. For months I did this, and when I finally asked Dun Loren what I was doing wrong, he laughed at me.

"'Worship should not always come in the form of prayers, Morgan,' he said to me. 'How you live your life and what you do with your devotion is just as important as prayer,' he said. When I finally understood exactly what he meant, I began to see things that had escaped my notice before."

"Such as?"

"Such as the fact that when Dun Loren and I went on field exercises, he neither slept nor ate, even if we were gone for a week. When I noticed this, I studied Dun Loren very carefully. The aura of Kasparow surrounded him in such greatness that he would actually begin to glow with a soft light when I focused my eyes on him. When we returned to the castle, I found that I was able to see this aura around all of the knights, and many squires. Some auras were bright, some dim. When I finally caught a glimpse of Dun Lian, as I expected, his aura was nearly blinding."

"You seem happy by this."

"Well, it is a fond memory. It was my 'coming-out ceremony.' I was amazed at what I had seen, and when I finally told Dun Loren, he exploded with laughter. 'So you've finally come out, eh?' he screamed at me. He slapped me on the back and yelled, 'Hey, Morgan's come out!' as loud as he could for all to hear. Every knight within earshot cheered and came over to slap me on the back. They all started chanting my name. Dun Loren came forward and started talking to me, but it was hard for me to hear, due partly to the noise, but also because the combined glow of Kasparow surrounding the knights was overwhelming.

"He started saying something about a great day and how we were off to celebrate. I was a little disoriented and stunned. They ushered me out of the castle, and by the time I got used to the effects of what I was seeing, we were in one of the taverns in town, and Dun Loren was ordering drinks for everyone. There were about fifteen of us.

"'My friends, I drink to the health of Kasparow for the first time tonight,' Dun Loren said. He picked up a small, nearly thimble-sized cup, if you can call it that, and drank his drink, as did the other knights in unison. They then turned to me and practically forced me to drink what they had put in my hand. It was an extremely-sweet-smelling liquor of sorts and burned very foully when I drank it.

"Almost immediately after I finished, another knight picked up another thimble and said, "I drink to the health of Kasparow for the second time tonight." He drank his drink, as did the others, again in unison. The roughness of the first drink had shocked me back to my senses a little. The glow of Kasparow was still there, but I seemed more myself, so, loving the attention the knights were giving me, I drank mine as well, as much in unison with them as I could.

"By the sixth or seventh drink, I was relaxed and in time with the other knights. I was able to look around me and noticed that we were being watched by the few patrons in the bar. Unlike the serving maids, they were very apprehensive and eyeing us suspiciously. It was at this time that I got my first glimpse of, well, of *evil*.

"They were sitting in the corner. Dressed in leathers, swords unbuckled, and sitting on the table along with huge tankards. There were two of them— unkempt, unshaven—and they looked dust covered, as if they had just arrived.

They too had a glow; I caught just a glimpse of it at first, and then another shot of that fruit liquor was going down my throat.

"I stared at them, focused my view on seeing that glow. They noticed me doing this. One of them grabbed his sword, at which time his glow flared into plain view. It was much different than what I had seen surrounding the knights. It wavered, as a cobblestone road will in the heat of midday. Their aura shifted from a deep red to a light black, wavering, shifting. It changed constantly, wasn't steady, not at all like what I had seen so far. I had a strange urge to pick a fight with those two.

"Then one of the knights grabbed me by the arm and said, 'I drink to the health of Kasparow for the fourteenth time tonight.' I realized that we had had a drink for every knight present. The knight holding my arm gave me another drink and stared at me knowingly. I looked to Dun Loren; he was motioning his hands slightly, seeming to urge me on."

"It was your turn to toast, I take it."

"Exactly. So I did. 'I drink to the health of Kasparow for the fifteenth time tonight.' By this time, the liquor was beginning to have a profound effect on me. The knights all cheered after we finished the drink. Dun Loren tossed a bag of coins to the serving maid, and they ushered me out of the tavern."

"What about the two men in the corner?" asked Jux.

"I don't know. I was rushed to another tavern. I never saw those two again. The thing was, however, that everyone we passed had some sort of glow to them. Again, some strong, some weak, some pure in color, some muted and dull in color, some white, some red, black, many different colors, everywhere I looked. The next tavern we entered was a very run-down, seedy-looking place. The kind of place I never would have gone into alone. I was glad to be in the company of fourteen knights."

"And the same thing happened at this tavern, I take it."

"Yes. But in this tavern, there were a lot more people. I found that just about all of them had an aura that was colored and nowhere near the white I had first experienced, and it was very hard for me to not fly into a rage and attack them. I felt as if I was almost *obligated* to walk over and stick a knife in half of them.

"Dun Loren must have sensed this because for the ten minutes that it took us to go through fifteen drinks, he never once let go of my arm. I remember leaving that tavern and entering another. This one had just as many evil people in it as the last one. At this point, the alcohol made it impossible for me to focus my eyesight very well, and I can't remember anything past drink number five."

"That is some ritual."

"Dun Loren called it a tavern crawl."

"Did you?"

"Did I what? Crawl? I don't know, I can't remember much past that point, except that I was continually catching glimpses of very different auras surrounding almost everyone we met. I remember that I felt like picking several fights that night, but I was too drunk to do much about it. The next thing I knew, I was waking up in front of a fire late at night somewhere in the woods, and I was naked."

"Naked?"

"Yeah, it was evidently a big joke to leave me naked in the middle of the woods. They wanted to see what I would do."

"What *did* you do?"

"Nothing for about three hours. My head hurt too much. When the sun rose, I got up and attempted to figure out where I was. I walked around for a little while but was a little too disoriented to go far, so I returned to the fire. Dun Loren was waiting for me."

"I bet you had a lot of questions."

"Certainly, but Dun Loren didn't give me much time. He started laughing when he saw me, which I didn't take too well. But before I could start to yell at him, he handed me my clothes. 'What's this all about?' I asked him.

"'It's your coming-out ceremony,' he said.

"'That tells me a lot,' I said. I got dressed as he explained.

"'When a squire or knight reaches the point in his tutelage when he really connects with Kasparow, the god Himself listens to the prayers and rewards the individual with His prolonged presence. The first side effect, if you will, of His presence is the ability to see the aura of *good*, or *evil*, that surrounds everyone. It is a big step in your becoming a knight and carries a great deal of responsibility.'

"'So we show this responsibility by getting drunk beyond remembering,' I muttered.

"'No, we do that because this newfound power has caused problems in the past. The sudden onslaught of such ability in untrained minds can have varying effects. It had a disastrous effect many years ago, near the time of the founding of the Dun Lian Brotherhood. Two squires, brothers—twins actually—were not supervised when they suddenly 'came out' and were 'aware' of those auras surrounding them. Did you see any other auras last night besides the ones surrounding the brothers?'

"'Yes, I did. Everyone had one. There were all sorts of colors, and they all were of different intensities.'

"'That's good. That's as it should be. Not everyone is *good* in nature. Some people are just as evil as you or I are good. And just because someone is a bad person does not mean they are evil. Sometimes even just thinking a good or evil thought can change a person's aura. You'll eventually learn to interpret these colors better.'

"'There was one man, near the beginning of the night—his aura flared a bright red, and I wanted to run over and stick a knife in him.'

"'That is why I say it can be dangerous. If you had been in that tavern alone and unguided, what might have happened? Would you have actually run over and stuck a knife in a total stranger for no reason?'

"'But if I am able to see evil, and if he was evil—'

"'Remember, sometimes just a thought can change a person's aura. Suppose that man was served a mug of mead instead of an ale, and he *really* hated mead, was allergic to it—just his getting mad and thinking he wanted to slap the serving maid could make his aura flare. Does that mean you should attack him for it?'

"'No.'

"'Well then, until you learn to control that urge to take down anyone evil, it's best if you are supervised. That is the main reason for the coming-out ceremony. The idea is to put the person in a situation where they are bombarded by all sorts of auras but are unable to do much about it.'

"'So you got me drunk.'

"'We find young squires more controllable when they are in that condition.'

"'What about these twins, what happened with them?' I had finished dressing and sat down next to the fire. Dun Loren removed some food from a rucksack and handed it to me.

"'You had better eat. It may be a while before you get the chance again.' I didn't like the sound of this. 'The twins—an old story, a tragic one. It's because of them that we have this ceremony. The twins entered training at the same time, under the same knight. They did very well and saw the light, if you will, quite quickly. In those times, gaining the presence of Kasparow was considered a personal thing. Squires were told that it would happen, but it was left up to the individual as to how they would deal with it.'

"I remember wondering at that time whether or not I myself had come out quickly."

"Did you ever ask Dun Loren?" asked Jux.

"No, I never did. Dun Loren had me stay in the woods praying and meditating until I felt that I had gained some control over this new ability.

Once I did come out, it seemed that my training went very quickly after that. I was a knight and off to explore the world before I knew it. A newly commissioned knight is supposed to go out into the world and find a just cause to ally himself with before he receives any post assignments."

"What about the twins?"

"Well, Dun Loren proceeded to tell me the story of the twins, the McAri brothers. Evidently, they came out very quickly, and while on field exercises, their sponsor was mortally injured and perished before he could receive any help. They made their way to a nearby city and contacted the Brotherhood. It took a while for a detachment of brothers to arrive. Meanwhile, the twins had chosen to take the edge off of the day's events at one of the town's taverns.

"It didn't take long for one of the bar's patrons to 'agitate' the brothers due to their newfound powers of perception. A large fistfight ensued that eventually was forced out into the street by the tavern's owners. It reached such a point that both brothers drew their Maltas just as the detachment of brothers was approaching. The fight was broken up, and the McAri brothers were forced to accept the Malta mark. That's just the beginning too. They went on to cause other problems for the Brotherhood."

"A *Malta*? They received a *Malta mark*?" asked Jux.

"It's a weapon." He concentrated for a second and brought up an image of a Malta and the information concerning its use.

"Ah, I see. Very nicely done, by the way. I believe you are getting the hang of things."

"That's not an accomplishment I feel like rejoicing in. Is there *any way at all* of getting out of here?"

"Only one."

"I know, if someone else touches the gem, I will enter his body. The last I remember, I was at the bottom of a lake when I touched the gem. There's nothing living in that lake, if Malchom was here for a thousand years, so I guess I don't have to worry about ending up as a fish. I guess I can only hope that Malchom somehow escaped drowning and took the gem with him. And then, what would he do with it?"

"Yes, well, there may be *one* other way to get out of here."

"How, how?"

"I am not exactly sure what would happen, but if the gem were somehow destroyed, then you would be released."

"But that's not something I have any control over, and besides, how would that help? I'd have no body!"

"There is that. You might not survive as a spirit without physical form." Morgan attempted a sigh. Jux didn't react to it.

"Who made this thing? Where did it come from?"

"I believe it was made to house the soul of someone named Durgolais. That was a long time ago, before I really came into existence. He was the first occupant of the gem. It is hard to remember anything about him. He came and went before I began to know what I was. His memories are faint."

"Well, let me see one. You can do that, can't you?"

"Yes, if I can find anything. As I said, I did not really come to be until several different souls were trapped here. But let me think . . ." Morgan waited as he felt Jux sifting through what seemed to be areas of *his* memories. Suddenly a vision flared into being.

He was looking at a group of men in armor. Nine of them were armed with long pikes and formed a semicircle around a tenth. The man behind the wall of pole arms stood very tall and proud; his hands were clasped casually behind his back. He *smelled* very confident, unlike his protectors, who reeked of fear. His armor was highly polished and extremely ornate, decorated with etchings and carvings. Instinctively, Morgan knew these etchings to be magical protections; they were there to protect the wearer from Morgan, from his breath.

"This is the most powerful memory of Durgolais. I believe it is the moment directly preceding his entrapment within the gem." Jux's voice cut through the memory without interrupting it.

"What do you want, Paladin?" he said. He was looking down upon the men. He must have been standing on higher ground. He was in a cave, the walls and the floor were very uneven, and there was an exit to the chamber behind the men. He could see the tracks the men had left when they had entered; they almost glowed with a faint red light. The men themselves glowed red. When he spoke, a wave of red light billowed in front of his sight like cold, condensed breath.

"I bring a gift," the Knight said; surely this was a knight. The armored man's voice was crisp, clear, and very distinct. Morgan realized he could hear everything—the men's breathing, the rustle of their armor, their heartbeats. There was a wind blowing outside. It was snowing; he could hear it.

"What do you bring me, little man?" said Morgan. He now saw that he had a snout, a very long snout, covered in rough brown skin.

"Just a little bit of tribute to ensure there will be no more raids on our town." The knight had been holding something behind his back, which he now brought forward. It was the gem, very large and green, and it was nearly the size of the man's head.

"How can he touch that gem?" Morgan asked.

"I think it might have something to do with his gloved hands," said Jux.

"A small bauble to you, no doubt," said the knight. "But a dear gift to part with for the town."

"Bring it to me." Morgan saw a large brown-clawed hand and scaled arm reach toward the knight. The knight hesitated, then stepped around the protection of his assembled entourage and strode, again confident, toward Morgan. He reached for the gem and caught a whiff of something new coming from the knight as he came closer to the gem.

"I'm a DRAGON!" said Morgan, stopping the memory.

"Yes."

"There haven't been any dragons for thousands of years."

"I know," said Jux. "Even in Malchom's time, they were long since gone."

"And this gem was made to house the mind of a dragon? I wonder if that affects things in any way?"

"I doubt it. Many humans and other races have been here, but whether or not the gem was designed to swap so many souls, I do not know."

"Please, continue with that memory."

"I did not stop it, you did. Can you find it again?"

"I did? I don't know how I did." He concentrated and with ease found the memory and started it going again.

He smelled something wrong, deceptive. He retracted his massive scaled hand.

"I do not trust you," he grumbled. "You are covered head to toe with magical protections. Have one of your *men* bring it to me." The knight considered this for a second, his scent turning less confident.

"Very well," said the knight as he bowed slightly and called one of his men forward. The man came forward, slowly, dropping his pike in the process. This man was terrified. The man's smell changed from utter fear to confusion and bewilderment and finally to shaken determination as he grabbed the gem, faltered, and then after a few seconds, stumbled forward. This man was certainly not as confident as the knight was. The knight himself was now apprehensive. He reached out for the gem a second time and felt a familiar draining sensation as he touched the gem.

"Wait a minute, back up a little," Morgan said as he rewound the memory.

"Very well," said the Knight as he bowed slightly and called one of his men forward. The man came forward, slowly, dropping his pike in the process.

"Look!" said Morgan. "That pikeman doesn't have any gloves on."

"You are right," agreed Jux.

This man was terrified. The man's smell changed from utter fear to confusion and bewilderment and finally to shaken determination as he grabbed the gem, faltered, and then after a few seconds, stumbled forward.

"There must have been someone else inside the gem. Durgolais wasn't the first occupant of this gem," Morgan said, stopping the memory. "They must have switched places when the knight handed over the emerald. How come you don't have any memories of *that* occupant?"

"I do not know. That was a *very* long time ago, you realize. It is hard enough to remember any of Durgolais' memories.

"And then that person carried the gem toward the dragon. He remained in contact with it for quite a few seconds. Morgan brought up the memory again.

This man was terrified. The man's smell changed from utter fear to confusion and bewilderment and finally to shaken determination as he grabbed the gem, faltered, and then after a few seconds, stumbled forward.

"Durgolais sensed the change right there. But it didn't happen at all while the man was approaching Durgolais, as if there were some sort of delay or reset time."

"Or perhaps a soul can be transferred *in and out* only once," suggested Jux.

"That would be a relief. If I ever get out of here, I wouldn't have to fear it happening again." He paused. "No, that would be bad. It would mean that Malchom could never be imprisoned here again, and I could never regain my own body."

"Do you really think you will get out of here and be able do anything about Malchom? Remember, he was here for hundreds of years. I do not think humans are that long lived."

"He'll slip up, if he still has the gem, if he's still alive. And I *intend* on knowing what to do about him. Show me *all* of his memories. I want to know him inside and out."

"I do not feel like showing you any of his memories. I had to deal with that very perverted mind for a very long time, I do not care to deal with it again. I would much rather get to know *your* fresh memories."

"If I am indeed trapped here for centuries, then we have a lot of time to go through my life. If Malchom somehow gets me out of here, I *have* to be ready. Show me what I want to know."

"No, I will not." If Morgan had had a physical body, he was sure he would be steaming at the collar, his face red with rage. He concentrated and began looking for Malchom's memories, which popped up quite easily.

"I said no," said Jux as the disembodied entity slammed the memories of Malchom shut.

"YOU WILL LET ME SEE WHAT I WANT!" Morgan exclaimed and reasserted his will to view Malchom's memories. Jux crumbled away from his probing.

"Perhaps we can both pursue our own desires at the same time," Jux said timidly. "Let me get you started." A memory, he was sure it was Malchom's, opened up for him. It must have been Malchom as a child for he was looking up at who Morgan felt was his father.

"Thank you Jux," he said apologetically. The memory began. The father figure turned his back and walked away.

"I must admit," interrupted Jux, "I never have been overpowered like that before. It was quite scary." Morgan heard himself laugh in the memory. The young Malchom ran after his father.

"I'm sorry."

"I know, Morgan. I can tell, you are a good person."

Good person? Morgan thought. *Good. I must spend some time in prayer. Perhaps Kasparow will hear me and help me.*

"For some reason, I do not think he will be able to hear you, Morgan. Altair never responded to Malchom."

"I must try." He fell silent and returned to Malchom's childhood memory. The feeling of Jux going through his memories almost completely disappeared as he engrossed himself in the life of Malchom Jamias.

CHAPTER 9

He awoke to the smell of curried beef. Zora was evidently still cooking. He rolled onto his side and waited for his eyes to adjust to the dim light. The smells of Zora's dinner were working their way into his stomach. It gnawed and churned acidly; he hadn't eaten since the morning. He rolled onto his back and rubbed his stomach. Even though he was hungry and his stomach screamed out to be filled, he felt bloated. He looked pregnant. Zora's cooking was going to kill him from obesity. He grunted as he struggled to sit up. He knew Zora was just teasing when she nicknamed him the Gut, but he had been getting more and more sensitive about his weight. He had decided sometime ago to ask Dun Loren to teach him a few of the exercise routines the squires went through. Of course, like everything else that didn't involve books, he hadn't quite gotten around to it.

Rosen Kirkland stood up from the large down bed and went to a scentwood chest next to his wardrobe. He opened the chest and removed a fresh robe, which he slipped on over his silk shirt and cotton breeches. He breathed deeply as the garment passed over his head. How he loved the smell that a good scentwood chest imparted to its contents. He would build a house out of scentwood if possible. Scentwood did not grow on his native continent. It wasn't until he arrived here and began his service with the Brotherhood that he even knew of the existence of scentwood. Indeed, half of the things in his apartment alone had been unknown to him back home. An indoor privy! Who would have thought it? Not once did he regret leaving his home and a depressing life in the mines that was sure to be his if he had stayed.

"Oh, you're awake," said his wife from the doorway. "I was just about to come get you." She walked over to him and kissed him lightly on the cheek.

"That's okay. I'll be back in a few minutes. Will dinner be ready then?"

"Yes, it will be, Rosie. We have to feed the monster, don't we?" she said playfully while patting his belly.

"Please don't." He took her hand away and left the room. "I'll be back shortly."

He knocked lightly on the door when he reached Dun Loren's apartment, loud enough if he was already awake. Getting no answer, he slipped inside and silently went to the bedchamber. Dun Loren was still asleep on the crude futon he used for a bed. Rosen often wondered why Dun Loren never bothered to put a more comfortable bed in his sleeping chambers. He didn't think he could ever get to sleep on something like that. He had had enough of such accommodations in the mining caves of his home.

He went back to the drawing room and opened the drawers of Dun Loren's writing desk. *At least he has a beautiful writing desk*, he thought as he sifted through the papers in each of the drawers. It didn't take long for him to find what he was looking for.

Dun Loren,

I write this letter to you for I know how close you are to Dun Lain. I did not disclose the following information to Dun Lian. I did not feel that it mattered. While the physical evidence is indisputable, I also knew Morgan quite well. Morgan and I spent a lot of time together drinking and talking at several of the taverns in Reitner before he was knighted and went off on his own. I know quite a few personal things about the boy, and I am disturbed by what one of the survivors here at Maralat had to say about him. The young lady was very shaken, but I believe her memory was intact and accurate. She claims that Morgan, or the knight who is responsible for the murders here, engaged her in very sexually oriented conversation and eventually convinced her to return with him to his room. She says, when they finally coupled, that "he was the most dominating, powerful, confident, and experienced man I had ever been with. It was the most pleasurable experience I ever had." I know for a fact that Morgan was a virgin and too timid around pretty women to ever be described as "dominating, powerful, confident, and *experienced*." I simply do not feel in my heart that Morgan is responsible for the murders here at Maralat or at the other sites. I know you will be held responsible for his actions if Morgan is convicted of these crimes. I have not received any new orders as of yet, and my services are at your disposal.

Dun Dison

Rosen hastily but carefully put the papers back as he had found them. *Murder?* He though. *MURDERS. Dun Lain had murdered people? Many people, by the sound of it. No wonder Dun Loren and the entire Brotherhood are so agitated over this.* He composed himself, meditated for a few seconds to clear his mind. He was sure Dun Loren didn't routinely check the auras of those he was friends with, but actively thinking of what he had just done might change whatever it was Dun Loren normally saw in him.

"Dun Loren?" he called from the bedchamber's doorway. "Dun Loren," he said, a little louder. The knight stirred, grunted a little, and rolled over onto his back.

"Is it time already?"

"Yes, Dun Loren," said Rosen. Best to keep the conversation flowing while he put his transgression behind him. "Dun Loren, I have been wondering, when you get the chance, could you instruct me in some of your exercise routines?" He patted his stomach. "Zora wants a bear for a husband, but I'm quite sick of being called the Gut."

"You have gained quite a few pounds since I met you, haven't you? Well, it may be a while before I return . . . and then I may not have any time." The knight raised his knees, put his hands behind his head, and sat up, bringing his chest to touch his raised knees. "Do this a hundred times a day.' He said as he repeated the motion a couple of times. "That should do the trick by the time I get back."

"Looks simple enough. Might I ask where you are off to?"

"Maralat, Morgan needs some assistance." The blond-headed knight stood, straightened his clothing, and looked around the room. "Well, my clothes and belongings are gone, so I guess Clerents and Justin have done their jobs well enough. Care to accompany me to the courtyard?"

"Certainly, Dun Loren." He followed the knight out of the bedroom and into the drawing room. Dun Loren went to his desk and removed some parchment, pen, and a bottle of ink. Rosen actively controlled his breathing and tried to keep his mind clear.

"Just in case the boys forgot. I'm sure I'll be writing a lot on this trip. Shall we?" The knight gestured for Rosen to exit the apartment. Dun Loren turned and locked the door behind him when they were both outside. He let out a sigh and followed the scribe down the dimly lit hallway. "Going to be a long, hard trip, my friend."

Rosen noticed that Dun Loren was studying him intently as they walked on. Nervously he hiked up his robe out of habit. He continued to concentrate on his breathing. He thought of his wife, he thought of his books. Dun Loren laughed.

"To get off the subject of your belly, what about these robes you wear? You're constantly tripping, and I see you walking around with them pulled up, like a milkmaid, all the time."

"Tradition, you know." He was glad the conversation had changed. He relaxed again. "Got to have the same type of robe that they wore a long time ago."

"Ah yes, the notorious Dun Lian traditions. I had no idea that they extended as far as to include the scribes."

"And the cooks, maids, gardeners, garners. Even the privy cleaners wear specific clothing, although for their job, I can see the functionality of what they wear."

"Now there's a job I wouldn't want to have. I guess indoor privies have their price. What do they wear anyway?"

"They have a suit of very thick, heavily oiled leathers that covers them nearly from head to foot. I believe it is supposed to keep the smell from saturating the skin or something like that."

"You know, I use the threat of joining the privy cleaners as a means of keeping unruly squires in line. You can't imagine how effective it is."

"Oh yes, I can. The toilet in my apartment has backed up several times. *You* probably have never experienced it as the putrefiers in the knight's apartments are emptied daily, regardless of what else needs to be done. Do you know how quickly those tanks fill when there is a knighting ceremony going on? Or how about during the feast of Dun Lian? Do you think any of the privy cleaners have the time to wander over to the servant's quarters and bother with the putrefiers there?"

"Hmm. Never even thought about it. Well, if it ever gets that bad again, feel free to use the privy in my apartment. You have a key, and I'm not there much."

"Oh right, I'm sure that would look good to any onlooker: 'Dun Loren was out on field exercises when I saw this squire come running down the hallway, fumble with some keys, break into Dun Loren's apartment, and rush inside. Then I heard this loud AHHH!' I don't think Zora would want to do the same thing either. You'll just have to hire more privy cleaners."

"You haven't eaten."

"What?"

"You're too grumpy and sarcastic to have eaten." They emerged into the courtyard and made their way to the front gates. Despite the time of night, the immense courtyard of Lianhome was awash with light. Some sort of the training was taking place nearly around-the-clock at the Dun Lian stronghold. The four three-storied towers at the corners of the courtyard each had bonfires ablaze at their base. *Miremoss* torches lined the walls and spotted the grounds of the courtyard. The plant produced a profuse amount of sweet-smelling smoke when burned and served to provide light, as well as deter biting insects, from flying freely around the courtyard. So much of the plant was used that a separate greenhouse had been constructed to grow the airborne moss. Dun Loren and Rosen Kirkland found a small group waiting for them at the front gates of the castle.

"Everything is in order, Dun Loren," said the twins in unison as he and Rosen arrived.

"Very good, boys." He found he was sweating despite his light clothing and the time of night and wondered if this was due to his nerves or if it was actually that humid. He looked at the faces of those gathered around him. The twins were buoyant and hyperactive, as always. They showed no sign of either stress or discomfort.

Dun Lian stood there, almost regally, in thin very light-colored cotton clothing. Dun Lian never wore anything other than simple cotton clothing, no finery, no silks, and no jewelry. Except on occasions of state when tradition demanded he be garbed in almost royal attire. This Dun Lian might have enough strength of character and popularity to introduce measures that would do away with some of the more mundane items on the long list of Dun Lian traditions. He would have to approach Dun Lian on this subject at a later time, if he was able to, if he was still a knight in three months' time.

Dun L'lsen stood behind Dun Lian. Oliver Olsen was an impressive figure of a knight. He was taller than any knight Dun Loren knew, and wider too. It was often joked that if Dun L'lsen were to lie on his side, he would still be taller than most knights. Dun L'lsen's long red hair was pulled back in a topknot. Dun Loren wondered what the big knight did with that hair when he put his helmet on. Dun L'lsen was almost as hairy as he was big. Thick red hair ran down his neck. Dun Loren doubted if it stopped there. His bare arms, originally fair skinned but now thoroughly tanned from years in the sun, were also covered with thick red hair. Dun Loren chuckled to himself as the image of a big hairy red grizzly came to mind. Dun L'lsen wasn't sweating either. Neither was his squire, who stood next to Dun L'lsen's massive mastodon-like charger.

Rosen Kirkland was sweating. But he was wearing a long thick cotton robe. Or was he nervous? Something was not quite right with the scribe. This man was so tan that he looked to be of another race. And glistening sweat was rolling down his tanned face almost in rivulets.

"This arrived with the evening dispatch." Dun Lian handed him a folded paper. "There was more to it, but this is all you need see." Dun Lian addressed the scribe, "Would you excuse us, Master Kirkland?"

"Certainly, Dun Lian. Dun Loren, Kasparow's grace be with you," he said, turning to the knight and shaking his hand in farewell.

"One hundred repetitions a day, and I will see less of you in three months."

"Gladly," Rosen said, almost lightheartedly. Dun Loren detected something in the response—was it *relief*?

"This new news is very disturbing and highly questionable," continued Dun Lian. Dun Loren scanned the paper as Dun Lian continued to speak. "Another town has been decimated, this time all but two are dead, 318, total. The two that remained could not describe the one responsible. They never saw him. They did know, however, that a Dun Lian knight came into town shortly before and set up a census office. He evidently posted papers all around the town stating that every citizen was to report to the 'Dun Lian Census Bureau' at a specific time the following day so that an accurate population count could be made.

"He also claimed that 'recruits' were welcome. The inn that he commandeered to conduct his 'census' was literally packed with all three hundred and eighteen bodies. All of their throats had been slit, and it appears as if their blood was allowed to spill on the ground. How exactly he was able to get all of the townsfolk without arousing any suspicion is beyond any comprehension."

"The village of Jourlean is nearly a hundred leagues from Maralat and almost fifty leagues from Dun Lain's last reported position," Dun L'lsen interrupted roughly.

Dun Loren had finished reading the report and was glaring at the big knight. "Perhaps this is a good sign, then. Would Dun Lain have such mobility? Perhaps something more complicated is happening. These wide-ranging and varied reports give me hope that the answer is not simply that Morgan has gone on a mad murdering spree."

"In either case," said the big knight as he turned to Dun Lian, "I request permission to accompany Dun Loren. Dun Loren, could you use another horse?" Dun Loren looked to the leader of his brotherhood. Dun Lian merely raised an eyebrow quizzically at him.

"I don't mind, Dun L'lsen. Are you ready to ride?"

"Both me and my squire."

"Well then," he said lightly, "at the very least, I could use you to scare off any beasties we might encounter." Dun L'lsen's grin was enormous.

*　　*　　*

Malchom woke from the trance with a start. They were after him. He delighted in knowing they would think it was Morgan who had committed the murders. The notion filled him with glee; it had been a thousand years since he cackled as much as he did now. After leaving the decimated dwellings of that puny village behind, he had called on Altair's avatar to transport him home.

He had been deposited on a mossy mound; his castle lay in ruins around him. A thousand years had not been kind to his former home. He spent the day roaming through the rubble. Somewhere was an entrance to the subterranean levels of his abode. The sun had gone down, and he still had yet to find it.

He now sat at a fire, eating a conjured meal and contemplating the powers he would pray for on the morrow. The food was bland, but he had no desire to chase down live game. Conjured food was always tasteless and was barely considered sustenance unless he spent extra time praying specifically for something a little more exotic. His prayers in the morning would be exhausting enough, no need to waste the gifts of the avatar. This second town should provide him with enough sacrificial power to get his operations off to the start they needed.

He must find the underground catacombs if they still existed. Simply asking for the knowledge of where the entrance was would work, but why not ask for something that would do more? The ability to be able to see through wood and earth and stone would help him find the entrance. It would also allow him to search for the many secret doors and hidden rooms that were a part of his now-ancient home.

Another *far sight* to be able to observe this Dun Loren character would do well. A permanent teleport ability, maybe the power of flight. If the upper areas of his castle were in ruins, the underground portions might be as well. A summoned elemental would aid him well in clearing any debris he came across.

Quite quickly, he was sure, the local law enforcement would begin to mobilize if he continued to obliterate whole towns at a time. It wouldn't take long for news to spread. He already knew the Brotherhood had begun its own investigation. A lot depended on his finding the entrance to and restoring the functionality of the caves and caverns that lay below him. They once served to house thousands of prisoners at a time. Fungi had once grown in these caves, capable of supporting a large amount of sacrificial worshippers while they waited to give their blood for the glory of Altair. He reminisced with a smile how easy and willing his followers had been in the past. He could begin collecting and stockpiling sacrifices again only if the catacombs were not destroyed. It seemed a vicious circle; any power needed to restore them would take blood, lots of blood. Large sacrifices couldn't be made unless he had a large number of people on hand, or was able to kill an entire village again, which was going to become impossible very quickly, he was sure.

A strange bleating reached his ears that sent a shiver down his spine. It was an earthy sound, which echoed around the ruin. The sound was loud; whatever made it must have been close. Malchom jumped to his feet and was reaching for his unbuckled sword when a figure exploded into the light.

The size of a man, the creature was hunched over, almost running on all four limbs. The creature's face looked as if it was contorted in pain. Tight thin lips pulled away from enormous fangs as the creature croaked in rage. It galloped on thick hind legs and long drooping forearms around the fire and reached Malchom with blinding speed. Caught off guard, he was unable to prevent the creature from smacking him backward with one huge-clawed backhand. Malchom staggered backward, falling to the ground, losing his weapon in the process.

Instantly the creature was upon him. The thing's flesh was leathery, green in color, and reeked of rot. Its thin wiry muscles showed surprising strength. He was lifted aloft with one arm and flung out of the firelight. Air rushed out of him as he collided with a tree. Gasping for breath, Malchom rasped the prayer that instantaneously transported him miles away.

The creature snarled in anger as Malchom vanished. Whirling, it sniffed the air violently, attempting to discern the whereabouts of its prey, but found nothing. Enflamed, it set about eradicating the contents of the campsite. The food was tasted and tossed into the surrounding brush. The backpack was emptied and discarded, spare clothing sniffed and tossed into the fire, metal utensils and tools banged against each other a few times, then dropped. A leather book was tossed aside. A thick woolen blanket was snatched up, sniffed, and discarded. The creature continued its searching until it came across a somewhat-bulky bag. Sharp claws ripped into pieces the leather straps that kept the bag closed. The creature upturned the bag, revealing only dirt. It grabbed the ball of dirt and sniffed, turning the packed sphere of earth round and round. The dirt cracked, revealing a glimmering green light that shone from within. The glow entranced the creature; he stared at it for several seconds before squeezing the ball of dirt, which barely fit into his huge hand.

Another of the creatures bounded into the campsite. Shorter than the first, it began screaming and grunting, waving its arms wildly at the first. Returning the ranting, the larger creature dropped the ball of dirt, shattering the dry shroud surrounding a gem, which glowed with a brilliant green light at its release.

The creatures ceased their arguing as the radiating light of the emerald entranced them both. The shorter one grunted several syllables and moved to pick up the gem. Yapping violently and possessively, the larger creature shoved the other away and snatched up the gem.

CHAPTER 10

"You have been quiet for a while. I do not even feel you searching through my memories. Has Malchom's life gotten to you?" Jux asked smugly. "I do not fault you for getting so upset. From what I have seen, you are a complete opposite to Malchom."

"That's not it," Morgan replied, the first time he had spoken in a long time, indeed. He had spent a long time going through Jux's memories, or Malchom's memories, *his* memories—whoever they belonged to didn't seem to matter anymore. He had learned many things. The most prominent was that Malchom *was* a truly evil person. From patricide to genocide, Malchom *enjoyed* killing. Malchom had been instrumental in increasing and cementing Altair's influence and widespread worship in the world a thousand years ago. One would think a religion that forced its followers to sacrifice its own members would eventually kill itself off. From what he knew of history, and now Malchom's own thoughts, that was not so.

Malchom had an efficient little operation going while he was alive. His base of operations, the Castle Altium, as Malchom had christened it, was built on top of a myriad of caverns and tunnels. There was but one entrance to these caves, and Malchom had found it by accident. With the help of powers granted by Altair, Malchom had transformed the caves into a complex designed to imprison thousands of people while they waited to be sacrificed. A fungus grew in the caves; Morgan could not be sure if it was a naturally growing fungus or one created by Altair for Malchom. This fungus grew very rapidly. It shed a dull yellow light, was nutritious enough to sustain life, and had a side effect when eaten on a regular basis. With enough of the fungus in a person's system, a continuing sense of euphoria developed. The person also became extremely susceptible to suggestion and became extremely submissive. Malchom had, at one time, several thousand people, of all races, simply sitting in his dungeons waiting patiently, willingly, to be sacrificed to Altair.

One of the ironic things about the whole situation was that these *prisoners* needed no guards. New *recruits* were kept in a separate area until the effect of the fungus took hold and the proper suggestions were given. Morgan and a handful of his brothers could have walked in, opened a few doors, and ushered the entire group out simply by uttering a few well-chosen words.

With such a supply of worshippers, Malchom had been able to request greater powers from Altair than most of his peers. Malchom had had an idea, which had formed just before his demise—a plan to *recruit* only women. He would gather thousands of women and make sure they became and remained pregnant. He would have eventually had a self-sustaining population of sacrificial fodder. It seems that Altair was partial to infants, as well as races other than human. There was no doubt, in Morgan's opinion, that Malchom would try and pick up where he left off as soon as he was able to.

"So you think Malchom will start killing again?"

"I think that's guaranteed. The real question is how many, and what will happen if he does it as a Dun Lian knight? He may not be one, but he certainly looks like one. If he were smart, he wouldn't do it openly. He'd wait, a few at a time, and gather his strength. He's got a good year before anyone begins to wonder what "Dun Lain" is doing. But then, there's no telling what he might do, after being bottled up in here for so long."

"Well, he is just one man."

"One man in the body of a Dun Lian Knight. And if Altair starts giving him powers again . . . You see, magic isn't widely used anymore, and I fear he will become quite formidable if he regains even a portion of his former power. And what about this mushroom? I've never heard of it before now. If he finds it again, that alone will give him great power over others."

"I think you need to quit worrying about it. Even if you were to get out of here—"

"Yeah I know," Interrupted Morgan. "I would end up in the body of a squirrel or some old man hundreds of years from now.

"So what were you doing just now, while you were silent?" said Jux, changing the subject rather bluntly.

"I had looked through enough of Malchom's memories and decided that it was about time I resumed my prayers to Kasparow."

"Really? I heard nothing. How do you go about this?"

"Well, I clear my mind of all thoughts and begin a chant, which I continue until I feel His presence. Then once He is listening, I begin my prayer. It is more of a song than a prayer, but I do not sing it out loud."

"May I hear it?"

"Prayer to Kasparow is still a private matter within the Brotherhood, but I guess conversation with you is about as private as one can get. From what I understand, everyone prays to Kasparow differently. Mine goes like this:

> I call on the grace of Kasparow
> For the first time this day.
> I call on the grace of Kasparow
> To bend an ear while I pray.
> I call on the grace of Kasparow
> For the second time this day.
> I call on the grace of Kasparow
> To bend an ear while I pray.

"And so on, until I feel His presence. Then I begin my prayer.

> You are my light, you are my faith,
> You dry the eyes, which bleed with tear.
> You are my blood, you are my breath,
> You still the hands, which shake with fear.
> You are my heart, you are my bone,
> You strengthen the body, which falls with frailty.
> You are my thoughts, you are my soul,
> You clear the mind, which clouds with senility.

"I'm not much of a poet. I know, the Brotherhood doesn't give much guidance when it comes to how a knight should pray. Kasparow is worshipped by many, not just the members of the Brotherhood, but within the Brotherhood, tradition demands that it be a solitary thing."

"The Brotherhood seems to be steeped in traditions."

"That would be an understatement, but it holds us together."

"Were you successful? In contacting Kasparow, I mean."

"No. I waited in meditation for a long time, longer than it should take for Kasparow to come."

"You say Kasparow comes to listen to you pray, is it *Kasparow* or an avatar of Kasparow, such as would deal with Malchom?"

"I don't know. I've never been physically visited by either Kasparow or one of His avatars. I guess that is a privilege left to more prominent knights."

"So you were unsuccessful. Perhaps Kasparow's influence does not extend into this place."

"Either that, or he has forsaken me. I truly hope it is the former. I'll need all the help I can get to bring down Jamias."

"How far did you get this time, with your meditation?"

"Seven hundred thirty-one. He usually responds by one hundred or so."

"I am surprised that I did not hear you praying, especially if you were at it for over seven hundred repetitions. That seems to me to be—"

Jux's voice abruptly faded. Morgan felt himself move; he felt as if he was being pulled through a siphon, squeezed tight to a point, then released in a rapid expanding of his soul. The remarkable thing was that he *felt* it happen. This could simply be another memory in Jux's vast repertoire of thoughts, but he seriously doubted it; it felt too real. He needed it to be real. He was beginning to think that he would go mad trapped as he was. A thousand years alone, even if he did have the memories of a hundred other beings to learn, would drive him insane. He clung to the hope that his salvation was at hand; perhaps Kasparow *had* heard him. After all, this was happening just after his period of prayer. He began his song to Kasparow anew, praying he would not end up as a fish.

He knew instantly that he was not a fish. He heard his own breathing—a shallow, rough, rasping sound. He heard crickets chirping a glorious choir all around him. He heard the rich rustling of wind in trees. He felt the same breeze attempting to cool his skin, which was being healthfully heated by a fire on his right side. He felt the dry ground beneath him, cold and hard and real. The smell of a beautifully burning wood fire filled his nostrils. The smell of dirt danced around him. Another smell—sweet, full-bodied—a smell that was unknown to him, hung heavily in the air.

While he was most definitely not inside a fish, he also knew he was not inside his own body. He had a bad feeling that he wasn't even inside a human body. His thoughts were jumbled, and he found it hard to think. Something was not right. His hearing and sense of smell were too powerful and too distinctive. He could hear, feel, smell, and *see*; he had definitely escaped the gem, but into *what*, and into what *situation* had he landed?

He could see, but it was completely wrong. His vision was bubbled and sectioned into twelve parts, as if he was looking through a dozen large glass beads. Eleven smaller images surrounded a twelfth larger one. There was no color to his vision. Everything was composed of shades of gray, black, and white. Though bland, he was amazed at how distinct shapes could be without the aid of color.

He was looking down at his own hands, at least he thought they might be hands. They were huge, at least they appeared to be huge. He was having a hard time deciphering what he saw. Twelve identical images were being imposed on his brain. He concentrated and tried to look through what appeared to be the center bubble; it was slightly larger than the other eleven.

These *were* his hands. They were connected to small but muscular arms, arms that seemed too long. The hands themselves were too large in comparison to his thin arms. They were clawed and had long bony fingers. Tough tendons bulged beneath what looked like tough, leathery skin. He could feel their power and strength as he flexed the muscles slightly. His hands and arms were completely alien to him, but what they held was not.

He was holding the gem. He had never really seen it before. The last time it had been in his line of sight, he was instantly sucked into the gem, and he was delirious and feverish as a result of touching the tainted waters of the Dead Pools. He knew it was the gem, however, from Jux's memories—*his memories?* He knew the look of that gem as well as he knew the look of his father or mother. The many memories of the gem that he had viewed while with Jux seemed to have come with him into his new body. He wondered if all the memories he had experienced while imprisoned within the gem had remained with him. He would have to find out; an intimate knowledge of Malchom Jamias would be invaluable now that he was free, but that would have to wait. There was something more immediately important he must do. He dropped the gem. It fell to the ground and rolled toward the fire. The flames were bright white and seemed to shimmer and give off waves of heat.

Movement caught his eye, or was it eyes? One of the smaller images surrounding his center view shifted and focused on a figure struggling to stand not ten feet away. He felt dizzy and nearly toppled into the fire with disorientation. It was difficult to believe that he could focus on more than one subject, with one eye even! He backed away from the fire and the gem; he was never going near that thing again. He turned and concentrated. All twelve images shifted focus as he looked at the figure that was just regaining its feet.

This thing looked familiar to him. It stood nearly four feet tall, or attempted to stand; a crouch was all that it could achieve. It was very thin and wiry while still appearing to be powerful and strong. It was crouched on huge half-bent legs that were the thickest part on the creature. The body looked emaciated; ribs protruded through a bumpy, leathery skin. Its arms were very long and would have dragged the ground had they not been flailing in the air. Huge, paddle-sized hands ended in thick dark claws. Its head was elongated and stretched out behind it, giving the creature a top-heavy look.

A tuft of thick black hair fell around extremely large dangling ears and a skull whose skin was too small to completely cover it. There was not enough skin to cover the mouth; the lips failed to stretch over a set of huge sharp, pointed teeth. The skin pulled away from its eye sockets, making the creature appear to be staring wildly. Its eyes were large, six-faceted and half circular in shape. In all, the natural appearance of the thing made the creature look as if it were contorted in pain, which was evident by its earsplitting shrieking and furiously flailing limbs.

Was it pain or *rage*? Was the creature in distress, or was it scolding him? Something about its movements and gestures reminded him of the way his mother would attempt to discipline his father. The thing was the most disgusting sight he had ever seen, and yet he was feeling a slight arousal between his legs. It was then that he realized this was a female of whatever species she was. He felt sick; the contents of his stomach flowed violently up his throat, out his mouth, and splattered on the ground. The female creature screeched and scampered toward him. Both the horrific sight before him and the sickening arousal within mortified him.

She was still swinging her arms every way she could, yapping noisily in what had to be some sort of language. She reached him and grabbed for his arms. Her touch was cold, tough. His skin crawled while his excitement grew. This disturbed him, and he reacted violently. He swung an enormous-clawed hand at her face. The speed and strength in his limbs took him, and her, completely by surprise. She crumpled before him, a wave of blood spilling from gaping gashes in her cheek. She stumbled backward, nearly twenty paces, not bothering to even brush a hand against her face, not bothering to wipe any of her blood away. Instead, the blood spurted from the wound with the force of a strongly beating heart. The blood looked odd, nearly white in color, but then he couldn't see color.

She howled a long, loud braying sound. Continuing to scream at him, she crouched and sprung forward, leaping the distance between them in one powerful flexing of her massive thighs. She landed on him, knocking them both to the ground, dangerously close to the fire, dangerously close to the gem. One of his 'eyes' shifted to his right, focusing on the gem; he was too close to it. Even if he was inside some sort of monster, he wasn't about to go back inside the gem. He was free, and he was going to stay that way.

She began to pummel him, beating his chest with the backs of her hands in wild arclike swings. In his prone position, he was able to catch a glimpse at the lower half of his body. His legs were proportionally as huge as hers were. His feet were webbed, clawed, and overly too long. Between his legs was what must be his manhood, if it could be referred to as *man*hood. His chest was beginning to hurt. Through some sort of instinct, he brought his massive feet up under her and raked her belly with the talons on his feet like a rabid cat.

Her skin was tough; the somewhat dull claws of his feet did little to disturb her assault. It only irritated her further. Her backhanded swings became closed-fisted cuffing. She was relentless; she showed no sign of stopping, or of even letting up. He wrapped a single enormous hand around her throat and squeezed. Her neck muscles were thick; he didn't think this would slow her down. He was getting desperate. His hand fell away from her throat; her beatings now targeted his face. Half in an attempt to fend off her attack and half through another strange instinctual response, he lunged upward and caught her throat in his powerful jaw. Without thinking, his mouth closed, blood spurted forcefully into his mouth, slipped sweetly down his throat. *Sweetly?* She struggled violently; he forced his teeth closer. She tried to pull away; he clung to her tighter.

Slowly, despite her struggles, she ceased moving. Pushing her off him, he rolled to his left, away from the gem. *Had his one eye remained focused on the gem?* He sprang to his feet, a bit more quickly and powerfully than he had expected. He looked at his hands, covered in the light-colored fluid, and realized that the creature, whose life was slipping out at his feet, was of the same species to which he now belonged.

He stumbled backward slightly and nearly tripped over a log. Without looking down, he sat on the log. *What am I?* he thought. *Obviously, I am one of whatever* that *thing is.* He studied the dead creature lying a few feet away. It certainly was horrific looking, yet why had he felt so aroused?

And why had the thing's blood tasted so sweet, so *good?* The blood still lingered in his mouth. He passed his large tongue over very sharp teeth. The sweetness remained. It did taste good, like the imported Chunyan melon candies that his father used to offer to his customers—hard candies that made your saliva thicken to the point of nearly becoming syrup. His stomach churned, not from disgust this time, however. He was getting hungry. Offhandedly he wondered if the dead creature was edible; after all, it seemed to taste good.

He breathed deeply. He could smell the blood on his hands, and he could smell the blood that was still dripping from the creature's throat. The smell made his stomach growl again. The smell of her blood reminded him of the sweetbread the castle caterers would bake round-the-clock at the Dun Lian stronghold. He should have been disgusted; this was the foul blood of a grotesque monster he was salivating over, but he wasn't. He *was* salivating. He wiped the dripping saliva from his chin, only to bring *more* of the sweet blood into contact with his mouth.

He sniffed the air again. Despite the overbearing pungent odor of the blood, there were many distinct odors that he could identify and point out. The ground smelled very dirty and dusty. The surrounding trees had a very stale floral odor. One of the trees, that one over there on the other side of the fire, smelled of what he thought was plums. Indeed, when he looked at the tree that the smell was emanating from, he saw little pieces of fruit dangling from its limbs.

There was a very crisp, sharp smell that he couldn't identify or pinpoint. It hung on the air and seemed to linger around the campsite like the way a heap of week-old garbage would linger, even after the refuse bin had been emptied. It was a strange smell, almost exotic, and started his stomach gnawing in hunger again. The smell was so faint that he couldn't pick out which direction it was coming from. The source of the smell was nowhere near, which disappointed him; whatever it was had to be food. It smelled like a mixture of tropical fruit, Chunyan spices, and tender milk-fed beef that had been slow-roasting in a fire pit for hours. There was another smell—bland, almost dusty, not unlike the smell of dirt. This smell was coming from his left, away from the fire. He stood, or attempted to stand. The leg and back muscles in his new body did not seem to be made for standing completely upright. He winced in pain as he stood, feeling the muscles stretch too far, feeling them rip. A groan of pain was generated from his throat, and he heard his new voice for the first time. It was higher in pitch than he expected. He tried to call out a hello; the sound came nowhere near resembling an intelligible word.

He found what he was looking for not far from the campsite. It was a chunk of dry bread. It was tasteless and hard, sort of like the field rations the brothers used. He bit into it and chewed. From where he was now standing, he could see the surrounding countryside. Two moons shed enough light to allow him to see for quite some distance. The nearby rolling, lightly forested landscape was speckled with the crumbling columns and fallen walls of an ancient castle, the stones almost completely covered with vegetation. Movement caught his eye. A white fox slinked silently through the rubble. Morgan sniffed; he could smell the fox *from here*! A bleating sound escaped his mouth involuntarily. The fox stopped, looked up, and bounded away, disappearing into the night. He tested the air again, nothing. His smell did have limits then; that, or every living thing in the area had vanished.

He found a discarded backpack, blanket, and empty leather bag on his way back to the fire. He sat on the warm log and continued to eat the bread he had found while examining the backpack. It was pretty well beat up, shredded a little. It looked like the backpack he had had with him at the Dead Pools. Of course it was his; Malchom had to be around. He paused in examining the rucksack and sampled the air again. Nothing. Nothing save that faint smell he could not find. Could that be Malchom's smell? He shuddered at the thought of Malchom's scent being so appealing to his appetite. Yes, this was without a doubt his backpack. What had happened to Malchom? Had these creatures eaten him? The campsite didn't seem like the sort of place they would create. The bread, metal utensils, forks, knives, tongs that were strewn about the ground certainly were not a regular part of these creatures' lives. Malchom had to have been here. The fire was beginning to warm him to the point of being uncomfortable.

He stood and grabbed the log in one hand to move it farther away from the heat. It was strangely colored, as if anything could be considered normally colored with his new colorless vision. The side of the log facing the fire was lighter in color while the backside, he found as he turned the log over in one massive hand, was much darker. He moved away from the fire. He had never felt so uncomfortable near flame, as if his entire body was overheating. The log was warm in his hand as well. At least the portion that was facing the fire was warm. He moved around the fire so he could see the front of the female creature, the side that was facing the flames, and found, as he was expecting, the color of her skin to be much lighter. Could he see heat? He moved away from the fire and dropped the log to sit. He was looking at both the back side and the front side of the log at the same time. He seemed to be getting used to this body's ability to look at more than one thing at a time.

Experimentally, he turned toward the fire and kept his center vision focused on the log at his feet. He moved one of his eyes to focus on the carcass before him. *That's two.* Concentrating, he brought a third eye around to focus on a tree far off to his left. *Three.* So far so good—the log, body, and tree remained perfectly in focus. He then focused on the gem. It was still glowing brightly. *Four.* A tree to his far right was next, and then his feet came into view. Next he focused on the fire, then one of the two yellow moons that were out tonight.

There were only two moons out, and they were *yellow*! That meant that the season hadn't changed. He had only been inside the gem for a month at the most! Unless an entire year, or years, had passed . . .

He was looking at eight objects at the same time. He felt slightly nauseated. He stumbled forward, his vision blurred, he almost passed out. He had to concentrate, keep his mind centered on what he was doing. The nausea faded, his vision cleared. He was concentrating so intently on keeping the eight objects focused that he did not realize he had moved forward several feet. It was the discomforting warmth of the fire that clued him in to how close to the campfire, and the gem, he had moved.

This time he sat. Clearing his mind, he started over, still intent on determining how much he could focus on at the same time. One object, two, three. *Keep focused.* Four, five. *Concentrate.* Six, seven, eight. The dizziness started to hum in his mind. *Concentrate, focus.* He slowly moved an eye to focus on a ninth object; this time it was the gem. *Concentrate, focus, concentrate, focus on the gem, the gem.* The humming began again in his mind. *Focus on the gem.* The humming grew, became a faint howling. *Focus on the gem.* The howling grew louder. It sounded vaguely familiar. His sight began to blur. *Concentrate on the gem, focus.* The howling filled his mind now, and he was sure he knew the source. It sounded exactly like the groan of pain he had let loose when he stood. *Focus on the gem, the gem.*

"Morgan?" His concentration snapped, and he reeled backward slightly. Okay, nine was not a good number to try. What had happened? He had heard Jux. He looked around him. The log was still beneath him; the crumpled body of the female monster was still on the ground next to him. The fire had died a little. The gem was still on the ground in front of the flames. He tried to close his eyes and rub them, but there was not enough skin on his head to form eyelids. That *had* been Jux he had heard, and what he thought was his new voice screaming, howling in fear, and yet he was still here. For a brief second, he thought he had returned to the gem, that he had somehow touched it, but it was still on the ground, next to the fire several feet away from him.

Perhaps he *had* touched the gem, touched it with his mind. He had concentrated on the gem, and then he had heard Jux. What if he was able to contact Jux? Jux's knowledge would be invaluable, or could that be the way your soul was transferred? He feared trying again, feared the possibility of being trapped within the gem again. His stomach growled once more. The sweet-smelling blood was becoming too overpowering.

Without thinking, he stood and dragged the carcass away from the heat. Grabbing one of the discarded knives, he awkwardly set about carving out a section of the female's thick calves. He was salivating again. But how to cook it? Setting the knife next to the log, he went to a nearby oak and, with one hand, ripped a long thin branch from the small tree. His strength surprised him as the limb came away from the tree like he was ripping paper, sending him sprawling backward. He picked himself up off the ground and recovered the piece of meat that had fallen from his hand. He sat back down and, depositing the chunk of flesh on the log, *by Kasparow did it smell good*, began to whittle the branch into a skewer for the meat.

It was a difficult job to accomplish. His hand would not grasp the knife properly to allow him deft use of its cutting edge. He moved his hand and arm in all sorts of contorted positions in an attempt to whittle the stick to a point. Giving up, frustrated, he tossed the knife down and shoved the hunk of meat onto the badly scored stick. Scooting in a squatting position, he plunged the bloody shank of flesh into the flames. It snapped and sizzled intensely. The blood burned foully, creating a black smoke that nauseated him.

The tree branch was not extremely long, perhaps four feet at most. He was too close to the fire. It felt as if the flames were cooking him as well. The fire seemed to warm his entire body, making him extremely uncomfortable. Not being able to stand the heat any longer, he shuffled back to his seat and sniffed his dinner. It smelled terrible; funny that the blood would smell so sweet and the flesh so bad.

He grabbed the light-colored chunk of meat with his free hand. It was hot, very hot, but the direct heat bothered him little. Instead, the heat entered him and dispersed throughout his hand. He marveled at this as he took a bite of the meat and marveled again as he reacted violently to the cooked flesh, spitting it out, forcefully, into the fire. It burned foully, sending out smoke that reached his nose and made him shiver. The meat tasted as bad as it smelled, and yet the blood was one of the sweetest and most satisfying things he had ever tasted.

Frustrated and hungry, he picked up the knife and flung it at the plum tree across the fire. His powerful long, thin arm swung gracefully, flinging the blade with an astonishing precision and speed. The knife hit its target with a solid *thunk*. Morgan stood to move and retrieve the knife, but stopped short. Remembering what the female had done, he decided to test his new body's strength further. He crouched low and jumped forward, leaping the fire and reaching the plum tree with ease. His landing was harsh. He fell flat on his face. Laughing, a sound that was altogether alien to him, he struggled to stand and regarded the distance he had covered. Nearly twenty feet, and he didn't think he tried half as hard as he could have. The knife was embedded deeply into the tree, nearly halfway up the blade, making it difficult for him to wiggle it free.

He spent some time tossing the knife around. He was unable to recreate the accuracy and deadliness of the first throw, but then, this was a simple cooking knife, not suited for a concentrated throwing effort. He would have to buy some real throwing knives. *Buy?* Why did he think he could buy anything? He had no money, and who would want to deal with him in the first place? People were going to run screaming from him the moment he showed this new bug-eyed face anywhere, if they didn't immediately try and kill him instead of running away in terror. This was almost as bad as being in the gem. Instead of being cursed to live forever with Jux as his only companion—trapped within the gem, without a physical body—he was now cursed to live as a monster, hated and feared by all of his kind. Or more accurately, shunned by those that *used to be* his kind.

In frustration, he angrily chucked the knife at the plum tree. It bounced off the bark and landed with a *clink* several feet away. He seemed to become frustrated quite easily, but then this was an extraordinary situation. He didn't think there had ever been a time that—wait, a minute, *with a* clink?

Morgan walked to the plum tree and began searching for the knife. The knife was easy to find. It had been slightly warmed from his handling of it and was lighter in color than the surrounding vegetation and ground. But what had it hit? A rock? No, it had made a metallic sound. He scanned the ground. Most everything he saw was the same in color, a muted gray. Some of the plants, especially those closer to the fire, were lighter in color. But the rocks, the dirt, most of the ground, looked so similar that it was difficult to distinguish separate objects.

When he found what he was looking for, his heart raced. It was long, somewhat thin, and barely a shade lighter than the ground. It *was* metal. Having rested on the ground for an unknown amount of time, the heat had leaked out of it, effectively hiding it from his view. He reached down and grasped its handle. It felt good in his hands, lighter than he remembered. Now he knew that Malchom had been here, wherever here was. This was his. He unsheathed the sword that Dun Loren had given him the day after his knighting, the golden studded sword belt clanging against the jewel-encrusted scabbard, and held the blade aloft. It reflected the light of the fire and seemed to glow.

Another growl from his stomach reminded him of his hunger. The smell of congealed blood drew him back to the female corpse. He knelt beside it, dropping both the sword and its sheath. Having been dragged away from the fire, the body had cooled somewhat and was quite a bit darker in appearance. The meat tasted bad, but the blood was sweet. Had he burned off all the blood when he cooked the meat? Was it the skin that tasted so foul? His gnawing hunger forced a gruesome decision. He had to eat.

Retrieving his knife, he clumsily sliced several slivers of meat from different areas of the corpse. Impulsively he plopped a small piece into his mouth and swallowed. Expecting to retch, he was surprised to find that the meat tasted good. Had he eaten from a different part of the body? No. And this piece was raw! Ravenously, he ate every piece he had cut away from the corpse, chewing the meat as long as he could, savoring the wonderful taste.

It wasn't until several minutes later, when he felt bloated, when there was not much more meat to cut away from the thin body that he sat back on the log and realized what he had done. He had eaten nearly the entire carcass, eaten it *raw*. He was disturbed by what he had done and thought he might get sick again, but his bulging, satiated stomach would not allow him to feel remorse for long.

He slipped from the log, grabbed the wool blanket, and stretched out on the ground. A comfortable distance from the fire, he felt warm inside, with a full belly, and completely content. Sleep overcame him. It felt good to get drowsy. This was genuine sleep, not the void he had experienced inside the gem. His muscles weakened and relaxed; his mind and thoughts became sluggish.

He was surrounded by a crowd of people, in what appeared to be the courtyard of a large castle. At first he thought it might have been the courtyard at Lianome, but things were subtly different. No, this was not the courtyard of his brotherhood's castle. He had a collar around his neck; he was leashed to a post in the center of the courtyard. Rows upon rows of people stood in a circle around him, and more behind them. He could see them all, as if they were standing on risers, row after row of people. If he had to put a number to them, he would have said they were in the thousands.

Dun Loren appeared next to him. "Morgan Mclain," he began, "you stand here accused of murder of the foulest kind. How plead you?" Morgan tried to speak, but only a light laughter escaped his lips. Dun Loren vanished.

The crowd began to laugh at him. Pointing, chuckling, giggling, shaking their heads, and speaking in soft whispered tones to one another as they laughed. At one time or another, they all seemed to be pointing at him, not at his face, but lower on his body. He looked down. He was naked. Embarrassment flushed his cheeks—could his cheeks flush with embarrassment? He tired to cover himself with his hands, and succeeded. His overly large talloned hands were twice as large as they should have been. He could have wrapped his midsection in them.

The crowd stopped laughing and gasped at his monstrous hands, some gaping in fear. Many of those in the crowd ran. They ran from him in horror. But for every one that ran away, he could see two take their place, ogling him as if he was some sort of wagon-show freak.

"Cover yourself properly. What kind of Dun Lian knight are you?" said Dun Lian, who popped into existence beside him, spoke, then vanished. Again, he tried to speak. Growls of anger were all that he could manage this time, snarls that bared his teeth, dripping saliva thickly down his chin to moisten the dirt below him.

More of the onlookers screamed and ran in panic. The crowd had grown; more were present than could possibly fit in the courtyard, yet he could see every single one.

"They will never let you go, you know that, don't you?" The voice of the speaker behind him was his. "You belong to them as much now, if not more than when you were simply a knight." He turned, but there was no one behind him. "I will never let you stop me. You haven't the power," came a whisper in his ear. Again, it was his voice he was hearing, behind him. He whirled again, turning just in time to see himself vanish. It was his body he saw, the one Malchom now resided in.

In front of him was Dun Loren. This time he was kneeling, bent over a headsman's chopping block. "Help me, don't just stand there. Admit your guilt, kill Malchom. It's your duty as a brother of the knighthood. Don't let me be held responsible for this." Morgan looked at the headsman, who raised his huge, broad axe, preparing to strike. "I beseech you, Morgan, don't let this happen." Morgan looked back to the headsman. His weapon had changed; he now held the great sword of Dun Lian. Startled, he looked at the headsman's face. That had changed also. He was now the headsman, or was it Malchom in his old body? He couldn't tell.

The crowd began chanting, "Headsman, headsman, headsman!" He, or Malchom—which was it? The body of Dun Lain raised the great sword and brought it down sharply.

"Nooooo!" he screamed, or tried to scream. All that came out sounded more like a mooing cow than a spoken word. The sword fell, and so did Dun Loren's head, which rolled on the ground and came to a rest at his big elongated clawed monster's feet. And yet it wasn't Dun Loren's face staring up at him—it was his own, or was it Malchom's? He looked to the headsman and found it was the female monster he had killed and eaten. She dropped the sword of Dun Lian and strode to him. She was nearly all bones; huge chunks of flesh were missing, the areas he had eaten. She approached him, ran a hand between his legs, and whispered into his ear, "You are mine." He screamed a loud, bloodcurdling animal's howl. It was *full of rage and fear and reminded him of the howling he had heard when he had made contact with the gem with his mind. It was a forceful scream, knocking all of the onlookers backward, who were nearly completely falling over each other. They all regained their balance as one and now looked upon him with awe instead of fear or amusement.*

The great brown winged body of Durgolais appeared before him. The crowd saw the monstrous dragon and fled. Nearly every single one of them ran terrified. It was a terror that sank into their bones. Morgan could feel them panic, could feel the blood drain from faces, limbs, vital organs. He could feel the terror literally eat away the bones of those that ran. They melted, sank into pools of bloodless, boneless flesh. He got hungry, and was suddenly eating the pools of people. They were still alive, screaming in ancient languages he shouldn't have known but somehow did.

He grabbed up the faces of people long dead—whom he couldn't have known, who lived thousands of years ago. He grabbed them up and shoveled them into an orifice the size and color of the gem that had appeared on his sloped, elongated head. He shoved them into his head, into his mind. They became a part of him, became a part of his memories, which were expanding at a frightening pace.

Durgolais spoke, and he was again standing, collared and leashed, in the center of the courtyard. "You will have my help." Something about the voice was familiar. Twice as many people surrounded him now. Despite having feasted on hundreds of boneless blobs of people, his hunger grew, his hunger for flesh gnawed inside of him. The people in front of him all turned into Chunyan pastries and candies. He salivated heavily, sending a wave of spit to the ground that splashed and became a small sea. Durgolais was swimming in the water. "You will find me, you will come to me." The voice was not Durgolais'; it was Jux's!

"You will find me, you will come to me." Durgolais changed, morphed into Morgan's old body. The crowd of people was standing behind Malchom; he knew it was Malchom. Malchom's face shifted, flickering between his face and what Morgan remembered to be Malchom's "You will come to me and be mine." Malchom raised his hand and tossed a large, yellow mushroom into the air. Morgan watched as it rose, reached its apex, and floated down, disintegrating into a yellow mist. The fine mist settled on the crowd, who were all munching on smaller versions of the yellow fungus. They appeared lost, far-off gazes in their eyes.

"You will come to me and be mine. You will perform for me, my little monkey. DANCE!" The command was intoxicating; he felt stupefied, euphoric. He danced like a marionette, long arms half limp, half upright, moving up and down mechanically, methodically, legs rising and falling as if strings were attached to his knees, head bobbing back and forth, not having enough strength in his neck

to be kept upright. The Malchom/Morgan face sneered. Malchom lifted a hand and pointed at Morgan, crooking a finger, "Come to me, my little capuchin." Morgan obeyed, ripping through the leash that bound him, advancing toward Malchom.

Dun Loren, Dun Lian, and every Dun Lian knight he knew appeared at his left. "By the grace of Kasparow, return to your post," they said as one. Morgan stopped, regarded them for a moment before he felt compelled to move. Malchom's command still rang in his mind. He took a step forward.

"Come to me, and I will show you the true path to follow," said Durgolais in Jux's voice. The dragon reappeared to his right. The dragon's appearance changed, morphed as Malchom's had. He took on the visage of all those boneless bodies he had eaten.

"Come to me, my little capuchin" echoed in Morgan's head. He took a step forward. Malchom continued to grin.

Everything vanished. He was standing in a void. There was no ground, no courtyard, and no onlookers. The Dun Lian knights had vanished, Durgolais had disappeared, and Malchom was nowhere to be seen. The only thing he did notice was a slight green glow that came from nowhere in particular yet permeated and illuminated a fine mist that hung in the emptiness.

The Malchom/Morgan figure solidified several feet to his left. Dun Loren coalesced from the fog a few feet to his right. Below him, an enormous Durgolais appeared with outstretched arms, the dragon's hands supporting Malchom and Dun Loren. The whole scene reminded Morgan of a set of merchant's scales.

"Choose," said Malchom.

"Choose," repeated Dun Loren. They both rose and fell slightly as Durgolais rocked his arms up and down, as if weighing them.

"Choose," all three said in unison. Morgan looked to Malchom. He was strangely compelled to walk in his direction. Altair's huge head, complete with fangs and bulging eyes, appeared behind Malchom. The god dripped yellow mucous on top of his disciple. A sweet, satisfying smell and feeling came over Morgan. He started to move in that direction; it felt so natural to walk toward Malchom.

Movement to his right caught his attention. Slowing his pace, he turned and looked upon Dun Loren. The knight was shining brilliantly, like the day he had first met him. Behind him, a figure appeared. The figure was strange; it looked to be two people at once. He couldn't make out the figure's features. It shifted too quickly for him to see anything other than bland, colorless, hairless features. The man—he thought it was a man; it was smaller than a man, a boy, perhaps not even a man at all. The man raised a dagger and made ready to plunge it into Dun Loren's back.

Morgan faltered in his steps and moved toward Dun Loren. After a few paces, he stopped. The smells of pleasure emanating from Malchom were too strong. He looked over his shoulder; hunger pains gripped him. He turned back to Dun Loren. The figure standing behind him was gleefully making stabbing motions at Dun Loren's back.

"The world will go on, no matter what you choose." Durgolais' whisper floated up from below him. Morgan glanced down. He was standing directly over the massive head of Durgolais the dragon. The dragon's eyes shone a brilliant green. His eyes flashed. "It has been nearly two thousand years since I was first entombed within the gem. Through it all, the gem has remained, and seen changes in the world. Changes for good, changes for evil. Do you decide to change things, or do you choose to accept what happens? Do you sacrifice yourself to follow one path, or do you give in to yourself and be led down another? If nothing else, remember this: questions always have answers, answers always have owners, and power always dictates the rights of sovereignty."

The glow of Durgolais' eyes flared slowly and consumed him, becoming brighter and brighter until he opened his eyes to a recently risen sun. He breathed deeply. Cold, charcoal-laden, dust-filled air filled his lungs. He coughed slightly and rose, looking around him.

The campsite was gruesome to behold, even to his colorless vision. A still-smoldering fire filled the little clearing with a low-floating cloud of smoke. The cold, dark-colored ground was littered with slightly brighter spots that were barely discernable. He was certain it was blood he was seeing. The female monster's body lay crumpled and twisted next to the tree he had used as a chair the previous night. Not much was left of her. A head, bones, and entrails had attracted dozens of light-colored *corpseflies*, which were busily eradicating the remaining edible parts. Having grown up on the fringes of civilization, he had seen many rotting carcasses and how efficiently and quickly a horde of corpseflies could strip them bare. That corpse would be all bones in a matter of hours, at most. The gem rested a few feet from the body. It still glowed faintly, glowed with what he saw as a white light. He had seen the gem in its green coloring in his dream

The dream! It was fading from his memory even as he fought to retain it. He tried desperately to remember it in detail, but all he could recall was Durgolais' face and eyes burning into him, eyes that were shaped like the emerald that rested near the almost-dead fire.

Jux had said something to him. What was it? He squatted next to the gem. Sitting back on his haunches seemed to be a very natural position; his leg muscles were tense yet comfortable. He felt the power they had exhibited

last night in the flexing of his thick thigh and calf muscles. He looked at the
nearly-completely-eaten corpse. Indeed, the leg meat had tasted the best, and
it had tasted best raw. That thought nearly made him sick anew.

He considered what he knew. Perhaps seven hours had passed since he
was released from the gem. From the two yellow moons in the sky last night,
he knew it to be no later than the end of the summer season. Had there been
a third moon, or had the two been orange in color, it would have been fall or
early spring, respectively. He was certain less than a month had passed since
this adventure first began. It was possible that a full year, or even years, had
gone by, but he felt that was not the case. He didn't feel as if he had spent a
year in the gem. No matter what Jux had said, he could tell that not much
time had passed. Which, *praise Kasparow*, he counted as a blessing.

He was now in the body of some sort of creature. A creature with surprising
strength, superb sense of smell, distinct visual capabilities, and an albeit-
disgusting appearance. The previous night, he had killed, in self-defense he
thought, what had to have been a mate or sibling to the creature that used to
inhabit this body, and then eaten her raw to satiate his stomach. Although,
remembering the flow of events, he was beginning to think that the female
had simply been scolding him and not attacking him. She had refrained from
using her claws and had not once done more than give him a sore chest.

He was sitting by a nearly dead fire in a small clearing. It was a campsite
that Morgan didn't think the creatures had set up. How would they have
started the fire? Around the fire, he had found his backpack, his cooking
utensils, the gem, and even his Dun Lian longsword. Either Malchom had
made it to this point, set up the campsite, began a meal of bread, and was
then attacked by these creatures, *or* the creatures had attacked Malchom
somewhere else; taken the backpack, gem, and sword; and then came here
to eat stale bread. He seriously doubted the later supposition to be true. Or,
he thought, these two creatures could have come across the items without
ever encountering Malchom. Again, how would they have started the
fire? There had to be something around this campsite that would betray
Malchom's presence.

He rose and roamed about the area, looking for anything that would
tell him one way or the other if Malchom had indeed been present at one
time. Amidst the brush, he found his journal. It was in good condition; the
leather-wrapped stick of charcoal used for writing was intact and still tucked
within the leather strings used to bind the journal together. It had no new
entries in it. Around the campsite, the hard ground, dusted with fine dirt,
held many light footprints, which were extremely difficult for him to see with

his colorless, heat-driven vision. Any distinct prints he could make out were obviously either his or the female's.

These creatures would not have made a fire, this he was sure of. His extreme discomfort near the flames last night all but assured him that these creatures would naturally shy away from any prolonged exposure to fire. Malchom, in *his* body, *had* to have been here. Where was Malchom now? He was going to find him, find him and smash his bones and drink his blood. Where had *that* come from? Had, he thought, these two *eaten* Malchom? No, that couldn't have happened. He doubted even these creatures would have finished off an entire corpse, bones and all. Malchom had retained the gem, somehow transporting it from the Dead Pools to wherever this was. Where was he now? It was about time to find out; he couldn't stay put here all day.

Morgan made use of what few possessions he now had. He started to stuff the backpack with the cooking utensils and his journal. Out of habit, he sat and carefully opened the journal, removing the charcoal pencil from its mooring, and started a new entry. His huge clawed fingers had a rough time grasping the instrument correctly. *Date unknown. Been released from gem. Been put in some sort of monster's body. Difficult to write. Going After Malchom, who is in my body.* It took six pages of rough, messy large script to record those five sentences. His terrible penmanship was going to limit the number of entries he could squeeze out of the remaining blank pages. Closing the journal with care—these bindings always ripped through the holes in the paper—he continued to gather his things.

Ripping the wool blanket in half, he passed it between his legs and held his knees tight, keeping the blanket from falling while he reached out and grabbed his sheathed sword. Disconnecting the sheath from the sword-belt he let the sword fall to the ground and buckled the belt around his thin waist. He then tucked the front and back of the blanket under the belt, forming a garment of sorts to hide his nakedness. Twisting the belt down upon itself several times, he succeeded in wrapping the blanket around the belt enough times to make it snug and secure enough that he was sure it wouldn't fall off him very easily. A monster he may be, but a modest monster at that.

He felt through the wrapped fabric for the clasp that would hold his sword and punched a hole in the wool with one of his sturdy claws. After clipping on his sword and stuffing the remnants of the blanket into his backpack, he caught sight of the gem with one of his eyes. What could he do with it? What *should* he do with it? If he left it here and someone came across it, they would set loose a monster in human form. Then again, if Malchom returned, what would he do with it? Visions of all sorts of evil acts that Malchom could accomplish with the gem flashed in Morgan's mind. He would have to take it with him. *Of course*, he would have to take it with him, how else did he think he would get his own body back?

The problem was in *how* to take it with him? Malchom had somehow brought it to this place, and from Jux's memories, he was almost sure that as long as his skin did not touch the surface of the gem, nothing would happen. He could wrap it in the blanket, stuff it in the bag, but for some reason, he just didn't trust that idea. With his luck, the gem would work its way free, and he would end up coming in contact with it somehow. He needed a container of some kind. Something thicker than wool or leather, something large enough to put it *in* and not simply wrap around it.

He looked around the campsite, and all of his eyes fell on the body of the female monster. Or at least, what was left of it. Most of the corpse was bone now. The corpseflies had done their job quickly. Many of them lay around the body, too fat to move, waiting for the time that their young, in larval form, would emerge into the world, eating their way out from the within the belly of the now-bloated flies. He wondered what would happen if a handful of corpsefly larvae were put inside a living person. The skull of the creature was completely bare, eyes eaten; only hard, thick bone remained. Thick, hard, durable bone. The Brotherhood used bone tubes to send messages that were important enough to guard against damage or unwanted eyes.

He moved to the corpse and plucked the dry, skull from amidst the stinking, bloated flies. They buzzed angrily around him, unable to take flight, as fat as they were. He squatted next to the gem. The skull was bigger than the emerald. Could he get it inside? Turning the skull over in his hands, he found a corpsefly within the skull, satiated on brain matter and not bothering to move. He shook the skull until he dislodged the fly and flicked it away with a clawed finger.

The fly had been quite busy. The skull was hollow on the inside, leaving a chamber large enough to house the gem—at least it looked to be large enough. He held the skull up and peered inside. The inside of the skull *was* large enough, but the hole at the base of the skull, where the creature's spine had once been, was nowhere large enough to let the gem in. He unsheathed his sword and used its pommel to pummel the edges of the hole with just enough force to chip it away. Several minutes later, he stopped, satisfied that the hole was large enough.

He carefully placed the skull over the top of the gem. It fit easily into the enlarged hole. Turning the skull over quickly, he trapped the gem within the skull. He stood and shook the skull; the gem rattled around slightly within the bony structure. Now he needed to keep it securely within the skull. Half of the remaining portion of the blanket, wadded and stuffed into the hole, served this purpose nicely. He then placed the skull within the leather bag and tore strips of wool to use as drawstrings. He put the bag in his backpack and slung it over his shoulder. Turning, he set out for the ruins he had seen the night before.

CHAPTER 11

Dun Lian remained and watched as the small group readied to leave. The humidity, even in the early night, was palpable. Dun Loren was sweating profusely, which was surprising. When you were used to sweating a lot, humidity was usually not enough of a catalyst to bring on such a sustained sweat. His silk shirt was weighted down and darkened with moisture. The knight wiped himself several times with the heavy cotton kerchief around his neck. The knight was worried, understandably. The threat of excommunication hung over Dun Loren's head. The weight of his situation was creating a heavy spiritual load every bit as real as if he had a sack of stones on his back.

Dun Loren was not responsible for what was happening, he knew that. Not only did he know it, he believed it. Unfortunately, there was no other course of action available to him. Tradition dictated that Dun Loren be the one responsible for bringing Morgan to justice. *Tradition.* It was called tradition, but Dun Lian knew it better as *law.* It may be ridiculous to strip a man of all his achievements and possessions for the deeds of another, but this was the Dun Lian tradition, and he wasn't about to break it. Traditions became traditions because they were done every single time a certain situation arose, year after year, decade after decade. By *not* engaging in a tradition even once, you began the first step toward a tradition of *not* following traditions. It may be wrong to enforce this particular tradition, but where one begins to crumble, many more will weaken, and the Dun Lian way of life was too steeped in ritual traditions to allow for any broad, sweeping changes without causing great chaos. There was a veritable bargeload of minor traditions that were absurd, antiquated, and just downright stupid. Watching Dun Loren's favorite scribe waddling away reminded him of at least one tradition that could be given the headsman's axe.

When a situation arose that was completely unique, a Dun Lian had the ability to make any decision he wanted. With no prior tradition do dictate the path he must follow, a Dun Lian was free to begin a new tradition, make his own mark upon the growing history of the Brotherhood. Unfortunately for Dun Lian *and* Dun Loren, this was the third time this particular tradition had been invoked. He had no choice.

As soon as he had learned of the rumor surrounding possible murders being connected with a recently knighted brother, Dun Lian had been bound to summon Dun Loren and charge him with the duty of bringing Dun Lain in for trial. He had been allowed the luxury of waiting to issue the order for the simple fact that Dun Loren had been on field exercises with his two newest squires. This had given him several more days—days to hope that fact would defeat rumor, days to be given enough room to defy tradition. When Dun Loren returned on the same day that Dun Dison's damning dispatch had arrived, Dun Lian had no way to stall any longer. Even Dun L'lsen, his chosen successor, had commented on the matter.

He was not surprised that Dun L'lsen, not his original choice of successor, had requested to accompany the overwhelmed Dun Loren. The dominant big hairy knight lived for adventure. It was his strength. Adversities, stress, the unknown were all things that made the big man shine. It was perhaps this ability that contributed most to his incredible popularity amongst the brothers. Only a couple of years after his knighting, it became evident that Dun L'lsen would gain the right of succession despite what Dun Lian personally thought of the man.

Dun L'lsen sat patiently on his heavy warhorse. The thickly muscled body of the charger was hidden beneath a scaled layer of finely crafted dwarven Ro'Havian barding. The weight the horse carried must have been smothering to the animal, yet it looked nearly relaxed, perhaps a little anxious to be moving; it stamped its feet occasionally.

Dun L'lsen himself was encrusted in an ancient coat of mail. Six months after his knighting, on his free deed tour, as it was now referred to, he had taken up the challenge of ridding a small border town of a couple of invading monsters. After dispatching the creatures, he had brought the bodies back to the Dun Lian stronghold to allow the resident sages an attempt at identification. The dead creatures turned out to be dragonnes, a distant relative to the long-disappeared dragon species. Hoping to find more of the creatures, or even a long-lost dragon, Dun L'lsen had used the remaining six months of his free deed tour to track where the creatures had come from. He had succeeded in finding their lair, but failed to find any more dragonnes, let alone a full-bred dragon.

Their lair was, however, filled with a mound of hoarded treasure. Coins, gems, jewelry, and, amidst the pile, a time-bleached skeleton encased in the armor Dun L'lsen now wore. The sages had placed the armor's age at nearly twenty-two hundred years old. What looked to be a taloned bird's foot was hammered very elegantly on the breastplate. Dun L'lsen had adopted it as his personal sigil.

That hoard had set him up as the wealthiest knight in active duty. There was no tradition against a knight having vast amounts of money, so long as he gave a certain percentage to the Brotherhood. Traditionally, 50 percent of any monies made while a brother was to be tithed to the Brotherhood's coffers. A great amount of coin had come in when Dun L'lsen had made his donation. From what Dun Lian knew, the big knight had invested most of the rest in local, and not so local, businesses. Dun L'lsen's yearly earnings on his investments were rumored to be vast. Dun Lian should have known exactly what amount those earnings came to, but Dun L'lsen had found a loophole in the tradition.

A brother was expected to donate 50 percent of any *money* made, earned, found, or given on a yearly basis. Dun L'lsen had invested his money in businesses that produced expensive, finely made goods. As a part of his investment agreements, his yearly compensations would be rendered in goods and services, not money, thereby completely sidestepping his need to donate half of his yearly income.

The knight had bought an extremely large parcel of land just outside the stronghold's walls. A construction company that Dun L'lsen was partnered in was continuously building and adding on to his estate. And of course, all the materials were of the highest imported quality. Almost two entire quarries of Andonesian red and blue marble had been hauled cart by cart from the far side of Andonesia, nearly six hundred miles away, just to construct a low-lying wall around the knight's property. Dun Lian had never visited the estate, but he was sure it was packed to the brim with very expensive accoutrements. He had even heard that the engineers of the estate had created a very elaborate indoor plumbing system that brought water in from a small river nearby. Supposedly, the indoor privies didn't use putrefiers. Instead, the waste was sluiced off and *piped* to an underground chamber well away from the estate, where it was allowed to slowly decompose back into the soil. Dun L'lsen said that it was an experimental invention, which he had also invested in and until, it became more popular, was very expensive to implement.

Dun Lian had erupted at Dun L'lsen when the knight informed him of his investment strategies. Doing what he had, Dun L'lsen had opened the door for a new tradition that could greatly hamper the Brotherhood's cash flow. What would happen if every knight were to begin investing all his money in such a manner? If he hadn't been as popular as he was, gaining momentum for a bid at succession, Dun Lian might have threatened to decommission the knight. But as it stood, Dun L'lsen himself graciously solved the problem by drafting a *last will* that, since he had no living family, proclaimed the Brotherhood, more specifically the Dun Lian, executor of his estate. Eventually, when Dun L'lsen died, all of his possessions, all of his business connections, would become the property of the Brotherhood. Indeed, his huge mansion would most likely become the new Dun Lian private residence. Very few knights felt the desire to follow with this tradition. Most wanted to be able to give their belongings to family members and loved ones.

Dun Lian studied the big knight. He was busy pulling his braided hair through an opening in the back of his helmet. The knight's topknot was nearly two feet long. It was bound by six inches of brass wires at the base, which, after the length of braid was through the hole in the helmet, could be forcefully pulled through the hole as well. This served to secure the topknot in place and make it stick nearly a foot in the air before cascading around the polished helmet.

Dun L'lsen was an impressive knight. It was no wonder his popularity had grown so quickly. As was tradition, Dun Lian had chosen a successor at his coronation as Dun Lian, just as the original Dun Lian had chosen Alexander Arjet as his successor. Dun Feld had been his initial choice. Dun Feld was a competent man and would have made a strong Dun Lian, but he was not a very likable man. So when Dun L'lsen came along, gaining popularity with each passing month, he had no choice but to name Dun L'lsen his successor. Dun Feld had no choice, as tradition dictated, but to step down. In private, Dun Feld had told Dun Lian that he was glad the change had come. Which surprised Dun Lian; he had thought the knight was looking forward to becoming the head of the Order. Dun Lian only hoped that Dun L'lsen would learn some restraint and become a little wiser before his ascension. At least the bequeathing of his property to the Brotherhood in an attempt to stop other brothers from following his investment strategies was a good sign.

Standing in front of Dun L'lsen's massive mount, his most recent squire held the horse's bridle, more to make himself readily available to Dun L'lsen than to actually steady the horse. Manney Petroiken was a small sandy-haired boy, not very physically adept or bright. Dun Lian suspected that he had become Dun L'lsen's latest squire out of some business arrangement. With his popularity, Dun L'lsen could have chosen any number of top-notch squires. Perhaps this little unremarkable kid had something going for him. Looking at the boy, Dun Lian decided it would have to be a *big* something.

Manney was completely unlike Dun Loren's two squires. It wasn't unusual for a knight to have more than one squire at a time, and a knight often took in brothers at the same time. Dun Lian was sure these two came close to being more than Dun Loren could handle. They had just finished settling Dun Loren in his saddle, and both went to their own mounts and, jabbering all the while, finished packing their supplies. The two seemed to move in unison; each had a feel for what the other was doing or about to do.

He had seen them in the courtyard practicing with weapons. They would make a formidable team someday. Justin's Malta mark was plainly visible even in the dimness of the miremoss-lit outer stable yard. The boy had shaved his head around the temple area, where the mark was situated. He was not ashamed of the mark. In fact, the boy acted as if it was a badge of honor. Dun Lian had no doubt that the boy would make it so.

The entire head of Dun Loren's other squire, Clerents, was completely shaved. A good idea, he had to admit, to have one of the brothers shave his head. Easier to tell them apart. Even if Justin decided to shave his head, his scalp would be nowhere near as tan as his brother's was. From what he understood, it was impossible to tell them apart when they first arrived at the castle. He didn't think one could ever be mistaken for the other now, especially considering that Clerents didn't have a Malta mark.

The twins had finished their packing and were mounting their horses. The five riders turned to face Dun Lian. They drew their swords and held them aloft, saluting Dun Lian before turning to leave. Attendants rushed to turn heavy wooden cranks that held the thick iron chains that operated the massive front gates of the Dun Lian stronghold. The thick, iron-reinforced gates moved outward over tightly packed iron rollers set in the ground surrounding the entrance to the castle. When the doors were open, the weight of the wood held the rollers in place, creating a metal walkway that even horses were not afraid to cross. When the gates were closed, however, the rollers were free to move. This had the effect of seriously hampering any attempt to approach the front gates with any sort of heavy equipment. Battering rams were useless, as the men who propelled the battering ram into the front gates could not get sufficient footing to apply any force to their attack. Oil could also be dumped into a small reservoir under the metal rollers, making them even harder to traverse. The entire system was quite a feat of engineering. It had been the brilliant idea of a long-dead Dun Lian knight. The engineering designs, and the knowledge required to maintain it, were a closely guarded secret. As it was, the contraption had yet to be tested outside of drills and attack simulations.

The group moved out in single file, with Dun Loren at the head, under the twenty-foot-long arched corridor that led outside. Dun Lian could see the twins look up at the ceiling, look up at the holes cut out of the arched roof of the passageway. They were called soup holes, after the souplike mixture of hot oil and poison that could be dumped down upon unwanted invaders.

Dun Lian had never seen those holes used. No Dun Lian, in the nearly thousand-year history of the Brotherhood, had ever seen those holes used. After the founding of the Brotherhood at the battle of Olmar, the Dun Lian of that time moved the base of operations to where this castle now stood. Having killed the wizard Kharrie, many nations were grateful enough to fund the building of the massive castle. It had never been attacked; the Brotherhood had enjoyed almost a thousand years of peaceful relations with the local government.

It was a strange government. When the wizard Kharrie died, the Brotherhood helped local nobles hunt down and kill Kharrie's remaining subordinates and generals. Kharrie had ruled Andonesia ruthlessly, and when the people found themselves without that restraining hand, they decided that such power should not be given to one or two men.

Many of the local lords with claims to the throne of Andonesia argued vehemently that the original monarchy should be reestablished. The people wanted an elected council. The Brotherhood had supported the people, and for their support, gained permanent tenancy within the boundaries of Andonesia. A large number of yearly recruits came from Andonesia and many knights of the Dun Lian Brotherhood currently held several appointments within the Andonesian government.

The Brotherhood enjoyed this comfortable relationship due mostly to the fact that Dun Lian knights stood for justice. Justice of a fair and right kind, no matter what position a person might hold. The powerful were just as responsible for their actions as the poor were. This went a long way at keeping the Brotherhood popular with the people. If the news of a

Dun Lian knight murdering *hundreds* of innocent people and slaughtering *entire* towns were to become common knowledge, the repercussions would be unpredictable. Capture, trial, and swift punishment of the accused in a "just and right" manner might diffuse any situation or bad publicity that could arise due to these murders. It *might* smooth over any problems, and it might not, especially if Dun Loren was unable to apprehend Dun Lain. Could he, could the Brotherhood, chance that? He began a prayer to Kasparow as he watched the five riders disappear behind the closing wood-and-iron gates.

*   *   *

"So do we head directly to Maralat?" asked Dun L'lsen, securing his helmet's visor in the open position. Light from the two moons bounced off the armor, illuminating the knight quite effectively. The knight had ridden up next to Dun Loren a few minutes after they had left the closing gates behind. Dun Loren still did not know how the big knight was able to wear all that stuff all the time. Rumors said that the armor was magical and weighed nearly nothing. It would have to be, he decided, for him to ever considering wearing it nearly round-the-clock like Dun L'lsen seemed to prefer.

"Actually," responded Dun Loren, "I want to start at the beginning. I want to follow his steps for the past month." He heard one of the squires cough slightly. It was nearing the end of the summer. It had been dry; the dust was rising as they rode.

"But where do we start? Wouldn't it be prudent to go to where he was last sighted and *find* him?" The squire coughed again. Dun Loren looked back; it was Manney who had coughed. He couldn't understand why Dun L'lsen would choose such a poor specimen of a boy as a squire. The sandy-haired youth was drinking deeply from his bota bag, obviously attempting to wash the dust away. Clerents and Justin were giving Dun L'lsen's squire an earful.

"We need to find out what has happened just as much as we need to apprehend him—"

"How can you say that!" Dun L'lsen almost yelled his interjection.

"And," irritated, Dun Loren continued without pausing, "considering the severity of these events, I don't want to put all my trust in rumors and reports. I would rather see everything for myself." He glanced at the dry road. It was packed barren earth. Even though there had been practically no rain this summer, the ground was still solid, not cracked with dryness as you might expect bare dirt to become in a drought season. There was no way that their five horses produced enough dust to choke the squire. This ground was literally as hard as rock. He surmised the amount of traffic to and from the castle had something to do with this fact.

"But that could take months, and you have only three. Who knows where all of this started—"

"I have an idea," he interrupted. Even at this time of night, he could see the slightly swaying illumination of carriage lanterns on the road ahead. He could make out six individual lights. It must be a caravan. It might be late, but the business that was the Brotherhood still trudged along.

"And what happens if he kills again while you're gathering facts?" It was a business, even if no one believed or admitted it. The Brotherhood was in the business of selling and enforcing its beliefs. No matter how many people said the Brotherhood stood for the rights of people or were the saviors of the oppressed, there were still huge numbers of brothers in the employment of nations and empires that only desired the troops for their expertise and deadliness at war making. Truthfully, Dun Lian and the Dun Lian knights would not hire themselves out or support a government that did not at least *attempt* to show signs of equal and humane rights for its people; but through it all, the money was coming in, and the coffers were growing.

"Nearly thirty knights are stationed in and around Maralat and the surrounding villages. I doubt another mass murder will be committed very easily." The big knight had very thoroughly rubbed his nerves from frayed to completely raw. His insistent continuance of this conversation was as rattling as the twins' incoherent, idle chatter, which always seemed to buzz around the pair.

"Regardless of that fact, you have a duty to bring him in. As he is your former squire, you are responsible for these murders he has committed. Need I remind you that tradition—"

"Dun L'lsen." He reined in his horse. The squires' horses came to a stop well behind the stationary knights; even the twins, who had seemingly remained oblivious to the conversation, ceased their chattering. "Need *I* remind *you* that since *I am* the one responsible for bringing Morgan in for trial, then *I* will be the one making the decisions? This is not a council. With my holdings and very *commission* in jeopardy, I am going to make damned sure that these charges are real. To do that, I need information. So things will be done as *I* say. Do you understand, Dun L'lsen?"

"Yes, Dun Loren." Dun L'lsen's squire's coughing resumed.

Dun Loren urged his mount forward. The road was entering a wood; the night became darker as trees grew thicker. The chattering from behind began anew. He was amazed at how the twins could just turn that useless prater on and off like that. He wondered if it was real, or just a convenient way of blending into a conversation without appearing intrusive. They had learned of the charges against Dun Lain somehow. "Your enthusiasm for adventure is well known, but I am surprised at your seeming readiness and willingness to damn Dun Lain. I know you didn't know him very well, but I find it hard to believe that you could think that anyone who made it through training, became a Dun Lian knight, and was graced with the light of Kasparow would ever be capable of murder, let alone mass murder."

"It *has* happened before, brother."

The swinging lanterns in the distance had been steadily getting larger. Dun Loren could now hear the faint creaking of carriage wheels and the clop of at least four horses. "A Dun Lian knight *has* been charged with murder before—twice, as a matter of fact—you are correct there. But this is not the result of some mead-induced bar brawl or jealous, adulterous rage. We're talking about the deliberate and brutal murdering of nearly four hundred people, including infants!" A gasp escaped the lips of one of the squires. Even without turning around, he was certain it had come from Justin.

"You must forgive me, Dun Loren." Manney's coughing was taking its toll on the boy's throat; it was getting worse, becoming more of a hacking. "I do become overzealous at times. Some people find that to be an asset. Your suspicions aren't unfounded. I also don't feel everything is as it seems, and to be honest, I do have another agenda. I mean to become Dun Lian someday. Our current Dun Lian could easily have another twenty years ahead of him, and popularity can fall just as quickly as mine rose. I must be involved in as much as I can, keep my fingers on the vein of the Brotherhood, if you will, if my right of succession is to avoid the headsman's axe." The carriages were close enough for them to make out the figure of the man driving the six-horse train of the front carriage. That was a lot of horses for a simple carriage. "And you must admit that this situation could have major repercussions. Consequences as yet unvoiced, or even unthought-of, could rear an ugly multifaceted head as a result of this situation. Who knows what traditions could be born or laid to rest if this thing is not controlled? By the grace of Kasparow, I will be in a position to see the Brotherhood through."

The carriage was not a carriage at all, but a massive enclosed square wagon and was the only one on the road. Lanterns swayed from elaborately wrought arms of wood that protruded from each corner of the wagon. Two lanterns

hung from poles affixed just ahead of the driver's seat. The driver's seat itself
was very large and almost ten feet off the ground. It was paneled from the
seat nearly to the smaller front wheels. Dun Loren suspected that a sleeping
compartment was hidden beneath the cushioned seat.

A low-lying flat platform extended at least ten feet behind the driver's
seat and ended in another set of small wheels. On this platform was hinged
the front half of the bulky square wagon, which continued backward a good
ten feet and ended in a final set of wheels, the only ones the wagon itself
possessed.

It was a wagon show, a massive traveling entertainment center that could,
and usually did, house any number of oddities that were gathered from all
over the world. The great wagon was impressive. The back was secured to the
extended platform at a single point. This allowed for easier turning, and the
two sections could be separated when setting up a show, providing a stage
and a separate carriage that could be used for transportation even without
the wagon. They were massive, heavy vehicles when fully assembled and
loaded. They were also commonly used for trade between the larger cities.
There was even a wagoners' guild that could train you in the proper handling
of the massive things. This, however, was most definitely a wagon show. It
was elaborately painted in gold and maroon, with strange images of exotic
animals on the sides.

By the grace of Kasparow, I will be in a position to see the Brotherhood through.
What did Dun L'lsen have in mind to do? *Another agenda?* Dun Loren did
not feel comfortable with that thought.

"Kasparow would not have accepted Morgan if he had such a dark side
within him. Something must have happened to him, and I have a very good
idea of where that thing happened." He could hear the twins talking about the
wagon show; they had recognized it for what it was as well. Between coughs,
Manney was busily asking all about the wagon show.

"You mentioned that once before." The big knight was paying no attention
to the approaching wagon. "What do you know?" The wagoner was a portly
man. In the glow of the swinging lanterns, he looked sick. They would meet
up with the wagon shortly.

"Morgan told me where he was headed when he left on his free deed tour."
Dun Loren could see now that the wagoner was sweating profusely. "I was
not very pleased at his decision." The fat man was dressed in brightly colored
silks; doubtless, they were a part of his act. The wagon show must be a good
one to allow the man to be able to afford silks. The driver had seen them and

looked as if he was about to stop his wagon and allow them to pass. "He said he had felt an irresistible pull toward the Dead Pools."

Dun L'lsen's horse came to an abrupt stop. "He went to the Dead Pools?" asked the knight, a little shocked. Dun Loren could not be sure that the wagoner had *not* heard. Manney coughed.

"Yes, and I would appreciate it if you would hold your tongue, or at least keep your voice down until this wagon show passes." The driver had pulled alongside the two knights.

"Greetings," bellowed the fat man. He was, indeed, sweating profusely; his face was covered in enough sweat that even his thin moustache glistened with moisture. Dun Loren was now able to see that the wagon show might not be as profitable as he had first surmised. The man's silk shirt was tight around his fat body and was haggard, coming apart at the seams the way silk does when pulled taut for too long. The colors were not as bright this close-up. "I couldn't help but overhear—"

Uh-oh, here we go, thought Dun Loren.

"Your squire's hacking coughs—it seems he might be a tad bit sick. That cough could be the first signs of pneumonia, you know." Dun L'lsen sat silently, almost ignoring the man. And if he wasn't fully ignoring the fat man, he was most certainly exuding an air of condescension.

The wagoner continued as if he didn't notice, or even care. "I just so happen to have a wonderful remedy all the way from the frozen wastes of Einiwetook." He reached under his cushioned seat and opened a compartment, the door of which was wide and tall enough to allow a person to slip into it. "Mara, will you hand me that pouch of cold remedy," he called into the darkness of the compartment. A hand emerged, holding a small leather pouch. "Thank you."

"You're welcome," said a nasally-stuffed-up feminine voice.

"Here." The fat man rose and, with a grunt and groan, leaned out to give the pouch to Dun L'lsen. "Mix a few pinches of this powder in his water flask, and that nasty cough will be no more." Dun L'lsen took the sack and started to untie the money pouch at his side. The fat man put a hand up in protest. "This is free of charge, my friend." He sat back down. "But you could tell me how much farther until I reach that wonderfully built castle of yours."

"It's just around the bend, just outside the tree cover," Dun Loren said, realizing that Dun L'lsen would not respond. "I'm sure Dun Lian would welcome a wagon show. It's been a while since he's seen one."

"Good, good. Well, good evening, and may Kasparow's grace shine on the both of you." The fat man bowed his head slightly and snapped his reins several times. The great lumbering wagon lurched forward. The three squires turned and watched it go. Manney had a disappointed look on his face. Dun Loren suspected the boy had never seen a wagon show before.

"Manney!" snapped Dun L'lsen to get his squire's attention. When the boy turned his mount around, Dun L'lsen tossed the sack of powder to him. The young squire quickly set about adding the powder to the water in his bota bag.

"The Dead Pools are a good week's ride away, are you sure you want to waste all of that time?" Dun L'lsen said, moving on. "And despite whatever you find there, it will then be another solid week of traveling before we reach Maralat. And from there, several more days to the village of Jourlean. At the rate he seems to be moving, he'll remain hundreds of miles ahead of you. You're going to waste a month just trying to catch up to him."

"And if I catch up to him tomorrow, and bring him in for trial next week, he'll be tried immediately. How is that going to help my situation? I have three months. I need all the information I can gather." They rode on in silence for a while. Manney's cough did not return. Dun Loren glanced back; the lights of the wagon show were still visible but had ceased their swaying. The fat man had probably come across another traveler and was attempting to peddle some more of his wares, but silence was all that reached him from the great wagon. Even the twins were silent as they rode through the nearly-pitch-black forest.

"Besides," he broke the silence, "we will ride straight through until we reach the Dead Pools. It should only take us three days at the most at that rate, unless you need to sleep, Dun L'lsen."

"No, but Manney will. He hasn't reached that point in his training yet."

"Has he even come out yet?"

"No."

"Then I hope you have taught him how to sleep in his saddle."

"What about the *horses*? They certainly won't be able to go nonstop for three days."

"We will exchange them when we reach the walled city of Panadar, and if the twins have remembered their training correctly, we will find fresh mounts waiting for us about a day's ride out of Panadar."

"What about your twins, can they handle this ride?" Dun L'lsen said almost snidely.

"My boys are doing quite well, thank you. They came out after only three weeks of training."

"Really?" Dun L'lsen said in disbelief.

"Yes, why do you think the rumors of them following in the footsteps of the McAri brothers are so numerous? Those two are the only brothers to have come out anywhere near as quickly as the McAri brothers did, and they only missed that record by a few days."

"Well, at least they *both* don't have a Malta mark. If they did, I'm sure the rumors would be far worse than they are. A new tradition of excommunicating squires might be born. No one in the Brotherhood wants to see something like *that* happen again."

"There is no need to remind me, Dun L'lsen. Believe me, I have thought long and hard on that subject. I even considered *not* enforcing the tradition and allowing Justin to sheath his Malta without dry-firing it. Now that, if it had become common knowledge, would have sent a wagonload of traditions to the headsman's axe." He paused for a few minutes. "I only considered it for a few seconds."

"How *did* he get his Malta mark?"

"The usual," responded Dun Loren. "He drew it in rage. It was partly my fault. Their training had been progressing so quickly and perfectly that I issued them their Maltas just a few days after they came out."

"You were treading dangerous ground, Dun Loren. Maltas are usually one of the last things given to a squire."

"I know, like I said, their training had been progressing extremely quickly. I swear to Kasparow they could be raised to knighthood now."

"Being knighted a little too quickly, like being issued a Malta a little too quickly, could only serve to cause problems."

"Do they wear the Medallion of Merit?" The two knights fell silent. No one spoke. The party rode the remaining mile to the village just outside of the Brotherhood's territory in silence. There was still activity in some of the taverns and inns that lined the streets.

This village had sprung up more out of the need to do business with the Brotherhood than out of any great gathering of people. Many of those responsible for the day-to-day running of the castle chose to reside within the village. A great bulk of the cooks, maids, groundskeepers, gardeners, and other menial laborers had practically founded this village long ago. Even the privy cleaners, despite the lingering stench, had found a place in this village. There were ten inns and at least as many taverns, all with plenty of rooms to let to the dozens of travelers that came to deal with the Brotherhood every day. Of course, important visitors such as nobles, governmental envoys, even princes, queens, and kings, were given lodging within the castle.

There was plenty of coin to go around. The Brotherhood's laborers were paid well, and they spent their earnings freely. Several of the taverns remained open around-the-clock. A groundskeeper or anyone else assigned a late shift at the castle could get a meal and a drink no matter what time he arrived home. There was such a constant steady traffic between the castle and the village that several people had suggested lining the road between the two with oil lamps to add light and safety for the late-night travelers. The village council was all for this idea; it meant more jobs, more income. The Brotherhood remained undecided. After all, the road was plenty safe. Who would consider committing a crime at the doorstep of the world's largest police force?

The group rode quickly through town. No one said a word, except for the occasional response to hails and greetings called from lighted, noisy tavern doorways. Yes, the Brotherhood was well liked in this town, in this country. They left the town behind them at a canter, the light from civilization fading quickly.

The miles peeled slowly away in continued silence. It was a mutual silence, each knowing that the others were engaged in traditional prayer to Kasparow. Dun Loren was grateful for the silence. He was sure Dun L'lsen would prove to be an annoyance to him in record time. He was having a hard time understanding why the big knight was so popular among the other brothers. He was opinionated, headstrong, rude, and slightly vain. There was no doubt that most of those who worshipped him had not spent a lot of time in a one-on-one basis with the knight. Dun L'lsen did seem to know, however, when he should remain in his place.

The following day was eventless. Other travelers were met and passed every so often, all of them shouting things like "Hail, brothers" or "May Kasparow grace you, kind sirs" or "Kasparow's praises to the Brotherhood." The twins continued to prattle and jabber in hushed tones to each other. Seemingly oblivious to everything around them except for the attention given to them by passing commoners, in which they basked like lizards sunning themselves on a hot summer's day. Manney wasn't faring so well. Even though the powder given to him by the fat wagoner had suppressed his coughing, it was evident that the cold still had a grip on him. His nose was runny, his face flushed, and he was forced to refill his bota bag as often as he could from passing travelers. The squire attempted to sleep at times, but it was almost of no use. Dun Loren had no doubts that the boy was running a fever.

He engaged Dun L'lsen in idle chatter, mostly about where the knight had grown up, what had pushed him to become a Dun Lian knight. He didn't learn much; Dun L'lsen's answers were always short and vague. He might have thought the knight was avoiding his questions, but it seemed more like Dun L'lsen was making things up as he went along. By the time they reached the Great Walled City of Panadar that evening, he didn't feel he knew the knight any better than before.

The Great Walled City of Panadar rose before them, silhouetted against the sky by a dying evening sun. Torches, oil lamps, and clumps of miremoss were just being lit along the walls and streets, hanging from doorways and rooftops, perched atop poles and towers to ward off the encroaching darkness. Dun Loren had seen the city in full night from this distance before. The thousands of small lights would bathe the city in so much light that it could be seen for miles around. Adding to that the fact that the city was built atop what some called a mountain, but in truth was just a hillock, and the city nightly became a beacon in the dark.

Panadar was one of six walled cities in Andonesia. After the original Dun Lian had erected a wall around the city of Olmar and defeated the wizard Kharrie, several other cities adopted the idea. Panadar was the largest and had earned the name the *Great* Walled City. Of the five others—Woodlands, Hunneck, Rendaran, Pitsy, and Origin, which was originally Olmar—only Woodlands came anywhere near the size of Panadar. Panadar's great size was mostly due to its location near the foot of the Purple Mountains, at the beginning of the O'kalakan pass. The traffic that came through the O'kalakan pass was almost nonstop, as it was the only way across the mountains. To travel from east to west, or vice versa, if you didn't make use of the pass, one would have to travel at least two hundred miles north to the sea or nearly three hundred miles south to where the Purple Mountains terminated at Lake Pren and the Pren River.

The Purple Mountains were not extremely tall; indeed, they were nowhere near as tall as the Majestics to the south, which bordered part of the Chunya Sea. Even the Lesser Majestics rose higher than the Purple Mountains. They were not tall, but they were steep and dangerous to traverse. Mostly cliffs, not many people could make it across the Purple Mountains alive. And if you were fool enough to attempt to cross the mountains at any point other than the O'kalakan pass, you would expose yourself to those things that *could* traverse the dangerous mountains. Creatures that were suited to life high in the mountains dominated the rocky crags. Large, giant-sized birds that were distant cousins to the long-vanished dragons dominated the skies. Carnivorous

tribes of trolls and ogres warred for domination of the mountain areas. The
Dun Lian Brotherhood had made a mountain of coin protecting the pass
and its travelers. They had also been asked to rid the mountains of the nasty
creatures that inhabited it. But the dangerousness of the terrain and the fact
that it wasn't *right* to engage in genocide had kept the Brotherhood from ever
accepting that commission.

The wall surrounding the city was twenty feet high and dotted with a
small guard tower, perhaps thirty feet in height, every few hundred feet or
so. Massive oil lamps and mounds of miremoss lit each tower like a brilliant
burning gemstone. From this distance, the wall, ringing the hilltop, looked
as regal as a jewel-encrusted crown resting atop a monarch's head.

They rode on in silence, a bit slower now; the horses were completely
exhausted. Even the twins kept silent. The road wound back and forth up the
hill and ended at the beginning of the Plakka. The Plakka was a makeshift
minitown that had risen around the entrance to the city of Panadar to meet
the needs of those coming to and going from the city. It was convenient for
a lot of travelers to be able to do business outside the city walls, but proved
to be a nuisance to those wishing to go directly to the city. The main road to
the entrance of the city ended at the Plakka; from here the shantytown placed
its buildings in the way of any direct movement to the city gates. To reach the
city proper, you had to negotiate a maze of shops and barkers' stands. Dun
Loren had often wondered why the city council allowed the dirty shantytown
to remain. It was Dun Lian who had pointed out the strategic value of the
shantytown. An attacker would either have to follow the winding maze of
streets and alleys of the Plakka or plough *through* the buildings to gain access
to the gates of the city. For this reason, only single-storied buildings were
allowed in the Plakka in an attempt to remove as many places where attackers
could take cover from arrow fire as possible.

They rode into the Plakka and were given a respectfully wide berth. Dun
Loren had been here one time before he had become a Dun Lian knight and
had been accosted by all sorts of barkers, tradesmen, hawkers, and hucksmen,
all attempting to part him from his coin. A normal citizen would be hounded
by these vultures from the time he entered the Plakka until the time he was
well within the gates of Panadar. This was not so for a couple of Dun Lian
brothers and their squires. Bows, greetings, and blessings were all that assaulted
them as they passed through the Plakka unmolested.

Once they were inside the city, Dun Loren began issuing orders. "I'll
check with our detachment here in the city. Clerents, Justin, you ready our
new horses at the Brotherhood's stables." He looked at Manney, then turned

to Dun L'lsen. "Take your boy to one of the temples of Kasparow and see about having him healed. That powder may have relieved his coughing, but he seems to be getting worse to me, and the last thing I want is to have to deal with a full-blown case of pneumonia. We are too pressed for time."

"Not possible," responded Dun L'lsen. "Manney needs to transfer my barding to the new horse, and I wish to accompany you. I too would like to keep track of Morgan's movements." He paused. "And I need to be seen as much as possible."

Kasparow, was this knight vain. "Do you intend to put that horse armor on every fresh mount you get for the next three months? We aren't engaged in war, or prancing around in a parade. That barding will only tire your horses out. If you wish to come with me to *be seen*, then so be it, but I will not have sick squires and heavy horses slowing us down. Clerents, you get our new mounts ready, *without* Dun L'lsen's barding. Justin, you take Manney to be looked at. They won't deny you." No Dun Lian knight would be denied healing by a priest of Kasparow, and that right extended to his squire as well. The priests might question whether or not Manney was a Dun Lian squire, but certainly not Justin, with his Malta mark proudly displayed as it was. They would be all right, and the boy would be healed. He addressed Dun L'lsen. "That would leave you to accompany me if you wish. I would suggest, however, that you remove that tin container you insist on wearing. We can have it shipped back to Lianhome with your barding. You'd feel much more comfortable in lighter clothing, I'm sure."

"In truth," the big knight said calmly. He didn't seem to be taken aback by Dun Loren's rudeness, nor did he seem to mind being given orders despite the fact that he was Dun Lian's chosen successor. He certainly did know when he was to remain in his place. He unwound the brass wire that held his topknot together and removed his helmet. "This armor is a part of who and what I am. I will not slow you down." He turned to Manney. "Go with Justin and be healed."

They rode to the building that housed the representatives of the Dun Lian Brotherhood in Panadar. It was a massive building, surrounded by a thin strip of well-kept grass that looked like the moat of a Chunyan Royal Castle. Nowhere else did the Brotherhood have such a strong presence outside of their own castle of Lianhome. The sheer numbers of knights needed to police the O'kalakan pass demanded such a structure. They dismounted, and several squires rushed to take care of the horses. Clerents followed their lead to the stables, talking all the time, of course. Justin had ushered Manney away, disappearing almost as soon as their feet hit the ground. Justin obviously knew it would take some time to reach a priest and persuade him to perform a healing on Manney.

Dun Loren looked up at the front of the building. It was four stories tall, encompassed nearly the entire city block it was on, and was made entirely of Andonesian red marble. It was an impressive sight. The radiating light of oil lamps set in sconces that lined the outside of the building accentuated the thick red veins that spiderwebbed through the gray-and-white rock. Several pots of glowing clumps of miremoss hung from chains suspended by retractable metal poles from the almost-flat roof of the building. Smoke from the miremoss floated heavily to the ground, creating a low-lying cloud that slowly dissipated around the building, keeping the area free of biting insects.

Dun Loren and Dun L'lsen entered the building and were confronted immediately with a knight sitting at a large desk in a small anteroom. A squire sat to his right. Four doors behind the desk were the only exits from the room. Each door was open, revealing a long corridor behind. An armored, pike-wielding knight stood between each door. At a moment's notice, those pikes could skewer anyone attempting to pass the front desk before they had stepped more than a few feet from the front door.

The squire at the desk put his right hand to his waist then raised it in the air as if drawing a sword and holding it aloft. Between brothers, it was tradition to allow the squire to perform the salute. As it was, Dun Loren and Dun L'lsen, at the same time, returned the salute.

"Greetings, brothers," said the seated knight. He was unshaven and round in the face. Dun Loren doubted if this knight had seen any field time in years. The somewhat-portly knight was busy furiously scribbling something on a piece of parchment and failed to even look up. The squire, however, had examined both Dun Loren and Dun L'lsen and came stiffly erect when he recognized the etched talon on Dun L'lsen's breastplate. "New recruits for the pass, I take it," he said a little condescendingly. "Is this your first assignment?" It was an honest mistake, two knights entering this building *without* squires most likely had not been in service long enough to have squires. He continued his writing. Dun Loren and Dun L'lsen exchanged a mildly amused glance when the squire poked the knight in the fat of his sponsor's ribs.

"Do that again, and I'll have you picking mushrooms by the moonlight!" the knight yelled, dropping his quill and making to slap the squire, who was nodding, wide-eyed, at the two new arrivals. The knight actually let out a squeal when he first laid eyes on Dun L'lsen.

"Dun L'lsen!" The Knight stood and saluted. "Please forgive me, I should have recognized you. I am Dun Mayden. How——"

"No matter, brother," Dun Loren said, interrupting the knight. He knew now that Dun L'lsen would sit by and abdicate the attention to him. "I require some information on a brother that may have passed through here recently." Dun Mayden stood silent for a second, looking with open mouth between Dun Loren and Dun L'lsen. When he realized that Dun L'lsen was neither offended nor the one in charge, he sat back down and addressed Dun Loren as he would have any other brother, except maybe for Dun L'lsen.

"You need information, then? Would this have been within the past week, or less *recent* than that?" His superior tone of voice was all but returning.

"At least more than a month ago," Dun Loren said shortly.

"A month. Well then." He picked his quill up, dipped it in an inkwell, and scribbled something on the parchment in front of him. "You need to go to the archives. The last corridor there will take you to the stairwell that leads to the fourth-floor archives. Brother Seguis will be able to assist you."

"Thank you, Dun Mayden." Dun Loren and Dun L'lsen left the anteroom.

"Interesting fellow," Dun L'lsen said when they were out of earshot. The corridor walls were pierced with arrow slits down the entire length of the hallway. He couldn't see them, but he knew there were brothers with crossbows behind the corridor's walls. The Brotherhood's internal security had always been formidable. He couldn't really understand why. He had no idea what could happen in *this* building, in *this* city that called for crossbowmen to be stationed, stuffed between these walls, around-the-clock. "I thought he was going to backhand his squire right then and there."

"I think the squire enjoyed poking him."

"I know he did," chuckled the big knight. "Did you catch his expression as we left?"

"No, I didn't." The corridor turned to their right and abruptly ended in a narrow spiral staircase. Dun L'lsen, with his broad shoulders and shining armor, had to turn himself slightly to ascend the staircase. The Brotherhood never made anything easy.

The four-storied spiral staircase tired him out. He had never been to the archives of this particular building and was amazed when he saw the soup hole in the ceiling of the stairwell.

Gaining the landing to the archives, Dun Loren entered a single room that occupied the entire top floor of the building. Well, he thought looking up at the soup hole, the *official* top floor anyway. The room was a maze of freestanding bookshelves that he would hate to have to enter. Dun Seguis met them at the entrance to the archives.

"Kasparow's grace be with you, brothers." This knight was slenderer than the last, but still was overweight—at least his attire made him look overweight. Dun Loren was surprised to see he was garbed in the heavy robes of a scribe. "Dun L'lsen, it is always an honor to be visited by the Successor." He bowed to Dun L'lsen then turned to Dun Loren. "Dun Loren, it is good to see you again."

"Have we met?"

"Yes, a few years ago, at Lianhome, during a knighting ceremony. It was my last knighting ceremony." Dun Loren still drew a blank. "I am sure I looked differently. I fear, after two years of sitting in this room, I have put on quite a few pounds. And I would have been in full armor then."

"You no longer train?"

"No." He tapped his left leg with an ink-covered hand. "A wound prevents me from most strenuous activities." It was only then when Dun Seguis turned and moved to a nearby table that Dun Loren noticed his limp.

"Why don't you have it healed?" he asked, following the knight.

"Well, you know the story," he said, sitting. "To remind me of certain events, honor, penance, that sort of thing. Your hands," he said, changing the subject. He may have met the knight before, but he still did not feel comfortable pressing the issue. Dun Seguis held his hands up, turning them over several times. His fingertips were black with ink, and both hands seemed a shade darker than the rest of his skin. Dun Loren noticed then that the man's lips were also a little blackened.

"Hazards of the job."

"I've never seen a scribe's hands so stained."

"Well, I don't exactly do scribe work here. It's mostly reading records and turning pages. The stuff tastes terrible. It's a shame we don't use ink made from poisonberries."

"What exactly do you do here?"

"Well"—the knight looked to Dun L'lsen, who nodded slightly—"as you know, the Brotherhood has been keeping records of all those that cross through the checkpoint at the base of the O'kalakan pass. Records of whom, what, and when have been meticulously kept for hundreds of years, practically since the Brotherhood began policing the pass. It's my task to put together a summary of trade and travel trends through the pass. As you can see"—he gestured behind him—"there are a lot of records to go through."

"Yes, I can see that."

"After two years, I am almost finished. But that is neither here nor there. What can I do for the two of you?"

"Well"—Dun Loren glanced back at Dun L'lsen, who had remained completely silent—"I need to know the last time a brother named Dun Lain came through this city or the pass, and what his stated destination was. This would have been anywhere from one to three months ago."

"Okay, well." The knight stood and walked among the bookcases. "Records that recent are kept right over here. If you will follow me, I think three of us will find it faster than one." Dun Loren and Dun L'lsen followed.

Half an hour later, they were leaving the archives, descending the skinny spiral staircase with no more information than when they had arrived.

"Are you sure this is the way Dun Lain came?" asked Dun L'lsen. Dun Loren didn't answer him. He was sure Dun Seguis would be able hear their voices echoing in the stairwell. After all, how had the man known to be waiting at the top of the staircase when they had first arrived? That ink-stained man knew a lot—too much, it had seemed. What had those exchanged looks between Dun L'lsen and Dun Seguis been about? Dun Loren wanted to keep this news as contained as he could. He even held his tongue in silence as they passed through the arrow-slit-riddled corridor. Any number of brothers could be lurking behind the walls. Emerging into the anteroom, he and Dun L'lsen ignored the guards, the squire, and a hastily standing Dun Mayden and left the building.

"To answer your question," he started once they got outside, "no, I am not sure." Clerents and four other squires were standing on the grass moat playing a game of *stretch*. It was Clerents's turn. He was standing with his feet about three feet apart; there was a dagger stuck in the ground at his left foot. Clerents picked the dagger up and tossed it, impaling it in the ground a few feet from his own position. He pointed at one of the squires, who grimaced. This boy steadied himself and, leaving one foot in place where it was, stretched the other to meet the knife Clerents had just thrown. The boy's feet were stretched at least four and a half feet apart. He had trouble keeping his balance and fell. He was disqualified from the game. Chuckling merrily, Clerents accepted the knife from the boy and tossed it again, picking a new squire to attempt to stretch to the knife.

"Then what makes you think Dun Lain went to the Dead Pools?" Dun L'lsen held his voice low, obviously aware of Dun Loren's desire for caution. Clerents heard the murmured voices and looked up. Dun Loren held up a finger, giving the boy a few more minutes to finish his game.

"Because Dun Lain came to me before he left and *told* me he was going to the Dead Pools. He confided in me that he had been dreaming of them and felt some sort of *pull* toward them. He must have headed straight for them."

"Must have. Do you still insist on wasting time tracing his steps instead of heading straight to Maralat?"

"Yes, I do. Clerents," he called to the squire, "bring our new mounts!" The boy tossed the knife one last time and sped off with several of the other boys to fetch the horses. Dun Loren played upon a suspicion and took a stab in the dark. "Why is Dun Seguis compiling that information for you?"

Dun L'lsen paused before answering. "Why do you assume I gave him the assignment?"

"Well, he did seem to look to you for guidance at times. Just a hunch, I suppose."

The big knight was busy pulling his hair back and binding it with a brass wire. He stopped and considered Dun Loren's statement for a few seconds before continuing to put his helmet on. "We can't continue as we have for the past thousand years. Eventually, the bottom is going to fall out of the sword-for-hire business. Even now our patrons are becoming fewer and fewer as ancient disputes over territorial boundaries are solved and laid to rest. There will come a time when arguments between nations will be solved purely by discussion and economic force, completely eliminating the need for armed conflict. Where will our services be needed then? As it stands, our largest numbers of troops are involved in the war against G'Zellan. What happens when that threat is taken care of?

"Things have gone so well for the Brotherhood in the past that not a single Dun Lian has bothered to make plans for the future. They just carry on as if tradition alone will keep the Brotherhood solvent. As I said, I mean to be Dun Lian someday, and I mean to make the Brotherhood a self-sufficient entity, not just the hired bully of any given monarch.

"For that end, I need as much information on the history and habits of trade as I can acquire. To be truthful with you, I have many such agents scattered around."

"But how are you able to give orders and use knights personally like that?"

"You would be amazed at what popularity and being the chosen successor can do for you."

Justin and Manney came running up at that point. "Sorry we kept you waiting, Dun Loren. It took forever to find a priest who would listen to me."

"No worries, Justin. How do you feel, Manney?" Dun L'lsen's squire looked much better. He was even full of energy and almost as talkative as the twins were.

"I feel great, Dun Loren. That was the first time I had been healed by a priest. I felt His presence. It was Kasparow, inside of me, and then all of a sudden, I wasn't shivering anymore, my headache was gone, I wasn't hungry or tired. Is this what it feels like to come out?"

"Very near it, Manney, very near it."

"I hope this will help me come out soon"—the boy looked to Dun L'lsen; Dun Loren knew of at least *one* person that did not worship Dun L'lsen—"as I have had such a hard time of it up to now."

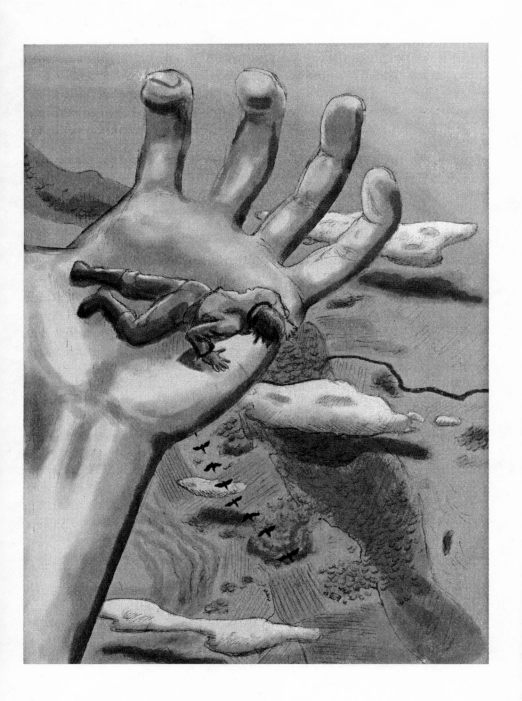

CHAPTER 12

Nearly all of the air in his lungs had been forced out when he had hit the tree. The rest had been used to speak the prayer that had saved his life. So when he materialized in front of a startled villager, just outside of a small town, breathing hard and fighting for air, it was no surprise that the old man fainted. The man had been carrying a large thick burlap sack, which released some of its contents to the ground when he fell. They were on a small road leading from the village to a field of crops that was cut out of the surrounding forest. In the light of the dual moons, Malchom could see several people in the distance, working the field.

It didn't take him long to decide what to do. He quickly grabbed what he thought were mushrooms and shoved as many as he could into the mouth of the fallen man, effectively gagging him, which brought the man to his senses, only to have him begin choking on the mushrooms stuffed down his throat. Unable to breathe or scream properly, the man sat up and began to struggle wildly. Malchom upended the sack and tossed the empty burlap bag over the man's head. With the strength of his new body, he crammed the rest of the man into the sack, breaking some of the man's bones in the process. He picked up the sack and quickly walked into the woods, away from the village and the field.

He went into the forest until he was sure he could not be seen, heard, or smelled and dumped the sack to the ground. The man had ceased his struggling. Either he had choked on the mushrooms to the point of passing out, or he had gone into shock, as long as he was still alive. Malchom drew a dagger from his boot and sliced open the burlap bag. The man stared at him wild-eyed, nostrils flaring in and out with strained grasps for air. Good, he *was* still alive. The man looked too terrified to even contemplate escape. Malchom left him alone and turned to his next task.

He reached up and pulled down several almost-dead branches to start a fire. Dead branches still on the tree were always the driest and caught fire easily. When he had piled enough kindling and drought-stricken brown leaves into a nice little pyramid, he untied the small pouch that hung at his waist and removed a decent-sized piece of flint. He squatted and used his boot knife to throw sparks at the pile of wood. A proper sacrifice to Altair required two things, blood and fire. Once before, he had made the mistake of not being able to produce flame for a sacrifice. Never again.

The dry leaves and dead wood caught fire quickly. He added more and more branches until the flames were self-sufficient and then turned back to the panic-frozen man. The man's eyes were bloodshot and beginning to gloss over; blood was seeping from his nostrils. He didn't have much time before the villager slipped away, and he needed the man alive.

In a hurry, he picked up the man and slung the almost-limp body over his shoulder, head forward and face down. Standing in front of the flames, his victim's head nearly five feet from the tip of the fire, Malchom pushed the man's chin forward with one hand and held his knife to the exposed neck with the other. Beginning the praises that would bring Altair's avatar, he slit his captive's throat. The fire sputtered in the night. The blood sizzled as it reacted with the heat, blending with the sound of his prayers. Sparks flew outward from the flames.

These were not ordinary sparks, and Malchom knew it. He heaved the now-completely limp form off his shoulder and kneeled in front of the fire as the sparks rose higher and higher into the tree-crowded night sky. They swirled round and round, coalescing into the form of a man. The sparks flashed brilliantly then died. The avatar of Altair remained, floating above the fire.

"Malchom," the figure said. Malchom knew the avatar could choose to take any form it wished. This time it pleased itself with taking the form of Malchom's former body.

"Nice form you've decided to take, avatar."

"You like it?" The hovering being turned around for Malchom to admire.

"Actually, I like *this* one better. It isn't as weak."

"Ah well, weakness is all determined by the soul within. You see, this may be a weak body, but"—the avatar flew at Malchom, knocking him to the ground. "With my most powerful soul inside, it becomes quite a juggernaut," laughed the avatar.

"Amusing, avatar, amusing."

"Ah, thank you, Jamias. I haven't been able to enjoy myself thusly for nearly a thousand years. Now what can I do for you?"

"Things have changed slightly. I am no longer where I used to be." He knew the avatar knew all of this. He was, after all, omniscient, but he felt more confident when he explained things. "I was attacked by a troll and had to teleport myself here. It makes no difference. It only means I will make my requests now instead of in the morning."

"You have decided what powers to ask for, then?"

"I have."

"Then begin."

"First," he said boldly and confidently. A few hundred sacrifices had nearly restored him to his old self. "I want the permanent ability to transport myself and as many people as I can touch at one time to any location of my choosing. I want you to summon an elemental, which will obey only me, to aid me in rebuilding my castle. I want to have the ability to use a far-sight spell at will to keep track of my enemies. I want the ability to conjure fire of any size and shape of my choice whenever it pleases me. And finally, I want the permanent ability to conjure any food of my choice." Malchom knew this was too much to ask for. The conjured elemental alone would take up most of his favor with the avatar today. In the past, he had not needed to worry about what he asked for; his power and influence with Altair had been great. The avatar floated to the ground and paced around the fire, deep in thought.

"I shall be generous to you today, Malchom. You shall have everything you have asked for"—Malchom's eyes widened—"but I shall require you to sacrifice one hundred humans by the first day of each month to maintain the powers I grant you today. I will also accept twenty dwarves or elves if you so choose. You know how Altair likes nonhuman blood."

"Thank you, avatar." He should have asked for more. This avatar was in a good mood today. "One further thing." The avatar eyed him condescendingly. "I want to know the whereabouts of the magical emerald that once housed my soul. It was amongst my possessions when I was attacked by the troll."

"You know the price for divinations, Malchom, or should I call you *Dun Malchom*?" The avatar chuckled. "One dwarf or elf child is to be sacrificed for each question asked."

"Yes, yes, I know. You just seemed to be in a good mood today."

"Well, I AM!" The avatar launched himself into the air and flew around the fire a couple of times before coming to rest in a relaxed, prone position, hovering on his side at eye level to Malchom. "Until you reappeared, I hadn't been able to walk this realm at all. Do you have any idea how good it feels to be active again after nine hundred and thirty years? Well, yes, I guess you do—"

"Nine hundred and thirty years? Is that how long I was imprisoned within the gem?"

"Actually, no. You were in for nearly a thousand. After you and your fellow wizards were killed, the Dun Lian Brotherhood slowly and efficiently hunted down and killed all of the followers of Altair. It took a good sixty years, but soon enough, there were no more worshippers of Altair left to summon any of his avatars. Altair lost interest in this realm and moved on, leaving me to keep a vigilant watch should anyone call."

"I see." Malchom noticed that the avatar was speaking in a hurried, excited manner almost as if he was stimulated by some sort of drug. The avatar continued restlessly.

"And to make sure I did my job, like there would be anything else to do besides watch, Altair took away my ability to leave this realm. Even traveling to our home plane of existence was denied to me. I couldn't even materialize myself in Altair's home temple, not that I *really* like it there, but it has prevented me from basking in His glory for the past millennium." The avatar *was* indeed in a talkative mood. Malchom decided to press the situation for all it might be worth.

"You said the Brotherhood was responsible for eradicating all of Altair's worshippers. How could they do such a thing? They worship the god Kasparow, and as far as I know, Kasparow doesn't grant powers anywhere near what Altair does. Even if my fellow wizards were killed, there should have been plenty of others around willing enough to step up and take our places."

"Oh, there were. But Kasparow *despises* magic and sorcery. He does whatever he can to quench its use. During the height of the battles, Kasparow gave the leader of the Brotherhood, the original Dun Lian, a sword that absorbs all magical energies around it. Armed with such a weapon, the Brotherhood was able to greatly stifle the power of Altair's followers."

"If there was but one sword, why couldn't Dun Lian simply be killed and the sword spirited away?"

"That was tried, but as soon as one would fall, another brother would assume the name and position of Dun Lian. They are quite skilled at combat. You have to understand that worshippers of Altair were not used to physical confrontation."

"Why didn't they simply ask Altair for protection from such a weapon?"

"They tried, but then ran into the problem of the mushroom and the spore. Which comes first? They were magically protected from the sword, but the sword nullified their magics. I fear they didn't phrase their prayers well enough to win out over Kasparow's power."

"Can it be done?"

"Yes, of course, it can be done," snorted the avatar.

"How would one have to phrase a prayer to gain such power?"

"Well, if you think about it . . ." The avatar paused, thinking. He smiled for a moment then his visage took on an evil, angry grin. "Nice try, Malchom. My jubilation at being free has loosened my tongue." The form of the avatar rushed into Malchom's face, growing in size until it was all that Malchom could see. "Do not test me, Malchom. I may be relieved to be active once more, but a mere mortal *will not* use me. You forget your place. A thousand years ago, you might have held enough sway with Altair to treat his avatars in any way you chose. That is not the case now. *I* am the only avatar of Altair left to this world. You must deal with me alone, remember that."

"Forgive me." Malchom did know where his place was. "You are right." His place was standing over this creature with his boot smudging the avatar's face, whatever form he decided to take. "I do forget my place. I am honored and humbled that you have decided to grant all of my requests today."

"Are you? For some reason, I don't think you are." Malchom began to protest. The avatar held up a hand and floated to the ground. "Let's just say that I don't think it fits with your character. Honored maybe, humbled never. More like surprised and stunned, if anything." The avatar glowered at Malchom. "You spent a long time as Altair's most prominent worshipper, and I remember that avatars would nearly beg Altair to be allowed to serve you."

"That was a long time ago now—"

"You're right," interrupted the avatar. "And things are not as they were. They never will be again. I never had the *honor* of serving you in the past, and it looks like I will never have to." The form of Malchom's old body suddenly grew in size. Malchom was scooped up in one massive hand and lifted off the ground with a speed that left him breathless. By the time he caught his breath, Malchom was hundreds of feet in the air. The avatar's body continued to grow at a frightening pace. Malchom looked down. The trees were dwindling in size rapidly, and a bird flew below him. He looked up to the avatar's face. It was nearly as far away as the ground. They passed through the cloud layer, and still they rose.

Nauseated, Malchom closed his eyes; he nearly vomited. The air was getting thin; he felt dizzy and euphoric. He was losing consciousness, his head lolled to the side. A thin veil of light passed across his vision, and he heard the rushing sound of wind just before his ears popped with a *fwoop*. Head dangling over the immense hand of the still-expanding avatar, Malchom saw the world, as he never had before.

It looked like a big orb made of Andonesian blue marble. Swirls of white clouds engulfed the globe. The blue of the oceans was immense, covering nearly the entire world that he could see. Quickly, too quickly, he was slipping further from consciousness.

"To emphasize my point, Malchom, I shall require you to meditate on your situation. When I feel you have learned sufficient humility, I will grant you the powers you have asked for tonight."

When he woke, his head was pounding like a dwarven blacksmith's hammer. He was lying next to the now-dead fire, the lifeless and partially burned body of the villager lay half in and half out of the cold ashes and charred wood. The avatar was nowhere in sight. He wondered what this avatar's name was. Usually, he never bothered learning. In the past, *they* had done his bidding, not the other way around. He would have to learn this avatar's name, and make him pay for the way he had been treated since escaping the gem. He was Malchom Jamias, after all. The avatar's last words came back to him. *Learn humility?* He'd show that avatar; humility, indeed. Omniscient he may be, but even gods couldn't know the private thoughts of mortal men, which had something to do with freedom of choice. Meditation—he would have to get a room at the nearby village and actually sit and *pray* to this avatar. Best to dispose of the body that was stiffening before him.

It took him until dawn, using only sticks, to dig a hole sufficient enough to bury the crumpled body. The drought-stricken earth was hard and compacted; he would have ruined his knife had he attempted to use it. As a result, he was extremely exhausted, sweating profusely, and covered in dirt and dust. All in all, as he strode down the packed-earth road that led to the village, he looked as if he had been traveling for days.

It was a small village he entered. About fifteen mud-brick and thatch-roofed buildings of moderate-size encircled a large sunken amphitheater. It was early, yet people were about their daily business. One woman to his left was beating the dust out of a collection of rugs strung between two of the buildings. Another group of women were arranging what he was sure were mushrooms along dozens of drying racks. They had their work cut out for them. Evidently, the previous night's harvest had been an abundant one, nearly four dozen bushels of mushrooms awaited to be unpacked and dried in the hot summer sun. Another group of four, this one all men, were busy loading small square crates onto a cart. The horse leading it stamped its foot and swished its tail at annoying flies. Nearing the sunken amphitheater, Malchom learned that the previous night's harvest had brought more than just mushrooms to occupy the townsfolk today.

"And not only that, but there were mushrooms spilled all over the ground near the fields." It was a short young woman who was speaking, he could barely see her as she was several steps into the amphitheater. She had dark hair and was quite pretty. She was speaking to two men—one old, one young, both tall.

"And you are sure no one has seen him since last night?" said the young one.

"I've asked everybody twice, once last night and once just now."

"Are there any horses missing? Could he have gone to the city early?" said the older man. What little hair the old man had ringing his head was long and white. The younger man, though not much past his second decade of life, was beginning to bald himself. These two were related, Malchom was sure of it.

"He's your brother Jansen, do you think he would do anything like this?" The old man folded his arms and picked at the gap between his front teeth with a thumbnail, mirroring the actions of the younger man.

"No, you're right, he wouldn't," said Jansen. He turned to the younger man. "I guess we should have a couple of the boys go look for your father, Raurin."

"I'll see if Collum and Ander are done loading the cart." Raurin unfolded his arms. "It won't take all four of them to get the mushrooms to market today, although they will be disappointed." He turned to leave and caught sight of Malchom. The tall muscular black-haired man said nothing; he just stood there looking at Malchom. The other two turned to see what Raurin was staring at.

"By Kasparow!" yipped the woman. She hiked up her dusty brown skirt and rushed up to Malchom. "What good graces are shining on us this day! Greetings, sir knight." Malchom was continually amazed at how easily he was identified as a Dun Lian knight.

"I am Dun Lain, I am on free deed. I have been traveling for quite some time and require a place to meditate." He had used this line several times before and found it to work quite nicely. Morgan's journal had been very helpfully informative. He hadn't quite finished it and hoped he could recover it. That is, if anything was left at his campsite after the troll attack.

"Of course, of course, come with me." The woman took his arm and started to lead him away. "You know, we have a problem that a strong and dedicated knight like you might be able to help us with," she said in a very soft tone of voice while stroking his arm. Was this woman flirting with him? He could hear Raurin and Jansen speaking in low tones as he was ushered away.

"Would you look at that," Raurin was saying.

"Easy now, she *is* your mother after all."

"Not by blood. And I think she *wants* my father to go missing. You know, I've always thought she was after our land."

"All I know is that you've always been jealous." Could this woman hear what was being said?

"I am Namara," said the woman. She *was* quite beautiful. Her long dark hair reached halfway down her back. Malchom found himself fantasizing about what he would do with that hair. "My husband, Geoffrey, and I own and run this little farm." It was a good thing these Dun Lian knights didn't take any sort of silly vows of celibacy.

"And how may I be of service to such a charming and beautiful young girl?" Namara blushed. Married or not, she did seem extremely receptive.

"Geoffrey was with the other workers in the field last night and simply vanished. No one has seen him or heard anything from him since then."

"This was last night?"

"Yes." They came to one of the larger buildings in the village. Namara led him inside. The floorboards squeaked a little. "Can I get you something to eat or drink?"

"I would be honored." Malchom despised having to engage in such pleasantries, but it was necessary to keep the people he met off guard. When the time came, he would drop the friendly chatter, take this woman, and then kill the two dozen or so inhabitants of this village.

"Have a seat, then. I won't be long." She nearly pushed him into one of the big chairs that occupied the central room. It was nicely furnished for such a dingy village. Three large scentwood chairs with down cushions took up most of the space in front of an Andonesian red-marble fireplace. Off to one side, near the doorway that Namara was exiting through, was a very nicely carved and gilded dining table and another set of cushioned scentwood chairs. He watched her exit the room. Her hips swayed with the grace of a queen and the experience of a tavern whore. Her dusty brown skirts did little to hide her shapely bottom. She returned after a minute with a ceramic mug in her hand, which she handed to him. It was cool to the touch.

"Its summer mushroom tea, ever tasted it before?" She sat in the chair next to him, scooted it toward him, and leaned in close.

"No, I haven't." He lifted the mug to his lips. There were a couple of mushroom buttons floating on the surface. He sipped the tea. It was sweet and tasted faintly of dirt. It was a bland drink, but the surprising and delightful thing about it was that it was cold. He grimaced a little.

"I know, not much of a drink, is it? It's the coldness of the drink that makes it unique. It's a natural property of the mushrooms, when harvested correctly. Geoffrey says the tea is going to be very popular and make our village famous."

"So you say your *husband* has gone missing?" He emphasized the word "husband" in a way that he hoped she would catch.

"Yes, well, like I said"—evidently, she did catch his meaning as she leaned in farther and placed a hand on his leather-clad knee—"he was in the fields with the others early last night. He went to make sure there were enough burlap sacks for the evening's harvest. You see, the mushrooms have to be stored in special sacks to keep them from deteriorating, and that was the last that anyone saw of him." She glanced around as if checking to make sure no one would overhear her, leaned in extremely close, and tightened her grip on his knee. "I suspect foul play," she whispered. Malchom was surprised; he leaned back in his chair.

"Why do you say that?" What could this girl know?

"Well, he wouldn't have gone anywhere during the harvest last night, nor right before taking a harvest to town. Making sure these mushrooms and the mushroom tea made this village famous has been his lifelong dream. I think he was kidnapped."

"Why would anyone do that?"

"For the secret of the mushrooms, of course! They only grow in this area, and only Geoffrey and a handful of the men here know how to harvest them without having them deteriorate at the slightest exposure to sunlight."

She was mistaken, of course, and Malchom knew it. He relaxed a little. "Do you have any suspects in mind? Anyone that might have mentioned anything out loud or coveted these mushrooms in any way?"

"That's where I thought you might be able to help. I would be most grateful to find out what has happened to my *husband* and whether or not he has met with his end." She kneeled in front of him, suggestively close. The door opened, and Raurin strode into the room. He had a disgusted look on his face. Malchom was sure Raurin had heard their conversation. The end of it, at least. Namara stood, a little embarrassed, and reflexively smoothed her skirt.

"I must speak with you, Namara." Raurin stalked into the other room.

"He's been full of jealousy since I met his father," she whispered in his ear. "I think he wants me."

"I can see why." She flashed him a smile that was more than suggestive as she left the room. Maybe he would keep her. Once he got his own mushroom production going again, she would become a willing servant. Yes, he would have to keep her. He could hear their argument from here but couldn't quite make out their voices coming from the other room. They were having quite an argument. When they returned, Namara was visibly shaken with a look of disbelief on her face. Raurin said nothing. He simply stalked out of the building, slamming the door as he left.

"Please excuse that little *family* discussion. You can understand how on edge we are at this time, can't you?"

"I certainly can, pretty lady." He felt confident and bold. It was best he press his advantage while she was still shaken. She blushed.

"W-would you like something to eat?" she stuttered.

"Yes, I am starved. And I would be honored to eat anything of yours." He raised an eyebrow at her. She blushed again. "Do you have a room where I can be alone to meditate?"

"Yes, of course, follow me." She led him out the doorway she and Raurin had used and into the kitchen. In the back of this room was a stairwell that was built into the ground and led downward and around into a long corridor that ran the length of the house. There was plenty of light streaming in through numerous windows set about shoulder height in the walls. The walls themselves were made of whole scentwood logs packed close enough to keep out the dirt and mud. The air was thick with the odor of scentwood.

"What happens to these chambers when it rains?"

"Well, scentwood likes water—it absorbs all it can, expanding during the process, which further helps to keep the water out. It's rare that our basements are flooded. We don't get enough rain for that. Besides, these rooms stay a constant temperature all year long. Our summers are much more brutal than our rainy seasons." She walked all the way down the corridor, passing several doors and stopped at the last one. "There should be enough light during the day, even if you close the drapes. There are two oil-lamp wall sconces if you need any additional light. It's a bare room, just a down-filled futon on the ground. I am afraid there isn't even a chair or writing desk."

"It will be fine. Kasparow's light"—he nearly choked on the words—"and the light of your face would be enough to last me for weeks." She blushed again.

"Go on." She batted her eyelashes. "You forget I'm married."

"Yes," he sighed, a much exaggerated sigh. "And on that matter, I shall pray diligently to Kasparow for guidance. I am sure that within a day or two, he will give me sufficient guidance to get to the bottom of your little problem. You should wait until then to do anything."

"Thank you. Shall I bring your food in, or should I place it at the foot of the door so as not to disturb you?"

"You may bring it in at your convenience. I wouldn't think of denying myself the opportunity to gaze upon your face again for any reason, Kasparow included." He was working it for all it was worth, and he was sure she was responding. This time she didn't blush but merely smiled broadly.

"Well then, I shall return shortly. Kasparow's grace upon thee."

"May Kasparow's grace shine upon thee as well." She turned and left, almost with a bounce in her step. Was she happy? He opened the chamber door and stepped inside. It was indeed bare. A small futon, barely large enough to fit his large frame, two wall sconces, and the curtains over the window were all that the room contained. No matter, he would spend the next day or two praying to Altair, eating free food and charming this young beauty into leaving with her. As an afterthought, he decided, when he left, that he would lead the villagers to Geoffrey's body just for fun. There is no way they would suspect him of the crime. There were times that he absolutely loved having been deposited into the body of this Dun Lian knight.

He opened the curtains of the large window so that anyone who wanted could look in on him. Let them watch him pray. It could only increase his legitimacy with them. Besides, no one would know exactly to which god it was that he was praying.

Unfortunately, Altair would not know either. If what the avatar had said was true, if Altair had moved on to other dimensions, then he would not hear any of Malchom's prayers. They would float out of his mind, up to the heavens, and into the ears of that pompous creature that was lucky enough to call himself an avatar of Altair.

Malchom had once had designs on attaining avatar status. He had been well on his way before the little war with his fellow wizards and his imprisonment within the gem. He moved to the window and stared out into the long shadows created by the still-rising sun. This house faced south, which he thought was an attempt to keep it as cool as possible. In fact, the only windows he had seen that faced north and the rising sun were here in the basement, in the corridor outside.

It was surprising that this house had windows at all. Glass windows were quite expensive, let alone ones so large. At least it was during his time, and all the scentwood. Scentwood had been a luxury even to his former standards. He wondered if it was only Geoffrey's house that had such luxuries or if all of these buildings were furnished thusly. That mushroom drink *must* be very popular.

Mushrooms. How ironic that the lovely Namara was after the rewards her husband's mushrooms brought. She would soon be slave to another kind of mushroom—if they still grew in the caves beneath his former castle, that is.

He caught sight of Raurin approaching Jansen. It looked as if Raurin had just come from the building Malchom was in. Jansen was talking with two young boys. After a few moments, the boys left. Malchom saw them climb into the front of the loaded cart and urge the two horses forward. They waved their good-byes.

"I'll send Ander back if we spot him in town!" yelled one of the boys. Raurin continued to talk with Jansen. They must have been arguing for Raurin's gestures were too wild and overstated to mean anything else. There was a knock at his door.

"Come on in, Namara."

"Um, my hands are full." Malchom moved to the door and turned the door handle. Namara was standing with a scentwood serving tray in her hands. The smells coming from the bowls and plates were very appealing, almost as appealing as Namara was, grinning at him devilishly. "Bed and breakfast. I hope you don't mind being served."

"I begin to wonder which of us is actually being served." She entered the room, smiling, and placed the tray on the floor.

"Its cold mutton-and-mushroom soup seasoned with cumin and a very spicy red pepper. I hope it isn't too spicy for you. The sweetbread and cheese should take some of the bite out of the soup if it is. And more tea, of course."

"Thank you, Namara."

"Well," she said after an awkward silence, "I'll let you alone then."

"I'll need at least two days to pray before I set about finding your husband, if he hasn't returned by then. You can bring food at the regular times."

"As you wish." Namara turned to leave.

"Namara." She stopped and turned. "I will get to the bottom of this for you, to *your* satisfaction." She smiled at him.

"I thank Kasparow for sending you to me." She left the room and closed the door silently.

You can thank someone else instead, he thought. Turning to the food, he sat on the down futon and consumed the meal. It was quite tasty and very spicy. The sweetbread did help absorb some of the spice's aftertaste, but he found himself having to save the tea for last, drinking the entire mug in one gulp in an attempt to quench the mildly irritating fire that was burning in his mouth.

He didn't really mind the burning sensation in his mouth. After a thousand years, he was having fun experiencing sights, sounds, smells, and tastes almost as if for the first time. And feelings, he remembered that woman who had thrown herself at him in that village not too long ago. The sensation of feeling was long missed. In his former body, women had had to be coerced into bedding him. That woman had wanted him, had been completely willing to please him in any way she could. The addition of that emotion added a lot to the experience. He wondered if he could lead Namara to that level of desire.

Regardless, he liked the way this new body felt. In the past, he had devoted his time to gaining power. This time he would concentrate a little more on the pleasurable side that his power could bring. Perhaps he would start a harem. A bevy of women from around the world to please his senses. Women of every shape, size, and race for him to pleasure himself with and to beget him as many offspring as they could. He would start a harem to produce a brood of loyal and trainable servants to be the generals in his new army. And Namara would be the first.

With those thoughts in mind, he folded the futon in half and propped it next to the door, against the wall facing the room's window. He sat on the puffy cushion, and it sighed as his weight forced trapped air out of the well-made mattress. Sitting, he recalled the prayers to Altair that he had not spoken or thought of for hundreds of years. Even when inside the gem, after perusing his mind once or twice, Jux had had no desire to repetitively go through certain of his memories.

Jux must be enjoying his new companion. The disembodied Jux certainly had not cared for Malchom. He wondered how many years in a row they had remained silent. Jux was definitely a creature of good, or at least one of order. Nothing at all like Malchom. This knight Morgan would probably keep Jux busy for hundreds of years.

Unless, of course, if he got out. Malchom wondered what had become of the gem. He had left it behind when the troll attacked. Could that disgusting thing have found it? He doubted it. The gem was stuffed inside a dirt-packed sack. All of which was inside his backpack. Trolls weren't that smart, and besides, it wasn't as if they were like dragons, only interested in gems and jewels. In fact, the only thing a troll cared about was fresh meat.

He sat back and forgot about the gem for now. Clearing his mind, he breathed deeply once and then left his body to breathe automatically as he began the series of prayers that would not reach his god's ears. That avatar would be the only one to hear his prayers, they both knew it. But still, he prayed to *Altair*. He called on Altair, speaking of His greatness, naming the wonders of deeds the god had done in the past. He prayed to Altair, calling for his return, begging to be heard. He prayed to Altair the entire time, never once thinking of the avatar that would be the only one to hear his prayers; he was not about to give that avatar such notice.

And so he sat and prayed as the light entering the room grew brighter and brighter until the afternoon sun itself poked into view and finally disappeared behind the other buildings, casting long shadows into his little room. Sometime before sunset, Namara knocked on the door and asked if she could enter. He reached up and opened the door from his seated position.

"Time for dinner." She turned, holding another serving tray, and smiled at him when she found him seated as he was. "Is this how all Dun Lian knights pray?"

"I wouldn't know. Prayer to *Kasparow* is a very private thing. Each knight does it differently, I am sure."

"I'm sorry, forgive me for intruding. I'll just put this down and let you be." She kneeled and placed the tray on the floor in front of him. She had changed clothes.

"That's okay." He grabbed her hand and stayed her. "Why don't you sit, eat with me, and tell me what has been happening today." She was now dressed in fairly tight-fitting wool breeches and shirt. Despite the fact that it was probably functional, her clothing was very revealing of the curves of her body. He had to mention it. "You've changed clothing."

"It's a little better suited for harvesting than the dress I was wearing this morning. Plus, the wool helps keep out the evening's chill."

"And a bit easier to get the dirt and dust out of, I assume."

"Yep. Just let it dry in the sun for an afternoon, take a switch to it, bang out all the dirt, then throw it in a scentwood chest for a couple of days. Hardly needs to be washed more than once a month."

"Well, they do nice things for your legs." Indeed, she had very shapely legs, and the tight-fitting wool accentuated that fact. "Tell me what has been going on. I saw Raurin and Jansen arguing earlier in the day. Any news of your husband?"

"No, no one has heard from him yet. And we've no word from Collum or Ander either, but they wouldn't normally be returning until tomorrow.

I've not let Raurin or Jansen do anything, as you requested. They are very upset. They wanted to go and send out a couple of search parties to look for him. I told them that you were spending the day praying to Kasparow for guidance. That seemed to quiet Raurin down, but Jansen is still making a lot of noise about sending men out. If we weren't in the middle of harvest and in need of every hand we have, I doubt I would be able to stop him from doing so."

"Raurin has faith in Kasparow?"

"Religiously, I dare say he has as much faith as any Dun Lian knight. He used to talk of Kasparow and the Brotherhood a lot when we first met. I thought it was just to get my attention and impress me, but after seeing how he relaxed knowing that you were praying to Kasparow today, maybe his faith is that strong."

"Faith in A—your god is a very important thing in life. It's the gods that give life meaning. Without them, we would be nothing more than animals procreating and filling up this world with useless bodies."

"What news have you then?"

"As a Dun Lian knight, I must spend a good portion of my day involved in prayer to Kasparow just to maintain my place in His eyes, when we need extra favors from him . . . It will take some time yet, at least another full day."

"I understand. I had better let you get back to it, then." She stood. "I will have a cool bath drawn for you in the morning if you require one."

"Thank you, but I think I will remain in meditation until my prayers are answered. I have a lot to do myself."

"As you wish, Dun Lain." She curtsied.

"Please, call me Malchom."

"As you wish, Malchom. I'll bring your breakfast bright and early." It wasn't until she left the room that Malchom realized he had given her his real name. No matter, she would be docile and compliant soon enough. His first name would not go beyond this village, that he was sure of. He continued his prayers to Altair until he fell asleep.

He awoke slowly, groggily, from a deep sleep with no dreams; the morning light temporarily blinded him. He had gone without dreaming for so long within the gem that when it first happened to him in his new body, he found that he had wanted to sleep all day. This past night disappointingly held no dreams for him. Drool was escaping from his mouth. It ran down his chin and soaked the wool pillow that his head was resting on. He decided go back to sleep until Namara came with his breakfast. He closed his eyes and was asleep instantly.

The second time he awoke, it was because someone had moved his head. He jumped up to find Namara sitting next to him still dressed in the wool clothing of the night before.

"Excuse me, I'm sorry. I shouldn't have done that." She jumped up and left the room. "I'll get your breakfast," she said as she closed the door behind her. Malchom smiled. She was his. If he persisted, he might not even need to use his mushrooms on her.

He went to the window and looked out. The scene was much the same as it had been the previous morning. Several women were drying mushrooms. Two young boys were packing another cart full of crates. And again, Raurin and Jansen were standing a few steps down in the amphitheater. At least he thought they were standing; all he could see were their heads and shoulders. Jansen was still agitated. Malchom could hear him shouting. What he was saying escaped him, however. It surprised him, considering the tension that was obvious between Raurin and Namara, that Raurin wasn't the one doing more of the yelling. His faith in Kasparow must be strong, strong enough that Malchom was sure he could use it to his advantage. After all, as a Dun Lian knight, he *was* a representative of Kasparow, in a manner of speaking.

As he was watching, Namara came stalking out of the house and headed toward the two men standing in the amphitheater. She had changed back into the loose-fitting, cool cotton skirts of the day before.

She walked up to the arguing men and jumped right into the argument herself, shaking a finger wildly at Jansen. Small in stature she may have been, but she could project her voice when she wanted to. She was saying something about Jansen having enough work to do and how he should let Dun Lain take care of finding Geoffrey. Raurin was nodding his head.

"After all, he has Kasparow on his side," she said loud enough for even Malchom to hear. He noticed that the rest of the villagers had stopped whatever they had been doing and were watching the three as well.

She left the two men standing there looking at her in disbelief. The entire village watched her return to the house. Malchom was sure she was close to tears. The avatar would have to grant him his powers soon. He may have Namara infatuated with him, and Raurin might be willing to wait for a sign from Kasparow, but Jansen, judging by the look on his face—and quite possibly the rest of the village—wouldn't wait much longer. He could just leave and come back for Namara later, but he wasn't exactly sure how far from his ruined castle he was. No, he should stay. This was as good a place as any to pray for his powers. If the avatar would only hurry up and grant them. And that wasn't going to happen as long as he left the avatar out of his prayers to Altair.

He looked back out the window. Raurin and Jansen were gone. The few people in sight were slowly doing their work while talking up a storm. Malchom had no doubt what the subject of their conversations was. There came a knock at the door.

"Dun Lain, it's Raurin. May I speak with you."

"You may enter." The tall almost-balding young man entered the room.

"Dun Lain, I wish to speak with you before Namara arrives with your breakfast. I fear she would not let me get near this room if she weren't busy preparing your food."

"She is quite domineering and outspoken, isn't she."

"Yes, that she is." Malchom saw a slight glint in Raurin's eyes when he talked about her. This young man was indeed infatuated with the pretty and petite Namara. He chuckled to himself—*young man*! He kept forgetting that he looked no older than the man standing in front of him did. *I am a young man too!* "It's no doubt you heard at least some of that conversation outside."

"I heard, some."

"Jansen will not wait much longer. While I strongly support your looking to Kasparow for guidance, the rest of the village doesn't. Well, the rest of the village besides Namara. This is the first time we have agreed on anything since . . ."—he hesitated—"since she and my father married."

"And what would you have me do?"

"Namara has said that you told her that nothing should be done until you received a sign from Kasparow. If you wish to remain here and pray, fine, do so—in fact, I will join you if you like, and perhaps two voices would be better than one. But please do not forbid or scorn Jansen for sending a couple of men out to look for my father."

"I will not prevent you from doing as you or Jansen sees fit." An idea began to form in his mind; he would be able to use this *man's* desires against him quite easily. "But I do ask this of you. Give me until tomorrow morning before anything is done. By that time, if Kasparow has not answered me, I will assist you in any way I can. Do you think Jansen will agree to this?"

"He might, if Namara and I yell at him enough. I would be most honored for your help, in either case." Malchom walked away from the window and approached Raurin.

"Namara tells me that you have great faith in Kasparow and once had the desire to become a Dun Lian knight." Raurin's eyes widened a little in surprise.

"Uh, yes, my faith in Kasparow is unmatched by any within hundreds of miles, save for those of the Brotherhood, of course."

"Of course. That's good to hear. Why then did you never become a knight?"

"Well"—Raurin relaxed a little—"my father was never able to find a sponsor. He was just as willing to have a Dun Lian knight as a son as I was willing to join the Brotherhood. And then, his discovery with the mushrooms and the tea simply took up too much time. Now, of course, it's too late."

"Why do you say that?"

"Well, this year I will celebrate my twenty-second birthday. I'm a bit old for a squire."

"Nonsense. Age never really matters, it's what's in here that makes a knight." He tapped Raurin's chest. "And if your faith is as strong as you say it is, then neither Kasparow nor the Brotherhood will care that you are twenty-two."

"Malchom, I have your breakfast ready," Namara called softly from behind the door. Raurin was startled and looked to Malchom as if asking where to hide.

"Come on in, Namara," Malchom said, which further startled Raurin, sending him fleeing backward to hide behind the door as it opened. He held a finger to his lips, imploring Malchom to keep his presence secret.

"All I have had time to prepare was some more cold soup." Which she carried in one hand in a metal-handled porcelain pot. "I know you must be tiring of it by now, but I promise I will do better by you in the future."

"It'll be fine, Namara. Would you shut the door, I have something I wish to discuss with you," he said. She obeyed, which revealed a very embarrassed Raurin.

"Raurin! What are you doing in here! I told you Dun Lain needed to pray and meditate and was not to be disturbed. You just march yourself right on out—"

"Hold on, Namara," Malchom turned her around and took the pot from her hand, setting it on the floor. "Raurin is here to help me. And actually, I am going to help him." He smiled at Raurin, who began to relax. "Raurin, because of his great faith in Kasparow, is going to help me pray for guidance. Two voices would be better than one, after all."

"But wouldn't that be almost like committing sacrilege? I mean, he isn't a knight, he isn't even a squire. Wouldn't the Brotherhood, or even Kasparow, be upset if they knew? Won't Kasparow know?"

"Possibly, but as of this morning, Raurin has become my new squire. And as his first duty, he will help me pray to Kasparow." Raurin and Namara dropped their mouths in unison.

"I'm a . . . I'm a . . . ," stammered Raurin. "I'm to be your squire?"

"Yes, Raurin, you are to be my first squire. Now"—he hurried Namara out of the room—"Namara, go tell Jansen what has happened and that he should wait until tomorrow morning. And see to it that no one disturbs us today. Even for dinner, Raurin will be fasting, as is tradition during his first few days as a squire."

CHAPTER 13

Morgan picked his way slowly among the fallen walls and towers of the ruins. He was no expert, but judging by the state of decay and overgrowth, this castle had been in ruins for hundreds of years, at least. The complex was huge. Nearly all of the fallen stone was red, blue, white, or black Andonesian marble. Even now, with commerce and trading as popular as it was, this amount of Andonesian marble would have cost a fortune.

Wandering around, he began to get the feeling that there was more to the ruins than that which he could see. For an unknown reason, he felt as if he should be digging into the dirt, as if he should be going underground. But not here, somewhere else within the ruins. He could almost smell cold, stale air that was seeping up from below. It was a very distinct smell and drew him forward through the fallen marble and low-lying brush as if he were following a guide rope. Whenever he would turn in a wrong direction, the intensity of the smell would drop dramatically. Eventually, he came to a pile of fallen stone that had to be the source of the smell. There could be no mistake; it even seemed like he could *feel* the temperature difference surrounding the pile of rocks.

He set about removing the rubble. It was easy for his new body to move the somewhat-small rocks that made up this pile. It might be luck that all these rocks were small enough for him to move, but he began to suspect that someone had placed them here. After what seemed like hours, the sun had risen nearly to its apex in the sky. He was finally removing the last rocks from a very sturdy metal grate. The edges of the latticework were embedded into more Andonesian marble that formed a four-foot-wide shaft that descended into the darkness. Without thinking, he gripped the metal and pulled with all his strength. The old marble gave way rather easily and sent him sprawling backward. The metal grate landed next to him, scraping his upper arm and cutting through his tough skin. A little bit of blood trickled out of the small wound.

He scrambled to his feet and inched his way to the shaft. He was sure it was deep. Reaching the edge, he peered over and sniffed. Cold, stale, earthen-smelling air wafted upward out of the shaft. With this much of an updraft, there had to be another opening to whatever chambers lay below. He picked up a small rock and dropped it down the shaft and began counting. He counted several moments before it sent any noise back to his ears. This hole was quite deep. He had no way to get down it. The shaft was only four feet in diameter. He might be able to extend his arms and legs against the sides of the shaft and shimmy his way down the hole, but the real question was, could he get back up?

The force of the draft coming up the shaft convinced him to look for the other entrance. He wasn't even sure there was one; it just seemed to make sense to him that there was. After all, this was the ruined complex of a once-large castle. It was quite common for castles to have vast underground catacombs. Even the main Dun Lian stronghold Lianhome had several subterranean levels that he knew of. The problem was finding this other entrance; it might not be anywhere in the vicinity. It could be miles away from where he was now. He returned to searching the rubble.

The fox he had seen the previous night was nowhere to be found, yet he could still smell the animal. Perhaps the creature made its home amongst these fallen blocks of marble. The scent of the fox was not the only smell that was prominent in his nose. That unidentifiable smell he had come across last night was stronger than ever. He let his nose lead him around the ruins in search of that smell.

The only thing he ended up finding was a burrow that, judging by the strength of the smell, had to be the fox's home. The smells were strong and inviting. He stooped down between two large fallen pieces of marble that hid the entrance from plain view. With an ease that continued to astonish him, he lifted one of the broken and weathered pieces of marble and flung it aside. He put his nose to the exposed hole and sniffed several times. There was more than one animal down the hole. And they were shaking with fear. He could almost smell the vibrations their bodies made.

His clawed hands were digging in the dirt, and before he knew it, he had shoveled open a huge hole that led right into the fox's den. A female fox chattered and screamed at him, terrified, as she protectively stood over two small kittens. The animal's screeching pierced his hearing with a sharp pain. The smell coming from the three animals was too overpowering. He reached out, his hand darting forward faster than he thought possible and crushed the throat of the female fox. Before he could control what he was doing, he had shoved the fox's head into his mouth and had cracked the creature's skull in half with the strength of his jaws. His tongue scooped the tender brain out of its shell and lolled it into the back of his throat. Realizing what he was doing, he vomited, sending bile, blood, and brains spewing over the cowering kittens. He backed away from the kittens, out of the hole. Emerging into the warming afternoon air, he grabbed his backpack and sword, which, even though he had no recollection of doing so, he must have removed before entering the fox's den. He buckled his sword and slung the backpack over his shoulder and began running.

He ran for quite a while, only slowing to vomit when his thoughts brought the sight of the dead fox to mind. Each time he remembered what he had done, the vision of the fox's head seemed to get more vivid. The bits and pieces of soft brain matter mixed with foul-smelling bile splattered against the faces of the helpless kittens and dripped into pools of disgusting goo. The blood seemed to take on a vivid red color in his mind. He might not be able to actually see color, but it was plainly evident that his mind could remember what the color red looked like. These memories were too vivid to be real. They were haunting him, teasing him, punishing him for the vile act he had committed. For the first time since being freed from the gem, he prayed to Kasparow. He prayed as he ran and wondered why he had not prayed before. Surely, Kasparow would be his salvation.

The sun was casting long shadows when he finally came to a rest next to a fair-sized slowly moving stream. He collapsed at the edge of the stream and attempted to vomit once more. A small amount of stomach fluid was all that escaped his lips. His stomach was empty. It ached with hunger; which nearly made him vomit again.

There were a few fish swimming lazily in the calm water. It was easy for his quick hands to snatch a fat fish from the water. He could eat fish, he was sure of it. He just hadn't been thinking when he—the thought came back to him in a wave of nausea—when he had eaten the fox. It must have been some instinctual response to which his new body was accustomed.

He flung the flipping fish over his shoulder and proceeded to catch and fling several more before he bent over the stream and caught sight of his reflection in the stilling water. The ripples of his recent actions made his reflection waver like a flag flapping in the wind. For the first time, he saw the true hideousness of his new form. The image of the female came to mind. When he had first awakened in this new body and had been confronted by the female, he hadn't realized how terrifying he actually looked. He had seen the female and knew he looked the same, but it had never completely sunk in exactly how repulsive this new form was.

Even with his black-and-white vision, he could make out the distinct features of his new visage. His elongated head was topped with a knot of snarled dark hair. His multifaceted eyes bulged on a face barely covered with tight bump—and mole-ridden skin. Sharp and jagged teeth protruded from a lipless mouth. He brought a hand up to touch his teeth. His fingers were long and were jointed with grossly enlarged knuckles. Claws that looked as sharp as his teeth capped each of his fingers. Flicking his front teeth with a finger, he found out just how sharp they were. His finger was sliced open. A light-colored liquid oozed out of the cut finger. He wondered what color the blood would have been. Remembering his earlier wound at the ruins, he checked his shoulder.

The cut was gone! He was absolutely sure he had cut his shoulder. Yes, he *had* cut his arm; there were light-colored bloodstains running down his arm, originating from a spot that he knew was where the cut had been. But the cut wasn't there. It was completely healed; it didn't even hurt. He looked back to the cut on his finger and squeezed it with his other hand. A thin trickle of blood seeped out of the cut and quickly stopped. He watched for a while and was amazed to see the small, little cut actually close and heal rapidly on its own. His new body was continually finding ways of astounding him.

There was movement in the trees to his left. One of his eyes caught it. He turned and studied the tree line. A small rabbit hopped out of the underbrush and into view. At least he thought it was a rabbit, it was hard to tell—the creature's coloring blended well with the surrounding brush, at least to his colorless vision, anyway. He sniffed the air but could not catch the scent of the animal. The breeze must have been blowing in the wrong direction. He sniffed the air again and caught the rabbit's scent this time. The rabbit was calm. It had no idea a hideous creature was so near. Saliva dripped onto his hand. He was actually salivating.

The rabbit was squirming in his hands, screeching with a high-pitched, painful voice that nearly made him crush the small animal's head. He looked over his shoulder with one eye. The stream, where he last remembered being, was several feet behind him. Again, he had acted without thinking or his knowledge. At least this time, he had not eaten the furry little animal before being able to stop himself. He held the rabbit aloft by the scruff of its neck. It struggled furiously; fear oozed out from it and into his nose. He remembered his reflection in the stream.

Was this how people were going to treat him? Were they going to be terrified beyond action at the sight of him? Running away in terror, alienating him from his race? He remembered the dream he had recently. Some people had run at the sight of him; some people had gawked in morbid fascination. And some had wanted to kill him. He knew now that he could never show this face in any civilized area. The monster that he was, he would be hunted down and killed, almost for sport. By Kasparow, he might even become the focus of one of his brother's free deed quests.

He held the animal up to his eyes and studied it. It was a solid light color. Two big dark widely staring eyes were all that stood out about the creature. Its eyes were huge, almost unnaturally large, and he realized the thing was staring straight at him. His gaze seemed to calm the animal. Either that, or the thing became too terrified to move. No, the rabbit was not terrified. He would have smelled it if the rabbit were terrified. Instead, the animal seemed to be calm, almost mesmerized. He continued to study the little thing.

He laughed. It was a guttural sort of laugh, contained almost completely within his throat. His movement startled the rabbit. It started to squirm again. He held the rabbit up at eye level and stared at it. Almost immediately, it settled down, and the smell of fear left it. He turned his head away. The squirming resumed. He turned back to the rabbit, and it relaxed again. Was this gaze effect a natural ability of this body he now inhabited? Or was he simply dealing with a confused, weird rabbit? The powers this body had were amazing. With the strength, speed, healing, tracking, and calming gaze abilities he now had, he could go after Malchom quite easily. He even knew what Malchom smelled like. That unidentified smell at the campsite had to be Malchom's scent. He would hunt the bastard down and eat him.

Eat him? Where had that thought come from? He shivered, the rabbit squirmed. If he could not control these bizarre thoughts and violent actions, he was going to end up with a lot of problems. What was it about being in this body that made such things happen? He studied the rabbit some more, and it relaxed. Inside the brain of the little animal was the mind of a harmless creature incapable, he was sure, of conceiving of or acting out such violent thoughts. Inside the gem was the mind of a natural predator and killer that acted and thought violently out of instinct. And now, inside the brain of this monstrosity was the mind of a complex human creature that could not only act on violent impulses, but was also capable of formulating ways in which to use those violent abilities as a means to an end.

He shivered, breaking eye contact with the rabbit and sending it into a surge of helpless struggles. The thought of plopping this thing into his mouth and sucking its brains out may make him nauseous, but there was nothing wrong with having a little roasted rabbit for dinner. He unslung his backpack and upturned it with one hand, emptying the contents to the ground. Never taking his eyes off the rabbit, he picked up the bag containing the gem, untied the leather strips, opened it, and dumped the skull on the ground. He then shoved the stilled rabbit into the bag and retied it. He set the bag on the ground. After a few seconds, the movement inside the bag ceased. He decided that cooked fish and rabbit would make a fine dinner and set about gathering kindling and wood for a fire. It had been a hot, dry summer, and even here near this stream, there were plenty of drought-stricken grasses and plants that would catch a spark nicely.

While gathering wood, his gaze fell on the skull-encased gem several times. What would he do with the monster in the gem? He could leave it in there. But if he were to lose the gem for any reason and someone were to touch it not knowing what it could do? He didn't want to think what kind of mess such a creature would cause in human form. And what would he do with the gem? He had assumed he would keep it until he caught up with Malchom, but what then? He was *also* assuming that he would be *able* to use it to get his old body back, like Malchom would just stand there and let him use the thing. He didn't really have any idea how he was going to go about getting Malchom back into the gem. Well, of course, it had been less than twenty-four hours since his release from the gem. What should he do now?

This brought him back to the dilemma with the creature now trapped inside the gem. Jux must be having a fit with the new occupant, considering how much he seemed to dislike violence and evil. That monster's memories would fill Jux's time with thoughts of violence and killing, if you could consider things like that violent. Was it violent or evil when one killed out of instinct and a natural need to survive? Was what he had done to the fox violent and evil? He decided that after he ate, he would spend the remainder of the day praying to Kasparow for guidance. He realized that he still, despite being free of the gem, couldn't feel Kasparow's presence.

By the time he had used his knife and flint to start a good-sized fire, he decided to put the monster's mind into the body of one of the two animals he had at his disposal. The question now became which one, rabbit or fish? In the end, he decided on the rabbit simply because he was in a mood to eat fish. Besides, skinning the rabbit would be a lot more of a hassle than a couple of quick fish fillets. He gathered the almost-dead fish and piled them near the fire along with a long stick he had picked out on which to roast them.

Morgan unbuckled his sword and used it to nudge the skull closer to the fire. Grabbing the sack, he sat as close to the fire as he felt he comfortably could. He carefully pulled the wadded-up blanket remnants out of the hole in the bottom of the skull. The cavity inside the skull glowed with a light-colored light. He knew it was a green glow. It would be the same green glow he saw when he had first come in contact with the gem. He knew it was no more than a couple of months ago, but that incident seemed to have taken place years in the past. He had only been in this body for almost a day, but he was finding it hard to remember what it had been like to be in his real body.

Inside the skull was the gem. An emerald the size of a large man's fist, it would have been worth a small fortune as a simple gemstone. As it was, the power of the gem made it a priceless artifact. He could use the gem for a multitude of things. He could become anybody, as long as he was able to touch his intended victim with the gem. With Jux on the inside recording all of the occupants' memories, he could learn anything they knew. Of course, he would have to have someone he trusted help him. He would have to go back within the gem to have access to the new memories that Jux would have. Or would he? He suddenly remembered what had happened the previous night when he was attempting to learn the limits of his new body. He had been concentrating on looking at several different objects at one time. Somehow he had come in contact with Jux, or at least that's what it had seemed like. He could have sworn that he had heard Jux's disembodied voice talking to him.

Setting the skull on the ground, he propped it up with a mound of dirt so the hole that gave access to the inside was facing him. Quickly he removed the rabbit from the confines of his bag and stared at it briefly to calm it down. This ability still astounded him. Holding the rabbit over the skull, he slowly lowered the animal toward the gem. He would hold the rabbit's gaze, to make sure it didn't squirm and make him come in contact with the gem as he lowered a dangling paw to touch the emerald. A strange fear came over him, and he stopped what he was doing. Not taking his eyes off the rabbit, he slipped his right hand inside the sack and transferred the animal to the burlap-protected hand. He resumed lowering the rabbit toward the gem. He realized suddenly what an awful risk he was taking and watched the rabbit closely as he lowered it, one eye focused on the gem, guiding a single rear paw toward the emerald. Even though all of his eyes were not focused on the rabbit, it still did not come out of its trance.

He saw the paw touch the gem and felt the rabbit give a quick start as the transfer seemed to take place. He had no real way of knowing for sure but was confident that it had happened. The calmness of the entranced rabbit suddenly disappeared and was replaced with several different smells at once. The animal became terrified, lonely, confused, and as angry as a hornet's nest all at once. The thing snarled in a way that Morgan knew could not be natural, baring teeth that he never knew rabbits had. He dropped the animal and watched as it bounded awkwardly into the surrounding brush. He was sure the monster was now within the body of the rabbit. This brought him back to the gem. Now Jux would have a nearly-thoughtless rabbit's mind to keep him occupied. He almost felt remorseful for having put the mind of a rabbit in with Jux. But perhaps he *could* contact Jux. Perhaps through concentration and meditation he could reach within the gem and speak with him. He was apprehensive about making the attempt. What would happen if he made contact and it switched his soul again? The prospect of being trapped in the gem again was terrifying, especially considering that he knew Malchom would not simply sit by and grow old. The ancient wizard would, without a doubt, begin making sacrifices to Altair again. It was in his nature; it was all the wizard knew. And with the visage of a Dun Lian knight, he could do a lot of damage very quickly. Impulsively he decided he had to try and contact Jux. The memories Jux had stored within the gem would be invaluable to Morgan in his quest to reunite himself with his body.

Morgan adjusted the skull so that he had a good view of the gem through the hole in the bottom. He stoked the fire and backed away enough to ensure he would not come in contact with the skull or the gem just in case anything should happen. Clearing his mind as he would if he had been praying to Kasparow, Morgan let his body and thoughts relax. The image of the fox popped into his mind. He felt himself salivate. He forced the image away, disgusted, and it was replaced with the image of the rabbit. He was finding it hard to concentrate. Even more bizarre thoughts came to mind. He assumed they were basic thoughts and instincts of survival. He felt the desire to seek out a dark place and sleep. He felt the need to hunt down that rabbit. Morgan decided that he might have a better chance of concentrating after he ate and his stomach was satiated.

He picked the knife off the ground and filleted the fish he had caught sometime ago. He was getting used to using the knife with his clawed hands and quickly had a dozen or so decent-sized fillets in front of him. Grabbing the stick he had chosen earlier, he skewered a chunk of fish, squatted on his haunches, and held the fillet over the fire. The meat sizzled and popped as it began to cook. The smell reached his nose, and he found that it did not smell as inviting as he thought it would to his starved senses. He remembered how vile the cooked meat of the female had tasted and wondered if this fish was going to turn out the same way. The raw meat certainly hadn't tasted bad. He shivered. The idea that raw meat was the only thing that his sense of taste would find appealing mortified him at the same time that it made his mouth water. He was having a hard time dealing with this apparent duplicity to his thoughts and actions. It had to be a result of being within this new body.

When he was satisfied the fish was sufficiently cooked, he removed it from the stick, allowed it to cool for a while, then placed it on his knee. It was hot, still too hot for his skin. He smacked it quickly to the ground and, considering his earlier discomfort with fires, came to the conclusion that his new body did not tolerate heat or flame very well. He wondered how many more things there were for him to discover about this body.

When the fried fish fillet was fully cooled, he took a bite. There was dirt on it, but he didn't seem to mind. It wasn't the worst thing he had tasted, but for some reason, he knew it would taste better uncooked. He discarded the burned fish and devoured the rest of the raw fillets. Emotionally, he could handle eating raw fish. His stomach wasn't full, and he was by no means satiated, but he did begin to feel much better. Turning back to the gem, Morgan cleared his mind once again.

This time he locked all of his eyes on the gem and visualized it as best as he could within his mind. Concentrating, he tried to remember what it felt like to be within the gem, or at least, what the complete lack of sensory input had been like. He remembered Jux's voice and the almost tingling he experienced when Jux would sift through his mind. He brought all of his Dun Lian—trained meditation techniques to bear and continued to concentrate on contacting Jux. His vision blurred, tunneled down to a point that the light-colored gem was all that registered in his brain. Color exploded in his mind. The same shade of green he knew to belong to the gem flooded his thoughts. He thought he was hopping out of some overly large vegetation when he was suddenly lifted up by the neck and held aloft high in the air, staring at his own ugly face.

"Morgan, is that you?" It was Jux's voice.

"Yes," he replied.

"How did you get back into the gem?" The image faded.

"I don't know, am I truly in the gem?"

"You must be, I can hear your thoughts. How else would that happen if you had not returned?" Morgan felt the familiar tingling as Jux began to look through his mind.

"Do you remember me contacting you briefly a short while ago?"

"Yes, I was examining the thoughts of this most bizarre creature when I thought I sensed your mind."

"I was concentrating on the emerald, and I think my mind briefly touched the gem. That led me to believe that it might be possible for me to contact you."

"Really? Let me see, show me the memory."

"No. First, I want to make sure I'm not stuck in here. I have to try to leave." Without another thought, he attempted to break off his meditation, to sever the contact he believed he had established. Nothing happened. He could sense Jux going through his mind. "Please don't! I have to know if I can get out of here." The sensation stopped. He concentrated again on severing the contact, tried to imagine the connection was cut. Again, nothing. He was getting excited, almost frantic. He continued to try; he *would not* get stuck in here again. Eventually, Jux interrupted him.

"You are attempting to break the connection by thinking it were so. I do not think that will work. Thinking and thoughts are things of this gem. Try concentrating on things of your other world." Without transition, he tried to move. The green in his mind wavered. He tried to taste the lingering flavor of fish he knew to be in his mouth; the green flickered on and off. He tried to remember the taste of the fox's brains and became nauseous as his colorless sight abruptly returned, sending him sprawling backward. An intense pain lanced through his skull. His head throbbed. Lightning seemed to be shooting in front of his eyes. It was a while before he felt strong enough to move. He stood up and looked around him. The fire was nearly all embers. The sun had just disappeared behind the tree line. Several hours had passed, but he was out, and he was safe.

He sat on his haunches in front of the gem. He was elated. He unconsciously started making a clicking sound in the back of his throat. Another strange quirk of this body, he thought. This ability was going to be extremely helpful to him. Hopefully the pain was not going to be a regular part of the experience although he could get used to that. He turned the skull around so he couldn't see the gem and tried again. Clearing his mind, he thought of Jux. He made the connection almost immediately this time.

"I see that it works," said Jux.

"Yes it does," he said happily.

"Will you allow me to go through your thoughts now that you know you can leave at any time? It would make it easier for me to understand what has happened."

"Of course." Morgan cleared his mind and brought up the memory of his first leaving the gem. It took on a life of its own as Jux replayed it.

"Something does not seem right."

"What do you mean?"

"I am not sure, exactly, but it seems as if your mind is not what it used to be."

"How so?"

"I do not know. It is almost as if you have lost some of your intelligence."

"Could it be because of the body I'm in now?"

"I do not know." The buzzing sensation increased as Jux tugged at his memories. The tug became a pull. The pull continued faster and faster. The pulling intensified into a rushing stream and was beginning to become painful. Jux sensed Morgan's discomfort and stopped. "You are experiencing pain?"

"Yes, a little."

"That must be because you now have a physical body. When you were in here before you had no body with which to feel pain, now you do."

"Is there any way to get around it?" Morgan asked.

"Well, I could take the memories from you slowly so as to cause as little discomfort as possible. Or I could take the memories all at once. There would be pain, but it would be over with quickly."

"Almost like tearing a scab away." He thought for a moment. "Well, several hours had passed when I was in here the last time. I don't feel comfortable sitting in the open like I am. Who knows what might come along? What I don't need right now is to be put back into this thing for real. Go ahead, take it all at once." He cleared his mind and steeled himself for the pain that was about to come. He felt Jux grab hold of his mind. The pain that followed was greater than any he had experienced before. He passed out.

When he regained consciousness, he found himself lying on the ground. He was extremely hot. He opened his eyes and was blinded by a noonday sun. He was too weak to move. Had he passed out for a day? Or perhaps longer? His head was throbbing. What was it Jux had said about becoming more stupid? It certainly was stupid to let Jux take everything at once. He was in the middle of nowhere. Who did he think was going to bother a monster like him way out here? He curled up into a ball and attempted to sleep, which he couldn't. His huge, lidless eyes continually brought light into his brain. He doubted he would ever be able to sleep during the day in this body. It was a couple of hours later that he finally felt well enough to pick himself off the ground and stagger over to the dead fire.

Everything was as he had left it, except for the discarded charred fish. A single corpsefly had found and quickly devoured it. It was bloated and unmoving. At any time now, the fly's children, squirming hungry larvae, would eat their way out of the fly's abdomen and consume their parent. He wondered how long the larvae would survive if he took them away from the fly as they emerged from its abdomen. They could then be force-fed to an enemy. One might not do much damage, just enough to cause pain before it was digested. Putting several into a victim's stomach would definitely be painful.

Morgan shook his head and forced the vile thought from his mind. He went to the stream and waded in. The cool water felt good, very good. Its chilling temperature invigorated him. He could feel his heartbeat rise; he felt the blood surging through his veins. His nostrils flared. He breathed deeply. He seemed to be more alive, more aware than he had been since he was released from the gem. In fact, he didn't think he ever felt this alive. It was as if the cold water intensified his senses. He found a very deep section of the stream and spent some time swimming. He found that his oversized hands and feet made him excellently suited to the water. He was even able to remain submerged for a remarkable amount of time. His black-and-white vision didn't even seem to hamper him that much. Emerging from the water, he felt a new energy, a new desire to get done what he had to get done. He saw the skull resting on the ground next to the dead fire. He wondered how far away from the gem he could be and still make contact.

Deciding to find out, he sat with his back to the slow-moving stream and attempted to contact Jux. After several minutes, he moved a few feet closer and tried again. It wasn't until he had moved to within ten feet that he seemed to pass over an invisible line. He felt calm. Was this an effect of the gem? He stepped backward, out of range, then forward again. Each time he passed that boundary, his thoughts seemed to become clearer. Finally he made contact with Jux.

"What have you figured out?" he asked.

"Well, I have been carefully examining what I pulled from you recently and comparing it to what I knew of you from before. It seems that the actual amount or potential for thought diminished when you voluntarily left the first time, that time when you would not let me view your mind for fear that something on the outside might happen."

"You mean the first time that I felt pain leaving."

"Yes. Here." Jux played the memory. "This is the time, I mean. By the way, do you feel pain now, since you have a physical body to experience pain, when I replay that memory?"

"No, not physically, not like I did that first time, at least. And definitely not like the last time."

"Well, that would lead me to believe that something happened during that first time you tried to voluntarily and forcefully leave the gem, almost as if you sacrificed part of your mind for the ability to be able to do so. I think you should try and leave again, to see if this happens every time. If it does, I would not suggest contacting me again. You could end up becoming too stupid to function."

"You might be right. But do you realize what a powerful tool and weapon this gem would become if I could come and go as I please?"

"Yes, I do. You forget that I know everything you know."

"Oh yeah. Well then, if you think it would be best to try—"

"You know I do. You forget that you also know everything I know. And by the way, I would like to thank you for getting rid of that vile creature. His thoughts were quite interesting but altogether too primitive. Not that the new occupant of the gem is any great conversationalist, but I think it was the right thing to do. You were right, you could not take the chance of that primal, naturally evil, instinctually driven monster ending up in the body of a sentient being."

"Which brings up another point. I have been having these very bizarre thoughts and uncontrolled actions now that I inhabit this body."

"Who knows what kind of effect that creature's instinctual thought patterns will have on your mind. I will endeavor myself to studying the possibilities. For now, I think you should leave."

"But for you to be able to figure anything out, won't I have to leave and then come back again?"

"Yes, I guess you would. I do not think *you* would be able to analyze the differences of your past and present mind."

"Well then, here goes." He thought of the physical world and attempted to break the contact.

"You're trying to think the connection severed again," interrupted Jux.

"Sorry." He tried to stand. And was back in his body, standing about ten feet from the skull, no pain, no discomfort. That was a relief. Now to go back in. Experimentally, he took two steps backward and sat. Almost as soon as he thought about contacting Jux, he found himself back in the gem.

"Now just remain silent and let me look through your mind." Morgan felt his mind being sifted through. There was a little discomfort, but Jux was taking his time. Morgan could see what Jux was looking at and what things he was comparing. Jux was right. Morgan never would have compared the images that Jux was.

"There doesn't seem to be any further degradation from that first incident. I think the gem ate some of your mind. It needed something of yours permanently here to allow this access you now have."

"But aren't all my memories already here, with you?"

"Yes, but I am a separate entity from the gem. Memories are one thing. The gem seems to have actually *taken* some of your intelligence to fuel this connection."

"Will it happen again? I mean, will this gem keep taking my mind from me?"

"It is hard to say. I did not find any evidence of it with your most recent traveling to and from the gem. If you continue to come and go, I will continue to monitor your progress as best I can. There is another thing that I have discovered, however. While you have lost a certain amount of intelligence, you seem to have acquired *more* intelligence."

"What? I've *gained* intelligence? How can I lose and gain it at the same time?"

"Well, it is not as if you lost an arm and then grew one back. You lost intelligence, became a little less smart, but you seem to have gained other abilities. You lost an arm but then grew two tentacles. Is that clear?"

"I've become stupider but gained new abilities? What kind of abilities?"

"Mental abilities. There is only one that I am sure of, but there seem to be more that I cannot identify."

"When I was holding that rabbit in my hands, I seemed to be able to calm it, or charm it by staring at it, is this what you mean?"

"No, that is a natural ability of the body you now have. I can let you into the mind of that creature at a later time. There are several significant things you need to know about that body. These abilities do not seem to have anything to do with your new body. I think they have manifested themselves as a result of your traveling to and from the gem.

"Ages ago, this gem was constructed specifically to house the soul of the dragon Durgolais. It was formed to hold the mind of a dragon, and while Durgolais was imprisoned for only a short while, his mind profoundly shaped the very nature of this gem. Another dragon sacrificed himself to free Durgolais and was imprisoned here for a *very* long time, so I have a large amount of knowledge on dragons.

"Dragons are natural telepaths. They are able to communicate over any distance with other telepaths. Even the isolated world of this gem poses no boundaries for telepathic thought. Durgolais might have been imprisoned within the gem, but he was able to communicate with his brood and coordinate a *rescue* attempt, if you will."

"That was a big mistake on someone's part."

"The creators of the gem obviously did not know the extent of a telepath's powers. I doubt they would have left Durgolais the ability to communicate with others of his kind if they had."

"Are you telepathic?" Morgan asked.

"No. And I do not think I can become telepathic, either, since I have no *real* intelligence to speak of. It seems that while consciousness may be an aspect of having a soul, intelligence is an aspect of having brain matter."

"So you have a soul."

"I have a portion of all the souls that have been imprisoned here."

"Back to these new mental abilities. You're saying that I'm now telepathic?"

"Yes, as far as I can tell, you have the same telepathic ability that Durgolais had."

"And is Malchom telepathic?"

"I do not know. I cannot be sure, but I do not think so."

"What makes you say that?"

"Because this is the first time that anyone has ever *tried* to use the telepathic nature of the gem to come and go."

"So if Malchom tries, he might be able to contact you as I have?"

"That remains to be seen."

"Well then, I'd better keep the gem away from him."

"For some reason, I cannot see Malchom ever wanting to come near this gem again."

"Not unless he realizes it potential. So I can mentally contact other telepaths?"

"You can also contact nontelepaths, but that takes a great amount of energy and would usually drain the sender of just about all his strength. I have a few memories of Durgolais doing so and barely being able to move for a few minutes."

"How is it done? Do you think I can do it when I am in my own body, or do I need to be within the gem?"

"If you are now a telepath, you should be able to do it in your . . ."—Jux hesitated—"*new* body just as easily as while in here. As to how to go about accomplishing a successful transmission, simply concentrate on the person you want to contact. If you make contact, you should be able to sense the other's mind, almost as if you were hearing an echo of their thoughts. When that happens, simply think of the images that you wish the other to know. You can even send entire memories if you wish. The better you know the person you are attempting to contact, the easier it is to make that contact."

"What else, you said you thought there might be more?"

"Well, dragons also have the ability to charm intelligent beings into doing what they want, as long as the being in question can understand the language being spoken. It is not a calming type of charm like the ability your new body has, but an actual mental charm. The charmed person basically becomes your best friend. It is amazing what kind of suggestions you can give to someone willing to do anything for you."

"Is that all?"

"Dragons also have a very powerful thought shield to protect against such mental attacks. From what I know, once this shield is in place, it remains there unless consciously taken down. You simply need to will it into being. You will not feel any different once it is in place so I do not know how you can be sure it is there short of being mentally attacked."

"Anything else?"

"That is all of the dragonlike abilities that you seem to have, but as I said, I sense that there are more that I cannot identify. Perhaps they are a part of the Mottapplan body you now possess."

"Mottapplan? Is that what this thing is called?"

"That is what it calls itself. The Mottapplans are close relatives of the G'Angeleppans. You are familiar with the G'Angeleppans, are you not?"

"You know I am," he said jovially. "Remember, I know everything you know," Jux continued without a pause. Obviously, the humor did not reach him.

"From Malchom's *memories*, I gather that you might know it as a troll." Jux brought up several images of trolls. The memories seemed to be from a couple of different beings. "It seems that several of the past occupants had experiences with trolls."

"So I'm a troll. I've never seen one before. Well, not until yesterday. Not before that female . . . Jux, I've done some very vile things the past day or two."

"I know. Remember, I know everything you know."

"I've been having a hard time controlling these urges that seem to come with this body."

"There is no telling what kind of effect being in that body will have on your mind. Certainly, there are some amounts of instinctual responses associated with every living creature. I would not be surprised if you eventually overcome these. As a matter of fact, I think you should see some of these images that I have from the troll's mind." Jux played a series of memories for him. Morgan stopped them every once in a while and would replay a certain memory to make sure he got the meaning right. In the end, he learned a lot about his new body.

Mottapplans were somewhat of a subterranean race, preferring to live in caves and only venturing out during the evening hours to hunt for food. Even though they were semi-intelligent, they ate only raw meat and thoroughly despised and shunned away from any other form of nourishment. They remained underground during the day due to their natural aversion to light and heat. They preferred the cold depths of caves and were very uncomfortable when exposed to the warmth of the sun. Fire was horrible to them, as he could guess by his reaction to the two fires he had been near the past day and a half. It seems they would venture near fire only if their life depended on it, that or if a choice piece of meat was to be had. Except for being burned, any physical injury they suffered healed incredibly fast, sometimes visibly. As he already knew, they—*he* was very strong and had extremely quick reflexes. His black-and-white vision, separated into twelve distinct images, could, with complete concentration, be focused on up to nine different things. Not only that, but his many-faceted, lidless eyes held the ability to confuse dim-witted smaller animals if he remained still, or at best moved very slowly. This trait was useful for sneaking up on tasty prey.

"I see what you mean about not being able to control these instincts," Jux said. "Perhaps returning to your Dun Lian regiment of prayer and meditation will help."

"I have been meaning to pray to Kasparow. Surely, he can help me. It's strange, I kept thinking that I would sit down and pray to Kasparow, but then I would completely forget about it. I wonder if that's a result of my lost intelligence?"

"More likely, it is a result of your situation. There was a lot for you to absorb in a very short amount of time. Or it could again be a result of being in your new body."

"I haven't felt Kasparow's presence at all in this new body. I know I haven't really tried praying to him yet, but it is still disconcerting to not feel His presence."

"Kasparow may be closed to you now."

"What?"

"Well, think about it. You now inhabit the body of a creature that is inherently evil in nature. Thoughts emanating from you are, at the very least, going to be tainted with that evil. Which, most likely, Kasparow will ignore. On the other hand, it could get His attention, prayers for help from an evil creature. You will never know until you try to contact Him. Perhaps that should be your first order of business."

"My first order of business will be getting my body back. I don't even want to begin to think what Malchom might be doing with it. He will suffer once I catch him."

"How so? You can't harm him, you need your body back."

"I can put him into the body of a fish, then serve him up cold with some nice Chunyan sea spices. He would be quite tasty."

"I think perhaps you should spend some time praying to Kasparow. This vengeful streak does not strike me as typical behavior for a Dun Lian knight."

"You're right. I can't believe that body is affecting me like this, even in here. As my sponsor, Dun Loren, liked to say, *If you can't be*—wait a minute, I'm now telepathic, right?"

"Yes."

"And I can, even if it is with difficulty, contact nontelepaths."

"Correct."

"Then why don't I contact Dun Loren? You said the better I knew someone, the easier it would be to contact that person. I can think of no one that I know better than Dun Loren."

"And by contacting him, you can let someone within the Brotherhood know what has happened."

"And possibly apprehend Malchom if he shows his face, *my face*, anywhere."

"That does sound like a prudent thing to do."

"So how do I do it?"

"Just think of the person in question and concentrate as hard as you can about contacting him." Morgan stilled his thoughts and brought up an image of Dun Loren. He was surprised to find the image to be from his first meeting with Dun Loren. Morgan was preparing a display at the front of his father's shop when the knight had entered. The morning sun was behind Dun Loren, and the light bounced off his armor so brilliantly that Morgan was sure he was an angel, or an avatar at the least. He concentrated on that image as hard as he could and thought of contacting Dun Loren. There was a brief flash and a quick, sharp pain that was over too quick to bother him.

The image he held in his mind shifted slightly. Dun Loren was still there, radiating light. He was still standing in the doorway of his father's shop in Rivingwyre but superimposed behind the knight was a desolate landscape. The land behind Dun Loren was barren, cracked dirt as far as the eye could see. He was standing at the edge of a motionless black lake. In his hands was a suit of armor that looked familiar. The blond-haired knight was getting ready to toss the exquisitely crafted suit of mail into the water. Morgan knew where Dun Loren was. He was at the Dead Pools. Morgan tried to speak out to the knight.

"Dun Loren, Dun Loren, this is Dun Lain . . ." Dun Loren turned and looked at him, at least it seemed like he was looking at him.

"Morgan, stop," came a faint voice. Dun Loren's lips moved slightly. Morgan couldn't be sure it was Dun Loren who had spoken.

"Dun Loren?"

"Morgan, stop now." This time the voice was louder. It was Jux's voice he heard. He felt a little discomfort when Jux spoke. "MORGAN, STOP WHAT YOU ARE DOING NOW!" The discomfort broke his concentration and brought him back into the familiar green haze his thoughts had while inside the gem.

"Why did you stop me? I did it, why did you stop me? It was Dun Loren's mind I contacted. I know where he is. I think he's looking for me."

"You are right. I think you did contact Dun Loren, but when you did, I could sense something going wrong. Once you made contact, you started losing memories. Something was darting around your mind draining you of your intelligence.'

"What? So even though you say I'm now telepathic, to use the power I have would let some unseen force dance around my head and eat away at my mind?"

"It should not happen this way. My memories from Durgolais gave no insight that this would happen. It could be because you were trying to contact a nontelepath. That sort of contact was physically draining for Durgolais. You are not a true telepath, and perhaps that kind of contact needs a different type of fuel to power."

"How much did I lose?"

"That is uncertain, but I felt it prudent to stop you before any real damage was done."

"But I was about to make contact with Dun Loren. A few seconds of brain drain would be worth being able to let him know what is going on."

"I at least thought you should know what was happening. If you choose to continue now that you know the risk, then please do so. I just thought you should know."

"What's a few more childhood memories compared to getting back into my own body before it's too late?" Even when he did contact Dun Loren, he began to think that the knight might not believe what he was being told. Morgan tried to clear his thoughts for another attempt and concentrated on making telepathic contact. He would need Dun Loren's help. Even if he didn't believe what his mind would be hearing, at least the knowledge of what was happening would be there. Sooner or later, Dun Loren would come to believe it. Dragons and trolls, Morgan wondered how many more surprises were in store for him before this was all over. To imagine that a dragon dead several thousand years would be so capable of hurting him was nearly beyond him. An image from his dream came to mind. Durgolais' massive face was staring at him, superimposed over his dream. That face had spoken to him in his dream. It had asked him to choose. Morgan had only the vaguest idea between what he was supposed to choose. It seemed as if Durgolais had been the mediator. In one of the dragon's outstretched hands was Dun Loren and in the other was Malchom. Morgan was standing in the center looking from Malchom to Dun Loren and back again when Durgolais had spoken.

"Who are you?" No, the dragon hadn't asked that.

"Morgan, be careful," came Jux's voice. Durgolais had simply said *Choose.*

"Again, WHO ARE YOU?" Morgan felt a familiar pull at his mind. It was the tingling he felt when Jux would search his mind for specific memories, but this felt slightly different.

"Morgan, you must stop—" The discomfort ripped into pain. He threw his hands to his head in an attempt to stifle the pain. Almost passing out due to the intensity of the pain, he looked around him and realized that he was back in his body, his new body. That pain must have severed his connection with the gem. It was dark out, nearly midnight, as far as he could tell; he must have been within the gem for at least twelve hours.

With a throbbing head, he rose and stumbled to the stream and jumped in. The cool water felt good against his skin. It made him urinate. This was the first time he had relieved himself since becoming a troll, probably due to all of his vomiting. He swam for a while. His head was clearing. The coolness of the water seemed to revitalize him.

So what had just happened? He was about to attempt to contact Dun Loren again and was thinking of his dream. Then all of a sudden, Jux had begun to speak to him, asking him who he was and telling him to be careful, then he had begun sifting through his mind. No, there had been *two* voices, and it wasn't Jux who had gone through his thoughts—at least it hadn't felt like Jux.

Morgan Mclain." There was no sound to the voice, but it boomed inside his head. He was underwater when the voice cascaded around his thoughts; he nearly gulped in cold stream water in surprise. Breaking the surface, he looked around him. There was no one. Why should there be? That voice had been inside his head.

"Morgan Mclain." The voice was very familiar. The voice seemed to lay itself over his thoughts. This must be another telepath trying to contact him.

"Yes," he thought, trying to project his thoughts to whomever was contacting him. There was no reply.

"I don't understand this," said the voice. He was sure he knew whom it belonged to; it sounded so familiar. Only, *something* was not quite the same. "A moment ago, you contacted me telepathically, and yet now I find that you are not telepathic." The voice seemed tired, almost exhausted. "I will have to search your mind further." Pain returned as Morgan felt a powerful mind ripping through his thoughts. He could feel the strength the mind possessed. With great difficulty, Morgan made his way to the edge of the stream and climbed up the embankment. With his head painfully beating with the force of a blacksmith's hammer, it was nearly impossible to climb the muddy stream bank. The pain continued as the unseen mind delved deeper into his thoughts. Finally he flopped onto the ground. Barely able to move or think, the pain paralyzed him. *Not a telepath?* he thought.

The presence in his mind abruptly vanished. The sudden removal of pain released him. He took a deep breath. Not a telepath? Then how had he been able to contact Dun Loren? Jux had said that he was a telepath, or at least had telepathic ability. Jux had also said that he was not a natural telepath. Perhaps . . . Jux! That was it! The gem was too far away from him. If he couldn't contact the gem from a distance, then maybe he couldn't use its powers from a distance either. Struggling, he stood and walked toward the skull. As he approached the gem, he seemed to pass a threshold. His mind cleared a little, the throbbing in his head lessened a bit. He was about fifteen feet from the skull-encased emerald. Experimentally he took a couple of paces backward and felt it as he passed over an unseen border. His thoughts clouded, and the thumping in his head grew louder. His range was growing. Before, he had to be within ten feet to feel that calming effect.

He moved to the dead fire and began gathering his things. He had spent over half a day in conversation with Jux. Time seemed to move very quickly while he was inside the gem. If he was going to research these powers further, he decided it would be best to do it at a more secure place. When he had finished packing everything else away, he carefully put his sack over the skull and securely tied it off before placing it in his backpack. He picked his sword up and buckled it to his belt. Now where would be a good place to rest?

"And now, you are telepathic. Interesting. I had not realized that the gem had been found." The voice was back. "You are Dun Lain, of the Dun Lian Brotherhood. Well, maybe not a knight any longer, considering you are now a *troll*." Morgan could sense the humor in the other's thoughts. "How is it that you were not telepathic moments ago and now are?" Morgan thought of his experiment a few minutes ago. "Ah, I see. This gem is quite interesting, indeed."

"Who are you? Where are you?" he thought.

"Ah, that is much better. Please, keep that gem near you. It is much easier for me to converse with you while you are telepathic."

"What did you do to me earlier?"

"Well, when you would not answer me, I simply took the memories necessary to figure out what was going on. As for your other two questions, you know who I am. At least your supposition is correct, though you have not figured it out yet. As to where I am, I am many miles south of you, near the Chunya Sea." Morgan knew he knew the voice but still couldn't place it.

"Chunya Sea? But that's hundreds of miles from here."

"Ah yes, well, distance matters not to true telepaths. It seems you are somewhat of a hybrid. That gem has conferred certain powers to you. It has been a while since I have seen it. If *you choose to do so*, why don't you bring it to me?" The words were heavy, thick, almost as if they had substance. They echoed in his mind. He moved forward slightly. *Choose?*

"You're Durgolais!" He wondered if he could shout telepathically.

"Yes, I am Durgolais, and yes, you can shout telepathically. There is a lot you can do, a lot you can learn. You will have my help *if you so choose. I will show you the true path to follow.*" Again the words weighed him down. He felt the need to start walking. "I can teach you much. Why don't you come to me and learn?"

"I . . ."—Morgan stumbled over his thoughts—"I don't know where you are."

"You will find me. *If you so choose, you will find me, you will come to me.*" The words were confusing him. He was having a hard time concentrating. Several images were placed in his mind. "That will show you how to get to me. Why don't you come to me and learn?"

Morgan studied the images. He saw enormous mountains towering majestically on the edge of a large landlocked sea. He was rushing over the water, flying at an incredible speed toward the mountains in front of him. Several cave openings appeared in the mountainside. Flying closer and closer, he was drawn to one that was all but submerged in the dark water of the sea. He knew where this was, where it had to be. This sea was too large to be anything other than the Chunya Sea. And those mountains were too immense to be anything other than the Majestics. He flew into the cave and plunged into the dark water.

"Now why don't you come and find me?" Morgan started running.

CHAPTER 14

"It was a dream," He said as he tossed a piece of wood on the fire. "I know it was a dream. At least, most of it was a dream. The other part seemed different."

"Who cares about the other part, why were you throwing my armor into the lake?"

"Like you said, it was just a dream. But that other part, I know he spoke to me."

"It's this place—it's evil, it's meddling with your mind." He grabbed another piece of wood and stirred the burning logs so that the fresh wood would lie as flat as possible. "Manney, put that pot on the fire," barked Dun L'lsen. He stood and turned to Dun Loren. "You ready for some tea? I brought a small amount of Chunyan Red for just this sort of gloomy morning."

"I wish you hadn't started that fire, I was actually thinking of packing up and getting back to Justin and Clerents. And I would have liked to have been able to look at that raft once in the daylight before you had Manney chop it into kindling."

"Relax, Dun Loren. The only clues the boat held are right here." Dun L'lsen pointed to a few chunks of withered, dry meat of some sort and a length of leather line with a coin tied to the end.

The big, muscular knight was right, of course. They had spent nearly a day walking from the edge of the woods to where they were now camped, on the edge of one of the Dead Pools. It would have been faster to ride, but their mounts had been pushed too far already, and besides, they became terrified to the point of fleeing as soon as they took two steps toward the Dead Pools. Dun Loren had heard of the bleakness of this place, but its effect on the horses took him completely by surprise. He left Clerents and Justin behind to take care of the animals.

He, Dun L'lsen, and Manney had continued on foot. It wasn't difficult to find Morgan's trail. Without the cleansing effect of rain, the packed dirt held a clear path to follow. Morgan had dragged something from the edge of the woods straight to the lake where they now were. Halfway to the lake, they discovered the carcass of Morgan's horse. Dun Loren had no doubt, by the reaction of his own horse, that Morgan's animal had simply died of fright. This place was barren of animals. Birds, jackals, there were no predators or scavengers around to disturb Morgan's fallen mount. Even corpseflies refused to live in this place. As a result, the animal was in nearly the same condition it had been when it died. It was dried and slightly shriveled from the heat and sun but was otherwise a perfect specimen to be examined. Morgan had evidently used his dead horse to restock his food supply. This explained the dried meat they had found. The boat explained the trail they were able to follow from the forest.

Nothing explained what had happened here or where Morgan might have gone. It was obvious, from the murders, where he ended up, but was that farmhouse his next stop from this point? Dun Loren was sure this lake held the key, but the question was what door did that key open?

"Manney, quit dallying around and put the water on the boil." Dun Loren noticed that the boy was hunched over the partially destroyed boat, a small axe in one hand. The boy wasn't moving. He was probably asleep. Dun L'lsen had been merciless the past day, forcing the boy to carry all of their supplies.

"I think we should pack up and leave. There is nothing more to be found here."

"Nonsense, Dun Loren. Come on, Manney. I for one would like to have hot tea with my breakfast. I think all of us could do with something hot to eat before we trek back across this Kasparow-forsaken place." Dun Loren was finding it hard to openly agree with anything Dun L'lsen said. This knight was becoming more and more irritating every day, but food would do them all a world of good. Dun L'lsen moved to his squire. "Come on, boy, there's work to be done. You do want to eat, don't you?" Dun L'lsen patted the boy's back roughly.

"No," the boy said, just before vomiting violently. "I . . . don't . . . feel good," he said shakily between retching.

"Oh my, looks like that cold has come back, Dun Loren." Something caught the big knight's attention, and he moved around to the other side of the boat. Dun Loren was amazed at Dun L'lsen's lack of compassion for Manney. He went to help the boy.

"Manney, are you okay?" Manney retched.

"Does it look like I'm—" He retched again. The boy was burning up and sweating profusely. Dun L'lsen's manners were rubbing off on the boy. Dun Loren took the axe from his hand and guided him to the fire. He placed a bota bag in the squire's hands.

"Drink, all of it." There was a slight odor about the boy. It was a putrid, sick smell. It was on Dun Loren's hands. He went back to the boat. Dun L'lsen was on his knees examining the ground near the dank water. Was he sniffing the dirt? The boat smelled as well. Why hadn't he noticed this before? It was a smell of death. If the boat smelled of it, then it must have come from the water. That in and of itself wasn't surprising for this place. And Manney must have picked up the smell from working with the wood. Could this be what had made the boy sick? Could the dank water of this lake carry some disease? Was it possible that the overwhelming sense of death this place exuded had entered Manney through the water? Could this be what had happened to Morgan?

"Dun Loren, come here." Had Dun L'lsen found something? "Careful, walk around this spot." He pointed to the ground. "I don't want you to mess up the tracks. It looks as if Morgan went into the water."

"What?"

"There are tracks here, leading into the water, and tracks there." He pointed again. "Leading out of the water." Dun Loren squatted.

"I see nothing."

"Trust me, they're there."

"Dun L'lsen, do your hands smell?"

"Yes, they reek of death. This whole place reeks of death. Are you just now noticing?"

"*Yes*, I am just noticing. That smell is all over the boat. It's on Manney, and now that I have touched Manney, it is all over my hands. Whatever comes in contact with that water gets that smell and transfers it to anything else it touches, like the wood, then Manney—"

"And now Manney is violently ill." As if to echo the statement, Manney retched again. "I see what you are getting at, but you're not sick, I'm not sick, and we both reek of it."

"Perhaps Kasparow's grace protects us. Manney hasn't come out yet. He wouldn't have that protection."

"So you're thinking that if this water could make Manney sick, then perhaps the same thing happened to Morgan."

"It would seem logical."

"But Morgan is a full Dun Lian knight—he *has* come out. He *does* have the grace of Kasparow's presence and protection."

"Yes, but as you just pointed out, he went *into* the water. Direct and overwhelming contact with the stuff might be too much for even Kasparow's grace to protect against, especially in one who had just recently come out, like Morgan."

"It would make sense, except for the fact that Manney isn't trying to cut our bowels out. He's just trying to vomit his out."

"But he didn't go for a swim in the stuff. Besides, if the evil of this place does enter the body through the water, who knows where it will lead?"

"Well then, I guess we have our lead. Morgan stumbled into the water, became *infected*, stumbled out of the water here, stopped at the boat, and headed off in that direction. It looks as if he went straight to the trees. I'll follow his trail. You and Manney, go get your squires and the horses and then follow the tree line south. We should be able to meet up where Morgan entered the woods."

Dun Loren looked at Manney. The boy was motionless. He looked catatonic. "Actually, I think Manney should be taken back to Panadar, I don't think *we* can do anything for him, and if the same thing happens to him that we think happened to Morgan, it would be better if he were surrounded by a host of knights and priests."

"You're right about that." He thought for a moment then stood. "We'll have your squires take him back. You and I will continue after Morgan." The big knight's insensitivity was finally too much for Dun Loren to take. He stood and confronted Dun L'lsen.

"*You* will take Manney back to Panadar. It's about time you treated him with a little respect and finally took some responsibility for the boy."

"I don't think so," stated Dun L'lsen flatly.

"You're forgetting *who* has been charged with finding Dun Lain."

"And you're forgetting a few things yourself." The knight stepped closer; he pointed to the ground. "Can *you* see those tracks? If *I* take Manney back, how will *you* follow Morgan?"

"I know where he went from here. I now know what has most likely happened to him. I don't need to visit all the other sites. I want to talk to the survivors at Maralat. It will take us several days to reach Maralat, and then at least a day or two talking with the townsfolk. That should give you plenty of time." He tapped the big knight's chest with his finger; he had been wanting to do that since forcing the knight to remove his armor. "You can take Manney. You *will* take Manney back to Panadar and meet us in Maralat, where *we* will pick up Morgan's trail. Understood?" Dun L'lsen was visibly shaking. He was red with anger. Dun Loren could have sworn there was actual steam escaping from the knight's ears. It felt really good to be able to push around Dun Lian's chosen successor in such a manner, especially since he had every right to, according to tradition.

"I understand, Dun Loren. I will follow your orders."

*   *   *

It was less than a day's ride to the site of Morgan's first murders once they rejoined his squires. It was not necessary for him to visit the farmhouse, but since it was on the way and since he would arrive at Maralat at least a full day before Dun L'lsen, he stopped anyway. He found himself morbidly wondering what the crime scene would look like. Apparently, Morgan had completely disemboweled three people in their own home and used their blood to decorate the walls with an unknown script. Dun Loren was certain there would be a Dun Lian knight at the farmhouse, possibly even a sage. Dun Lian would want to know what the strange writing said.

He was right. A saddled horse grazed peacefully in the front yard of the single-storied building. In a situation like this, when speed could mean everything, the Dun Lian knight who was here would leave his horse saddled for as long as he stayed at the farmhouse. It may not have taken that much time to ready his horse, but training, as well as tradition, required the knight to be ready at a moment's notice. The three of them rode up to the building and dismounted. Dun Loren asked the twins to check on the other horse and wait outside until he called for them; he wanted to see the mess before deciding to let the twins into the house. The twins looked at each other, then shuffled off to do his bidding.

His nose was assaulted by the strong, pungent odor of decay as soon as he stepped inside the house. Corpseflies were everywhere. A dozen or more were startled by his entry and buzzed loudly, rising into the air, forcing him to shoo them away.

"They seem to be feeding off each other. Quite a lot of them, aren't there?" said a man seated behind what once was this family's dinner table. He was a small man, wearing what Dun Loren swore had to be leather armor that was padded to give the impression of bulk. There was no way this diminutive knight was that muscular. "Dun Loren, I presume."

"Yes." The man rose and crossed the room, stepping over two corpses, which were all bone at this point, and presented himself before Dun Loren.

"I am Dun Dahra." The knight raised his hands, shoulder width apart, palms facing upward, and saluted Dun Loren. This salute was meant to imitate the symbol of the Dun Lian Brotherhood, the Scales of Justice, but a more learned person would tell you that it originated to show your enemy that your hands were free of weapons. The salute took Dun Loren by surprise. There was very little hierarchy within the Brotherhood. Most knights were of equal rank. Only very old or very new knights held any greater or lesser position within the Brotherhood, although a brother would yield authority to a knight who was stronger in the presence of Kasparow than himself. Once a knight completed his free deed tour, he was pretty much an equal and need not salute his brothers. Dun Dahra was obviously new at this.

"I was told you might arrive and was ordered to wait for you. I was all ready to head overseas for my free-deed tour when Dun Lian asked me to come and look at these writings."

"An overseas tour? Wouldn't that take longer than a year in the long run?"

"Yes, but I don't mind. The G'Angeleppans have been very forceful about expanding their territories. Those filthy muckbeetles need to be contained. We need all the brothers we can muster in that war, and to my delight, Dun Lian has decreed that newly commissioned knights may serve overseas for their year tour."

"I was not aware of that."

"Well, Dun Lian approached the squires individually at first, to see what kind of response he would get. I believe he has only recently made the decree public. I guess my background in languages made me the perfect choice for this job." He wrinkled his nose. "Not one I would choose to do again. I have been here for only a day, and already feel as if I will never be rid of this stink." He turned and faced the opposite wall. It was covered in blood. The Dun Lian Scales of Justice, painted in the blood, dominated most of the wall. Below the scales was a single sentence written in a script that Dun Loren could not make out.

"Can you read it?" The blood had dried and was beginning to peel away from the hardwood walls.

"It's written in an old religious tongue, which hasn't been seen since near the end of the second age and was never widely used outside of religious ceremonies. The literal translation reads, 'Condemned thee entire beneath Altarium . . .'" He paused and turned back to Dun Loren. "Which basically means 'All shall perish before Altair.'"

"Altair?"

"Why anyone would want to invoke the name of Altair, let alone be able to do it in this script, is beyond me. I was unaware that there still were any worshippers of Altair around. I thought that religion was dead a long time ago."

"It is. This is just the ranting of a madman."

"But how did he learn to write in that language, and why paint the Scales of Justice?"

"It's no secret that the Brotherhood almost committed genocide on the followers of Altair. Obviously this nut holds a thousand-year-old grudge." Dun Loren was sure that this knight knew nothing of the real identity of the murderer. Dun Lian would not have let that information be known. As far as this knight was concerned, the culprit was some backwater farm boy. Knowledge of the true events would be suppressed as much as possible. Even the surviving inhabitants of the village of Maralat would be kept from leaving their hamlet until this situation was solved.

"But where did he learn that script?"

"That's one of the mysteries to be solved, Dun Dahra." He was beginning to formulate an idea of the answer to that mystery. "There were supposedly *three* victims here? I only see two skeletons."

"The other is down here, in one of the bedchambers." The young knight exited the room and led Dun Loren down a hallway.

All shall perish before Altair? Dun Loren was beginning to think he knew what had happened to Morgan. For a brief second, the rank smell of death vanished as a slight breeze blew in from a window at the end of the hallway. Could the twins handle seeing this? Did it matter if they saw it? They entered one of the rooms. The smell of decay returned; it reminded him of the Dead Pools.

Morgan had gone to the Dead Pools. He had entered the water and then headed to this farmhouse, where he killed four people and an infant—three inside the house and an elf and child in the woods nearby. Did Dun Dahra know of these two? Morgan had then written "All shall perish before Altair" in their blood upon the wall before heading off to Maralat to murder seventy-seven more people.

"The brothers who first found her brought her in here to make her more comfortable." There was a skeleton sitting up in the bed. Strangely enough, there was very little blood on the thin cotton sheets. "She was nearly dead when they found her. Her eyes had been gouged out. Evidently, she was unable to talk or tell our brothers who was responsible." Information was indeed tight. Dun Dahra didn't even know of the Medallion of Merit that was found here. "They were all bone by the time I arrived."

"Do you think there is anything else you can learn here?"

"Not that the other brothers haven't already discovered, no. The writing was the last bit of evidence that needed to be examined."

"And you are sure of what it says?"

"Unmistakably."

"Okay"—he paused—"then burn this place. Burn it to the ground." The bulky young knight looked startled and took half a step back in surprise.

"What of the corpses?"

"You're right," he sighed. "There is that." It would be proper to bury them. He would have to retrieve the elf's and infant's bones as well. Should he allow Dun Dahra to do this? How much information was too much information for this knight to know? "I'll have my squires help you. Remove the bones, burn this place, then prepare a gravesite. They shall receive a proper burial."

"As you wish, Dun Loren." The knight saluted him again before he began his task of gathering the bones on the bed. Dun Loren left the building and was immediately confronted by his squires.

"Can we go in?" they said in unison.

"There are two bodies in the woods to the south of here. Find them first and bring back the bones." Dun Dahra came out of the house carrying the dead woman's bones wrapped in a bedsheet. He saw the two boys headed toward the woods.

"Two squires? Where are they headed?"

"There are two more bodies in the woods. It seems whoever did this didn't want anyone to escape."

"Really? Well, where do you want me to make the gravesite?"

"How about right here, in front of the house, but far enough away that it won't be harmed when we set the house on fire?"

"As you wish, Dun Loren." Dun Loren was relieved this knight wasn't giving him the same hassle that Dun L'lsen had. Then again, not many knights would. Dun Loren went to his horse and unpacked a small sack of supplies to draft a letter. He went inside and sat down at a relatively clean area of the table in the main room, placing the sack on the bloodstained table and removed a pen, ink bottle, and several pieces of paper and one piece of sheep's-hide parchment. He absentmindedly chewed on the wooden end of his metal-tipped imitation quill. The man-made quill was an expensive one. Imported from Chunya, it was a luxury that most passed over. Dun Loren had to write with them; chewing on the feathered end of a natural quill pen just didn't achieve the same calming effect for him.

So Morgan had gone to the Dead Pools, which were formed from a battle waged nearly a thousand years ago by the mightiest of Altair's worshippers. He had evidently entered the water and then come here to slaughter an entire family and write, with their blood, upon a wall in a language that hadn't been used since Altair's time. He knew the water had made at least one person sick. Could some ancient evil have entered Morgan through the water and possessed him and pushed him into committing these murders? Was he strong enough in Kasparow's presence to fight back? Was there anything left of him? He said a quick prayer to Kasparow for Manney's soul. If Morgan couldn't withstand this evil, Kasparow only knew what would happen to Dun L'lsen's mistreated squire. At least, after Dun L'lsen left the squire at Panadar, the boy might get the proper attention he deserved.

He was sure Morgan had tried to contact him somehow. The sound of his voice, the feel of it, the familiarity of it was too strong and real to have been a dream. Dun Loren chuckled as he remembered the dream. He had thrown Dun L'lsen's armor into the water of one of the dead pools. He had taken a perverse sort of pleasure in telling Dun L'lsen of the dream. Of course, the big knight had dismissed the *entire* thing as nonsense. "That type of ability is gone from the world. Telepathy is no more real or used than magic is these days." Dun L'lsen had been quite adamant when he had made that statement.

But the big knight hadn't known then what Dun Loren knew now. If something had possessed Morgan, something with knowledge of ancient languages, then couldn't this *thing* also have ancient powers as well? He needed more information on what might now be residing within Morgan. He turned to the table and began writing on the thick piece of sheepskin parchment.

> The person carrying this letter, Dun Dahra, is a knight of the Dun Lian Brotherhood. He is on a mission for the Brotherhood and acting on Dun Lian's direct orders and in his behalf. No hindrance and complete aid should be given to Dun Dahra while pursuing the goal of his mission. May Kasparow's grace shine upon all.

He put the letter aside to dry and began another.

> Dun Lian,
> The investigation, in my eyes, goes well. We began in Panadar, where we found that Dun Lain had completely bypassed the city on his travels. Before starting his free deed tour, he informed me of his desire to investigate the Dead Pools.

With Kasparow's speed, we made the pools within two days and found evidence that Morgan had indeed been there. Manney, Dun L'lsen's squire, came in contact with water from one of the pools and fell deathly ill. I had Dun L'lsen, after much "discussion," take the boy back to Panadar to be treated by our priests in the city. There is evidence that suggests Dun Lain may have become immersed in the same water that made Manney sick.

I am currently at the scene of Morgan's first murders. The reports are true, five dead, including an infant. The brother sent here to decipher the writing on the wall of the farmhouse has completed his job. "All shall perish before Altair" is written with the blood of the dead in an ancient religious script. It occurs to me that there must be a correlation between the Dead Pools, an area where the greatest of Altair's worshippers obliterated each other, and Morgan's mentioning of Altair's name.

This, I feel, is our best lead to working out this mess. I have asked Dun Dahra to delay his free deed tour and do some research for me on Altair and the Dead Pools. I fear an evil has come over Dun Lain, and I need all the information on Altair that I can gather. I have taken the liberty of drafting a letter of marques for you to sign that will aid Dun Dahra in completing his new charge. As this research may take some time and as a gesture of good faith toward the man, I request that you allow him to forego the required year of free service and bestow full brotherhood upon him.

From here I will proceed to Maralat, where I wish to interview the survivors. It would be helpful if you could provide me with information of Dun Lain's last known position. After Maralat, I plan to visit Jourlean. Dun L'lsen is to meet me there as well.

He stopped and chewed on the end of his pen. If there was only some way that he could keep Dun L'lsen from continuing on with him. Dun Lian's chosen successor was nearly intolerable. If it weren't for the big knight's tracking skills, he would have completely declined the man's request to join the party at the onset of their journey. He dipped the metal-tipped pen into his ink bottle and continued.

As I sit and think about it, if this evil can control a brother as strong in the presence of Kasparow as Dun Lain is, what chance does a squire who has not yet come out have? It may be wise to have Dun L'lsen look after his squire until we are sure that the boy is out of danger.

In any case, I will have Dun Dahra deliver this message before continuing on the mission I have charged him with. I will send another dispatch when I reach Maralat.

May Kasparow's grace never leave you.

Dun Loren

He sat up straight and waved the two pieces of parchment it had taken to write his dispatch to Dun Lian in the air to dry faster. This was more out of habit than out of any need to dry the ink. Most of the ink had dried by the time he finished drafting the letter. Pulling a letter tube from his supply sack, he rolled up the letter to Dun Lian and stuffed it inside the small metal container. He had no fire to melt the sealing wax, so he worked the wax between his fingers until it was pliable enough to stuff into one end of the tube. Into the other end, before he plugged it with wax, he wound a small cotton string that would allow Dun Lian to easily remove the wax plug when pulled. He put the tube aside.

Grasping his metal-tipped pen in one hand, he grabbed the now-dry sheepskin and skewered it twice, punching two holes near the bottom of the letter. Through these holes, he tied another piece of cotton string and then folded the letter, using the string to tie the letter shut. He tossed the letter to the table, hitting the metal letter tube and nearly knocking it to the ground. Returning the tube to a more stable position, he sighed, folded his arms, and lay his head down to rest. Even though the presence of Kasparow kept him alert and allowed him to forgo sleep—he hadn't slept since leaving Lianhome—he closed his eyes and let sleep come. It was Dun Dahra who woke him what seemed like an instant later.

"Dun Loren, we're ready to light the house on fire." The knight nudged him slightly.

"Uh, okay. Are the graves dug?"

"Dug, filled, and ready for Kasparow's grace."

"Where are the twins?"

"Waiting outside."

"Did they see this?" He motioned to the wall behind him.

"They helped me remove the last of the bones from this room."

"I guess that would be a yes." He was still a little groggy.

"Uh, yes. Sorry, Dun Loren."

"How long was I asleep?"

"About two hours."

"This is for you." Dun Loren stood and handed the sheepskin to Dun Dahra. "And this"—he picked up the metal tube—"is for Dun Lian's eyes only." He paused as he moved around the table to the front door. "So you are a student of languages?" He handed the letter tube to Dun Dahra.

"Yes, amongst other subjects."

"What do you know of Altair and his religion?"

"A little more than most other Dun Lian knights."

"Which is probably a lot more than I know." Dun Loren looked out the open door. The twins were standing near the freshly filled graves tossing two knives between them. They were as good as a juggling act in a wagon show, but every now and then, one of them would yelp and shove a cut finger in his mouth. "This is also why I have another duty for you to perform in this matter." The little knight looked at him despondently.

"I had hoped to get on with my free deed tour, Dun Loren."

"And you shall. Rest assured, the actions you perform for me now will count toward your yearlong tour. In fact, such is the urgency of your next task that Dun Lian may waive the tour entirely and take you straight to full brotherhood."

"With all due respect, Dun Loren, I *was* actually kind of anxious to join in the war against the G'Angeleppans."

"That war isn't going anywhere. It'll still be around when you finish your tasks." Dun Dahra was intent on joining that battle. If he wasn't a newly commissioned knight, he might have been able to refuse Dun Loren's orders. "And besides, wouldn't you rather go into that situation as a full brother?"

"There is that." He stopped and thought for a few seconds. "What would you have of me?"

"I need information. I want you to learn all you can about Altair, his religion and his followers. I want you to pay specific attention to anything that concerns the Dead Pools and whatever might have happened there in the past. Panadar has a rather vast library. You should start there, unless you know of a better place to look?" Dun Dahra looked to the writing on the wall.

"Altair? Yes, Panadar would be as good a place as any to start."

"There is a brother in Panadar, Dun Seguis, I believe, that may be able to steer you in the right direction."

"I know of Dun Seguis, doesn't his area of research deal more with *recent* history than with *ancient* history?"

"Yes." Dun Loren wondered if the little knight knew what Dun Seguis's real mission was. "But all he does is keep his nose in a book." Indeed, his hands and lips were stained black from years of turning ink-filled pages. "He'll at least be able to get you started." The smaller knight turned away from the bloodstained wall and joined Dun Loren in gazing out the doorway.

"*Two* squires. It must be nice to have someone look up to you the way they must. I can't wait for a squire of my own."

"Well, if you survive a year of fighting with the G'Angeleppans, I doubt it will take long for dozens of potential squires to flock to your side. That's a very high-profile war you want to run off and join."

"And a difficult one, from what I hear. I hear they can take the shape of any creature they want to, even look like men! Can you imagine, being in the middle of combat and having a fellow brother turn to you and stick a sword in you?"

"Well, just keep the faith. Kasparow will protect you from such sorceries."

"Speaking of sorceries"—he turned to face Dun Loren—"what exactly is going on here?" Should he tell Dun Dahra the truth? What if Dun Seguis were to tell Dun Dahra that it was Morgan he was interested in? Would the knight be able to put things together? "If you don't mind me asking," said the knight after Dun Loren's silent pause.

"Well"—Dun Lian might want to keep a lid on this matter, but he decided to make use of this young and malleable knight—"the information I tell you now must never leave your lips unless you are speaking with me or Dun Lian. Understood?"

"Yes."

"Swear on your faith."

"I . . ." He paused and straightened up, composing himself. It wasn't often that a Dun Lian knight was asked to swear on his faith; it was an extremely serious oath to take. Breaking it could see the knight decommissioned. "I, Dun Dahra, knight of the Dun Lian Brotherhood, swear on my faith never to speak of the information I learn on this matter to anyone other than Dun Lian or Dun Loren." He sighed. "Is that good? I've never taken such an oath."

"You did fine, as long as you realize the seriousness of that oath." Dun Dahra nodded. There was a long pause before he continued. Outside, the twins had stopped what they were doing and were looking in their direction. "It was a brother who committed these crimes." From the look on the young knight's face, he thought Dun Dahra was going to faint.

"How could one blessed by Kasparow even think of doing such things?"

"That is why I need information on Altair and the Dead Pools. The brother in question recently visited the Dead Pools. I fear some evil entered him while he was there."

"That would fit—the Dead Pools, Altair, the writings. Was it a brother I know?"

"It was a former squire of mine, Dun Lain."

"I'm sorry, Dun Loren. I guess that would explain why you have been chosen to pursue this matter. I guess you have a lot at stake, then."

"That"—he said slowly—"is an understatement." Dun Loren looked out the door at the twins standing next to five freshly filled graves. *Hundreds* dead at this point, and it would be his responsibility if Morgan could not be brought in.

"I don't mind telling you, Dun Loren, that there are many Dun Lian *traditions* that I find absolutely absurd. I would do away with half of them were *I* Dun Lian."

"And what traditional precedent would you quote that would give you the power to get rid of hundreds of years of traditions? Most brothers believe it is those very traditions that have kept the Brotherhood strong all these years."

"It's our faith in Kasparow that has kept us strong."

"We had better get started." He motioned to Dun Dahra to lead the way. *I hope we can all keep the faith.*

CHAPTER 15

The mundane way of traveling by horse certainly was a nuisance. Malchom was glad that his new body seemed to be used to spending days seated on a hard leather saddle. He was sure his old body would have fallen apart by the second day. He could have transported both he and Raurin instantly back to his ruined castle, but he did not want to perform too much magic around the young man just yet. After all, he *was* supposed to be a Dun Lian knight, worshipper of Kasparow, and Kasparow absolutely abhorred magic. Altair's avatar certainly had played his part well. That memory played in his mind, reminiscent of how he had viewed memories in the gem . . .

"Greetings, Dun Lain," the avatar said as he materialized directly in front of a stunned Raurin.

"Greetings to you, avatar," he said. If Raurin hadn't already been on his knees, Malchom was sure he would have fallen to them. As it was, the man slumped against the wall, awestruck.

"I see you have brought a new worshipper into the fold."

"The first of many more. My squire and I have been diligently praying the past day to be graced by your presence. I take it by your answer to our *prayers that my penance has been met."*

"Well, your recent"—the avatar looked to Raurin—"achievement has me intrigued."

"I take it then that my previous prayers will be granted."

"Yes." Malchom was flung backward by the sudden rush of force as the powers he had requested days ago flooded into him. "Your prayers have been answered." With those final words, the avatar vanished, leaving a confused Raurin staring blankly at Malchom as he slowly got to his feet.

"Was that Kasparow?"

"It was an avatar. Do you know what those are?" he said weakly.

"No."

*"The gods rarely deal directly with mortals. Instead, they send avatars—agents,
if you will—to interact with us mortals."*

"Is that what we wanted? Is that why we were praying?"

"Yes, it was, exactly. I just wasn't ready for it."

"For what? What did he do to you?"

"He infused me"—Malchom paused—*"with the knowledge of where your
father is."*

The appearance of the avatar had erased any doubt Raurin might have had
as to the validity of Malchom's knighthood. Raurin had run out of the room
to distribute the good news that "Kasparow" had shown "Brother Morgan"
the light and given him the knowledge of his father's whereabouts. Raurin
had run out of the room before even finding out from Malchom what had
happened to his father. So profound was Raurin's religious experience that
he didn't open his mouth once in protest to any of Malchom's requests or
commands from that time forward. The only words that did seem to escape
his lips were "Certainly, Dun Lain," "Yes, sir," or "At once, Dun Lain."

So when Malchom had asked for two of the village's strongest mounts
to be readied and fully loaded with supplies, "Yes, Dun Lain" was the only
response offered. Even the rest of the villagers had sat in silence awaiting "Dun
Lain's" next move. Malchom had decided to take it as far as he could.

Raurin had returned with two horses. They had mounted and left the small
town, with the villagers in tow. No one had said a word. They had marched
on in silence to the spot where Malchom had spilled Geoffrey's lifeblood to
the ground. The assembled group stood motionless as Namara had walked
to the slightly raised mound of relatively freshly disturbed earth and sank to
her knees. She had bowed her head and began to mumble. The assembled
crowd had done the same.

She may have been fooling the others, but Malchom had figured her out
almost from their first conversation. She wasn't truly interested in *where* her
husband *was* more than *what* her husband *had*. With him now dead, she was
the sole owner and operator of his potentially big business. She had stood,
walked toward Malchom and Raurin—both had remained in the saddle—and
said loud enough for everyone to hear, "Go with Dun Lain and make your
father proud."

With that, she had left the clearing, but not before she paused before
Malchom, placed a hand on his knee, and spoke so only he could hear, "Bring
us back a Dun Lian knight." He knew the comment was meant for him, not
Raurin. She had then silently left the clearing, followed by the rest of the
villagers; and as a group, they all walked back to town, without so much as

a single "Why?" or "Are you sure?" muttered between them. None of them had bothered to dig up the corpse. After all, the knowledge had come from a Dun Lian knight, who had received it directly from Kasparow. There was no need to question it, in their minds; just accept it, and no one, especially Namara, was going to begin to doubt Dun Lain.

So he and Raurin had spent the next three days in the saddle. They had ridden almost nonstop until they reached Malchom's ruined castle, until they reached the spot where whatever that thing was had attacked Malchom.

As he had feared, the days-old campsite was in ruins. None of his belongings could be found, which he did not really care about. His cooking utensils, backpack, sword, journal—all these things were gone. They were all replaceable; they had been replaced before leaving the village. Raurin had even produced a sword for "Dun Lain" to wear. It was the gem he was concerned about. He needed it. The magical emerald was going to be instrumental in his return to power. Nothing was left of the campsite—well, almost nothing. The creature was still there; at least, its bones were still there.

"Is that what attacked you? Those look like troll bones, don't you think?" asked Raurin several minutes after arriving at the campsite. He had remained silent and mounted as Malchom made a preliminary search of the area for the emerald and now dismounted to examine the bones. Of course, Malchom had no intention of letting Raurin know exactly what had happened, or what he was looking for. Not yet anyway, not until he had started production of his own mushroom drink and had Raurin subsisting on a regular diet of the stuff.

"It appears so." Malchom joined Raurin in examining the corpsefly-cleaned carcass. "I wonder how it died?" he muttered, poking through the bones.

"Why didn't it chase you? Trolls aren't known for giving up on their prey."

"I tossed it the rabbits I was skinning and preparing for dinner," he lied. "I was then able to flee. I suppose it could have choked on the dead animals." What *had* happened? Had it found the gem? Had the creature touched it? Something or someone had found it. The creature was here, and yet nothing else was. Something had walked away with the gem.

"I doubt that," said Raurin. "If it had, wouldn't there be rabbit bones here as well? Something else must have come along after you left. I mean, look, where's the thing's head?"

Where indeed? thought Malchom. "Most likely, it stuck around long enough to digest the rabbits and then was attacked by something else, probably

a local hunter, who kept its head for proof of bounty. Dun Lian knights are
often called in to assist in such hunts when troll attacks are reported." He
was reaching, but he knew Raurin would not question this. "In any case, it
is dead, and we can now continue with my charged task."

"Which you haven't said much about."

"Your training as a squire officially begins now," Malchom said as he deftly
mounted his horse. "The first bit of wisdom I have to impart to you deals
with *silence*." Raurin breathed heavily and cast his eyes downward. "I am not
chastising, you Raurin. You've done nothing wrong. It's just that, normally,
it's not a squire's place to question his patron. Your place is to learn from me,
and you will learn better by watching and listening rather than by talking."
He paused. Raurin was still gazing at the ground. It seemed to Malchom that
some of Raurin's earlier fascination might be seeping away. "Don't get me
wrong, Raurin, I enjoy conversation. Just try to do better at distinguishing
when you should *ask* for information and when you should let information
be offered *to* you."

"Yes, Dun Lain."

Malchom whirled his horse around and pointed to the vegetation-covered
ruined castle not far off. "You see those ruins?" Raurin jumped into his saddle
and looked. He started to respond but then simply nodded his head. Had
Malchom damaged his relationship with Raurin by reprimanding him as he
had? How did Dun Lian knights normally handle their squires? He knew that
tradition played a large role in the life of a Dun Lian knight. Did the general
populace know this as well? What he did next disgusted him completely,
but he felt it was necessary. "Raurin"—he reached over and patted Raurin's
knee—"I was not yelling at you or ordering you to be silent. I just wanted
to establish a few basic things." Raurin tried to smile. "And as a Dun Lian
knight, there are a lot of traditions you will have to live your life by now . . .
It's always better that you get started off on the right path."

"Oh great, I've heard about those traditions."

"Really? Like what?"

"Oh, just that there are a *lot* of them."

"That there are, Raurin, that there are." They fell silent for a few moments.
Malchom urged his mount toward his ruined castle. "What do you know of
gods, Raurin?"

Raurin looked at Malchom, then away, quickly, almost meekly. "Not
much, actually, just that Kasparow is the accepted deity almost all over the
world. I hear the Brotherhood is in a war somewhere on another continent
with a race that believes that *they* are gods."

"What about other gods?"

"Other gods? There's only Kasparow."

"Ah well, there *were* other gods, long ago. Long ago when the world was quite different than it is now. *Chaos*—" He had to consciously keep his feelings of ecstasy from seeping into his voice. "Chaos was a way of life back then. It was a turbulent and exciting time. Then *Kasparow* came and vanquished the other gods. And now we have all this order." He sighed.

"You seem as if this is a bad thing," said Raurin timidly.

"Bad?" Malchom composed himself. "No, I'm just a little weary." Malchom rubbed his eyes. "The first tradition you will absorb yourself in is prayer. As *Dun Lian knights*, we must pray to, our god, every day. Not just normal prayer, or even prayer resembling what you and I did three days ago. We will pray in a way that every Dun Lian knight has prayed since the inception of the Brotherhood nearly a thousand years ago." Now came the crucial part. "Prayer within the Brotherhood is a very traditional and well-guarded thing." He stopped his horse and stared intently at Raurin to emphasize his point. "Those outside the Brotherhood are not to know of the more serious of our traditions."

"Yes, Dun Lain," Raurin said confidently.

Malchom continued riding toward the ruins. "Prayer is a private thing and, except for group rituals, is done in a solitary manner. You must pray every day. When is up to you, but it must be every day, and it must be for at least an hour at a time, though the more you pray, the closer you will be to Him." Now for the big leap, he hoped he would land on his feet. "Within the Brotherhood, when we pray to our god, he is known as *Altair*. Kasparow is more of a . . . *secular* designation. When you pray, you pray to Altair. In your prayers, you will confirm your *belief in* and *servitude to* Altair. There will be times, in the future, when you will be required to make certain . . . *sacrifices*. These will be made known to you when the time comes. For now, at least an hour a day, on your own time. The more you pray to Him, the more Altair will listen."

"Yes, Dun Lain."

That went well. Raurin questioned nothing; he even seemed to really understand what he had just heard. Malchom decided to move on quickly. Let this little victory lie as undisturbed as possible. "On my current free deed tour, as you were asking after earlier, my current charge is to investigate these ruins. It was built hundreds of years ago, near the time of the founding of the Brotherhood. Our scholars believe there may be a complex of caves and caverns beneath the surface that may still be intact. The possibility of retrieving

valuable information is great." Malchom paused and watched Raurin out of
the corner of his eye. "The castle used to belong to a powerful man named
Malchom Jamias before he disappeared nearly a thousand years ago." There
was no reaction. Raurin kept riding and listening, as if this were just any
other history lesson. "Malchom Jamias was a very powerful and prosperous
man in his time. He mercilessly ruled a good portion of this land from this
very spot. All lived in fear of him."

"Then why do we seek knowledge of him, if he was such an evil man?"

Raurin's comment surprised Malchom. He had half expected the young
man to sit there and simply listen. Malchom looked down at his hands before
replying. They were big, powerful, and young looking. He continued to forget
that the body he now had was young, probably no older than Raurin's. He
may have felt hundreds of years old, but the world would see him almost
as a child. "To know our past is to know our possible futures. Knowledge is
always a good thing. The more you know . . . Were you even aware there was
a person who used to rule the land from here named Malchom Jamias?"

"No, I wasn't. I don't see how learning about an unknown, long-dead
tyrant can help me now."

Malchom took a breath in an attempt to steady an urge that was rising
within him to smack Raurin. "Well, what were the times like? How did Jamias
rise to power? How did he keep power? Could something similar happen today,
and what would it take to achieve that kind of power? Would the forces that
exist today be able to deal with such a man? Knowledge of your enemies, real
and potential, is always a good thing." They were nearing the ruins and fell
silent as they slowly picked their way among the first few boulders.

The moss-and-kudzu-covered Andonesian marble still held a small
amount of beauty, even in decay. Malchom had spent large amounts of
money to import the marble needed to construct his castle. It was the finest
castle ever made, or at least it had been. Even while looking at the ruins, in
his mind, he could still see his castle standing. This would have been the
southern portion of the castle, the barracks and slave quarters. Most of his
slaves he had sacrificed to Altair at one time or another. Just about all of his
slaves were kept below, almost directly below this spot in fungus-covered
eerie-yellow phosphorescent-lit caves, but a few slaves were needed on the
surface to help run the castle.

There had been an airshaft, between the slave quarters and the barracks,
that led down to the caves. It was one of several that helped to ventilate
the subterranean complex. These would, if any of them were still intact,
probably be the easiest way to access the caves. If not, he could always

summon an elemental to dig straight through the earth, which was how he had fashioned the caves in the first place. He was praying to Altair that the airshafts were still in place. He didn't want to start flinging magic around Raurin just yet.

The debris became too thick and jumbled for them to easily maneuver their horses any farther. Malchom stopped and leapt out of his saddle. He continued to be amazed at the strength and agility of his new body. "We'll make a camp in this little area here. These fallen boulders will provide some protection should bad weather arise." His old body had been frail, small, and almost sickly; he felt he could do anything in this new body. He removed the sword Raurin had furnished him with from its resting place on his saddle and buckled it around his waist. Soon the boy would wonder why he wasn't being trained for combat, why there were no sparring matches between them. With a little luck, he would have Raurin drugged beyond reason before that happened.

"Unpack our supplies and then find a place to tether the horses. I'm going to look around a little." Raurin nodded and began his duties as Malchom started to scramble over the boulders in front of him. Whoever had destroyed his castle certainly had done a complete job of it; everything was just a big pile of boulders. This worried him a little. Would the underground areas have been left intact?

There was no semblance of any actual buildings left, just a big pile. It was difficult to gauge where the shaft between the slave quarters and barracks should be. However, after only a few minutes of searching, he found the shaft. It was there, plain as day, uncovered and out in the open. How had he missed this before? He dropped to his knees and peered over the edge of the shaft and was assaulted by an updraft of cold air. This was promising. The air wasn't stale, which meant that the cave system was most likely intact. A horde of elementals had originally constructed the cavern system with several entrances and these airshafts to encourage a self-reliant ventilation system. Fresh, circulating air was a necessity. At the height of his power, the cave system had housed nearly two thousand people, most of them pregnant women.

Altair demanded blood as sacrifice for the powers he bestowed. Demihumans, such as elves and dwarves were preferred, but any sentient, two-legged creature's blood would suffice. Malchom personally held the belief that Altair had a special taste for infant blood. Many of his former constituents didn't think so, which was their loss. Malchom believed he was favored in Altair's eyes due solely to the number of children he sacrificed on a regular basis.

It had been quite an operation at one time; nearly two thousand men and women living in the caves, subsisting on light and nourishment provided by the yellow fungus that Malchom had conjured into being. He still believed that the idea to create the mushroom had been his greatest achievement ever. Instead of forcing his followers to be sacrificed or attacking his neighbors to take captives, as he and his peers had done for decades—after all, that was a self-defeating practice—he had come up with the plan to create his own self-propagating clan, whose sole purpose for living would be to produce as many offspring as possible. All of which would die on Altair's altar within months of their birth. How to keep his little "clan" subservient, alive, and separated from the rest of the world had been a difficult problem to solve. Solved it he had, with great success. He had asked Altair for a plant that would thrive in the caves, provide light and nourishment, and help keep the inhabitants under his control. Even Altair had liked the idea when Malchom had proposed it. The big, fanged, floating head that was Altair's favorite representation in this world had laughed and grinned evilly. It was the only time Malchom had ever heard the god laugh. That yellow mushroom had served him well in the past. *And it will serve me well now!* He was almost giddy as he leapt to his feet and headed back to where Raurin was making camp.

"Dun Lain," Raurin said as Malchom approached, "I've started a fire. I thought we could use something to eat before—"

"No time for food just yet, Raurin. I've found an entrance to the caves. I hope you've brought some rope."

"Yes, yes, I have. What else will we need?"

"Just a lantern, or some torches. Do we have any of those?" Raurin nodded and rushed over to a pack he had placed under one of the larger boulders and began digging through it. "Great, hopefully we won't even need it."

Raurin stepped up to him and, slinging a coiled rope over his shoulder, handed Malchom a small lantern. "There isn't much oil, probably enough for five or six hours' total."

"That should be sufficient." Malchom handed it back to Raurin. "Perhaps you should light it from the fire first."

"Uh, yeah." Raurin adjusted the rope and obediently bent down to light the lantern.

This is too easy, Malchom thought. *I almost don't need the mushroom to control Raurin. I wonder what I will be able to have him do once I have the drug to reinforce my commands?*

"Done." Raurin stood. "Are the horses going to be safe?"

"Of course they will. This is a fairly deserted area."

"A deserted area with trolls wandering around."

Malchom turned and started for the airshaft. "They will be fine, Raurin. That troll is dead, remember?" He didn't really care if the horses were safe or not. With any luck, in the amount of time it would take to burn all of their lamp oil, his squire would be drugged, under his *complete* control, and he would have no further reason to use the horses to travel. They would die, tethered to those trees, as far as Malchom was concerned.

They approached the shaft, and both young men got to their knees and peered into the blackness of the hole. "How deep do you think it is?" asked Raurin.

"Sixty feet." Malchom felt Raurin looking at him. "If our sages are correct, the first of the caves is about sixty feet underground."

"Great, this rope is only fifty feet long."

Malchom stood up and folded his arms. "Well then, I guess we'll have to jump the last ten feet. Or if we had some spikes, we could hammer them into the side of the shaft and make a ladder of sorts. Besides, the shaft is skinny enough that we could always shimmy our way down."

"But if we do that"—Raurin was still peering into the shaft—"how will we get back up?"

Malchom grinned. *You won't need to worry about getting back up,* he thought. "There are other exits from the caves. This is a man-made structure, after all. There will be obvious ways to get out." He was lying, of course. First, the caves were fashioned by summoned creatures, and second, the exits were hidden. He had covered them with powerful illusions granted from Altair. After all, he couldn't have people and animals wandering into his secret garden. Would the illusions still be working after a thousand years? Would they still be functioning without Altair's presence? He hoped so.

"Someone's been here recently."

"What do you mean?" Malchom said; a sinking feeling began to form in his stomach.

"Well." Raurin stood and dusted his hands against his breeches. "Look around you." He motioned to the boulders around them. "These rocks don't look like the rest of the ruins. They're not covered in vines or half buried in dirt. And that grate over there." He pointed behind Malchom. "It's kind of teetering on that rock. It's not settled like it should be if it had been there longer than a month or two." Malchom took a good look around him. This would explain why he had missed the shaft the last time he was here. "And here." Raurin bent down to the edge of the shaft. "Around the edge of the shaft, there's dust and fresh bits of marble from when the grate was ripped away. I would think, if this was done a long time ago, that the debris would have been washed or blown down the shaft by now." Malchom bent down and pinched a small amount of marble dust between his fingers.

"You may be right, Raurin." What could have ripped the grate away, the troll? It was dead. He patted Raurin on the back. "Good eyes, my boy. My sponsor, Dun Loren, would be impressed. He's an excellent tracker himself." Could Dun Loren have tracked him this far this fast? That couldn't be possible, could it? Was Dun Loren down in the caves now? "Well, how did they get down, then? I don't see any ropes or ladders."

"Could they have found one of the other entrances you mentioned?"

"I doubt it. They're over a mile from here."

"Then perhaps they shimmied down the shaft like you suggested."

"Perhaps." It couldn't have been Dun Loren. How would he have known to look for the caves?

"Well, whoever it was, they either had a lot of people, or they were very strong. I doubt that together you and I could move *half* of these marble slabs." They both fell silent for several seconds as they looked around them. Eventually, their eyes fell on each other. Raurin was looking at Malchom with a slightly quizzical look on his face.

"There's only one way to find out. Tie that rope around this boulder here. I'm going down."

"Yes, Dun Lain." Raurin almost leapt into action. He scrambled over some of the marble debris and began working one end of the rope around the boulder Malchom had indicated. "I hope you are right about being able to get back up. I mean, what if there *is* someone down there?"

"Not to worry, Raurin. *If* there is someone down there, then it would have to be another Dun Lian knight. In either case, we won't have to worry about getting back up."

"Done!" Raurin walked over to the hole and tossed the rope down into the dark depths of the shaft.

Had Raurin even been listening to him? Malchom stepped to the edge and wrapped the rope under his bottom and then back up, over his left shoulder. Letting the rope slowly slide through his right hand and instinctively guiding the rope with his left, he began to walk down the side of the shaft. *How had he known to do this?*

"Dun Lain, what about the lantern?" Raurin picked up the lantern and brought it over to the shaft where Malchom was already several feet down.

"Well, I don't have any free hands. When I get to the bottom, I'll have you lower it down." Of course, Malchom knew he wouldn't need the lantern if the mushrooms were still thriving. Raurin started to protest but then fell silent. Malchom was sure his *squire* was reviewing the "Don't question your patron" speech he had given earlier. Ignoring Raurin, he continued down the shaft.

The way he had wrapped the rope around him created a seat that gave him surprising stability and control over his descent. His new body continued to surprise him. He wondered again how many more unknown abilities he had available to him.

The light from above dwindled to a pinpoint as he lowered himself into the cool confines of the shaft. Within a very short amount of time, he was engulfed in darkness. Before he knew it, the end of the rope passed through his right hand. Had he not reacted quickly, clenching the rope in his left hand, he might have fallen. Bringing his feet up, he pushed his back against the shaft and wedged himself into place. Letting go of the rope, he looked up at the small circle of light above and called up to Raurin.

"I've reached the end of the rope. Take it back up and lower the lantern down." Raurin complied without a reply. He felt the rope slide past his legs. He *felt* the rope, he couldn't *see* it. He couldn't see his legs. He had expected light from the mushrooms to have reached this far. Perhaps the mushrooms no longer existed. Perhaps this particular shaft was not the one he thought it was. Perhaps this shaft was deeper than sixty feet. If he only had a rock, or a coin, he could drop it and get an idea of how deep the shaft was. He knew that a minute had barely passed when he caught sight of the lantern slowly making its way down to him, but it had seemed like an eternity in the darkness.

It took several seconds for his eyes to adjust to the light. The metal-hooded design of the lantern was perfect for this situation. It reflected its light downward, and Malchom's gaze followed.

He nearly lost his footing when he laughed at what he saw.

The shaft made an abrupt ninety-degree turn about four feet from where he was. Sighing a little, he jumped down to the floor of the shaft. He untied the lantern and squatted, shining the light as best he could down the now-level tunnel. It continued for about fifteen feet before angling downward again.

"Come on down, Raurin," he called back up the shaft. The rope moved violently, and Raurin appeared quicker than he had expected. He entered the tunnel to give Raurin room at the bottom of the shaft. With his large frame, it would have been difficult to turn around so he entered headfirst.

"Wow, how far does this go?" Raurin asked from behind him.

"Only about fifteen feet, then it slopes downward." Malchom shoved the lantern behind him. "Here, you carry this." With that, he began crawling forward.

When he reached the slope, he stopped and peered over. With Raurin and the lantern behind him, he shouldn't have been able to see very far. The tunnel sloped downward sharply for a few feet and then turned to his right. He could see a yellow glow feebly attempting to shine its way past the turn.

The mushrooms! "Douse that light, Raurin." If he was correct, this shaft led into his *waiting* room. Again, without questioning him, Raurin extinguished the flame of the lantern. Malchom waited for his eyes to adjust.

"What's that glow? *Is* there someone down here?"

"You'll see." In the past, Malchom had commanded several of his drugged cave dwellers to bring a number of infants to this waiting room on the same day each month to await being taken to Malchom's chapel in the castle's main building. Back then, such was Malchom's influence with Altair that he needed to sacrifice only once a month. Granted, that monthly ritual was a grand one. Upward of forty infants would be "harvested" each month. Their blood, much of it nonhuman blood, spilled in Altair's name, on His altar.

He still marveled at the setup. Over fifteen hundred women voluntarily, through use of the mushroom, getting pregnant as often as they could by the few hundred male occupants of the cave created a constant flow of newborns to sacrifice. He slid headfirst down the incline and scrambled around the corner. The glow was definitely getting stronger. He could see a grate-covered opening a few yards in the distance. All the beings that had lived in this huge cave system, all of them addicted to a drug that kept them under his control, all this effort had accumulated once each month in the room he was about to enter.

Crawling up to the grate, he looked into the chamber. It *was* the waiting room! The roughly rectangular room was fully covered by the yellow light-producing fungus. Malchom smiled and sighed in relief as he gazed on a pile of mushrooms in the center of the room that was several feet thick. There was plenty to go around, more than there had been in his time. He surmised that several hundred years of unchecked growth was responsible for the huge mound of mushrooms on the floor.

He grabbed the grating and shook it. It was loose. It would probably come free easily. Bringing his feet up under him, he rolled onto his back and kicked the grate with all the strength of his new body. The metal grating popped loose and landed on the floor with a soft thud, releasing a cloud of mushroom spores that were quickly sucked out through the airshaft. Malchom reacted quickly by closing his eyes and holding his breath. He wasn't sure if the spores alone would do anything to him, but he didn't want to take the chance. He could feel the spores as they wafted past him. The cloud dissipated quickly enough, and he resumed breathing. He flipped onto his belly and slithered to the edge of the shaft. It was at this time that he caught a good look at Raurin's face.

His *squire's* face looked a little flushed. The young man was rubbing his eyes as if something stung them. Raurin coughed. "Are you all right, Raurin?" Malchom asked with a slight smile on his face.

"Uh," he coughed again. "Um, that dust seems to have made me a little lightheaded."

"Is that all you feel?"

Raurin nodded

A little lightheaded? Not euphoric? Perhaps inhalation of the spores wasn't enough. "It will pass." Malchom looked below him. His feet were about three feet from the pile of mushrooms. They would provide a soft landing, but they would also send another cloud of spores billowing into the air. He looked back to Raurin, who was staring red-eyed at him. Raurin hadn't seen the pile of mushrooms yet, had he? For all he knew, it was a simple dust cloud that had irritated his senses. "Here I go," he said and, holding his breath, dropped from the ledge without further comment.

He was expecting a cloud of spores and a soft landing on the nearly two-foot pile of mushrooms. What he got was a cloud of spores and a shaky landing on an unstable surface, almost as if he had jumped on a pile of loose firewood. Losing his footing as the mat of mushrooms and several small objects shifted out from under him, he landed on his bottom with a larger puff of spores and a clatter of what he now saw to be bones. He shut his eyes, which had begun to sting, and held his breath as he waited for the cloud to dissipate. Some of the spores had succeeded in infiltrating his respiratory system, causing him to cough lightly and accidentally inhale more of the spores.

He felt dizzy. Several times in the past, he had ingested the mushroom; after all, it was a drug with some pleasant side effects. This was nothing like the very satisfying feeling he experienced when he had eaten the mushroom. This was more of an annoyance.

It didn't take long for his mind to clear. He had never known the mushrooms to give off spores like this when disturbed. Could this be a natural mutation? Would they still work as they had in the past? They still gave off light, but what about their druglike qualities? Were they even still edible?

With the mushrooms he had landed in disturbed and pushed aside, he could now see that the pile that filled the room was a pile of bones that were covered with a thin layer of the mushroom and not one big mound of fungi.

Bones? He picked up a bone and examined it. It was human; small, but human, or at least, humanoid. All of the bones looked to be diminutive in size. Judging by the size of the bones and the size of the pile, there must have been enough corpses in this room to make thousands of fleshed people, albeit small people.

What had happened here? Had there been some sort of massacre? Had his enemies invaded his castle and, finding the cave system, killed all of his followers? Why would they put them all in this room? But then, these bones were too small to belong to the followers he had left behind.

"Dun Lain," Raurin said from the shaft. "Are those *bones*? And where is all this light coming from?"

"Come on down, Raurin. Just be careful where you land." Malchom moved to a corner of the room where the mushrooms and bones weren't so thick, taking care to kick up as little dust as he could. "I don't think the spores from these mushrooms will hurt us, but it's best not to kick up too many of them." Raurin lowered himself over the edge. "These mushrooms, one of the things I was expecting to find down here, are supplying the light. I wasn't expecting to find all these bones." Raurin dropped to the floor, sending a somewhat-smaller cloud of spores into the air.

"Would you look at all these things!" Raurin said, bending down to inspect one of the mushroom-covered bones. "Do these things cover all the walls down here?"

"Yes, well, they should—at least, that was what I was led to believe."

"Well, I guess you were right, then. We won't need the lantern. We won't even need our food supplies, if it comes down to that." He plucked a mushroom from a small bleached femur. "These things are edible."

"How do you know that?" Malchom's heart quickened. Was it going to be *this* easy?

"I come from a village that was founded on mushrooms, remember?"

"Are you sure?" Malchom was hoping his squire's desire to impress a Dun Lian knight would lead to what would normally be considered a rash action.

To prove his knowledge on mushrooms, Raurin popped the small yellow fungus into his mouth.

"Wasn't that a bit foolish? How can you be so sure they are edible?"

"Well," he said, plucking another mushroom from the bone in his hand, "as my father taught me, and he knew *all* about mushrooms, any mushroom that has these serrated edges that line up with these fanlike flaps here underneath is edible. At least, any mushroom currently known." He stopped and stared at Malchom, a worried look coming into his face as he finished chewing the mushroom and swallowed stiffly.

"I don't think you should worry. These mushrooms have been around for a very long time. How does it taste?"

"Quite good, actually." Raurin dropped the bone and turned the mushroom he was holding over and over. "I see none of the obvious features that denote poisonousness. And these serrations, it has to be edible." He sniffed the mushroom and shrugged, plopping this one into his mouth as well. "Is my mouth glowing?" Raurin opened his mouth after chewing a few times, revealing the mashed-up mushroom. He giggled slightly when Malchom didn't answer. "Sorry," he said, covering his mouth to keep from spitting out the mushroom bits. "These things *are* good," he mumbled through a mushroom-full mouth.

Malchom couldn't keep himself from smiling. His face almost hurt; he was smiling so broadly. This was too easy. Hopefully, this was a sign of things to come. "Well then." Smiling? No, he was positively *grinning.* "*If you are hungry, eat lots more mushrooms,*" he said in a suggestive voice. The mushroom had never been this quick to be effective, but who knew. Perhaps time had strengthened their potency.

Raurin stopped chewing. "I *am* hungry." Without further thought or hesitation, he knelt and began mindlessly plopping mushrooms into his mouth. He looked up at Malchom and chuckled. "Why do you have such a sinister-looking grin on your face, Dun Lain?"

"Finish eating, and I'll tell you all about it."

CHAPTER 16

Dun Lian stood on the balcony that encircled his war room. He had been spending too much time in this room as of late. Several serving trays filled with empty bowls and plates littered the balcony. Two large down-filled sturdy-cotton pillows had been brought in to augment the comfort of his chair. He had actually fallen asleep in that chair last night.

He was awake now, staring down at the huge map that was the table that occupied nearly all of the room below. Dozens of small metal and wooden figures were littered across the table. They represented troops, armament, ships, and special occurrences that concerned the Dun Lian Brotherhood.

One of those special occurrences was this nasty business with Dun Lain. There were tin skulls marking the areas where he had struck. Skulls to represent death. Tin to represent the meaninglessness of those deaths. There was a cork carving of a knight on foot. It represented Dun Lain and was made of cork to signify that his exact whereabouts were not known. A wooden carving of a knight on horseback representing Dun Loren and his party rested only a few inches from the cork figure. It was wooden to signify Dun Loren's detachment from the normal business of the Brotherhood.

In his hand was a letter. It was the second letter he had received from one of his knights in the field today. The first had been brought in by Dun Dahra and was from Dun Loren. It seemed Dun Loren believed that some evil presence, or at least a nasty disease, had infiltrated Dun Lain and was at the root of his recent actions.

As interesting as all that was, it was neither the cork nor wooden figures on the map nor Dun Loren's letter that currently held his attention. It was the second letter, the one he held in his hand, that was making him more and more agitated.

The letter had arrived in the afternoon's mail. He looked at it again. The sunlight streaming in through the stained glass windows of the war room had faded since he had first read the letter. Now as he reread the letter, the dimming light echoed his sinking feelings.

Dun Algen was the commanding officer of the Brotherhood's Eastern Forces. The bulk of the Eastern Forces was involved in the war against the G'Angeleppans. Since it was a very active campaign, he received regular reports from Dun Algen. News of troop movements, supply lines, intelligence reports, gains and losses were sent from Dun Algen on practically a daily basis. Today's letter shouldn't have upset him more than Dun Loren's letter, but it did.

Dun Algen's latest dispatch reported of several victories. On any other day, this would have brought a smile to his face. The instant he had finished reading the letter for the first time, he picked up the wooden rod used to manipulate the figurines on the table and adjusted the appropriate pieces. Dun Algen had reported that the Eastern Forces had taken three villages and their accompanying keeps. These were key victories. The strategic positioning of these keeps help to solidify the Eastern Forces front lines. He was sure that G'Zellan was aware of this fact. The G'Angeleppans had vehemently defended those three villages in the past. Intelligence reports had shown that G'Zellan had gone so far as to bleed away a number of troops from other positions just to shore up the defenses of these villages.

The keeps that guarded the villages had proved to be nearly impossible to overtake. Besieging them was useless. Whenever the Brotherhood would get close to breaking the resolve of those inside, those damned G'Angeleppans would just tunnel into the ground and change personnel. Fresh soldiers and supplies once a month completely eradicated all effectiveness of a siege. It was a good thing the G'Angeleppans had little to no knowledge and skill at engineering or castle building. It was a standing policy amongst all the nations of the eastern continent that no more keeps or castles be built until the G'Angeleppan situation was resolved.

The news that they had taken the three villages wasn't what was bothering him. Dun Algen had let him know weeks ago that plans had been set to mount a major push to take all three keeps at once. The fact that they had succeeded was great news. It was Dun Algen's description of *how* they had taken the villages. *Our forces overran the G'Angeleppans in all three attacks. Little resistance was met. They were practically retreating as we advanced. Why their resolve faltered now, allowing us to take the keeps, is beyond me.*

Why, indeed? He couldn't understand why G'Zellan would just give up these areas, as it appeared he had. Dun Algen had written that perhaps it was an indication that they were winning the war, that the G'Angeleppans were being contained and pushed back. Dun Lian couldn't believe this. He couldn't believe that any G'Angeleppan would give up, unless they were dead. Some small part of him, a miniscule idea stuck in the back of his head, spoke with the loudest voice he had ever heard. It was telling him that his recent "victory" was connected with the Dun Lain incident somehow.

But how could G'Zellan know of the killings already? He answered the voice inside his head. Even with the Brotherhood's well-established and very quick mail system, this letter had taken at least two weeks to reach him from the eastern continent. That would place the date of the victories a day or two after Morgan's first kill at the farmhouse outside of Maralat, if not the same day or before! He didn't think G'Zellan's information-gathering capabilities could be that good, could they? The G'Angeleppan race had the ability to project illusionary visages, which, praise Kasparow, had no effect on Dun Lian knights. Could they have other powers as well? Or could their apparent retreat have been simple coincidence? It had to be. What purpose could *retreat* serve? If G'Zellan did know of the possible internal problems associated with Morgan's actions, then wouldn't that nasty creature press the issue and *attack*? That little voice was telling him that the Brotherhood's resources were soon to be stretched to the limit. He decided to institute a renewed aggressive recruiting policy.

He descended the spiral staircase to the room below and sat heavily into his pillowed chair. Pulling the cord that summoned servants to his war room, he sighed and dropped Dun Algen's letter on the massive table. He wished Dun L'lsen was with him at the moment. His chosen successor's ability to see every angle of a situation was uncanny, even if the big knight rarely considered anything other than exactly what he personally wanted or believed.

It didn't take long for a squire to arrive.

"Yes, Dun Lian," said the youth, barely poking his head in through a slightly cracked door.

"Fetch Rosen Kirkland for me."

"The scribe? At once, Dun Lian." The door closed quietly, leaving him alone in the massive room once more. *Do you think I should move a bed in here?* he asked the voice in his head, which remained silent. He propped his feet up on the table, attempting to get more comfortable while he contemplated exactly what he would have Rosen Kirkland put to paper for him.

*   *   *

"Enter!" he called over the din that the three giggling females created as they frolicked under the coverings of his bed. He remained sitting at his table, looking at the moving mound of furs as the messenger entered and dropped a letter on the table. The young G'Angeleppan never looked up, never glanced at any of the naked body parts protruding from the bed furs. He simply walked in, placed the paper on G'Zellan's table, and then left. Was the boy afraid to look him in the face? Was he embarrassed to look at the naked women? Or was he nervous about being in the presence of his living god? His people were such spineless creatures when it came right down to it.

G'Zellan sighed and picked up the paper, ignoring the antics of the females. Maybe the young messenger just wasn't interested in the women; *he* certainly was bored with them. He glanced at the paper. It was another request from Lord Corrain. The young lord was ambitious, nearly too ambitious. He was beginning to think that the alliance with Lord Corrain might have been a mistake. It *had* been Corrain's idea to let the Brotherhood finally take the three villages to the south of Corrain's territory. Was this a mistake?

Lord Corrain had noticed the strategic value of the villages. Not that G'Zellan hadn't, but the young lord had proposed allowing the Brotherhood to take the villages and instill in them a sense of power and urgency that would hopefully goad them into advancing farther. Lord Corrain wanted to allow the Brotherhood's forces to push even deeper into G'Angeleppan territory so that his forces could attack from the north, shearing through the Brotherhood's support lines like a scythe.

G'Zellan had initially liked the idea, thinking it would prove a fatal blow if it worked. He was taking a huge risk. To be as deadly effective as possible, he would have to let Dun Lian's forces get deep within G'Angeleppan territory. Would Dun Lian fall for it? The Brotherhood's leader was proving to be quite competent in battle strategies. Would Dun Lian or his commanders on this continent even consider that another human would ally himself with the G'Angeleppan army? Lord Corrain had expressed his dislike of foreign forces holding such power in his lands enough times in the past. Although he had openly denounced the Brotherhood's presence, Lord Corrain had always remained neutral in the war. G'Zellan was sure that Dun Lian kept Lord Corrain's neutrality in mind when making decisions. But would he see this trap, and would he advance his front lines as Lord Corrain was counting on?

Now with their recent internal problems, the Brotherhood might not take the bait. Had G'Zellan given up three very important keeps for nothing? Well, he really didn't believe it was for nothing. The benefits of the alliance with Lord Corrain were definitely worth the temporary losses.

He crumpled the paper and tossed it into the fire blazing in the center of the room. The letter said something about housing arrangements for the masonry specialists that Lord Corrain was sending to teach his subjects. Humans were such pathetic creatures.

He felt the tingling in his mind before he heard the voice.

Sire.

He clapped his hands together loudly and shouted, "Out! I've had enough! I wish to be alone!" The three females shrieked almost in unison and rushed to exit the room, not bothering to clothe themselves; after all, why did females need clothes?

"I can hear you. Report," he said out loud. He didn't have to speak since he was communicating with his thoughts; he just couldn't get used to the idea of having a conversation with someone else solely inside his head.

Dun Lian ordered a major increase in recruiting only hours after receiving news of their victories from Dun Algen.

"Really, so then, do you think he's eaten the muckbeetle?"

It would appear so. What else would he want with more troops? Although I don't know how soon this edict of Dun Lian's will generate enough men to mount a military response to their recent victories, as we hope it will.

"What of T'Lanizen? Has he reported in yet?"

No, Your Majesty.

"Very well, keep me apprised as soon as he contacts you." The person G'Zellan was conversing with knew this was a dismissal.

As you wish, Sire. The tingling vanished as the other mind left his. *How soon this edict of Dun Lian's will generate enough men to mount a military response . . .* It was beginning to seem as if his agent within the Dun Lian stronghold was becoming smarter as he continued his direct contact with humans. Perhaps he should send more of his people out into the world like this; they certainly could use more intelligence.

So Dun Lian seemed to have fallen for his little ploy. Either he needed more knights for the war, or he was worried about what Dun Lain's murders might do to the Brotherhood, or both. G'Zellan was starting to get worried. A renewed force of Dun Lian knights could do some serious damage to his plans for undisputed rulership of this continent. He needed more information. Damn that T'Lanizen.

CHAPTER 17

He was tired. He was definitely very tired. He hadn't stopped moving for four days. Again, he was amazed with his new body. Several times, he had caught himself thinking that it might not be that bad if he had to stay in this form. What was so wrong with it? He could handle the food part, as long as he had an easy supply of fish available to him. His new body was strong, quick, had a built-in endurance that easily surpassed any non-Kasparow-enlightened person. He could only begin to imagine what augmentations Kasparow's presence would give him once he reestablished himself in his god's eyes.

Damn it! He should have been praying to Kasparow these past four days! With nothing to do but run and swim, he could have been meditating at the same time. He didn't even need to think about where he was going. The information placed in his mind by Durgolais was leading him forward.

Durgolais had contacted him once each day, to check on his progress and urge him on. Not that he needed any urging. He felt an almost-disjointed need to go to Durgolais. Every now and then, he would begin to wonder why he needed to meet Durgolais; but then the ancient dragon's voice would resonate in his mind, and his determination would return.

The way to Durgolais was an easy path to follow. He had been running for nearly a day when he came to the Chunya River. The Chunya River was an old river, yet still flowed rapidly southward and was void of the oxbows and meanderings that were typically associated with older rivers.

Up until that point, he had been traveling through deserted countryside. When he surprised a young boy playing on the riverbank, he decided to use the river for cover as well as speed. The boy had screamed as loud as anything Morgan had heard before and ran away faster than seemed possible for the little lad. Of course, the boy's speed was no match for Morgan's new body. In one muscular lunge, he sprang past the fleeing boy and spun to fiercely face the young lad, smacking him with a large-knuckled backhand. The boy had crumpled to the ground like a discarded garment. It was around this time that Durgolais had contacted him for the first time since he had started running. At the dragon's insistence, he had left the boy behind and jumped into the river, continuing his journey.

He stopped swimming. He found that he was extremely buoyant. While his huge hands could keep him well out of the water with a very minimal amount of paddling, he found that he could float on his back without effort. He decided to take his time and float lazily toward the cave opening that would lead him to Durgolais. It wasn't until now, swimming in the Chunya Sea, as the snow-dusted peaks of the Majestics disappeared into cloud cover before him, that he thought about what he had done.

He felt like vomiting. He felt he *should* have vomited. He had eaten that boy. The memory of the boy's scent came back to him; he started drooling. KASPAROW SAVE ME! He rolled over, face in the water, and rinsed his mouth for several minutes. Taking a deep breath, he dove powerfully downward until his ears began to hurt. There was little sunlight this far below the surface, and most everything was the same cold temperature. There was little for his multifaceted eyes to focus on. He was becoming a little disoriented.

When the pressure became too great, he stopped swimming and screamed as loud and as forcefully as he could, expelling all the air in his lungs. Only after doing so did the thought occur to him that without air to make him buoyant, he might not be able to tell in which direction the surface was. On one level, he didn't care if he drowned, Kasparow would not take his soul for surely He would damn him for his crime. Morgan knew Kasparow would never enter him now. He went limp and found himself moving, presumably with the added weight of his sword, downward. What seemed like minutes passed. Whatever air was left in his lungs was keeping him alive during the slow descent. Eventually, the pressure became too great, and he instinctively swam in the other direction. He swam slowly to the surface, the dimness lifted, his ears no longer hurt. When he broke the surface, he was barely breathing.

He was facing south, toward the Majestics. They were the tallest mountains in the world, and they butted up against the Chunya Sea, the smallest inland sea in the world. The mountains were aptly named. They rose with such a vertical steepness that traversing them was nearly impossible. Well, impossible for most. There were a few Dun Lian records of nonhuman races that inhabited the Majestics—ogres, trolls and the like.

Trolls? Could he find others of his kind in the Majestics? He shook his head. *His kind?* He was not a troll. He may be trapped in this body, but he was *not* a troll. He remembered the boy. It was time he started acting like a man.

Despite the fact that it was still summer, snow had started to collect on the higher elevations of the Majestics. Somewhere out there, Durgolais the dragon was waiting for him. He would go to Durgolais, but the dragon would have to wait a little while longer.

He rolled onto his back and cleared his mind. Almost as soon as he thought about it, he made the tingling connection to the gem. At least *that* was getting easier.

"I know I said that I was finding this *rabbit* a refreshing change of mind, but I think I could do without it."

"Nice to talk to you too, Jux, and yes, I'm okay."

"I mean, it has no concept of communication, even on a basic level, and it is constantly shouting random thoughts and desires. Despite the fact that I cannot shut these things out, I feel alone. I have never been alone since my creation, and I have to admit that I do not find the experience appealing."

"You're becoming more and more human."

"Please do not tease me. I rarely experience emotions of my own. I guess this is what you would call a mood swing, or possibly a temper tantrum?"

"Maybe just a little."

"Yes, I was worried about your safety. I simply took your memories as you appeared. It is not like I had much else to do."

"Then you know what happened."

"Yes."

"Wasn't that truly ghastly?"

"Well, it *is* in your nature to do such things."

Morgan was appalled at Jux's statement. "By Kasparow, it is not!"

"Sure it is. You are now in a troll's body. It is only natural to assume that you will be subjected to and follow the same urges as any other troll, regardless of what your consciousness might be used to. What was the first thing you did when you saw the boy?"

"I jumped in front of him."

"Why?"

"I don't know, I just did."

"And what was the first thing you did after knocking him down?"

Morgan paused. "I ate him."

"Why?"

"I don't know, I just did." If he were in his body, he would have vomited. His proficiency with the gem seemed to be getting stronger. Five days ago, the desire to physically vomit would have broken his concentration and the connection.

"It is apparent that the natural urges to attack that boy and eat him overpowered any aversions you may have had."

"But that's completely horrid! I can't go around committing such crimes! Kasparow will damn me!"

"You should realize that it is not a crime to do what is natural for you to do."

"But it's not natural for me to eat people!"

"Yes it is. Remember, you are a troll now."

"I am NOT a troll!"

"What did you see the last time you saw your reflection?"

Morgan remained silent, but the memory of leaning over the streambed several days ago flashed in his mind. Jux saw this image as well.

"And that would be the visage of a troll. Thus, you are a troll."

"A troll with a human mind." He fell silent again and thought about the boy. He would have to find the boy's family and explain. "A troll with a human mind," he repeated. "Or more accurately, a human *soul* trapped within a troll's body."

"But a troll, nonetheless."

"It may be this body's natural responses to attack and eat little boys, but I don't share your belief that my body's natural instincts will overpower my conscious decisions."

"I know you do not."

"And I will do everything in my power to prevent anything like that from happening again for as long as I am in this disgusting, vile body. If there is one thing Dun Lian knights are known for, it's our mental discipline."

"You may have no choice in the matter just as you have no choice in seeing Durgolais."

"What do you mean I don't have a choice?"

"You are being coerced into going to see him."

"I am not!"

"Yes, you are. I would bring up the memory of what he said to you four days ago, but I fear it might compel you to leave and continue on your journey. There is still much we must discuss. Think about it. He suggested you go see him, and you immediately set off without thinking about it and did not stop for four days even when you had done something as vile to you as eating that boy was.

"He is a natural telepath. He can project his thoughts into your mind, and he can plant suggestions there as well."

"You mean he can control what I do?"

"To an extent. You see, you had no objections when it came to going to see him. He cannot make you do something you really do not want to do. If his commands are against your nature, or are extremely vile to you, they will not work. Keep that in mind—it will help you when you face him."

"Well, now that I know, why don't I just not go?"

"I am not so sure that would be wise. As I said, he is a natural telepath. There is much you need to learn now that you are a telepath yourself, as I have ascertained from examining your mind before and after your attempt to contact Dun Loren."

"This is new, when did you figure this out?"

Jux continued without answering him. "By utilizing the gem to contact Dun Loren, you sacrificed a small portion of your intelligence. It was simply absorbed, eaten by the gem. It gave you all the powers and abilities of a natural telepath with certain limitations. The amount of intelligence you lost directly corresponds to the amount of *reserve* telepathic energy you have.

"Whenever you engage in telepathic activity that would normally physically exhaust or require extra effort from a normal telepath, instead of drawing on physical strength, you draw on this *reserve*."

"How much energy is in this reserve?"

"I do not know. But I do believe that once exhausted, it can only be replenished by sacrificing more of your intelligence."

"So the more I use these abilities, the dumber I'll become."

"Essentially, but only when you use those abilities that require extra strength—"

"And those abilities would be . . ."

"That I do not know, which is why I think it may be prudent to actually go and see Durgolais."

"Before, I didn't think there was anything wrong with that. But now, knowing he was telepathically compelling me against my knowledge makes me wonder exactly what he has in mind."

"I wonder that myself. However, the vague memories I have of dragons leads me to believe he is a fair and just creature."

"Then why were the dragons feared and hated so? They were hunted to extinction, or at least so everyone has thought for two thousand years."

"Ignorance is usually the sire of fear. I do not know why they were hunted. Perhaps you can ask him that when you see him. Just keep in mind that he cannot make you do anything you truly do not want to do."

"You say he isn't able to make me do anything that is against my nature. Do you think then, since *I am now subject to all the urges a troll would be subjected to* that he can compel me to do something that is within a *troll's* nature?"

"I do not know."

"A fine lot of help you are," he said unhappily.

"I am sorry, but this is the first time I have dealt with anything like this. And since I have no experience with it, I am sure Durgolais does not know what to make of it either. As you said, dragons have been extinct for two thousand years. Why would he contact you and risk changing that?"

Morgan thought on Jux's point for a few minutes before addressing the disembodied voice.

"He wouldn't, unless he was sure that I wouldn't be able to bring that fact out into the open. Now I'm really not sure I should go to him. Although *I* contacted *him* first, even if it was by accident. I guess he feels he *has* to do something about it."

"I still have the feeling that he is an honorable creature. And I still think his experience in this matter will be to your benefit, especially when it comes to tracking down and regaining your own body. Malchom will be a formidable foe. Gods do not die, they are only forgotten. If he regains power, you may need these telepathic abilities to defeat him."

"By Kasparow!" Morgan shouted. "I just realized something. Does *Malchom* know of the gem's powers? Couldn't he become telepathic if he came close to the gem?"

"I do not know, possibly, but I would think that he would have to know of the gem's powers before he could utilize them. You found out by accident, and were purposefully attempting to force your mind inside the gem. After only a few months of freedom, I do not think he will be in any hurry to get anywhere near the gem physically, let alone mentally."

"I just hope nothing happens to my body before I have a chance to confront him. That's another reason why I'm not so sure I should go see Durgolais. I don't think I can afford to waste the time."

"But can you afford to waste the knowledge he might be able to give you?"

"I don't know. What I *do* know is that I need to know what is going on. I should contact Dun Loren. If he was at the Dead Pools, then Malchom has done something that would prompt Dun Loren to go looking for me, and *that* can be a very serious charge for a Dun Lian knight."

"Dare you waste away your reserves contacting him?"

"As my sponsor, he is responsible for my actions until I finish my free deed tour."

"I know."

"I can't let Malchom's actions put Dun Loren's life in jeopardy."

"I also know that you have made you mind up on this decision."

"At times I wish there were some way of blocking my thoughts from you. I'd find it more interesting to have a normal conversation with you. As it is, I might as well be talking to myself."

"Well, in effect, you are."

"I know." Morgan thought himself back into his body, into the troll's body, severing the connection instantly.

He was still floating on his back in the middle of the Chunya Sea. He wasn't any closer, as far as he could tell. It was still light out. Whether or not it was the same day, he couldn't tell. The last time he had spent any time within the gem, almost a full day had passed. Eventually, once he got his body back, he would have to experiment with the gem, find out exactly what it could do.

But was this magic? Dun Lian knights weren't *forbidden* to use magic. The Brotherhood traditionally did, however, echo Kasparow's abhorrence of magic. Would Dun Lian allow him to study the gem, or would the leader of the Brotherhood order it destroyed? He didn't think there would be anything wrong in studying it. He would have to present a strong case to his fellow brothers.

Fellow brothers? Was he still a Dun Lian knight? He hadn't felt Kasparow's presence since leaving his own body weeks ago. He hadn't even prayed to Kasparow since then. Would Kasparow accept him as a troll? He should pray now. He didn't have to go anywhere. Durgolais could wait. But what of Dun Loren? If he were truly looking for him, he should know what was going on. He should be forewarned just in case he did catch up to Malchom.

He would pray to Kasparow first. He would float here for a few hours and hope that Kasparow heard his prayers. Then he would contact Dun Loren. The cost of using that power was well worth what it would accomplish.

He closed his eyes and breathed deeply. He might be in a new body and many things might be new and alien to him, but the routine meditations and prayers he had been practicing for years were still second nature. His mind cleared almost instantly. All thoughts were washed away. Only a single thing remained. He visualized the word, began speaking it within his mind, over and over. *Kasparow, Kasparow, Kasparow.* There was nothing except the word.

As with the gem, time had no meaning while he meditated. Thus, he had no idea how long he had been praying before his concentration was broken by Durgolais' voice.

"It is not wise to open your mind so completely. Anyone could enter you and wreak havoc on it while you are thusly laid bare."

Morgan did catch one thing before his meditation stopped that lifted his spirits. He saw himself, in his new body, holding a set of Dun Lian Sales of Justice. What the image meant, he did not know. It wasn't the image that had given him a hint of hope. He *felt* that the image had come from Kasparow. He hadn't actually graced him with His presence, but the image was unmistakably sent from Kasparow—he knew it, he felt it. Morgan allowed himself a few moments to rejoice in that feeling.

"What do you mean?" he replied to Durgolais' statement.

"When you clear your mind so completely like that, you remove any barriers that might otherwise protect you. Just now, while you were contemplating that image from Kasparow, I could have run rampant through your mind and done nearly anything I pleased. It is very dangerous to meditate in that manner."

"But Dun Lian knights have been doing it this way for a thousand years without any problems."

"There has never before been a Dun Lian knight who was also telepathic. Dun Lian knights also have the added protection, which you do not, of Kasparow's presence."

"Kasparow will grace me again," he replied.

"Still, there is much you need to learn. To start with, when you converse with another telepath, *project* your thoughts. If you do not, and simply reply, you keep the conversation within your own mind, which again can be very dangerous. Yes, there is much you need to learn. So *continue your journey and come to me now.*" The command tugged at Morgan's muscles. He righted himself in the water and nearly began swimming again.

Just keep in mind that he cannot make you do anything you truly do not want to do. Jux's voice echoed inside his head. His muscles relaxed.

"Why should I come to you?" he projected outward, or at least he thought he projected outward.

"Good, you learn quickly. You shall be an excellent student. *So take no further actions except to continue your journey and come to me now so that I might teach you.*" Morgan began swimming again.

When he reached the southern end of the Chunya Sea, he knew that time had passed. The sun had set, and the moons had risen. He had started swimming, and now he was here; he had no recollection of anything in between.

Before him was a massive cliff that rose out of the summer-warmed water and became the Majestics. It was a good thing that the entrance to Durgolais' lair was accessible from the water. Even if his kind—even if trolls did inhabit these mountains, he was certain he could never scale them.

Durgolais' implanted directions had steered him to this point. He wasn't sure where to go from here. He seemed to be on his own now. On his own, was he really on his own? Evidently, he wasn't totally against the idea of meeting Durgolais.

He had allowed Durgolais' command to control him again? How could he stop this? *Just keep in mind that he cannot make you do anything you truly do not want to do.* Would Jux know?

"Jux." This *was* getting easy.

"Yes?"

Morgan projected the memories of the past few hours. "How do I keep Durgolais from controlling me like that?"

"Just do not let him."

"How do I do that?"

"I do not know, how did you contact Dun Loren?"

"I don't know, I just did."

"Then just do not let him."

"That doesn't help me." If Morgan could have sighed, he would have.

"What exactly did you do to contact Dun Loren?"

"I thought about him, thought about contacting him, then it happened."

"Then why do you not try that? Think about Durgolais, then think about not allowing his commands to work on you."

"If that works, will I have to continually be thinking that, or can I start after he tries it again?"

"I do not know. It seems to me that you need something more permanent, something like a wall."

"But what kind of thoughts are permanent?" There was a long pause. Was Jux silent, or was he thinking something? If he was thinking something, why couldn't Morgan hear it?

"When Kasparow filled you, you did not need to continually think of him?"

"No."

"What did you do then, to pray to Kasparow?"

"You know."

"Yes, but it is the train of thought that helps us figure things out. What did you do when you prayed to Kasparow?"

"I would visualize His name and His face. Then I would think of nothing but Him until His presence was with me."

"Well then, perhaps you should visualize a wall and then think of nothing but this wall surrounding your mind."

"For how long?"

"I do not know."

"Can I do it in here?"

"I do not know."

"Well, a lot of help you are," he replied before severing the connection. He wasn't going to give Jux a chance to mention that he *was* actually helping.

The motion of the water had pushed him closer to the nearly-smooth rock of the cliff. The moons were still out, so he didn't think much time had passed. Perhaps, as he became more proficient with the gem, the actual time spent within it was reduced.

He paddled backward, putting a large distance between him and the rock. If he was going to spend an undetermined amount of time meditating, he didn't want to be interrupted halfway through by the water nudging him against the cliff.

Closing his eyes, he began as if he was praying to Kasparow. This time, instead of Kasparow's name, he visualized the wall that surrounded the Dun Lian castle, Lianhome. What more suitable wall could he use?

When the vision of the wall was vividly planted in his mind's eye, he began to talk to himself. *This wall surrounds my mind, this wall surrounds my mind, and it protects my mind from outside thoughts. It will remain until I take it down. This wall surrounds my mind, this wall surrounds my mind, and it protects my mind from outside thoughts. It will remain until I take it down . . .*

When he stopped and opened his eyes, it was light out. The sun had recently risen. There was still a slightly damp chill in the air from the colder nighttime temperatures, evidence that fall was approaching.

Would the wall work? There was no way of knowing unless he confronted Durgolais. He could try to leave, continue his search for Malchom. He could try and find Dun Loren, or at least contact him telepathically. But then, would he ever learn to use these new powers of his? Could he figure things out on his own? Even with Jux's help, he might never discover the things that Durgolais could teach him. His dream came back to him . . .

Durgolais spoke, and he was again standing, collared and leashed, in the center of the courtyard. "You will have my help." The dragon had been in several parts of his dream. *"Come to me, and I will show you the* true path *to follow."* Later in the dream, the dragon had offered what seemed to be advice. *"The world will go on, no matter what you choose."* Durgolais' *whisper floated up from below him.* Morgan glanced down. *He was standing directly over the massive head of Durgolais the dragon. The dragon's eyes shone a brilliant green. His eyes flashed. "It has been nearly two thousand years since I was first entombed within the gem. Through it all, the gem has remained and seen changes in the world. Changes for* good, *changes for* evil. *Do you decide to change things, or do you choose to accept what happens? Do you sacrifice yourself to follow one path, or do you give in to yourself and be led down another? If nothing else, remember this: questions always have answers, answers always have owners, and power always dictates the rights of sovereignty."*

What did Durgolais mean by all that? Was it really Durgolais, or was it simply a dream that held no meaning whatsoever? The dream seemed to be prophetic in nature; one thing had 7already come to pass.

At one point in the dream, Dun Loren was kneeling to a Dun Lian headsman's axe, pleading with Morgan: *"Don't let me be held responsible for this!"* Morgan knew now from his brief telepathic contact with his mentor that Dun Loren was indeed being held responsible for whatever Malchom was doing. What *was* Malchom doing? Was this really prophetic? Every Dun Lian knight knew that a sponsor was responsible in all ways for his squires until they finished their free deed tour.

Whatever the dream meant, Durgolais was obviously involved somehow. The dragon had been a living set of scales, with Malchom in one hand and Dun Loren in another. Whether Durgolais was to be an active participant in the events to come, or whether he was, like a set of scales, simply a tool for him to utilize, was a decision Morgan hoped to have control over.

Therefore, the decision to continue on to Durgolais was his. *Or was it?* As if he had been here a hundred times before, he dove down and headed for the cave opening he knew was there, thanks to Durgolais' implanted memories. He almost felt as if he *had* been here a hundred times. That was another reason to confront Durgolais and settle these issues, to stop second-guessing himself.

The cave opening was there, several feet below the surface of the water, exactly where he knew it would be. He swam into it. The water inside the cave became lighter and clearer as he swam along. It also got warmer.

It was large, more like a tunnel than a cave. Morgan couldn't see the walls of the cave—not that he would have been able to, with his heat-dependant eyesight, if the walls had been closer. The tunnel carved a straight line back into the mountain and eventually began to angle downward. He knew this because the sloping ceiling slowly came into view as he swam along. The rock was evidently colder than the water. Wherever this tunnel led, there was a heat source somewhere ahead. Were the Majestics volcanic?

He continued along, swimming slowly, enjoying the warmth of the water. He could at least allow himself a little bit of relaxation before he confronted Durgolais. There were no fish swimming around, no plant life floating through the water or clinging to the tunnel's walls, at least none that he could see. The tunnel seemed barren and desolate, and yet warmly inviting somehow.

He swam downward for a good fifteen minutes before the ceiling curved and angled sharply upward. He approached the opposite wall and was amazed at how the tunnel was now almost completely vertical. Now anxious, he swam powerfully to the surface.

Violently, he broke the surface, the sounds of his arrival echoing in a large lit chamber. He exhaled. *After all that, I'm not even breathing hard.*

The pool of water he waded in was in the center of a large cavern. This place was not natural. The floor was flat and smooth. The walls angled inward in a uniform, worked manner as they rose into a tapered dome.

A massive chandelier hung from the apex of the dome. A chain the thickness of his leg provided the support. Two dozen torches, if they could be called torches, rested in the chandelier, providing enough light to fill the chamber. They looked like torches, were the same size and shape as torches, yet they were not burning, and the light they gave off definitely was not from fire.

There were four exits from the room. They were all perfect three-quarter circles. Columns had been carved on either side of each of the exits. Three were small tunnels about six feet in diameter. The fourth was larger, much larger. It was at least forty feet tall, and even wider.

He paddled to the edge of the pool, expecting the water to get shallower and shallower as he got closer to the edge, much like a riverbank would. This was not the case. The edge of the cave floor, where it met the water, was almost a perfect ninety-degree corner, as if someone had simply punched a huge hole in the ground to create the access tunnel.

He pulled himself onto the cave floor. The floor was made of marble and was definitely not indigenous to this mountain. *Is this Andonesian marble?* The floor appeared to be a single piece of marble; he could find no cracks or joints anywhere in the floor as he made his way to the largest of the exits. If Durgolais were a dragon, then it would be most likely that this was the tunnel he used. *Wouldn't it?* When he approached the tunnel, he discovered that the walls of the chamber were not smooth, as he had originally thought.

An enormous mural had been carved into the walls of the chamber. As far as he could tell, the engraving covered the entire dome and depicted a tropical scene. It was a beach scene. There were huge palms, laden with large fruits of some sort. A flock of birds was in one area of the sky. Several tropical animals peered out of the carving at him, half hidden by stone foliage. A mountain rose in the background, smoke was rising from its summit. There was a large sun carved just above the chandelier. The entire mural was different shades of light and dark. *Were the walls painted?* He wished now that he had more than his limited black-and-white vision.

Peering down the forty-foot-long tunnel, he could now see that it went back into the mountain for quite some distance. Somehow he knew the tunnel led deeper into the mountain, away from the Chunya Sea. He began walking down the tunnel.

One of the strange torches was set in a sconce every hundred feet or so. He stopped and examined one. It was bright enough to hurt his eyes if he looked straight at it. Although it provided light, it did not change the color of the rock around it, as a hot torch would have done. His eyesight picked up no changes in heat on or near the torch. Indeed, when he put his hand up and tentatively touched it, it was cool, almost cold.

The walls of this tunnel were carved as well. It retained the same tropical motif, but the palm trees and smaller bushes thickened as he progressed down the corridor. He was amazed at the complexity and beauty of what he had seen so far. It must have taken decades to create this complex, but then, if this was Durgolais' lair, the dragon would have had centuries to complete this work.

He continued walking, cautiously, attempting to stay as alert as possible.

Several times something on the walls caught his attention. At first he simply continued walking as he could see nothing unusual. It was just a wall. The third time it happened, he walked over to the spot and examined it.

It was just a wall, but it did not look right to him for some reason. He put his hand up to feel the rock.

It went straight through!

He jerked his hand back. *A fake wall, an illusion?* Now that he knew it was there, he concentrated on the wall and was able to see right through it.

There was a small room behind the illusionary wall. It was the size of a small bedchamber. *Some sort of observation post? Was this Durgolais' version of a soup hole?* Now that he knew what they were, he was able to see every hidden chamber along the tunnel's walls. There were quite a few of them.

He must have walked two miles before he noticed that he was coming to the end of the tunnel. He could now see another large chamber at the end of the tunnel. He took a deep breath, steadied himself, and decided that there was no reason to attempt to conceal his approach. He walked boldly forward, as best as he could with his bent legs, and stepped into the largest room, above ground or below ground, that he had ever seen.

He thought he could have fit the entire Dun Lian stronghold into this chamber.

Despite its immense size, he could see the entire chamber as clear as day, as if there was daylight streaming in. In fact, there did seem to be daylight streaming in!

The walls rose what must have been several hundred feet and curved inward slightly and disappeared into a bright summer sky! This room had no ceiling but was instead open to the sky. Wispy clouds floated overhead; the sun, almost at its zenith, glared down at him. A bird flew across the sky.

This was impossible. He knew there should be miles of mountain above him. Some inward instinct knew which direction and how far he had traveled into the mountain and knew that there should be rock above him. And yet, here was the sun, the clouds, and a bird!

This was not right. He lifted his head to the sun; there was no warmth. *Could this be another illusion?*

One of his eyes caught movement near the center of the chamber. He began walking slowly toward the movement, which was a good quarter of a mile away.

As he walked, he noticed that these walls were carved much like the walls in the entrance chamber. The carvings in this room depicted thick jungle plant life. The floor again was a single piece of marble. *How could this be possible?* he thought. *Where could one find such a large single piece of marble? And how would you get it here? It's just not possible.* He concentrated on the floor as he walked; perhaps this was another illusion.

As he got closer, he was able to make out what occupied the center of the room.

There was a single table in the center of the room. It was a massive table. It was rectangular in shape and hollow in the center. A break on one side of the table allowed access to the center so that a person might walk around the inside. Even with this accessibility, a person could not reach every part of the table's surface from either the outside or inside of the table without assistance.

There was a short man standing in the center of the table, intently looking over some objects on its surface. He paid no attention to Morgan.

Morgan stopped a few feet from the table. He was now able to examine the table better. Each length of the four-sided table was roughly fifteen feet in width. A map had been painted on the tabletop and depicted every continent and island that Morgan knew of, as well as several he could not identify.

Hundreds of objects littered the surface of all four sides of the table. There were figures, numbers, blocks, flat chips, and dozens of other objects on the table. They looked to be made of all types of material—wood, stone, clay, bone, ivory, porcelain, and half a dozen different metals. It looked exactly like Dun Lian's battle map, only much, much larger.

The man continued to study the map in silence. He was looking at an area that Morgan knew to be Lianhome and Panadar. He was a short deeply tanned man. His skin was smooth and taut, not what Morgan would have expected in someone who evidently spent a lot of time in the sun.

The man had no hair. His bald head was even more tanned that the rest of him and had a dark stripe that ran from his eyebrows, up over his head, and back down his neck and disappeared under a small red silk tunic.

He couldn't have been more than five feet tall. He leaned against the table, supported by very muscular, tanned, hairless limbs. Even his legs were strong and stocky, as well as hairless and unshod. Morgan noticed that both the man's fingernails and toenails were in need of trimming—they were long, thick, and yellowed as if they hadn't been attended to in months.

Morgan felt a slight pressure against his mind. The man recoiled slightly in what seemed to be surprise. He turned to face Morgan.

"You've put a shield around your mind. Did you do this on your own?" Morgan was startled from the pressure against his mind and the man's reaction. Had the man actually spoken out loud to him?

Morgan tried to respond but could only manage a garbled growl from vocal cords that were as yet untried.

"Yes, I did," he responded telepathically, immediately, almost instinctively.

"Good, good," said the man as he walked out from behind the table and approached Morgan.

Morgan felt the pressure against his mind again. It lasted for only a second before forcefully increasing to a concentrated push that felt like a pin swiftly pricking his skin.

"But not good enough," said the man's voice in Morgan's mind.

"Who are you?"

"I"—the man looked up at Morgan and stared at him with powerful yellow-and-red eyes—"am Durgolais."

CHAPTER 18

"Dun Lian told me that you would be headed in this direction. His last dispatch was just over a week ago. I have heard nothing since then. He told me you had complete authority in this matter. I take it that Dun Lain is to be formally charged with these crimes?"

"Yes," Dun Loren sighed. "No recent news from Lianhome? Dun L'lsen hasn't shown up?"

"No, Dun Loren, on both accounts."

"I half expected him to make it here before me," he muttered quietly, sarcastically. The other knight acted as if he hadn't heard Dun Loren's last statement.

"The Successor is coming here? He's helping you in this matter?"

"Yes, Dun Dison, I have the privilege of being saddled with the mighty and influential Dun L'lsen, chosen successor to Dun Lian." This time he spoke loudly and didn't bother to hide his sarcasm and obvious dislike of Dun L'lsen. He heard one of the twins attempt to stifle a snort.

The knight glared past Dun Loren, obviously at the twins. Dun Dison probably worshipped the man.

"It will be an honor to meet Dun L'lsen."

"If you say so," said Dun Loren, dismissing the line of conversation by looking around the small village.

The village was nearly deserted. From reading Dun Dison's dispatch, he knew that Morgan had slaughtered over seventy of the town's inhabitants in a ritualistic manner. There couldn't have been more than a dozen villagers left alive. He saw at least that many brothers walking about the small gathering of buildings that was the town of Maralat, or used to be the town of Maralat.

Dun Dison had been ordered to seal off the village, preventing all but Dun Lian knights from entering or leaving the village. It wasn't uncommon for potentially harmful diseases to break out every now and then. Since it was the priests of Kasparow that usually tended to such sicknesses, no one would question or come near a quarantine enforced by the Brotherhood.

"Come," said Dun Dison, patting the neck of Dun Loren's horse. "You must get down off these animals and let them rest before you are charged with murders of your own."

The younger knight smiled up at Dun Loren. Dun Dison might be well over two decades younger than Dun Loren, but his comment was not out of place or disrespectful. He and Morgan had been squires at the same time, but Dun Dison had been commissioned a season earlier and had obviously already finished his free deed tour. He was a full knight and, in all respects, Dun Loren's equal.

He dismounted and adjusted his silk shirt. It was soiled and stank. He wiped the sweat from his face with the cotton kerchief around his neck. Neither he nor the twins had bathed since leaving the burning farmhouse two days earlier. The farmhouse's well and water bucket had provided a shower of sorts to the three stripped-down travelers. That cleaning had been the first they had since leaving the Dun Lian stronghold. Even though they had been afforded the luxury of one bath, their clothes were still carrying the original dust from Lianhome.

He turned and addressed his squires, who had dismounted and were leading their horses toward his. They were already ready to lead his horse to the town's stables.

"When you're done, bring our clothes so we can become human again."

"Yes, Dun Loren," said the twins in unison. Clerents grabbed the reins of his horse. He knew that the twins already knew to do this; they were very bright and, after a month of living with him, knew him as well as anybody.

"My squires need to take care of the horses." He turned back to Dun Dison. "I would like to have three baths ready for us when they are finished. You can brief me between now and then."

"Very well, Dun Loren." The young knight turned and walked off, talking as he went, assuming that Dun Loren would follow. "I have wondered, ever since Morgan told me that you had taken on squires who were twins . . . ," He paused and glanced backward slightly to see if Dun Loren had followed.

Dun Loren was patting the shoulders of his squires.

"You were saying?" he said as he caught up to Dun Dison.

"I was saying"—he lowered his voice as he turned around—"ever since Morgan told me that you had taken on twins as squires, I've wondered what they were like."

"You mean, you've been wondering if they are like the McAri twins."

"Well"—Dun Dison glanced back at the twins to make sure they were out of earshot—"yes, I was wondering that. The McAri twins began a very bloody chapter in our history. Some say that it wasn't just the fact that they were commissioned too early. There are some that say the very nature of being twins who came out together caused the problems."

"Just because our order is steeped in traditions does not mean that history will repeat itself. I will agree with you that there are many similarities. The same knight is training them both, they both came out at the same time, and they are both ready to be commissioned well ahead of the normal amount of time." He stopped and said loud enough to make Dun Dison think the twins might hear. "But do I have any fears they will make the same mistakes as the McAri twins? None whatsoever." Whether Justin and Clerents could hear was not his concer; he just wanted Dun Dison to wonder.

"Forgive me, Dun Loren, I didn't stop to think that this might be an old, rehashed subject for you." The younger knight caught sight of someone and called out to him. "Nathan, come here please."

Dun Loren looked over his shoulder and saw a youth approaching. Did Dun Dison have a squire already?

"Your squire?"

"Oh no." Dun Dison chuckled a little. "He belongs to one of the other knights. We had so much to do here when we first showed up that the few squires we had sort of became common property." The boy trotted up to them.

"Yes, Dun Dison."

"This is Dun Loren." He motioned to the blond knight. "He and his squires are in need of cleaning. Please draw three hot baths for him in one of the empty houses. Be sure to let us know which one. I'm sure Dun Loren is anxious to get clean and wouldn't want to wander around looking for his bathtub." The squire bowed and ran away without a word. "There are a lot of empty houses in this village these days," he explained.

Dun Dison walked up to a large gazebo that was in the center of the village and sat on one of its benches.

"Are you thirsty?"

Dun Loren shook his head as he sat.

"Then I guess you would like to know what happened here."

Dun Loren nodded.

"Well, from the reports of the few survivors, of which there are only eight, and from our own investigations, we can say for certainty what happened." He paused and observed Dun Loren.

"Dun Lain came into town, now about two weeks ago. He was, of course, greeted with open arms. This town is no stranger to Dun Lian knights. So he was shown respect and treated to a meal, many drinks, and a room for as long as he stayed.

"During his dinner, he met a woman, Rylla. They eventually became quite comfortable with each other and ended up getting to know one another in the privacy of his room. When she said good-bye the following morning, it was the last time she would see him.

"The inn at which he was staying has a front common room and a back, more private, dining room. The dining room has a central fireplace and hearth equipped with stone and metal fixtures for cooking.

"It appears he called everyone that was at the inn into the dining room and knocked them out. We are pretty sure of this—all of the corpses have fractured skulls. We believe he used the pommel of his sword as they all have the same rounded indentations. Most likely, he did this one at a time. I don't think that even a veteran knight could take on several people at once without raising suspicion.

"We believe he then tied these people up and one by one called the townsfolk into the inn, where he did the same to each of them. The eight survivors all reported either being asleep or out of the village proper.

"When he had abducted all that he could, he began the killing." Dun Dison paused, looked over his shoulder, and pointed at a large two-storied building.

"That's the inn there." He motioned to the other buildings. "You can see that it stands well away from the other buildings. Only the stables are close to it. Who knows how long it took him to get all the townsfolk into the inn, but once he did, we don't think it took long to kill them.

"One by one, they were tied to the spit that hangs over the fireplace. Their throats were cut and their blood allowed to spill onto a very small fire. We know he didn't use a big blazing fire, for none of the corpses were burned that badly. All except the one that was found left tied to the spit, that is. It appears he just left that poor person there when he was done.

"It looks as if he simply spilled their blood on the fire, then moved on to the next one. I don't know how he was able to keep a small fire burning while being constantly doused with blood—"

"Were there any markings on the walls?" interrupted Dun Loren.

"Markings? You mean like writing?"

"Writing, or symbols."

"No, there was nothing on the walls. There was a lot of blood on the floor, all drippings, nothing meaningful, nothing coherent, that is. Were you expecting something?"

Dun Loren wondered exactly how much this knight knew. The fewer people who knew the truth, the better, but this was one of Morgan's closer friends.

"You can inspect the inn yourself," said Dun Dison when Dun Loren didn't answer right away. "Besides putting the dead to rest, we've left things as they were."

"How was it that you were able to examine the bodies before the corpseflies got to them?"

"Well, he evidently fled as soon as he accomplished whatever it was that he was doing. I came along shortly thereafter and found the bloody mess before the corpseflies had a chance to infest many of the bodies. When some of the townsfolk returned, I had them shoo the flies away while I rode to Lianhome to inform Dun Lian. I must admit, their arms had to have become tired very easily. They were in too much shock to do much else though—"

"*You* came along? What were you doing in this area?"

"As I said, this town is no stranger to Dun Lian knights. I grew up here, which is probably why Dun Lian granted my request."

Dun Loren waited silently for the young knight to continue. Dun Dison was having a hard time keeping the tears away. It took him several minutes to continue.

"I left this village when I was twelve." He sniffed and rubbed his eyes, gazing downward. "It took me three years as a serving boy at Lianhome before I found a knight to sponsor me. Morgan and I met during my yearlong training. I was commissioned before him, so I haven't seen him since.

"I was nearing the end of my free deed tour when this happened. I begged Dun Lian to let me handle the quarantine."

He looked up, into Dun Loren's eyes.

"He did, and raised me to full knighthood. It was especially hard when I heard Rylla describe Morgan with unwavering accuracy, very hard."

They fell silent. Dun Loren gazed across the village. The twins were exiting the stables. They walked half the distance to the gazebo and stopped. They both looked Dun Loren in the eyes, then looked to each other. Dun Loren knew what was coming next.

The twins looked back to Dun Loren and bowed slightly in acknowledgement. Clerents and Justin then each drew two daggers from hidden boot sheaths and began expertly juggling the small blades between them.

He decided that Dun Dison had a right to know what was going on, or at least what he thought was going on.

He watched the twins as he told the story.

"Morgan left on his free deed tour about a month and a half ago. Before he set out, he told me what he intended to do. For some time, he had been having dreams that centered around the Dead Pools. You and I both know that the Dead Pools and the Barren is an area that is avoided by all living things. Neither he nor I could fathom why he would feel the need to go there." He sighed. Justin dropped one of the knives. "I should have argued against it more than I did, but he was determined to go.

"Then about three weeks ago, Dun Lian summoned me and handed me one of your dispatches. It was a devastating letter. I don't think I have ever felt such an utter sinking feeling before." He glanced at Dun Dison; the knight was staring off in another direction.

"Knowing where he had intended on going, I left immediately. Dun L'lsen had asked for permission to go along, so, accompanied by his squire, Manney, the five of us set out for Panadar. I wanted to make sure that Morgan hadn't headed in that direction first.

"There was no record of him passing through Panadar, so we headed, with Kasparow's speed, to the Dead Pools. We reached the edge of the Barren in two days—"

"Two days!" exclaimed Dun Dison, his vision refocusing on Dun Loren. "You must've killed your horses!"

"I had the twins arrange for replacements to be waiting for us a day's hard ride out of Panadar." The twins were still tossing the knives back and forth. *Had Justin cut himself?*

"His trail was easy to follow. He had constructed a small raft at the edge of the Barren and used his horse to drag it to the pools. We found the carcass of Morgan's horse several miles into the Barren. It was still roughly intact. Even corpseflies won't dwell in that area.

"When we reached the pool, we found the raft, and a couple of other items. Dun L'lsen was able to determine that Morgan had, for some reason, wandered into the water."

He looked back to Dun Dison. The other knight was staring at him.

"The smell of decay that permeated everything in that area was overpowering."

Dun Dison turned away.

"Manney had used parts of the raft to start a fire and was making some tea when he became violently ill. He vomited until there was nothing left in his stomach. A fever followed.

"The smell of death was on Manney, it was on the raft, it was on everything that came in contact with the water. It was even on Dun L'lsen and myself—after all, we had touched the wood that had touched the water, just as Manney had."

"Then why didn't the two of you get sick?"

"Kasparow's grace. Manney hasn't come out yet. He wasn't afforded the protection of Kasparow's presence."

"So you think that Morgan became sick even though he, like you, was protected by Kasparow's presence?"

"There was evidence that he entered the water. We merely came in contact with wood that had come in contact with the water some two weeks earlier. Its potency was no doubt reduced.

"Having a good idea of what was wrong, I had Dun L'lsen, take Manney back to Panadar to be healed by our priests." He thought about telling Dun Dison of Dun L'lsen's lack of concern for his squire, but decided otherwise.

"The twins and I headed for the farmhouse. Dun Dahra had been there for days, translating the writing on the wall and waiting for me to show up. When we were finished, we buried the dead, burned the place to the ground, and left for Maralat.

"Here is where things become disturbing." Still watching the twins, he heard Dun Dison shift positions on his bench.

"You remember that Morgan"—he nearly stumbled over the name—"drew the Dun Lian Scales of Justice on a wall of the farmhouse with the blood of the victims." He heard Dun Dison grunt in recognition. "That, and there was other writing on the wall as well, which Dun Dahra had been able to interpret."

He paused for a while. The twins had stopped and were looking in his direction. They weren't looking at him to see if he was done talking with Dun Dison; there was no inquisitive look in their faces. They seemed to be awaiting his next words as if they, fifty feet away, could hear him.

He turned away from the twins and focused on Dun Dison. The two locked eyes as he continued.

"*Morgan* had written in blood, in a tongue that has not been uttered for nearly a millennium, the phrase 'Condemned thee entire beneath Altarium.' Which basically means 'All shall perish before Altair.'"

"Altair?"

"You know what event shaped and formed the Dead Pools a thousand years ago, do you not?"

Dun Dison stared at him blankly. How could a Dun Lian knight not know this? It was the battles against Altair's worshippers that formed the Brotherhood. Perhaps the young knight was simply too stunned to reply.

"The final battle between all but one of Altair's mightiest worshippers took place in the Barren. The magics released during that battle formed depressions in the earth that would eventually fill with water and become the Dead Pools." Dun Dison continued his blank stare.

"Morgan visited the Dead Pools." He felt as though he was leading the young knight like a bull by the nose ring.

"And then he began his killing spree, writing praises to Altair in Altair's religious language."

Dun Dison broke eye contact and stared after the twins, who had resumed their juggling, apparently oblivious to the conversation taking place.

"So you think that Morgan isn't simply sick, like Manney, but that something else has hold of him. Something old, something evil, perhaps even one of Altair's ancient priests. Perhaps even Altair himself?"

Evidently, Dun Dison did not need to be led by the nose.

"It would explain everything. Morgan wasn't a scribe or a scholar or a sage. How else would he know a language dead for nearly a millennium? And do you really think that Morgan himself could be capable of murdering several hundred people?"

"Several hundred?" Dun Dison turned back to Dun Loren.

"He attacked another village. Evidently, this time he simply walked into the village and proclaimed that *the Brotherhood* was taking a census and all the townsfolk were to report to the local inn to be counted. He even encouraged recruits.

"Needless to say, he slaughtered them in the same manner as he did here."

"Kasparow have mercy on his soul." Dun Dison bowed his head and sighed.

"Worshippers of Altair were required to make blood sacrifices during their prayer. If I remember correctly, the greater the sacrifice, the more power Altair would bestow upon the priest."

"So you think that Morgan is trying to contact Altair? You think he's trying to call back Altair's power?"

"I think *someone* is trying to worship Altair again."

"Kasparow have mercy on his soul."

"If he *has* a soul left."

That was the end of their conversation. The twins approached a couple of minutes later.

"Are you ready to become human again, Dun Loren?" they asked in unison.

"Did you bring our other set of clothes?"

"Yes, Dun Loren," they said.

"Good, because we smell like a trio of muckbeetles."

*　　*　　*

Dun Lian,

It is with a heavy heart and reluctant admission that I send this letter. It is becoming more and more painfully clear that Dun Lain is the person responsible for the recent murders. I arrived in the town of Maralat early yesterday afternoon. After consulting with Dun Dison, I spoke with the woman claiming to have shared the suspect's bed. Not only did she describe Dun Lain exactly, but she was also able to identify certain skin growths on his thighs that I am sure only his mother and I have had the opportunity of seeing.

After interviewing the woman, I inspected the crime scene. Dun Dison informs me that no mutilation other than the slitting of throats was done to the bodies. He was fortunate enough to have arrived before they began to decompose or fall victim to corpseflies. The possibility that these people were killed in a sacrificial ritual to Altair is a strong one.

Knowing what we do of the Dead Pools, and of Morgan's sudden knowledge of Altair's religious language, I am beginning to think that an evil presence has taken a grasp on Dun Lain. Inwardly, I pray for this to be true. If an outside force is indeed directing Morgan's actions, then at least his soul may be salvageable.

Today we will search the surrounding area. It may be a waste of time, but I hate not to be thorough. Dun Dison and the other brothers here have had their hands full simply attempting to keep the quarantine working smoothly and have not been able to do much investigative work.

As far as the village and townsfolk go, I recommend continuing with the façade of a quarantine as long as possible. Eventually, this town will either have to be left alone or destroyed completely. It may be wise to relocate the survivors to Lianhome and burn the village to the ground in the outward appearance of containing the disease.

Either this evening or tomorrow morning, we depart for the village of Jourlean. I do not expect to find anything new there, but as I said, I hate not to be thorough.

Have you news from Dun L'lsen? How fares his squire, Manney? May Kasparow grace him with His presence. Kasparow knows the boy needs some direction.

Dun Dison awaits your orders. As always, may Kasparow's grace shine upon thee.

Your servant,

Dun Loren

Dun Loren picked up a bone tube and inserted the rolled-up letter. He should have brought Rosen Kirkland along with him. The scribe's handwriting was much better than his was; besides, the fat little man needed some exercise. He had told the scribe to do a hundred sit-ups a day. He smirked. The rotund scribe would probably be able to do ten before his back would start to hurt.

He had just finished sealing the ends of the bone tube with wax when Dun Dison and the squire Nathan entered the building. The squire put a tray of food, pitcher of water, and an empty wax-lined leather mug on the table that Dun Loren had been writing on.

"It's bizarre," said Dun Dison. "To find all these houses so empty. Dun Loren examined the recently raised knight. Stress, or perhaps sadness, showed in the few lines that appeared in the young face as the knight attempted a weak smile.

"No doubt." He tossed the bone tube on the table in front of him and watched as it nearly rolled off the edge. "Can you have that sent in the next dispatch?"

"Of course." He nodded to the squire. Nathan picked up the bone tube and left the building. Dun Dison sat in one of the wicker chairs around the table. "Shall we breakfast together?"

"By all means," replied Dun Loren. Dun Dison plucked the leather mug that was hanging from his belt and poured himself some of the liquid from the pitcher.

"Flavored with sassafras, I hope you don't mind." Dun Loren shrugged and poured himself some as well. The two knights sat in silence for a few moments before Dun Loren reached out and grabbed a piece of the bread that had been supplied. It was freshly baked, still a little warm. He raised an eyebrow at this. Dun Dison noticed his surprise.

"The few remaining villagers are more than willing to cook for us." He sighed. "It seems with nearly everyone else dead, they have little to do."

"They should be taken to Lianhome." He took a bite of the warm bread. "And this village burned to the ground," he said through a mouthful of bread. Dun Loren snatched an apple off the serving tray.

"That would hold true with the appearance of a quarantine." The other knight had acquired his own piece of bread and was busy swabbing it with a dark liquid in a small shallow clay bowl.

"Is that Chunyan Chianna?" The acrid smell of the liquid reached Dun Loren's nostrils and confirmed his question before the young knight could answer.

"I love this stuff," he said, saturating another piece of bread. "This particular bowl has been used for nothing else for the past ten years. It was my mother's."

His mother's? Dun Loren hadn't thought about it before, but if this was the village Dun Dison grew up in, then it would stand to reason that his parents probably were now dead.

"It *was* your mother's? I take it they were among the victims?" He pulled out a knife, sliced off a portion of the apple, and dipped it in the spicy liquid. He liked this stuff as well. There was silence. Dun Dison had been staring at the knife.

"No," he said faintly. "They died before I left to become a knight, one of the reasons I did leave." He stared at the knife a bit longer. "You don't like Dun L'lsen," he changed the subject. "Why?"

"Well," Dun Loren said, enjoying the taste of the liquid. Typically made of vinegar, oil and Chunyan spices, this was a particularly strong-tasting batch. The clay bowl must have contributed to its taste. Years of saturating the porous clay with Chunyan spices had to be enhancing the liquid's flavor. "Dun L'lsen is a fine knight." He dipped a piece of bread in the Chianna. "But the man is lacking in the area of amicable personality traits."

"Really?"

"Most certainly," he said, nodding slightly. "I don't think I have ever met another Dun Lian knight that was more self-absorbed or interested in his personal affairs more than Dun L'lsen."

"But, I mean, I've never met the Successor before, but he is very highly spoken of. You're the first brother I have heard of that *doesn't* like him. In fact, everyone I've met sings his praises."

"Dun L'lsen does have a way of charming those around him, I'll give you that." The taste of Chianna was becoming a little overpowering; he cleansed his throat with some of the sassafras-steeped water. "He seems to radiate charm as easily and effectively as his damned armor reflects sunlight. But don't be fooled by that charm when you meet him. Dun L'lsen has his own agenda, apart from the Brotherhood, that he follows quite blatantly.

"He was with me for several days when we first set out. I think you would be surprised by his actions and treatment of those around him." Dun Dison thought for a moment.

"Well, I'm not saying you're wrong, but I think I will hold my judgment of the man until I meet him."

"That"—he bit into the apple—"is an excellent policy to follow."

*   *   *

Dun Lian,

There was nothing more to be discovered at Maralat. We spent a day searching the surrounding countryside, but other than the freshly dug graves of the villagers, nothing in the immediate area had been disturbed or was out of place.

I must commend Dun Dison for his handling of these events. Even though he had no blood relatives still living at the village, it had to be difficult to see his hometown decimated so. He awaits your orders. Having now seen the village, and having had time to think this through, I strongly recommend that we burn the village to the ground and relocate the survivors to Lianhome.

The news from Jourlean, except for the number of dead, is not much different. Over three hundred were slaughtered in the same ritualistic manner. This time *Dun Lain* commandeered a local inn and set up a fake census bureau and was able to convince the entire town to show up at the at structured intervals. It is a feat beyond comprehension. The only survivors were a couple of boys that had left to go camping the day Dun Lain arrived.

We spent the entire day today searching, in vain, for any clues. It almost seems as if Dun Lain is able to come and go as he pleases. Besides the dead, and the experiences of the living, there is no trace of him anywhere.

Considering the totality of this massacre, I recommend burning
this village to the ground as well.

There was a knock at his door. It opened before he could reply.

"I'm almost finished," he said, keeping an eye on the parchment as he
finished it and signed his name. He rolled up the paper and looked up. "Do
you have a dispatch leaving tonight—"

Dun L'lsen stood on the other side of the table.

"I don't know, brother," Dun L'lsen said. "That is a question for someone
else to answer." The reflection of a dozen candles off his flawlessly polished
armor made him look like a walking chandelier.

"Ah," he said sullenly. "How nice to see you, Dun L'lsen. Could you summon
a squire for me?" He looked down, turning his attention to packaging the letter in
a bone tube. It was several seconds before he heard Dun L'lsen turn and leave.

He's caught up with me already, he thought. *And the worst part of it is that I
can't think of a reason to dismiss him. Although his tracking abilities may be useful.
I wonder if he would be able to find any traces of Dun Lain around here.*

Dun L'lsen returned all too quickly, a squire in tow.

"I believe Dun Loren has a message to go out as soon as possible." The
squire stepped into the small room and waited for Dun Loren to hand him
the segment of bone.

"Tonight's dispatch then?" he said. The squire bowed and hurried out of
the room. "Sit down, you must be tired. You must have ridden nonstop to
catch up with us."

"Not really," said the knight as he sat. "I went straight to Panadar, dropped
off Manney, then headed for Maralat and evidently just missed you."

"Manney is all right, then?"

"I'm sure he is. I dropped him of at the temple, ran a few errands, and then
continued after you." Dun Loren wanted to scream at the man. "I probably
would have caught up with you, but I didn't have the added benefit of being
able to acquire fresh horses."

"Dun Dison wasn't accommodating?" He found that hard to believe,
unless the younger knight *had* formed a new opinion of Dun Lian's chosen
successor. "I find that hard to believe."

"No, Dun Dison was quite supportive. He offered a horse, but I declined.
I'm not sure what Dun Lian has in store for that village, but I'm sure Dun
Dison will need all the resources he has."

*He's got his armor back . . . he probably adorned his horse with that damned
barding as well.*

"Besides, I'm partial to my own horse. I don't think another horse could keep up with me."

Or would want to keep up with you, he thought. "So tell me, Dun L'lsen, you actually have no idea how Manney is doing?"

Dun L'lsen stared at him blankly for a moment before replying. "The priests will take care of him."

Dun Loren returned the blank stare.

"I *did* leave instructions for them to notify me of his progress." Dun L'lsen leaned back in his chair. "I'm not that much of a monster, despite what you think."

Dun Loren sighed and sat back as well.

"I just think you could treat your squire a little better. I'm sure he, like many others, idolizes you."

"Well, I've never had any complaints from squires in the past." He relaxed a little. "To change the subject, we've had good news from Dun Algen. It seems we have gained a considerable amount of ground lately. The G'Angeleppans have pulled out of several key positions—"

"Pulled out?" That didn't sound like something G'Zellan would do.

"Well, Dun Algen reports that they have beaten the G'Angeleppans back, but Dun Lian doesn't trust this description. He doesn't think G'Zellan would give up three almost completely intact keeps so easily."

"Nor do I. Those damned earth-burrowing muckbeetles don't give up such fortifications easily."

"He thinks it has something to do with Dun Lain."

"He told you that?"

"Since I was to be meeting up with you, he thought you should know."

"How could G'Zellan retreating be linked to whatever is going on with Morgan?"

"He thinks G'Zellan is attempting to draw more of our forces overseas, away from Lianhome."

"Does he think G'Zellan knows exactly what is going on here?"

"He fears it, yes. He's stepped up recruiting, nearly quintupled it. In fact, all those knights at Lianhome who currently have no squires have been instructed to take on two."

"Just as long as they're not twins," said Dun Loren.

Dun L'lsen let loose with a very deep, earthen, throaty laugh.

"Praise Kasparow Oliver, where did that come from?"

"Haven't I ever told you? I'm part dwarven, you know how they like to laugh." The two knights looked at each other for a moment, then both began laughing.

"That's the first time you have ever called me by my first name, Dun Loren. Or should I say *Grant*?" Dun Loren stopped laughing and fell silent.

He sure does have a way of loosening you up, he thought. He studied his folded hands.

"Do you think G'Zellan knows of what is going on here?"

The big knight seemed to be contemplating something, perhaps the exchange that had just taken place? It took him a while to respond.

"How could he? So few know of what has happened that it would have to be someone involved with this investigation or someone high up in the Brotherhood. Someone like you . . ." His voice trailed off. "Or me," he said after a pause.

Dun Loren looked up.

"I doubt it could be a fellow brother. Their aura would give them away the instant they thought of such treachery." He looked away slightly, concentrated on the big knight. Dun L'lsen's own aura was impeccable.

"What about non-brothers?" asked Dun L'lsen.

"The only ones involved that have any knowledge of the murders are trapped within quarantine. And a layman would be even less able to hide his aura.

No, I don't think there can be any leak from within or around the Brotherhood. I've never had the distasteful pleasure of seeing one, but G'Angeleppans are reputed to have certain mental powers. Who knows what kind of information-gathering capabilities they possess?"

"Indeed . . . who knows?" They fell silent for a time again. "I take it we next head for Dun Lain's last known position?"

Dun Loren sighed to himself—*we*. "Yes, *we* will head south in the morning, although there hasn't been any news of him for a while. If his mobility is as good as it seems, he might not be anywhere near there."

"Indeed. Well"—Dun L'lsen stood—"it's time for me to pray. I'll see you in the morning."

"Good night, Dun L'lsen." Dun L'lsen turned and started walking out the door. "Kasparow's grace upon thee," he said, almost as an afterthought. The words almost stuck in his throat. *Was Dun L'lsen really all that bad a person?* He sighed and rose to retire to one of the building's bedchambers and begin his own prayers. Morgan would be among them this evening, as he had been for several weeks now.

*   *   *

The morning air was thick, full of moisture, but still somewhat chilly. Dun Loren swayed slightly in his saddle. The twins were asleep, their mounts following Dun Loren's horse out of training, or was it instinct? It was just the three of them. Dun L'lsen had been removed from their party two days ago, before leaving Jourlean, which he had hoped for all along, but now he was beginning to think that Dun L'lsen's tracking ability was going to be sorely missed. Dun L'lsen had argued vehemently that the letter did not pertain to him, but eventually relented. He was mortified by the events that drew Dun L'lsen away, but at least the annoying man was gone. He prayed that Dun L'lsen could make a difference where he was going.

He pulled a folded piece of parchment from his belt pouch and read the letter again for what must have been the tenth time since leaving Jourlean.

Dun Loren,

Please see to it that the knight ferrying this message receives any and all aid, as his mission is a dreadfully urgent one.

As for the knights involved with the quarantine of Jourlean and Maralat, they shall proceed with your suggestion of burning the villages to the ground. They shall post appropriate plague markings and bring the survivors with them when they return to Lianhome.

It is hauntingly ironic that your suggestion should so precede the events that have now come to pass. There is no denying that what has happened has a direct correlation to your pursuit of Dun Lain, and I pray to Kasparow that it goes no farther.

A plague, a very mercurial and malignant plague, has broken out in Panadar and along a path that leads toward the Dead Pools. Our priests have no doubt in their minds that Dun L'lsen's squire, Manney, is the origin of the epidemic.

I use the word "epidemic" because it will undoubtedly become one. The disease appears to have a very short incubation period and is extremely contagious. Those who were near Manney's presence while he was being healed at the temple and were not protected by Kasparow's grace were showing signs of the disease within mere hours.

As of yet, we have had only one death. The disease is treatable. Our priests have been able to cure anyone infected, and relapses have not, thank Kasparow, occurred.

Besides that one bit of bright news, all else in this matter is grim. Because of the quick incubation period, the numbers of infected are growing at an alarming rate. Our priests predict that they will be overwhelmed within a matter of days.

We have no way of knowing how many outside of Panadar have been affected. We fear that unless contained in the next few days, this plague could become the worst ever known. Panadar itself has been quarantined. Only the sick are allowed to enter, and only those graced by Kasparow's presence are allowed to leave.

Therefore, with the exception of yourself and the twins, I am hereby ordering all knights and their squires to return to Lianhome immediately and without detour. It will take all of our manpower to contain this evil.

There have been no reports of those who are protected by Kasparow's grace transmitting the disease, but regardless, you must remain in the village of Jourlean for at least eight hours. It may be cruel, but I order you to spend those eight hours interacting with the two surviving villagers. If, after eight hours, they are showing no signs of the disease, then you can be certain that neither you nor the twins are carrying the disease. I am sure that they would be sick by the time you read this letter if you were infected. I simply feel it prudent to make sure.

You witnessed what happened to Manney, so you have an idea of the initial symptoms of the disease—dripping nose, fever, profuse sweating, and repeated vomiting. In later stages comes uncontrolled defecation and urination. A distinctive green-yellow ring develops around the eyes as they retreat into the skull from lack of moisture in the body.

I know that your quest now takes you to Dun Lain's last reported position. From this point on, I fear that there will be no support for your efforts. Our need at Panadar is too great. Please send an update as soon as you are able.

May Kasparow protect us all.

Dun Lian

It was a grim letter. Rereading it never helped. Plague. Could it really be as bad as Dun Lian said? Of course it was. Why would Dun Lian lie? He wondered if the whole thing could have been prevented if Dun L'lsen had treated Manney's situation differently. Dun L'lsen could not have known how serious Manney's condition was . . . but he could have gone directly to the priests at Panadar. Dun L'lsen probably stopped several times along the way. *That damned self-absorbed man probably stopped off to get his armor and barding* before *taking Manney to the priests*, he thought.

He returned the letter to his belt pouch and removed another piece of parchment. He studied the map that Dun Lian had included in his latest dispatch.

The road they traveled south from Jourlean was packed dirt. Despite a hot, dry summer, little dust was being generated by their passage. Soon they would be leaving the road and heading east, into the woods, toward Morgan's last reported position.

He glanced back at the twins. They slept as they rode, their thick dark cotton kerchiefs wrapped around their heads to block out the light and heat of the day. Summer was nearly over, but the day could still be oppressively hot and bright, which never lent itself to sleeping in the saddle. The bulk of the day had passed, and the sun would be going down soon. Should he wake them? Should they stop for the night? They couldn't push their horses as hard as they had in the past three weeks, as there would be no replacements for quite some time.

He caught the smell of burning wood; the hairs on his arms stood on end. It smelled like—a campfire? It had to be; he could also smell cooking meat and roasting Chunyan spices. He couldn't see a fire anywhere nearby; there was nothing on the road ahead of him.

He stopped, silently drew his sword, and lightly prodded Justin with its tip. The boy woke with a start, and Dun Loren silenced him with a finger to his lips. He motioned to Clerents. Justin quietly woke his brother. Dun Loren sheathed his sword.

They sat and listened for several minutes. The twins had smelled the fire as well; they continued to inhale the tantalizing aroma as if there had been no food in their stomachs for days.

The daylight seemed to be fading rapidly. He couldn't find where the smell was coming from, and the twins, with a simultaneous shrug, told him they couldn't either.

He urged his horse forward slowly. Step-by-step, they eased down the road, eyes wide, searching the forest on either side for any hint of the source of the smell. He stopped and motioned the twins to come up alongside of him.

"I don't know why this bothers me," he said in a whisper. "It will be dark within the hour. We'll stay put until then. The lack of light might give away whatever campfire these smells are coming from." The twins nodded.

Eventually, after standing in stillness for nearly half an hour, the daylight having almost completely faded into night, Justin motioned to a point ahead of them to their left, a little ways into the woods.

"I think I see light, there."

Dun Loren saw it as well.

"Okay," he said. "You two dismount. Justin, follow the tree line on the other side of the road and sneak past that point. Signal me when you get a few yards beyond where you would leave the road to reach the campsite. Clerents, you stay here, along this side of the road. I'll casually walk the horses up to that point and take a better look. I don't expect any trouble, but be ready for my signal."

"Yes, Dun Loren," they whispered. Justin jumped from his saddle and was off, hurrying down the road with a quietness that was impressive considering the speed at which he was moving. Several minutes later, he signaled, chirping like a cricket in a code that Dun Loren taught all his squires. Dun Loren nodded to Clerents and continued, noisily, down the road.

He came to a wide path cut into the woods, leaving the road in the direction of the fire. From this vantage point, he could see the fire easily enough.

A clearing opened up about twenty yards into the woods. A small campfire reflected light off some sort of wooden structure. There was a figure seated between the building and the fire. He thought it was a woman.

He chirped, ordering the twins to advance slowly and quietly toward the fire.

Turning his mount off the road, he led the three horses down the path, grabbing some branches that hung in his face, purposefully breaking them.

The woman at the fire looked up sharply, but not startled, as if she had been expecting someone to walk down the path. He continued his noisy approach, hoping that his passage would mask any sounds the twins might make.

When he came into the light of the campfire, her eyes widened, brightened.

"Praise Kasparow," she said. "A Dun Lian knight!" She leapt to her feet and ran to Dun Loren's horse. "Praise Kasparow you're here." Dun Loren looked down at her. With her back almost completely to the fire, deep shadows danced across her visage.

She was absolutely stunning in the veiled dimness of the campfire.

"I was sure it was them again, but now you're here to protect me." Her voice held a certain nasal quality. It seemed to penetrate his senses. Dun Loren shook his head. Her beauty had entranced and almost dazed him for a moment. He glanced around him.

The clearing was in disarray. Dozens of objects, debris that looked like personal effects, were strewn about the clearing. The place was a disaster. He was sure there was more outside the immediate light of the campfire.

What he thought was a wooden building was actually a massive wagon. It too was a disaster. It was obvious that someone had tried to destroy the huge thing. Every wheel, even the spare that was normally kept underneath the wagon, was broken in some manner. The ten-foot-long rear wagon had been ripped open at several places; the side doors and panels that normally opened to reveal the wagon show's secrets were ripped from their hinges. The double doors that allowed entrance to the rear of the wagon were on the ground. The sides of the wagon, originally painted in gold an maroon depicting exotic animals, had been splashed with what Dun Loren was sure was blood.

The carriage itself, besides a large number of bloodstains and smashed wheels, was relatively untouched. Someone made sure this wagon show would put on no more exhibits.

He looked back to the woman. She was turned around, examining the campsite as he had done. He could see her face in the full light of the fire. She *was*, indeed, a fine-looking woman.

"They certainly made a mess of things." She sniffed, wiped her nose, and turned to look at Dun Loren. He recognized her voice. He knew this wagon show. He had seen it just outside of Lianhome.

"Where's your wagoner?" he asked.

She blanched and shivered. Was she sweating?

"He's dead," she said; her nose was stuffed and runny.

Could it be the plague, here, already?

He dismounted, chirped an all-clear to the twins, and let the horses wander off to the side. Dun Loren moved to the woman and grabbed her by an arm. He put the back of his hand to her forehead as he guided her to sit down by the fire.

"How long have you been sick?"

"What?" She looked at him with a confused stare.

Clerents and Justin emerged from the surrounding trees. Again, she looked up quickly, but not as if she was startled, almost as if she was expecting someone.

"They're back!" she screamed and leapt behind Dun Loren with an amazing agility.

Dun Loren forced her around front and sat her down again.

"Clerents, Justin, tether the horses." He grabbed her chin and made her face him. "They're my squires." She seemed to relax instantly.

"I knew you would protect me," she said. The words punctured his thoughts. Her eyes bored into him. She was beautiful.

"How long have you been sick?" he asked again.

"What?" she stumbled over the word. "Weeks, at least." She continued staring at him. "Why?"

Justin came up beside him.

"This is the wagon we passed at Lianhome."

"I know."

"Does she have the plague?"

"I don't think so, but we should wait and see, to be sure. We need to stop for the evening anyway."

Clerents joined them then.

"Does she have the plague?" he asked.

Dun Loren looked at Clerents. He had to laugh.

His laugh was cut short. An explosion of noise and motion blew out of the trees. A hideous thing stumbled into the clearing. Its skin was pulled tight across its face in a snarl that made him shiver. Multifaceted eyes seemed to stare at all of them at the same time. An eerie moan slipped passed huge teeth.

"By Kasparow, what is that?" breathed the twins in unison.

Dun Loren drew his sword. "Troll" was the only word that came to mind.

CHAPTER 19

M alchom reasserted his hold on the fingers tucked into his fists. He and four others kneeled in the small room. They were all fairly young. It was time for them to pray. Malchom laughed to himself. *They* would be praying to Kasparow; *he* would be thinking the thoughts that would transport them to his castle—his ruined but ever-improving castle.

"Remember," he said, "if Kasparow blesses us, he will take us to a place where you will begin your devotion to him. You must keep your eyes closed, think of nothing, and remain still until I tell you what to do next."

"Yes, Dun Lain," they responded in unison as they bowed their heads.

It's good to be finally free, he said to himself and thought of the holding cells in the catacombs beneath his ruined castle.

In an instant, they were no longer in the small village that the four girls had called home. They were now kneeling, hundreds of miles away, in a small mushroom-lined and mushroom-lit room. Two other girls, dressed in plain brown robes, were standing in the room, waiting with a distant, almost-empty look in their eyes. Malchom nodded his head at the two standing girls, who produced small leather drinking bags and stepped up to the kneeling girls.

"We are in luck, girls. Kasparow has graced us. Remain still. Shortly you will feel a flask pressed to your lips. Drink deeply for it is a holy consecration of which you must partake. This elixir will open the way for Kasparow to enter you."

Within a short time, the four girls had drained the flasks dry. Malchom instructed them to open their eyes and stand. Even though the drug would take several minutes to begin working, they obeyed without question. The girls gazed wide-eyed at the small room. There were four exits to the room, a door in each wall. All four females looked to Malchom.

"This is Tara and Lorna," he said, motioning to the brown-cloaked girls. "They will be your teachers for the first few weeks, while you become accustomed to serving Kasparow. You will listen to what they say and obey their words as if they were coming from me. Do you understand?"

The girls nodded. None of them spoke.

"Good." He kissed each of them on the lips. "You will enjoy your service." He smiled and motioned to Tara and Lorna. They came forward, and each took two girls by the hand.

"If you are hungry, feel free to eat a mushroom off the wall. They are quite safe, and quite tasty." The training began immediately as the two groups were led in opposite directions, into the rooms that had usurped their village as the girls' new home.

He left the new *recruits* in Tara's and Lorna's capable, albeit drugged, control and exited the room. This had been, quite luckily, his third trip of the day. In the scant two weeks since finding his catacombs, he had collected almost a hundred people.

He needed a hundred people by the beginning of the month to keep the few powers he had been granted. He was pacing himself well then, to have a hundred people ready for sacrifice and still have many left over to begin his breeding process again.

The men would be sacrificed first, a hundred of them. He needed the females to bear children. He still had a very long way to go before he had enough women to provide a continual supply of infant sacrifices.

He maneuvered around a pile of fallen rock and dirt. This area of the caves had almost completely collapsed a week ago. It had taken his elemental quite a while to open the passageway again.

The summoned creature was working tirelessly around-the-clock under Raurin's direction to completely restore the catacombs. In time, he would eventually turn the elemental's labors toward the castle above ground, but not until he had reestablished most of his power.

On almost a nightly basis, he watched the progress of Dun Loren. The magical divination ability that Altair's avatar had bestowed upon him was proving to be most handy. He knew that Dun Loren was following his trail from the first two villages and would soon be literally right on top of him.

He had sent the elemental to the surface to hide the airshafts with massive boulders too large to be moved by Dun Loren's group while still allowing the airshafts to function normally. Even if Dun Loren brought with him a team of Dun Lian engineers, it would still be nearly impossible to clear the debris away.

He passed by the room that he and Raurin had originally entered some two weeks ago. The pile of bones had been cleared away, and Raurin had taken over the room and turned it into a laboratory of sorts. The young man was in the room now, fooling with the experiments he had expressed an interest in pursuing.

"How goes the excavation?"

Raurin looked up. He was chewing something.

"The avatar is still clearing out one of the southern tunnels," he said with a mouth full of fungus. Malchom had originally told Raurin the elemental was an avatar. He didn't think summoning elementals would have fallen within the Dun Lian realm of abilities. "It was severely damaged. He'll be there a while." Malchom hadn't needed to force Raurin to continue to eat the mushroom; he seemed to like them, or perhaps he liked the euphoric side effects of eating the mushrooms. "I thought I would come and work on the mushrooms some more."

He must like them. He was working on selectively growing a more potent mushroom.

"This goes well," he said as he plucked a small mushroom and ate it. "I'm using the same procedure my father used on his mushrooms, and I think I'm making progress. This latest batch tastes much better and seems to give off more light."

He is definitely addicted, Malchom thought. *He doesn't even realize that he's improving the potency of the mushroom—at least he won't admit it.*

"Be sure to get back to the . . . avatar. If he finishes, he will need direction."

"Of course, Dun Lain."

He left Raurin then and continued down the hallway, thinking that carrying the boy away from that village had been one of his best ideas, which reminded him of Namara. She had stirred feelings in him that he had not had for well over a thousand years. Even before his entrapment within the gem, he had never felt as strong a desire as he felt for Namara. He didn't know if it was anything other than a purely sexual attraction, but he did know that he wanted her.

And why not? She was a very beautiful woman, and she had shown interest in him. Well, Namara had shown interest in *Dun Lain*. His old body had been so frail and homely that no woman would even think about bedding him without being drugged with the mushroom. Malchom was sure she was simply after the Dun Lian title. No matter, any interest on her part would serve his desires well.

Why couldn't he go get her now? Raurin was too far gone to care, even if he was attracted to her as well. Besides, the complex was large enough now that he need never see her. She would, of course, stay in his private apartments, and he could easily keep Raurin out of that area.

He turned around, went back to Raurin, and asked for a handful of the young man's newest, biggest, and best mushrooms.

Minutes later, he was materializing in the woods just outside Raurin's home village. Ironically, it was the same spot where he had killed Raurin's father. Someone had erected a small headstone. Something was etched into the Andonesian marble, but Malchom didn't bother to read it.

He made his way to the packed dirt road and was spotted by one of the villagers as he emerged from the trees. The sun may have gone down over an hour ago, but the twin moons, rising early as they did in the late summer, gave off plenty of light.

"Dun Lain! Greetings!" said the man as he bowed slightly, spilling a few mushrooms from the basket he was carrying. "It pleases me to see that you remember the death of Geoffrey and honor him by visiting his grave."

"Um, yes, of course. I couldn't travel in this direction without paying my respects. The headstone is very beautiful, and the epitaph is very . . . thoughtful."

"Thank you, Dun Lain. I chiseled those words into the marble myself. I am Jansen, Geoffrey's brother."

"Well, Jansen, walk with me to your village? I have come to see Namara and tell her of Raurin's progress."

"It would be my honor to do so, Dun Lain." Jansen turned slowly and started down the road. Malchom now saw that this man was old, much older than Geoffrey had been. He also learned, through the idle conversation the man made as they walked, that he was a very simpleminded man.

*   *   *

He materialized in a very dark alley. An alley that he knew, despite the size of the city, would be void of people, especially at this time of night. It was nearing the midnight hour, and anyone still awake was either drinking or sitting at home. There would be no one in this alley to see him take form out of thin air.

Namara had been very surprised and extremely glad to see him. They had talked for a while, spoken of Raurin briefly, but mostly laughed and flirted with each other. The sexual tension between them was so thick it almost became a thing he could grab. He had given her a small sack containing the mushrooms and told her it was a present from him, for her only.

He had told her to eat the mushrooms the next day, a few hours before sunset, and that he would return to see her again that evening. Malchom held no doubts that she would follow his instructions; her eyes had told him that much.

That brief encounter with Namara had led him here, to the walled city of Origin. It wasn't the largest of the five walled cities in Andonesia, but as its name suggested, it was the oldest. This decadent old city, which suited him so well, was where he would find what he was now looking for.

He strode out of the alley with a confidence provided by his tall well-built frame, which his old body never could have afforded him. This particular alley provided a shortcut between a large bakery district and Glyphada Street. He was confident that no one saw his arrival. He knew that until nearly three in the morning, there would be no one in the bakery district, and anyone entering the alley from Glyphada would be doing so to relieve themselves, in which case they would be in no condition to comprehend anything they might see.

Despite the time of night, the street was awash with light and activity. Miremoss and oil lamps cast flickering shadows that added to the dancing gaiety being displayed by hundreds of revelers. Glyphada was a wide, albeit short, avenue that was lined as tightly as possible with taverns and saloons of all sorts. It was to one of these inns that he strode, polishing the emblem on his breast that identified him as a Dun Lian knight.

So intent was he on satisfying the desires Namara had aroused within him that he failed to notice the figure that literally coalesced from the shadows of the alley and continued to shadow his every move.

Even though the main room of the tavern was nearly overflowing with people, it didn't take Malchom long to settle on a woman and lead her, almost dragging her, upstairs. No one protested when he simply grabbed her, tossed a coin to the bartender, and headed for the stairs, not even the pair of young men she had been flirting with.

"Room 7," the bartender had yelled, but no one else paid attention to him. Everyone had noticed what Malchom was when he walked in through the door with a very loud greeting to all and paused dramatically to allow every eye to find the Dun Lian Scales of Justice prominently displayed, and freshly polished, on his left breast.

A Dun Lian knight could do nearly anything he wanted. Such was the respect that a Dun Lian knight commanded that even when he acted rudely, people were honored to do as he desired. Plus, why shouldn't they trust a Dun Lian knight?

So with all eyes watching, as the pair hurried upstairs, no one noticed the leather-clad silver-haired man who nonchalantly hurried after them.

Malchom came to the door to room 7 and, as he turned to open it, caught a glimpse of something out of the corner of his eye. He thought he saw a man, but the image disappeared as he turned.

Thinking only of Namara and the beauty he had brought up here in her place, he dismissed the vision and locked the door behind them.

*   *   *

It was still dark out. A little light from dying oil and miremoss lamps filtered past the curtains. There was very little noise coming from downstairs or outside. So little noise that he could hear his bed partner's light breathing. The night crowd had dispersed; it must have been very close to dawn.

Malchom wasn't sure why he had awoken. He remained motionless, kept his eyes shut, concentrated on listening.

There, near the door, a sound his ears knew. Well, a sound that this body's ears knew. It was so familiar to him, like the way a sword felt in his hand, but he couldn't quite place it. He cracked his eyes open the width of hairs, allowed his vision to adjust as much as possible.

Nothing, even though he could see the door plainly. There was no one there.

The sound came again. It was near the door, but this time a little closer. He continued to watch the door but saw nothing.

Again, this time a little farther to the left. Whatever it was, it was moving to the pile he had made of his discarded clothing. It sounded like . . . like leather . . . soft leather being rubbed against something . . .

Leather boots shuffling against the floor? he thought; his heart was thumping. He didn't dare move but decided to see if he could startle whoever this invisible intruder was.

He snorted loudly and faked a snore for a few seconds. He closed his eyes and let his new body instinctively take over.

The Dun Lian—trained body relaxed immediately. His breathing slowed, deepened, his heartbeat steadied. It was several minutes before the intruder dared to move again. This time, in his relaxed, heightened state, Malchom was easily able to decipher what he heard.

Although he couldn't see him, there was definitely a person walking ever so slowly toward the pile of clothes to Malchom's left.

Whatever kind of thief this was, he would have to come within inches of the bed to reach his booty. He would have to come very close to Malchom's long powerfully muscular legs. It was a good thing the late summer's heat had kept him from sleeping *under* the covers.

Instinctively, Malchom's leg shot out and slammed into a body that was thrown against the wall. Malchom jumped from the bed and landed on an arm, or at least he thought it was an arm. Either his eyes hadn't adjusted to the dim light at all, or this arm was invisible.

The person on the other end of the arm struggled wildly and swung his free arm up to strike Malchom.

Malchom's body, the Dun Lian training kicking in full force, felt the intruder's movements and blocked the blow with his left forearm. His body refused to hesitate. Malchom thrust his right hand forward, open palmed, and connected with the head of the invisible intruder. The body went limp beneath him.

Almost immediately, a form materialized before him. It was a man, clad in soft leather. His face was deeply tanned and lined and was framed by a moderate amount of distinctly silver hair.

Malchom put an ear to the man's chest. He was still alive and breathing. Not knowing how long the silver-haired man would be unconscious, Malchom hefted him into a chair and turned to rouse the woman.

"Get dressed!" he shouted. She nearly jumped out of the bed in surprise. How had she slept through the scuffle? "Get dressed." He tossed her clothes to her. "I need to be alone, I must pray to Kasparow." He hurried her out the door before she could dress herself or even see the man slumped in the chair. Before he closed the door, he gave her one last deep kiss. She turned and walked away, lost in bliss, as he slammed and locked the door. He had locked it in the first place, hadn't he? He turned back to the thief.

The man was still unconscious. Malchom went to the bed and snatched up a linen sheet and, ripping it, used it to gag and tie the man down. When he was done, he propped himself up on the bed and waited for the thief to wake.

How had this man made himself invisible? It had to be done magically. He had heard of certain creatures that could blend into their surroundings so as to become virtually invisible, but none that could assume human form.

Yes, it had to have been done magically. Which would be of great interest to Malchom. From what he had seen in the past month, magic was taboo and its use completely eradicated. He was becoming more and more anxious to talk with this silver-haired thief.

The sun came up. Malchom was staring out the window. The streets were empty. Unlike the bakery district a block over, Glyphada Street didn't get started until nearly noon. The man was still unconscious, was completely still.

A little too still, Malchom thought.

"How long have you been awake?" he gambled, addressing the unconscious man.

"For quite some time," the man said as he lifted his head slowly. "I was about to give up anyway." He twisted his head to each side, cracking his neck several times. "My neck is killing me."

"Speaking of killing," Malchom said boldly, with authority, "how dare you try to pilfer the room of a *Dun Lian knight*?" The thief rolled his eyes and looked down to the floor with a slight sigh. Malchom sat up on the edge of the bed.

"What's your name, and how did you manage that invisibility trick of yours? Kasparow frowns on the use of magic, you know."

"*Speaking* of names, what's *your* name?" asked the man, his head still bowed.

"I am Dun Lain—"

The man snorted at this and looked up.

"You can drop the charade, you are *no* Dun Lian knight."

"How dare you?" Malchom said, rising to his feet and taking a step toward the man.

"Sit down!" The confidence and command in the man's voice stunned Malchom; he sat back down on the bed. "If you're a Dun Lian knight, then I am a giant muckbeetle."

This man was becoming more and more intriguing. Malchom studied the man for a moment.

"What makes you say that?"

"I just know Dun Lian knights when I see them, and *you* are not one. You do fight like one, though," he said, exercising his jaw muscles.

"I don't see how you can be so sure of that. I can go downstairs right now, and two dozen people would bow to me as if I were their king."

"Yeah, just because you dare to wear that emblem on your chest."

"My name is Dun Lain, and you will show me the proper respect!"

The man simply laughed.

The chair was within easy reach of Malchom's long legs. He put his foot under the chair and toppled the man to the floor, which stopped his laughing. Intriguing or not, he was losing control of this situation. This man was proving to be bold, arrogant, and annoying. Malchom couldn't help liking the man. He left the thief where he was until the man decided to speak on his own.

"All right!" said the man several minutes later. "I'm called Frost."

"Frost? What kind of name is that?"

"It's a name." There was a long pause. "Look, my arm is starting to kill me, could you please lift me up?"

"But 'Frost' isn't a name—I mean, what kind of mother would give her son a name like that?"

"Please! This is really starting to hurt."

"But *'Frost'*—"

"Okay!" yelled Frost. "I gave the name to myself."

Malchom waited.

"I don't like my real name," Frost said in a very controlled, almost-calm voice.

"What is your real name?"

"Gayman Darkenye," Frost said quietly after a pause.

"What's wrong with that?"

Frost sighed. "Do you know how much I was teased as a kid because of my name?"

"I don't see what's wrong with your name."

"Forget it, you didn't grow up in the same area I did."

"At least you got that one right."

"Please, would you sit me up straight?" begged Frost. Malchom liked the tone of Frost's voice; he felt he had control of the situation again. Malchom stood and set Frost's chair on its feet.

"Now, *Frost*," he said, standing over the man, "tell me how you managed that trick of yours."

"Tell me how you are able to go around masquerading as a Dun Lian knight."

Malchom backhanded Frost across the jaw.

"Now why did you go and do that?" Frost whimpered and ran a tongue around his cheek.

"Because you are tied up, and I am not." Malchom struck him again. "What were you looking for in here?"

"Your gold," he said sarcastically.

Too sarcastic; Malchom struck him a third time.

"Would you quit doing that!"

"Start acting like what you are, my prisoner, and start answering my questions, and I might." Just to exercise his control, Malchom tipped the chair backward. Frost's head struck the floor with a thud that almost sounded hollow.

"I was looking for a clue as to who, or what, your are, since I knew you were no knight," Frost said after a while, almost meekly.

"And how do you know I am not a Dun Lian knight?"

Frost remained silent.

Malchom walked over to Frost, put his large bare foot on the man's exposed neck, and pressed down firmly. Frost gasped and wheezed. Malchom continued until the man was beginning to turn purple.

"I will never tire of this," he said as he sat back down on the bed. "Though I do have someplace to be tonight and a lot to do in between." For the first time, Malchom realized that he was naked. He stood and dressed. He was about to strap on his sword belt but stopped, and drew the sword slowly, noisily. "So I guess I will just have to step up my efforts." He tossed the scabbard and belt on the bed and went to stand over Frost again.

"Time to get," he said as he lowered the sword point to Frost's midsection, "creative."

"Now I *know* you're no Dun Lian knight."

"How do you know that?" Malchom rested the sword point on Frost's groin.

"First off, no Dun Lian knight would threaten a person such." Malchom pressed the sword forward slightly. "Secondly," Frost said with a jump, "I saw you materialize in the alley last night." Malchom withdrew the sword and tossed it on the bed. "No Dun Lian knight would use magic like that."

"Magic not unlike yours," Malchom said as he set Frost upright again.

"Exactly what I was hoping to find out. Very few people these days can do magic, let alone actually practice it in the open like that."

"Yourself included." He sat on the bed.

"Well, it's a professional necessity."

"So you're a common thief."

"My word! Thief, yes. Common, no. I am the most noted and notorious thief in Andonesia, if not the world!" Frost was getting cocky again. "Why, I am wanted by all the—"

"I could push you over again."

Frost fell silent.

"So now"—Malchom leaned forward on the bed—"how is this magical invisibility of yours achieved?"

"The ability to turn invisible gives me a great deal of power."

"Power, you like power?"

"Power is good. Invisibility is good, especially in the hands of the greedy. Greed is good."

"And just how do you become invisible?"

"I don't know how you do it, but I, well"—a smile came to Frost's lips, his cockiness returned—"rings"—he brought his unfettered hands forward and showed Malchom a gold band on one finger—"aren't just for binding lovers." Malchom stood up violently.

"I could pretend I was tied up again," Frost said quickly, shoving his hand behind him."

"What did you just say?" Malchom asked, leaning over Frost menacingly.

"I said I could pretend to be tied up again," Frost said timidly.

"No, before that."

"I, um, I said rings aren't just for binding lovers?"

Malchom laughed and retrieved his sword belt, buckling it around his waist.

"Frost, my friend,"—he sheathed his sword—"you may have just saved your life."

"Really? What did I say? What did I say?"

Malchom stepped over to Frost and slapped him on the shoulder. "Rings aren't just for *binding* lovers." He thought of his private quarters.

Instantly they were in the catacombs.

Frost, who had been sitting in a chair, fell to the ground. "My word!" he exclaimed as he stumbled to his feet. "So when you appeared in the alley, you weren't just becoming un-invisible?"

"I was traveling instantaneously from one place to another."

"Where are we?" Frost asked in astonishment as he looked around him.

"About a hundred or so miles south of the city of Panadar."

Frost gaped at Malchom.

"Now *that* is power, what I could do with such an ability."

"And such power you shall have."

Frost walked over to a wall and lightly touched the mushrooms that covered it. "Are these things giving off light?"

"Yes, and they're edible too, but you are *never* to eat one."

"Where are we?"

"This is my home." Malchom walked to a table against one wall and picked up a flagon of wine. "Are you thirsty?"

"Yes, very," said Frost as he wandered slowly about the room.

"I am in need of some, help." Malchom held out a goblet. Frost accepted it.

"What kind of help could a man with your obvious power need?"

"Oh, don't get me wrong. I have plenty of . . . *servants* to do my bidding. But none of them have much . . . free will, shall we say. I need someone with a *clear mind* that I can trust to do things for me. And of course, I would give that person enough power and ability to do what I ask of him."

Frost drained his goblet and held it out for more.

"How do you know you can trust me?"

Malchom refilled Frost's goblet.

"Rings aren't just for binding lovers," Malchom quoted. Frost snorted; a few drops of wine came out his nose.

"This doesn't have anything to do with my name, does it?"

"I will perform a binding ceremony—a *magically* binding ceremony that will bind you to me, making it impossible for you to harm me or go against my wishes in any way possible."

Frost upended his goblet. *Is this man a drunkard?* Malchom thought. *No worry, I'll simply incorporate that into his binding.* Frost motioned to the container of wine.

"We're all out. We'll have to go get another bottle." Malchom left the room, confident that Frost would follow.

"So we're underground," Frost said as he caught up to Malchom. "Do these mushrooms cover all the walls?"

"Yes, they do. They provide light, air, and nourishment for a selected few."

"That's right, you said they're edible. Why is it that I'm not to eat any?"

Malchom stopped and turned to face Frost. "Because they contain a potent drug that will make you nothing more than a befuddled idiot." Malchom raised an eyebrow.

"Right, and you need someone with a *clear mind*."

"Exactly." Malchom continued on and did not stop or even speak, although Frost kept talking, until he reached the apartments that held one of the recent additions to his family.

He opened the door to the suite, and two young girls clad in brown robes stood as quickly and as steadily as they could; both were chewing on a mushroom.

"Dun Lain," they said in unison, "you honor us with your visit."

"Yes, of course." He heard Frost stifle a giggle. "Tarna, you will come with me.

"Of course, Dun Lain." The three left the room.

When they next stopped, Frost eased up beside him and whispered.

"Now I see why you don't want me to eat the mushrooms."

Malchom ignored him and opened two large doors.

"This," he said, striding quickly into the room, "is the ceremony chamber." He closed the door once all of them had entered. He then locked the door.

"Am I to take part in a ceremony today, Dun Lain?" asked the wide-eyed girl.

"Yes, you are, my sweet." He cupped her face in his hands. Such delicate features—the angular jaw, the high cheekbone. She would do nicely for this sacrifice. She was part elven. Nonhuman blood would be required for him to get what he wanted from Altair's avatar. "Please, remove your robe and lay facedown on the altar."

Frost's eyes brightened as he watched the girl disrobe. When she turned and started for the altar, he looked around for the first time.

The room was very large. It was almost the size of a large outdoor amphitheater and was designed much in the same way. Row after row of tiered seats descended nearly a hundred feet to the altar below.

The altar itself stood above and slightly in front of a blazing fire. The flat surface of the altar was large enough to hold a person and had a small break in one side. What looked like a sluice was positioned below this break and ran directly into the fire.

As the girl neared the altar and climbed onto it, lying facedown, her neck over the break, Frost realized what was about to happen.

"What kind of ceremony is this?" he asked, a little shocked.

Malchom whirled on him quickly.

"This binding must be voluntary, or it will not work. You see now what I am about to do. I will not lie to you. This will be just the beginning. You will see many more things, do many more things that will make the next few minutes look like a gathering of choirboys. You must decide now if you want to do this, for it must be done of your own volition."

The thief stood motionless for a few minutes. He appeared to be gazing at the girl. Malchom waited patiently. The voluntary portion of a binding ritual was the most important part. Frost rubbed his still-sore jaw.

"You say that this binding thing will make it impossible to do you harm?"

"Yes, you may think of it, you may desire it all you want, but you will be unable to physically do anything about those desires or do anything contrary to what I tell you to do."

"And in return, I get powers such as yours."

"To an extent, yes."

"And what is it you will have me doing?"

Malchom turned away from Frost and advanced toward the altar slightly. He stopped at the steps that led downward.

"Your primary duty will be to abduct females and bring them here. Women, girls, all races. You will kidnap as many as you can each day. I need at least a thousand."

"Bring them here so you can drug them and do with them as you wish?"

"More or less. You have an idea of what I am about to do with this one. The ones you bring to me will be impregnated, and kept pregnant, so that I—"

"So that you can have a growing supply of sacrifices."

"Exactly." Malchom nodded.

"Will I be able to partake in this . . . 'breeding' process?"

"If you wish, so long as the number of births reaches a satisfactory level."

"So those that I kidnap will not actually be killed?"

"After a while, no." He turned around and walked up to Frost. "Blood is what drives my power. Until we are . . . *producing* enough of our own, we will need to sacrifice regularly from our stock."

"So you're talking about thousands of people." Frost stepped past Malchom and started down the stairs slowly. "Won't that arouse suspicion? Won't the Brotherhood come looking after a mass murderer, especially if its one of their own?"

"They already are. Which is one reason why I need another to help me," Malchom said as he followed the thief down to the altar.

"It's interesting that you chose to impersonate a Dun Lian knight." He touched the altar; it was unexpectedly cool. He ran a hand along the soft skin of the young girl's thigh.

"That is a story that I wouldn't actually mind telling someone." Malchom stepped up to the girl's head.

"Is there any way out of this binding?" Frost asked as his hand worked its way up the girl's body.

"Death." Frost looked up at Malchom. "Or the proper blood sacrifice," he added.

"Do what you must, then," he said as his hands caressed the girl's buttocks, "*wizard.*"

"I am not a wizard," replied Malchom. A knife was suddenly in his hands. He slit the girl's throat in one smooth motion. Her blood poured down the sluice and spilled into the fire. Frost watched, transfixed as Malchom started the chant that would entice Altair's avatar to take shape before them.

The fire started to sputter and pop. Coals leapt from the fire and sent sparks flying in all directions. Malchom knew the avatar was putting on a show for Frost's benefit.

A piece of wood lifted itself and hung above the fire for several moments before exploding in a shower of sparks that danced all around them.

The embers didn't die. Instead they continued their dancing, twirling and spinning around the altar, then around Malchom, and finally made their way, sputtering and sparking, to fly around the head of an astonished Frost.

"My word!" Before his eyes, Frost saw the glowing embers of wood spin into the form of a face. A face that Malchom knew well.

"Greetings, avatar."

"Greetings to you, Malchom." The face turned and looked directly at Frost. Those fiery eyes seemed to burn into him as if the coals were actually touching his skin. "Do we have another convert?"

"Well, this is Frost. And I would like," he glanced at Frost, "to bind him."

"Ah, a binding, just as good."

Malchom knew that the avatar knew all of this, and he was aware that the avatar "knew" that Malchom knew the avatar was aware of all of this. It was a game they played. The avatar liked to pretend that he wasn't nearly omniscient out of some perverse desire to actually *talk* with someone.

"Where are your sacrifices, then?" The avatar glanced around the empty chamber.

Malchom sighed.

"Here is my proposal." The avatar wouldn't know this, however. "The blood of the firstborn to the elven king as payment for the binding."

Frost choked audibly. The shimmering, fiery face of the avatar smiled and turned to stare at Malchom.

"Elf blood, and *royal* elf blood at that. Agreed!" The form started to turn back to Frost.

"And as for the sacrifice given today . . ." He had to put up a strong front now. He had to let Frost see that he wasn't intimidated by the avatar. "You will give Frost the ability to transport himself to the elven city and then back to this chamber with the firstborn when he has accomplished his task."

"Done!" cried the avatar, his attention fully on Frost. Malchom grinned at what would happen next.

Caught unaware, Frost was flung backward, into the first row of seats, by the powers the avatar was infusing him with. He landed roughly and fell backward into the second row. A very faint "My word" could be heard from the fallen Frost.

"I just love doing that," said the avatar.

*   *   *

Namara lay sleeping in his arms. He had pulled her long dark hair up and placed it around his head like a cap; several strands lay across his face, and he could smell the faint scent of some sort of fruit. He had known she was a beauty, and last night he had found out how beautiful she actually was. Never, neither in this body nor in his previous body, had he known such pleasure. She had done everything he had asked of her.

Of course, unfortunately, she was in the thralls of the drug and not enslaved by her love for him.

Malchom had never known love. Was he in love with this woman? His desire for her was obvious, but was it anything other than a physical attraction?

He turned his head and buried his face in her mass of hair.

What is that fruit?

He remained as still as possible, not wanting to wake her. He wanted to savor this moment for as long as he could. Soon she would wake, look at him with her eyes, and he would feel the desires again. At which time she would succumb to his every whim. Not that such events were unpleasant; they were just a little too empty, almost completely void of any real emotion from her.

He could simply *tell* her that she was going to enjoy it, *tell* her to show him how much she enjoyed it, and she would, without hesitation. But somehow, that wasn't good enough for him. Having tasted even the slightest amount of what he thought must be love, any implanted feelings he gave her would seem pale by comparison.

All of this worried him. He wanted more than the drugged-up, stuporous, wide-eyed, dull looks she gave him while influenced by the mushroom—he needed her to be under its control to ensure his hold on her. Would she love him if she wasn't drugged? Could he afford to let her be free of the drug? What would she do with a clear mind? Leave? Find Raurin and tell him of the drug?

In his wildest dreams, she would turn to him, state how much she loved him, and stay at his side no matter what he did. As it was, she would probably run and hide as soon as she found out what he truly was.

He could always bind her. Once bound, she would be unable to betray him or do him harm and still have some amount of free will to do as she pleased. She could be freed from the witlessness the drug imparted. But would she love him?

He heard a faint knock on the door to his apartments. He propped himself up on his arms and roused Namara. She woke easily despite lack of sleep. She looked up at him with a drowsy, dull look and smiled.

"Umm . . . is it morning already?"

"It's well into the afternoon," he said, running his fingers through her hair.

"Umm," she said sleepily, "how do you keep track of time down here?"

"You'll become accustomed to it soon enough. But for now, I want you to *stay here. Do not leave my apartments. If you get hungry, eat some mushrooms.* There is wine and water in the other room. Would you like me to have a bath drawn for you?"

"Umm"—she stretched and yawned—"yes, a nice hot bath with some Chunyan bath spices would be nice." He kissed her lightly on the lips and left the bed, donning a nondescript brown robe as he headed through the many rooms of his private apartments.

A young girl, gaze downward, dressed in similar brown robes, was behind the door when he opened it.

"Forgive the intrusion, Dun Lain. I know you have orders for no one to disturb you in your private quarters but . . ."—she looked up then—"there is a man and a woman in the ceremony chamber. The man is screaming for you. The woman is . . . well, is just screaming."

"Thank you, my dear." He bent down and kissed her on the forehead. "Would you do me a favor?"

"Of course, Dun Lain," she said excitedly; her whole face seemed to brighten.

"I want you to draw a hot bath for the woman in my chambers and attend to her needs. *Tell no one who I have in here or describe her in any way.* If they ask, simply *tell them I have a woman in my apartments.* Do you understand?"

"Yes, Dun Lain."

"Good. You may come and go from my chambers as you need. Now off with you." The girl hurried away, no doubt consumed with the task of finding hot water. There were several underground streams running through the complex that provided for fresh drinking and bathing water, but no one ever took a hot bath. In fact, Malchom's apartment was the only area equipped with a tub large enough to bathe in.

He shut the door and made his way to the ceremony chamber.

A man and a woman, he thought. *Could Frost have returned already?* It had to be. Who else would have simply appeared in the ceremony chamber, but him, with a woman?

The binding ritual was going to require the blood of the elven king's firstborn. Was the firstborn a female? There might be adverse consequences if this was the case. Sacrificing an elven prince is what had been agreed upon, or had it? All he had said was the firstborn of the elven king, who, he had assumed, was male. Perhaps a childbearer of elven royalty *would* be better.

His thoughts drifted back to Namara. *Her* binding might be a problem. A binding was usually very costly; a large amount of blood was needed to complete the ceremony. Abducting such a prominent figure for sacrifice might be worth doing once, but twice? Would that draw too much attention? He was going to have enough problems with Dun Loren. What problems would he stir up if members of royal families started disappearing?

No, Namara's binding would have to be done the old-fashioned way, lots of blood. It might take months for him to gather enough people to bind Namara *and* continue with his plans.

What if she wouldn't agree to the binding? Would the avatar accept the acquiescence of a drugged Namara?

He came to the double doors that led to his favorite sacrificial altar and flung the doors open violently.

She will have to agree! Either that or stay drugged, I don't care which. I'll have her either way, he thought.

The thief had indeed returned. Frost was staring up at Malchom, a little startled by his rough entrance. There was a nearly-naked female on the altar. Her features looked to be elven.

"Get her off the altar!" he called down to Frost.

"I thought she was needed for the binding," returned the silver-haired thief.

"Yes, but we need another just to summon the avatar. Stay here." Malchom turned and left the room without waiting for an answer. He didn't have to go far before he found a girl wandering around in a drug-induced daze. Malchom guided her to the ceremony chamber. He hated wasting perfectly breedable females but was in no mood to search out one of the few males he had collected so far.

Frost had the girl slumped in the seats of the first row by the time he returned.

"I had to knock her out, she was being loud," Frost said in response to Malchom's quizzical look at the elven female.

"This is the elven king's firstborn?"

"Yes, don't you recognize her?"

"No, I don't," he said sharply. "I'm sorry if I'm not up on my current events."

"What muckbeetle crawled into your bed this morning?"

Malchom glanced hard at Frost. "Women," he said to no one in particular. "You," he addressed the drugged girl, "disrobe and lie facedown on the altar." She obeyed without a sound, obviously *very* drugged.

It wasn't long before Malchom was instructing Frost where to dump the drugged girl's lifeless body for later cremation. The thief obeyed, keeping a fearful eye on the summoned avatar the entire time.

"Are you sure you wish to proceed with the binding, Malchom?" asked the avatar.

Did the avatar know something Malchom didn't?

"Why would I not? This *is* the firstborn of the elven king," he said as he motioned Frost to place the elven girl on the altar.

"Yes, it is, but *only* the firstborn is required."

"What exactly do you mean?" asked Malchom, puzzled.

The avatar only grinned. There *was* something else, and the avatar was playing his little 'I'm omniscient, I'm not omniscient' game.

Malchom sighed audibly, as much for Frost's benefit as out of frustration.

"You ask me if I am sure we wish to proceed as we put the sacrifice on the altar." He folded his arms and walked slowly past the altar. "I say of course, this is the agreed-upon price." Malchom turned and stared at the avatar. "You say that only the firstborn is required, implying that I am about to sacrifice more than was agreed upon, which means that either she is more than just the firstborn, or . . ." He smiled and turned to Frost, whose eyes widened.

"Or she is pregnant," finished Frost.

"Which means we have another sacrifice, possibly to use for another binding?" Malchom cocked his head, raising an eyebrow quizzically at the avatar. This could solve a lot of problems for him.

"Not quite. An unborn child would not be enough to fuel a binding, even though it is royalty."

"Then why do you banter with me over the price of the binding?"

This time it was the avatar's turn to raise an eyebrow. "Oh, I don't know." The fiery form fingered the edge of the altar.

Malchom sighed again, frustrated this time for real at the avatar's continued insistence at playing his little game. He walked to the front row of seats and sat, slumping against the second row. Both the avatar and Frost stood silently as he thought.

"Frost," he said several minutes later, "please wait outside." The thief hesitated for a few seconds. He had begun to shift his feet nervously during the eternity that Malchom had sat silently thinking and now seemed reluctant to move. What was Malchom going to do in his absence?

"Frost, please, I have a few things to discuss with the avatar," Malchom said calmly. He stared intently at the thief. Frost seemed to visibly shake as he acquiesced and sprinted up the steps, suddenly eager to leave the room.

When he heard the doors at the top of the amphitheater shut, Malchom stood and strode to the avatar, stopping less than a foot from the creature's noncorporeal form.

"No more games today, avatar. Here is what we will do about this situation, and I think you will find pleasure in my idea."

The avatar listened intently, not bothering to look up at slightly open double doors. He knew Frost was listening, he knew everything. That is, he knew everything that happened; he didn't always know what individuals were thinking, which was why he listened closely as Malchom outlined a very interesting idea, indeed.

CHAPTER 20

Morgan stood motionless and watched as the creature moved back to its original position behind the massive table. Morgan was amazed at how similar this table was to Dun Lian's battle table, only this one was much, much larger.

"You can't be Durgolais," he thought, assuming the other was reading his thoughts.

"Oh no? And why not?"

"Durgolais was a dragon. You don't look anything like a dragon, and there haven't been dragons around for several thousand years."

"How do you know I am not a dragon? If there haven't been any dragons around for thousands of years, then how do you know what one looks like?" This creature continued to speak audibly, which disturbed Morgan for some reason.

"I've seen paintings, seen pictures in books," he thought.

"How do you know those pictures are accurate?"

"Why wouldn't they be?"

"You tell me."

"Books are for storing information, why store false information?" Morgan thought for a moment. Could this creature read his mind when he was thinking to himself? He remembered the commands that *Durgolais* had implanted in his mind, which had brought him here. This creature was attempting to manipulate him.

"Besides, I have seen a dragon . . . in my mind, through the gem. Durgolais was a huge brown reptilian-like creature with scales and large wings . . . nothing near what you are," he thought.

"Ah yes, the gem. Keeping that in mind, I say this to you: you look nothing like a *human* knight of the Dun Lian Brotherhood. You look like a troll."

The audible words, not just their meaning, seemed to hit Morgan like a slap in the face. He stumbled backward slightly then stepped forward and steadied himself on the table. His mind was swimming. He felt a little disoriented; his eyes refused to focus on Durgolais alone. Images of the table, the frescoes on the wall, the impossible sky above him, even the image of Durgolais, floated amongst his many eyes like butterflies.

He shook his head.

"You must excuse me, that was uncalled for," said Durgolais.

"What do you mean? What did you do to me?" Morgan steadied himself and stood on his own, stepping away from the table, away from Durgolais.

"You can, if done correctly, project enough force with your thoughts so as to cause physical disorientation. This is one of the things that you will need to learn."

Morgan walked around the table. Durgolais remained still, following Morgan with his head. He could accept that Durgolais could be in a different body. After all, *he* was in a different body; but how did he know this was Durgolais? And if this was Durgolais, that body would have to be thousands of years old. How could he be sure, especially if this creature could read his thoughts? He could simply be saying everything Morgan wanted to hear.

"You can be sure of who I say I am," said Durgolais, almost on cue.

"Are you reading my thoughts, everything that I am thinking to myself?" thought Morgan.

"Yes, to an extent, I am. Deep thoughts can't be read without a more serious effort."

"Then you probably know my doubts and expectations. You're simply telling me what I want to hear. Durgolais lived thousands of years ago. That body of yours doesn't look to be that old."

"You can be sure I am . . . that is, *there is a way* you can be sure I am who I say I am," said Durgolais.

"How?"

"You can put a shield around your mind and protect it from other telepaths."

"I tried that already, remember? It didn't work."

"That was a very impressive attempt, having done it yourself. With proper instruction, you could form a shield that I would be unable to penetrate without a fight."

"And who would teach me? You?"

Durgolais simply nodded.

"Why would you do something like that?" he thought.

"Someone needs to teach you, and I must admit that there are *benefits* that I would profit from."

He wondered if he could trust this creature. Obviously, he couldn't be sure until he was able to keep the other out of his mind. He could ask that Durgolais refrain from reading his thoughts while he learned to produce a shield.

"But how would you know I wasn't reading your mind? You would have to take it on faith all the way through the learning process that I was keeping my word."

"My thoughts exactly," he thought.

"There is another way," said Durgolais.

Morgan remained still. He didn't respond in any way, but his mind automatically thought, "How?"

"I can *place* the knowledge in your mind, much as I placed the compulsion for you to come to me. In that way, you would forego the learning process altogether and instantly know how to protect your mind."

"You can do that? Place bits of knowledge in my mind?"

Durgolais nodded.

"What would prevent you from placing other things in my mind? What would prevent you from completely owning my mind, then?"

Durgolais shrugged. "That's where the trust part comes in."

An idea began forming in his head. Morgan thought of Jux immediately, hoping to enter the gem and hide the idea before his thoughts betrayed him to Durgolais. The connection was instantaneous.

"Jux, I have a favor to ask of you." Could Durgolais hear his thoughts now? He opened his mind to Jux and projected his idea.

"It will take a bit of time for me to rummage through your mind and catalogue it as it is."

"But do you think it would work? Would you be able to notice any changes that Durgolais might make?"

"Undoubtedly."

"Then do it, and do it quickly." Morgan opened his mind. He knew it would hurt a little, as it always did, when Jux forcibly removed large amounts of information from his mind.

The tingling he normally experienced when Jux sifted through his memories was immediately replaced with a sharp pain that shocked him back into his own body. Had there been enough time for Jux to do what he needed?

Almost instinctively, he began visualizing the wall around the Dun Lian stronghold. Perhaps he could reinstate the shield. He concentrated on the wall and imagined it growing taller and thicker. Durgolais was moving around the table toward him, but he didn't notice. He was lost in concentration. The wall continued to grow.

"That is a very crude way of constructing a shield and requires a lot of time," said Durgolais. "I can show you an easier way." There was a push against Morgan's mind, and the image of the wall was swept away, without pain this time. Durgolais tapped Morgan's forehead with a long yellowed fingernail.

"And the shields I can show you to erect would not be as fragile."

"Do it," Morgan thought quickly, hoping Durgolais was still unaware of his idea.

"Relax, breath deeply, think of nothing, open your thoughts to me. On the count of three, I shall proceed. One . . ."

A lancing pain shot through Morgan's mind and ricocheted around the inside of his brain, almost blinding him with the pain. It was short-lived, however, and when the pain receded, Durgolais stepped back a few paces and folded his arms.

"I see they count differently where you come from," Morgan thought as his mind was clearing.

Durgolais shrugged. "Think of the picture of your Dun Lian stronghold, and that memory will lead you to the knowledge I placed within you."

The image of the Dun Lian stronghold came into Morgan's mind, and almost without transition, he became aware of the ability to protect his mind with a very formidable shield. Without hesitation, he thought them into existence. It also seemed as if he pushed another presence from his mind. *Durgolais?*

"Now since that is done," said Durgolais, "you will have to project your thoughts to me, as I can no longer idly pick them up.

Could he trust Durgolais? Had Jux been successful? What did Durgolais know of his plan? Thoughts and questions came to him a little more easily. He felt a little more secure with the shield up, even if he didn't as of yet completely trust Durgolais.

"Give me a second to check things out?" he thought.

Durgolais made no response.

"Give me some time to check things out?" he projected.

"Certainly," said Durgolais.

Morgan took that as a good sign and thought inward to the gem again.

Pain assaulted him as soon as he made contact, thrusting his awareness back into his troll body. He shook his head and attempted to relax, tried again.

This time Jux spoke to him before anything else happened.

"I must apologize for that," said Jux's disembodied voice. "I was not sure if speed was of importance, so I decided to take the information first and ask questions later."

"You could have warned me." Morgan shot forth a vision of the pain he had experienced.

"Again, I apologize."

"What news, then?"

"Oh, I have barely been able to start."

"But you can do it—I mean, this wasn't a wasted effort, was it?"

"I can do it. I took . . . an *imprint*, if you will, of your mind before and after the event. I now need to sift through them completely, which is a very large task."

"How long will it take?"

"I . . ." Jux paused, looking for the right words. "I have no idea of the *time* it will take to accomplish this task. How long were you outside the gem just now?"

"Only about a minute," replied Morgan.

"Then taking that into consideration, I can only guess that it will take me"—he fumbled with the words—"*days* to be sure."

"Days? What am I to do until then?"

"I suggest letting him teach you. Knowing about your new abilities can only help."

Morgan brought up the image of him pulling his hair out.

"That is an interesting way of telling me you are frustrated. And what I find more interesting is that you pulled up an image of your new body, not your human one."

"Well, wouldn't that only be natural?"

"It is not natural for you to be in a troll's body. I wonder what other *natural* things you are acquiring?"

For some reason, Jux's statement irritated Morgan. He willed himself to return to his body without comment.

Durgolais was still standing, arms folded, several paces in front of him. He decided to go with Jux's suggestion.

"Everything seems to be okay," he thought. "What do we do next?"

"First," said Durgolais, turning and moving away from the table, "you must accept who I am."

"How can I believe you are a dragon, let alone Durgolais? The dragons in my memory were much larger creatures than yourself."

Durgolais had stopped a fair distance away from the table. He looked up, at the impossible sky above him and spoke, projecting his voice loud enough for Morgan to hear.

"When I left the gem, it was because one of my kind came to rescue me. Even though he was a young dragon, he was willing to give his body up for me. We are very long-lived. He had a long life ahead of him."

"Then how did you get into this body?"

"When it was learned that I had escaped the gem," continued Durgolais without answering Morgan's question, "they came in force and recaptured the gem. I learned later that they put his soul into the body of a muckbeetle." Anger welled within Durgolais; he started to shake. "A MUCKBEETLE!" He turned and looked at Morgan, almost pleaded, "We're not evil creatures, but they couldn't understand that. They only saw us as monsters." He looked up again, searching the sky. Morgan would have to find out how the ceiling of this cave was possible.

"They came after us with a fierce vengeance after they learned I had been freed. We were hunted, pursued, and most of us were forced to flee this land. Some of us hid. They had hunted us nearly to extinction.

"In terms of your generations, it has been very difficult for us to recover. Not only are we long-lived, but we give birth so rarely, and gestation takes . . ." He paused and looked at Morgan. "Well, it takes a very long time."

"I still don't understand how you got into this body, especially if the gem had been taken from you."

"Not only are dragons true telepaths . . ." He smiled. The smile seemed to elongate, widen, and grow in size. Durgolais' entire body began to expand. It started with the smile, worked its way to his head and down through the length of his body, which began to stretch out behind him.

In seconds Durgolais had grown to immense proportions; he now filled a large portion of the room. Despite the change, some of his bodily features remained the same. He still had very dark rough skin with the distinctive markings on his head that started down his extremely long neck. Spiked ridges rose halfway down his neck and continued down his spine to the very end of a long, thin tail.

The creature delicately spread a set of leathery wings that were as wide as he was long. They practically touched the opposite walls of the chamber. Durgolais crouched forward on two large clawed hands. The hands had yellow talons nearly as long as Morgan was tall. A huge reptilian head confronted Morgan.

"Dragons are also true shape changers," came Durgolais' voice in his mind.

This was the image of what Morgan believed to be a dragon.

"Shape changers?" projected Morgan. "That's impossible!" Morgan's vision wavered slightly, and Durgolais' long brown body began to rapidly shrink. In moments the huge creature dwindled to the size of a normal human.

Morgan was stunned; Dun Lian now stood before him. Morgan reflexively tried to straighten himself. It was a poor attempt, in his new body, to come to attention.

"Relax," said Durgolais. Durgolais chuckled and changed once again, this time returning to the form Morgan had first met. "Still think it impossible? Still doubt that I am Durgolais? I may prefer this form, but I am still Durgolais. It's just much simpler to be in this form. Easier to get around, and I don't have to eat as much." Durgolais smiled, showing long yellowed teeth. At least some things seemed to remain constant.

Morgan shook his head and paced around the massive table. He stopped and leaned against it on both hands. If this was Durgolais, then he would be able to describe things that only that ancient creature could. He did seem to know about the gem, after all.

"Describe to me how you were first imprisoned within the gem," he projected.

Durgolais closed his eyes and paused before he replied. "There were ten of them, but only one of them wanted to be there. He was in the back, surrounded by the nine, who were armed with long pikes." He breathed in deeply. "I can still smell their fear. They said they brought a gift, an offering of peace. It was then that the Paladin held out the gem. It was very large, indeed—a prize any dragon would cherish. I didn't trust this Paladin." Durgolais opened his eyes and looked at Morgan. "He smelt too confident, plus, he was saturated with magical protections.

"So I had one of his puny, fearful little men bring the gem forward. I was right, because as soon as that man touched the gem, his scent changed. I knew something was wrong, but I touched the gem anyway." Durgolais walked behind the table. He was shaking a little.

"The memory of that prison will haunt me forever. All that darkness, loneliness." Loneliness? This wasn't right; Durgolais should have been kept company by Jux. "It was only a matter of weeks before I was freed from the gem, but time held no meaning in that void. It seemed an eternity.

"I learned, when I finally entered the body of the young dragon that sacrificed himself for me, that they had been using my body to make attacks upon our kind. Evidently, the knight who took control of my body liked what he was doing."

Why didn't Durgolais know of Jux? Morgan searched his thoughts, sifted through the memories he gained while inside the gem, and found what he was looking for. Jux had said that he hadn't come into being until several minds had been trapped within the gem. Durgolais was the first; there was no way he would know of Jux's existence. This was a positive thing for Morgan, he was sure of it.

How lonely and terrifying the gem must have been for Durgolais.

"I was determined to get my own body back. But that never happened. We were taken by surprise when they attacked in force, slaughtered. My body was destroyed, and the gem was retaken." Durgolais bowed his head. "I pleaded for us to stay and continue the fight, but we were divided. My brethren were too proud to take human form and continue the fight in hiding." He looked up into Morgan' eyes. "My pride had been broken long ago. They fled, I hid. They fled to other lands, other continents, but only found that persecution followed them wherever they went. It seems your kind's terror is universal." He sighed and stood up straight, folding his arms against his chest.

"I finally convinced them to come to me. We built this place and started working, in secret, for our return. Someday, your kind will grow enough not to fear us. Especially if it is found out that we have been among you for thousands of years."

"There are more of you here?" projected Morgan. He looked around at the chamber again. No wonder it was so big, if it needed to house a horde of dragons, even if they could change shape. A W-shaped wing of birds flew across the sky. Morgan could hear their combined squawking.

"Not presently. They are *on assignment*, scattered throughout your civilization."

"You mean they're in human form and walking among us like regular people?"

Durgolais simply nodded.

"How many?"

Durgolais glanced around the table. "Only a few dozen. As I said, we were nearly hunted to extinction."

"But that was thousands of years ago, at least!"

"Only three have been born since that time." Durgolais sighed. "It will be a long road back."

Morgan looked down at the table. There were perhaps two hundred figures positioned in various places around the large-sized map. Which ones represented the dragons? There were metal figures, wooden figures, porcelain figures, plus a few others whose composition he couldn't quite determine.

If there were a few dozen dragons out there, then shouldn't there be a larger representation of whatever material their pieces were made of on the table?

Morgan studied the table more closely. He counted nearly sixty gold figurines. These had to represent Durgolais' dragons. There were two figures sitting atop the area that Morgan was sure was Lianhome.

"There are dragons in the Dun Lian stronghold?" he projected, confronting Durgolais with his eyes.

Durgolais shuffled his feet. "You can read the map," he said, avoiding the question. "Good." He pointed to a group of three figures to the south of Lianhome. "You see these figures? That's Dun Loren." The three figures were made of iron.

"You have two dragons at Lianhome?" he asked again. Durgolais ignored him.

"Dun Loren is hunting Jamias, thinking it's you."

"How do you know Malchom Jamias is in my body?"

"It was a part of the images I took from your mind when we first made contact."

"Why are you telling me all this? If your operation is so secret, why let me in on it?"

"You're not aware of what Jamias has been up to since being released from the gem. He has committed crimes, many crimes that your brotherhood believes you have committed." Durgolais pointed to several porcelain skulls. "Malchom has murdered several hundred people."

Morgan's heart sank into his stomach. He made the connection almost immediately. "He needs sacrifices."

Durgolais nodded; Morgan lowered his head. "So far, spread of this news has been tightly regulated. Not many outside of the Brotherhood even know of the murders, some of which were massive." A tone of disgust entered Durgolais' voice. "Two villages were almost totally slaughtered."

Morgan let out an audible moan. "If it were to become common knowledge," continued Durgolais, "that a Dun Lian knight was responsible for the brutal murder of hundreds of people—"

"But a Dun Lian knight is not responsible!" shouted Morgan telepathically. Durgolais recoiled slightly. "*Malchom* is responsible for those murders."

"Yes!" Durgolais pounded on the table; he was annoyed. "You know that, and now I know that, but no one else does! And who, besides someone who has experienced the *pleasure* of the gem, would believe it?"

"He has to be stopped." Morgan was more determined than ever to get his own body back. But what would happen if he did? Would *he* then be held responsible for the murders?

"The distance between the murders, between the known murders, suggests that he has regained some of his power. This is what frightens me. No one in this world wants Altair to turn his attention this way again."

"No one except Malchom."

"And those converts he is able to pick up along the way."

They were silent for a while. Morgan tried to imagine what would happen if Malchom's power were to grow close to what it once had been. He shuddered at the memories that came to mind, Malchom's memories.

"So you want me to go after him."

"You are a Dun Lian knight, and Malchom is using your body, doesn't that make you bound by tradition to go after him?"

"I think tradition can be ignored on this one. I'm not sure if Dun Lian traditions still apply to me. I haven't even felt Kasparow's presence since I left the gem."

"Then you will need all the help you can get, which is why I want to teach you."

They stared at each other.

"Tell me one thing." He paused. "We're under the tallest mountains in the world," he projected. Pointing to the ceiling, he asked, "How is that possible?"

Durgolais smiled.

CHAPTER 21

The creature made a noise that resembled that of a bleating goat, which seemed to hit him almost with physical force. The woman screamed and rushed to hide behind him; her high-pitched screaming hurt his ears more that the troll's bleating. He shoved the woman back, just enough so that she would stumble backward several feet before falling to the ground. Fool woman. Dun Loren whirled to face the creature directly and drew his sword, whistling a command for the twins to protect the woman and the horses. Trolls liked horseflesh, did they not? The creature moved with astonishing speed. Before he could even raise the tip of his sword, the troll was on top of him.

Fearful of the huge thickly clawed hands attached to very long, thin but muscular arms, Dun Loren decided not to give the creature a chance to strike at him.

Clerents had moved to the horses while Justin was busy pulling the woman farther away from the creature. Dun Loren whistled for Clerents to come up behind the creature and tumbled backward, toward the fire; trolls were afraid of fire.

The troll continued to advance, slowly, fearful of the fire. The creature had two large multifaceted bug eyes that reflected the light of the fire like huge gemstones. The thing seemed to be experiencing some sort of torture. Its face was twisted and taut; a snarl of pain was plainly evident on its thin lips. It was grunting and growling loudly. Dun Loren whistled another command for Justin to put the woman on one of the horses—too late, he realized, as Justin passed through his peripheral vision, quickly leading the horses and the woman to the road. He was sure the horses were all too happy to leave the clearing.

The creature crouched, ready to leap, and raised its hands to strike, screaming at what had to be the top of its lungs. Dun Loren whistled, instructing Clerents to strike in unison with his next actions. The troll cocked its head slightly and poised himself, ready for a strike from behind. Did the troll know that Clerents was behind him?

The reflected light from its eyes shifted slightly, as if he was looking behind him at the boy. The creature *was* aware that Clerents was behind him.

Another whistle, this time telling Clerents to move to the creature's left. Perhaps they could pin it next to the fire. Where was Justin? They needed a third person to corner the troll against the fire effectively.

The troll moved with Clerents, to his left away from the fire. Yes, the creature could definitely watch them both at the same time.

The creature started to move. Both Dun Loren and Clerents raised their swords in anticipation of an attack. The troll backed down and returned to a squatting position. It looked as if the creature was about to leap forward, but after several seconds, Dun Loren concluded that this was merely a comfortable standing position for the twisted creature.

The creature was definitely aware that it was outnumbered, but did it feel outnumbered? If they could hold it at bay until Justin returned . . .

The thing's head turned halfway to its left; the reflection of its eyes almost betrayed where it was looking. Was half of its one eye looking off into the woods behind Dun Loren?

A whistle came from the direction Dun Loren thought the creature was looking. Justin had somehow circled behind them, and this creature knew it.

Dun Loren whistled for the twins to take up flanking positions; they would corner this thing against the fire now.

When Justin slid out of the tree line, Dun Loren shifted to his right, thrusting his sword forward, forcing the troll to back up against the fire. All four of them moved in unison until Dun Loren and the squires were positioned neatly around the troll, the twins on either side, with Dun Loren directly in front of the creature. He had closed in on the troll slightly, pushing him back against the fire while remaining well out of range of those long arms. The twins stood poised, ready for Dun Loren's next command. A single short whistle would start their attack.

The troll stood up straight, or attempted to stand straight, and raised its arms, holding its palms upward. What was the creature doing? Dun Loren chirped instinctively at the movement.

His training paid off; the twins reacted to his command immediately. They both lunged, one attacking high, the other swinging low. Dun Loren stepped forward and prepared to thrust the point of his sword at any opening the creature gave him. That opportunity never came as the creature again reacted with blinding speed.

The creature sprang backward, through the flames, and landed several feet on the other side of the fire. The twins faltered for a few seconds, amazed, before they began circling around the fire, coming to a stop several feet to either side of the troll.

With those thickly muscular legs and that low crouch, Dun Loren realized that the creature could probably leap completely out of the clearing in one jump if it wanted to. This changed things immensely. With only three people, they would no longer be able to contain the thing very effectively. By Kasparow, even if they had ten knights, they probably couldn't keep this thing from escaping if it wanted to.

What was that movement the troll had done? Something about the thing's actions worried him. Dun Loren relaxed slightly. The twins had moved to either side of the troll and were awaiting his next command. The troll had returned to its squatting position.

The thing wasn't making any threatening movements. Did it want something? What was it waiting for? Was it simply afraid of being outnumbered? He couldn't begin to believe that such a creature, with its obvious strength and speed, would feel threatened in this situation. And what was it that continued to bug him about the thing's actions?

Dun Loren reviewed the past few minutes in his head. On one level, all of the thing's actions had been somewhat nonthreatening. One could argue that the troll hadn't attacked them, merely had approached them. With the thing's speed, there had been several times when it could have swung at either Dun Loren or the twins.

All four of them had remained still for several moments now. Dun Loren took the opportunity to ask a few questions.

"What did you do with the woman and the horses?"

"I took them to the road. You can still see the fire down the path. I gave her instructions to flee at the slightest sound or movement unless it was one of us specifically calling to her," replied Justin.

Dun Loren nodded. He didn't like leaving the woman or the horses alone, but three against one was far better than two against one.

The troll was moving his head back and forth between Dun Loren and Justin. Was the thing following their conversation? That couldn't be. Still, the troll made no advances or threatening motions.

All of a sudden, the thing raised its arms again, palms upward. Justin jumped at the movement and lunged with his sword at the thing's head. The troll leaned back slightly and swiftly reached out with its long appendage, grasping Justin's sword arm by the wrist, easily hauling the squire off his feet.

Clerents, seeing his brother dangling in the air, lunged at the creature himself. Dun Loren had begun moving as soon as Justin had attacked but would get there long after Clerents's first blow would fall.

The troll, keeping its head forward, flung a hand backward. The long-armed backhand struck Clerents's sword midblade with such force that it was smacked out of the squire's hand. The force of the blow caused Clerents to lose his balance and tumble to the ground, his hand reaching for his Malta.

Dun Loren was around the fire and, staring into the thing's eyes, charged the troll. The creature held a hand up and stepped back a pace. Dun Loren stopped short, mesmerized by the light reflecting off the troll's multifaceted eyes. He was only disoriented for a second, but it was enough to prevent his attack.

Justin was still dangling in the air. Justin began to scream. His hand was shaking; the thing was crushing the boy's wrist.

Clerents regained his feet. Dun Loren held a hand out to hold the squire at bay. "Clerents, hold!" Something about the creature's actions continued to eat away at him; they still were not threatening.

Justin's grip on his sword faltered; the weapon began to slip from his hand. He let out another painful scream.

Clerents couldn't stand it any longer. Damn Dun Loren's commands. The squire drew his Malta at the same time that Justin's sword fell to the ground.

The troll dropped Justin and whipped its head around to stare directly at Clerents, crouching in tense readiness. It uttered a deep, grating sound. Did it just say stop?

"Clerents!" yelled Dun Loren. "I said hold!" Clerents, keeping his eyes fixed on the troll, lowered his Malta slightly.

After a few seconds, the thing relaxed a little and turned back to Dun Loren. It seemed to Dun Loren that the troll was looking at all three of them at the same time.

A low, guttural sound escaped from between the thing's taut lips, if you could call them lips. No one moved. Justin's eyes widened; he was busy massaging his wrist. Dun Loren hoped that it had not been broken.

The sound came again—this time it was slower, more distinct. Was that a word? Was it trying to talk? Justin obviously thought so; he shook his head and spoke.

"Did that thing just speak?" The troll looked to Justin and repeated the sound, waving to himself in the process. Clerents's jaw dropped. Dun Loren slowly moved closer to the creature.

"It did! It just tried to talk," cried Justin. "I distinctly heard two separate words."

"What did it say?" asked Clerents.

"I'm not quite sure . . ."

Almost as if the troll understood what was being said around him, it grunted and waved to himself again. This time Dun Loren was closer. He too thought he heard two separate words.

"There!" Justin pointed with his unhurt hand. "I swear he just said 'organ clean.'"

The troll slowly stood as straight as it could and raise its arms again, palms upward.

"Did that thing just do what I think it did?" asked Clerents in wonder.

"What did it do? What did it do?" asked Justin, whose vantage point on the ground and being slightly behind the creature had kept him from seeing the troll's gesture.

Dun Loren lowered his sword slightly and stood in a more relaxed position.

"He just saluted me in the Dun Lian fashion," said Dun Loren, amazed.

*   *   *

"Yes, I am certain there are no more areas that were tampered with."

"And you're sure this *trap* will work?"

"From what Durgolais taught you of telepathically attacking someone, yes."

"That's good, but I want you to continue to examine things, just in case there is something you missed. And take a look at what Durgolais taught me. Perhaps you can figure out a few more things."

"Certainly . . ." Jux was still speaking, but Morgan ignored him and returned to his own body.

He stood and sprang out of the small stream he had been resting in. Cooling his body in the running water of the stream while he talked to Jux had been a good idea; the summer might be nearly over, but the nights were still somewhat sweltering. He had been swimming and running since he left

Durgolais several days earlier, and his overheated body needed the cooling rest stop.

He had spent nearly a week with Durgolais. The dragon had started to teach him things about his new abilities. Every waking moment had been spent learning, testing, exercising his knew telepathic abilities. He had spent the entire week doing everything Durgolais had told him to do. That is, until Jux had told him that Durgolais had lied to him and *had* done more to him that first day than simply giving him the knowledge of telepathic shields.

Jux discovered what the disembodied ancient voice had called a *hidden trapdoor* in the shield that Durgolais had taught him to erect. Jux was certain that it would allow Durgolais to bypass Morgan's shields anytime the dragon wanted to. After a lengthy discussion with Jux, Morgan had decided to leave Durgolais' cave as soon as possible.

The opportunity had presented itself on the day that Durgolais had shown him how to use his new abilities to view someone from afar.

If you are familiar with a mind, Durgolais had explained, *then you can look in on what they are doing from just about any distance. We call this astral viewing. If done properly, you can even physically transport yourself to that person's location.*

After several hours of initial instruction, Durgolais had left Morgan alone, telling him to try and follow Durgolais' actions throughout the day. After only a small amount of effort, Morgan had found it quite easy to follow Durgolais around as the dragon went about his business. In his mind, he could see everything Durgolais was doing; he was even able to change the perspective of his viewing, to look in on Durgolais from any angle.

Then after an hour or so, Durgolais turned, looked straight at him, straight into his mind, and said, "A telepathically aware creature will be able to sense the viewing. You cannot hide from this. An experienced telepath will be able to view you through your own astral window, and with only a slight push of thought . . ."—it was at that point that the vision shattered, sending pain sparking through Morgan's mind—"the experienced telepath can shatter the connection and prevent you from viewing him again, at least until he initiates mental contact with you, thus reestablishing the link."

All that day, they had practiced establishing, viewing through, and destroying the link, in each direction, from Morgan to Durgolais and from Durgolais to Morgan.

It was near the end of the day. Durgolais was busy at his map table, and Morgan had been watching the dragon for about ten minutes when

Durgolais moved a golden figure into the same spot that Dun Loren's figure occupied. When Morgan finally realized that there was a shape-changed dragon with Dun Loren, he had decided that it was time to leave. Dun Loren needed to be made aware of the presence of the dragons. By Kasparow, he needed to be made aware of the *entire* situation! He had waited until Durgolais had left the table for his own sleeping chambers and rushed quietly out of the caves, taking one last look at the impressive ceiling of the massive map room as he left. Durgolais had said the ceiling was made possible by magic.

You mean like what Malchom does? he had asked.

No, the dragon had replied, *there are several types of magic, What Malchom practices is not true magic. He gets his power from his god. A true magician taps a huge storehouse of energy that resides on another plane of existence. This ceiling was made long ago. There are a few left that can still accomplish this, but not many. No, the practice of true magic is a rare thing, indeed. Your brotherhood has seen to that.*

He left that night and didn't stop. Several times, he had attempted to view Dun Loren but was unable to, either because Dun Loren was not a telepath or because Morgan didn't know his sponsor's mind well enough to initiate contact. That was one thing he had never asked Durgolais.

Morgan was surprised that Durgolais hadn't tried to contact him, either telepathically or with an astral viewing. There had been nothing from Durgolais—no thoughts projected for him to hear, no attempts at breaching his shields, no astrally projected viewing windows to follow him around since he left the caves and the Majestics behind.

This had been the first time that he had stopped to rest. He had stopped, rested for a bit, then contacted Jux and learned of the idea to place a trap on Durgolais' back door into his mind.

Durgolais had taught him how to project his thoughts so as to cause physical disorientation. It could be done to anyone, but was most effective against other telepaths. Jux had suggested putting a trigger on Durgolais' trapdoor so that Morgan would instantly and automatically initiate that telepathic punch whenever Durgolais attempted to circumvent Morgan's shields.

You know how to do that? Place that trigger, I mean? he had asked.

Yes. Durgolais provided that knowledge himself when he placed the trigger that led you from thinking of Lianhome's walls to the knowledge he placed in your mind.

Well, then, see if you can figure anything else out, he had said.

Neither he nor Jux thought their trap would stop Durgolais, but it would alert Morgan to Durgolais' presence in his mind and just might give him a chance to do something else.

Why not just take it out and erect a shield without that door? Morgan had asked.

Do you know how to do this? Jux had responded.

No . . . I only know how to erect the shield as Durgolais showed me.

Well then, until you learn otherwise, what else can you do?

So now Morgan was running again. It was a low, crouching run; he was almost on all four limbs. Branches and undergrowth whipped past him with alarming force. If it wasn't for his tough skin, he was sure he would have been a bloody mess by now.

He was almost there, or so he thought. He could smell a fire. It was faint and still far off, but he was sure it was Dun Loren. There was another smell, something familiar. It was strange, almost a blend of half a dozen smells. Was that Chunyan spices he smelled?

He thought of what Durgolais had told him as he ran.

Dragons were real! Not only were they real, but they had been around for thousands of years. They had the ability to assume the form of any creature they wanted, and a few dozen had worked their way into the world as people. Not only that, but several had even infiltrated the Brotherhood! Dun Loren was with one at this very instant!

Durgolais had said that they were not evil creatures and that all they wanted was to reintroduce themselves into the world. Why the big hiding game, then? Durgolais had said that the general populace would be terrified by the presence of dragons. Because of this, Durgolais had said the dragons needed to hide amongst people and gain their confidence. Did they need to do this for more than a thousand years? And why spread themselves all over the world? Morgan had seen the golden figures that represented Durgolais' dragons on every continent. There were several placed suspiciously close to where the war raged with G'Zellan. Morgan was certain he had seen one in the heart of G'Zellan's territory.

From what he could see, Durgolais had agents in every major government and society that he knew of. By Kasparow, Durgolais' map had even shown him some areas of the world he never knew existed. It seemed to Morgan to be a plan of domination and control more than of reacquaintance.

During the five days they had spent together, Durgolais continually talked of the necessity to control the balance between good and evil. Good and evil, he had explained, were both necessary for life to thrive and impossible to be rid of completely. It was the intelligent, civilized being that actively strove to maintain a balance of the two. *Barbaric and unevolved is the person that fights for the advancement of one over the other,* Durgolais had said.

In that one statement, Durgolais had condemned the Brotherhood and solidified Morgan's resolve that the dragon's plans needed to be exposed. How could he call the Brotherhood barbaric? Didn't Durgolais realize what he had said? Didn't Durgolais realize that the Brotherhood was the largest force in the world that actively worked for the betterment of life, for the *good* of people everywhere? Was Durgolais so caught up in his own designs that he couldn't see how such a belief affected Morgan?

Durgolais wanted Morgan as an ally, that was obvious—or at least he though it was. What other reason could Durgolais have for teaching him like he had? Why would the ancient dragon tell him of their operation?

Unless . . . Morgan carefully worked his thought through. Unless Durgolais desperately wanted Morgan to go after Malchom and bring him down. Durgolais himself had said that no one would want the return of Altair. Such a strong force for evil would almost have to topple the balance that Durgolais was trying so hard to maintain.

But didn't Durgolais know that he was going to go after Malchom anyway?

He caught another scent. Horses . . . three of them—he started to drool—and three, no four people. And something else . . . He stopped and sniffed deeply, scanning the area with his heat-driven vision. Something around here was rotting. He could definitely smell Chunyan spices now, and the smell of the fire was nearly overpowering. He became nervous for some reason; he could feel his hackles rise. His nose led him in the direction of the fire.

With the speed at which he was moving through the underbrush, it didn't take him long before he could see the fire. Its white-hot intensity assaulted his vision with a vengeance. Even with the brilliance of the fire and the thickness of the trees, he could see a group of figures moving around the fire.

His ears caught a crisp, clear chirping sound. He knew that whistle! That was an all-clear signal! This was Dun Loren! His heart began to beat faster.

Two of the figures were just emerging from the trees into the clearing, obviously Dun Loren's two new squires. The other two figures were standing by the fire, talking. Their words were garbled, barely audible at this distance.

The tall figure was obviously Dun Loren. The other—a woman, from her smell—had to be the shape-changed dragon. Urgency fell in step with his pounding heart.

"Dun Loren, be careful, she's a dragon!" he projected with his thoughts. Wait a minute, he wouldn't be able to hear that. Morgan rushed forward and burst into the clearing. Dun Loren's laugh stopped short.

For the first time in a long while, Morgan attempted to speak. He backed his attempt with a little telepathic push. Dun Loren needed to know what this woman really was.

It was a miserable attempt. What he thought would have come out as "Dun Loren, stop" sounded more like an irate sheep being sheared.

Knowing Dun Loren would have no clue what he was trying to say, Morgan walked up to his former teacher and tried to speak again, more bleating.

Dun Loren drew his sword and tumbled backward, whistling a command for Clerents to come up behind him. Morgan followed Clerents with two of his eyes. Two more eyes were watching Justin move the woman toward the horses.

"Wait, Dun Loren," he tried to say with no better coherence than before. He moved forward very slowly, grimacing at his inability to talk. Dun Loren was obviously afraid of him, as well he should be! *I'm a troll after all,* he thought. He decided to slow down and not give Dun Loren any reason to fear him. They did fear him, though; he could smell it.

Dun Loren whistled again, telling his squire to take the woman and the horses to safety. They were well trained. Morgan noticed that Justin was well ahead of Dun Loren's commands. He followed Justin out of the clearing with two of his eyes.

Clerents had moved behind him and was very close; his smell was strong. He couldn't speak very clearly. Dun Loren and the squires had no idea what was actually going on. He would have to show them in some other way.

Show them! He would show them who he was.

Morgan relaxed, stood as comfortably and nonthreateningly as he could and lifted his arms, palms upward, saluting Dun Loren in the Dun Lian fashion and tried to shout "Hail, brother!"

Dun Loren whistled at his movement, instructing the squire behind Morgan to strike in unison. This was not good; he didn't want them to attack. He turned his head slightly so he could focus several of his eyes on Clerents. If the boy *was* going to attack, he would want to see it coming.

They didn't strike. Instead, Dun Loren whistled for Clerents to move to his left. They wanted to pin him against the fire! One eye drifted to the fire. It was hot, almost unbearably hot. He moved with Clerents, away from the fire. Was that surprise he saw on Dun Loren's face?

He stood and tired to salute Dun Loren again. Both the knight and the squire raised their swords. He sat back down and tried to relax. They sat in silence for several moments.

He saw a light-colored figure coming toward them through the tress. He focused two eyes on it; it was Justin, returning without the horses or the woman. The squire whistled just before he emerged from the trees.

Dun Loren commanded the squires to take up positions around him. All four of them moved in unison until they were neatly arranged around the fire. Morgan let himself be positioned thusly. He needed time to let them settle down. Their fear was still oozing from their pores like Chunyan spices. After a few moments, he tried to salute Dun Loren again. He watched all three as he moved.

The knight reacted immediately and whistled for the twins to attack. Morgan saw the attacks almost in slow motion. Justin swung high, at his head, while Clerents brought his blade in low. He saw Dun Loren waiting for an opening to strike.

Morgan didn't give him that opportunity.

He sprang effortlessly backward, over the fire, and landed lightly on his feet, returning to his relaxed position. Dun Loren and the squires faltered, stunned at his movements. Morgan remained motionless as the twins again flanked him. Dun Loren appeared to relax a little. The knight's fear was fading. Was he finally figuring things out?

After several moments, Dun Loren finally spoke, "What did you do with the woman and the horses?" Morgan watched the two as they spoke.

"I took them to the road. You can still see the fire down the path. I gave her instructions to flee at the slightest sound or movement unless it was one of us specifically calling to her," replied Justin.

Dun Loren nodded. The twins were still terrified, but he could tell by Dun Loren's scent that he had calmed down considerably. He seemed perplexed. He was working something through in his mind. In his mind . . . If he could only contact Dun Loren telepathically . . .

But he could! Jux had told him it was possible, and he had done it once. It would eat away part of his intelligence, but it might be worth it if he couldn't make Dun Loren understand what was going on.

Morgan decided to try one more time. He raised his arms in salute to Dun Loren. The twins were definitely not as relaxed as Dun Loren.

Justin lunged forward with his sword, aiming for Morgan's head. He didn't want this to happen. He didn't want to hurt them! Morgan leaned back slightly, grabbed hold of the squire's wrist and hauled the boy into the air, squeezing his wrist in an attempt to get him to drop the weapon.

Two of Morgan's eyes saw Clerents react to this. The other twin initiated his own attack. Dun Loren rushed around the fire, shouting.

Rage began to well within Morgan; he didn't want any of this to happen! He focused two more eyes on Clerents and slapped at the squire's blade with such force that he thought it might break. Pain shot up his arm. The boy fell to the ground, reaching for something at his side.

Dun Loren had made it around the fire and was charging him, sword ready. This was not right! Morgan stepped back and held a hand up. He brought all of his eyes to bear on Dun Loren and stared the knight with all the rage that was building within him.

Dun Loren stopped his charge. Morgan focused on the three of them at once. Clerents was regaining his feet. He heard Dun Loren call for Clerents to back off. Justin still hadn't dropped his sword. He squeezed the squire's wrist with conviction this time. Justin screamed and dropped the sword. Morgan saw Clerents draw his Malta.

He dropped the shaken squire and whirled to face Clerents, crouching, ready to spring past the boy if he attempted to fire the Malta. He shouted for the boy to stop. The words came out a little clearer this time. Could he eventually learn to talk?

"Clerents!" yelled Dun Loren. "I said hold!" Clerents, keeping his eyes fixed on the troll, lowered his Malta slightly.

After a few seconds, when he was sure Clerents was going to obey his sponsor, Morgan turned back to Dun Loren, keeping two eyes fixed on each of the squires. He let himself relax. Dun Loren seemed to be waiting for him to do something. He finally had their attention.

"I'm Morgan Mclain," he tried to say. It was a low, guttural noise, sounding nothing at all like what he wanted to say. Justin was still on the ground, massaging his wrist. He breathed deeply and concentrated, tried again.

"Morgan Mclain," he said again, a little better.

"Did that thing just speak?" Morgan looked to Justin and repeated the words, waving to himself in the process. Clerents's jaw dropped. Dun Loren slowly moved a little closer.

"It did! It just tried to talk," cried Justin. "I distinctly heard two separate words."

"What did it say?" asked Clerents.

"I'm not quite sure . . ."

Now they were paying attention. He concentrated again and spoke. "Morgan Mclain," he said, again gesturing to himself.

"There!" Justin pointed with his unhurt hand. "I swear he just said 'organ clean.'"

Morgan slowly stood as straight as he could and raised his arms again, palms upward.

"Did that thing just do what I think it did?" asked Clerents in wonder.

"What did it do? What did it do?" asked Justin, whose vantage point on the ground and being slightly behind Morgan, had kept him from seeing the gesture.

Dun Loren lowered his sword slightly and stood in a more relaxed position.

"He just saluted me in the Dun Lian fashion," said Dun Loren, amazed.

"That's impossible!" shouted Justin, slowly climbing to his feet.

"Well, you just heard it say 'organ clean,' so the thing can obviously talk. How much more impossible can it get?" said Clerents.

"By Kasparow, it can't be. What does 'organ clean' mean? Is that supposed to be its name or what it wants to do with us?" replied his brother.

"What I want to know," said Clerents, "is why is it wearing a sword and a backpack?"

Morgan chuckled; he had forgotten all about the sword buckled at his side and the pack strapped across his back. Dun Loren was looking at him, shocked; evidently, he hadn't noticed either.

"And why is it wearing that cloth like an undergarment?" said Dun Loren.

"That thing just laughed at you, Dun Loren," said Justin.

Dun Loren sheathed his sword. With the exception of Clerents's Malta, they were all now unarmed. Dun Loren looked at the Malta. Clerents would get a mark for drawing that and not firing it—at least that was the tradition. "This, indeed, is very strange," he said.

"I-am-Morgan-Mclain," Morgan said very slowly. It was nearly useless; the sounds were barely discernable. He was getting frustrated at his inability to talk.

"You see," said Justin. "It is trying to talk."

"Well, if it can talk," said Dun Loren, "then it can understand what we are saying." The knight leaned forward and spoke directly to Morgan, "Know that I will not hurt you if you do not hurt us." Morgan sighed and nodded.

Dun Loren raised an eyebrow in surprise. "Will you let me see that sword?" asked Dun Loren as he held out a hand.

Morgan hesitated for a second, glanced at Clerents's Malta, then slowly unclipped the sword and handed it hilt first to an astonished Dun Loren.

Dun Loren took it and turned it over and over, examining it very closely. "This looks like Dun Lain's sword."

"I. Am. Dun. Lain," Morgan said carefully.

"What did it say?" asked Clerents. Justin shrugged.

"How did you get Dun Lain's sword?" asked Dun Loren.

"It is my sword. I am Dun Lain," replied Morgan, a little too quickly.

"What?"

"I-am-Dun-Lain. That-is-my-sword," Morgan said slowly. It was of no use; he couldn't pronounce the words correctly.

"Slow down, say that again. I can't understand you." Dun Loren spoke slowly and loudly. "Where-did-you-get-this-sword?"

Morgan stomped his foot in frustration; Clerents and Justin jumped. "By-Kasparow, it-is-my-sword. I-am-Dun-Lain!"

"Did it just say 'I *Kasparow*'?" asked Clerents.

"No!" he raged, throwing his long arms up in the air in complete frustration. Justin and Clerents jumped backward, startled by his abrupt movements. Justin regained his weapon; Clerents held his Malta up high.

This was getting nowhere; he would never be able to speak so they could understand him. In frustration, he lashed out with his thoughts, forging a link with Dun Loren's mind. Dun Loren recoiled a step as his mind was assaulted.

Morgan caught a glimpse of a shimmering that appeared next to Dun Loren. Was that an astral viewing?

"Dun Loren, *I am Morgan Mclain*," he thought.

"How can that be?" stammered Dun Loren. "You're a troll." Justin and Clerents stared at Dun Loren questioningly.

"Listen to me, I *am* Dun Lain, trapped within this troll body," he thought.

He focused several eyes on the shimmering that had quickly grown in size. Was Durgolais finally looking in on him?

"Impossible," Dun Loren said weakly. He almost stumbled forward. The twins started to move toward Dun Loren.

Morgan had had enough. He gathered his memories of entering the gem and the troll body and flung them into Dun Loren's mind. Dun Loren screamed in pain and fell to his knees, dropping Morgan's sword.

Morgan could see a figure through the shimmering. It wasn't Durgolais.

Clerents reached Dun Loren and helped steady him. Justin advanced on Morgan. Morgan retreated.

Morgan could see the figure through the viewing window better. He was looking at himself! It was Malchom! Morgan thrust his mind forward and shattered the link the way Durgolais had taught him. He caught a glimpse of surprise from Malchom as the shimmering winked out of existence.

Justin was attacking. Morgan had put so much effort into blasting away Malchom's viewing that he had forgotten the charging squire.

Justin's blade drove deeply into his side.

Morgan screamed and forcefully punched the squire square in the chest. The boy was flung backward several feet. Morgan yanked the sword from his side and, still grasping it, leapt from the clearing, disappearing into the woods.

Steve Baumler was born in Washington, D.C., in 1966. He has lived in the DC metropolitan area for most of his life, with some time spent in England, Greece, and road trips throughout the U.S.

The works of J.R.R. Tolkien, Stephen R. Donaldson, and C.S. Lewis inspired Steve to start writing. In addition to writing Inherent Nature (2009), he has also written numerous short stories and poems.

As a stay-at-home dad, Steve enjoys the rigors of raising his two sons. In his spare time, being an avid gamer, he can be found playing nearly any type of game from board games, computer games, console games, and poker.

Steve holds a bachelor's degree in English, from James Madison University in Harrisonburg, VA.